# 3 1/2 YEARS

Jeremiah Jones

*This book would not be possible without the many supportive friends and family in my life. To those I give a hearty, THANK YOU! But there are four personal thanks I want to pass along. First and foremost, I thank Jesus Christ for His indescribable gift. Second, I thank my incredible wife, Lindsey for encouraging me to get back on my horse and write this book. Third, I thank my parents, Dale and Melanie Jones, for always loving me and sticking with me despite the endless reasons I gave them to write me off. And finally, I thank Kim Neuman for her excellent job of editing the chaos I dumped in her inbox.*

*For the time is near...*

# CHAPTER ONE

*"It is appointed unto man once to die, and after that...judgment."*

-Hebrews 9:27

A solitary, cold wind howls across a snow-covered field like a lonely ghost looking for something to haunt.

Up ahead, a feeble doe trudges across the same field, hunting for sustenance—she hasn't eaten for days. Her outlook is bleak; if food isn't found soon, this doe's story will have a sad ending.

Bracing against the biting cold, the doe waits out the wind's frigid fury. As the wind subsides, the deer looks up to find an unexpected blessing—a small patch of uncovered grass.

Gratefully, she trots over to dinner. While dining, she eyes the desolate field, keeping her ears tuned for predators.

A light snowfall begins, quickly switching to a whiteout. Her nervousness overrides her hunger pains. Senses tingling, she scans the field. The wall of snow creates a sound barrier, making it hard to hear. Anxious breath billows from her nose. Agonizing seconds stretch out. She knows she smells something. She knows she smells danger. At last, the suspense crescendos as a chorus of bells signal from the ashen sky.

***

The bells invade the silence as though an air raid siren hollers. This analogy isn't far off. For the once peaceful nights have turned like a beloved dog gone rabid.

Silencing the cellphone alarm's agony, a man scoots against his headboard in time to square off with a new noisemaker—a meowing cat. Allowing his hand to be assaulted by the famished feline, he sifts through the concluding dream. In his forty-plus years, he cannot remember a longer, more strenuous season of bedtime terrors. But, truthfully, the dream wasn't that bad. It was just a deer trying to survive. However, based on previous nights, he's certain something WAS hiding behind the cascading snowflakes, waiting to leap out like a madman from a closet.

The man coaxes the melodramatic cat away as he crawls out of bed and heads for the shower. Ten minutes later, the shower curtain whips back introducing a reinvigorated human being. His name is Joshua Mendel. His friends call him Josh—not a big stretch. Well, they *would* call him Josh if any of them were still around. All his closest friends are gone and with them any clear understanding of what truth is except for one irrefutable certitude: God does NOT keep His promises. If He did, Josh would not be picking up the pieces of a shattered existence.

Because of this why for and many more, he hates God. But all that is putting the cart before the horse; there's plenty of time to delve into Josh's bitterness later. For now, the minutia of his new life serves to distract him.

One of those distractions—an orange tabby cat continuing his earlier demands of, "FEED ME!!"

"Alright, settle down. Stop yelling at me," Josh commands the meowing cat who's joined him in the hallway.

Entering the kitchen, Josh prepares the mouthy cat's breakfast and plants the food bowl on the floor. The cat pounces while offering a "thank you" meow.

"You're welcome."

With that chore over, Josh begins his daily intake of caffeine. K-cup inserted, button pushed, and seconds later his Keurig servant provides cup number one. Sipping while leaning against the kitchen counter, Josh gazes into his living room, admiring its elegant features. While lost in his thoughts, malevolence slinks in.

"Toby! No!" he yells to the cat shredding his antique couch.

Launching into the living room, he shoos away the upholstery killing machine. Offended, the cat scurries off, leaving Josh to examine his prized couch. To the untrained eye, the couch looks valuable, which it is. Most of his living room décor appears inestimable; it's like he lives in an upscale antique store.

Glorious chimes from a grandfather clock call from the corner of the living room. It's 6:00 a.m. With Toby in step, Josh heads to his office. This too is an antique-filled room. Some of the pieces are so stately they'd reduce any serious collector to a babbling fool.

Toby jumps onto the mahogany roll-top desk while Josh plops in the companion piece: an antique swivel banker's chair. His attention turns to the only modern item in the room—his laptop. As Josh waits for the laptop to start up, Toby busies himself with knocking everything over.

*Crash!* Down goes Josh's desk picture frame. Irritated, he scoops up the little hellion and anchors him to his lap. Toby purrs victoriously, settles down, and drifts off.

Josh picks up the knocked-over frame and wipes off the glass. He stares deeply into the picture, traveling back in time. As though heralded from the morning sky, exposition dawns. The picture is of a beautiful woman cozying up to Josh; and judging by the emotions on present-day Josh's face, this mystery woman is quite dear. Where is she? Did she leave him? Did she die? What dubious event achieved bachelor status for this poor man?

No clichéd words are spoken. No lamenting vows are promised. Thus, no clues are revealed... sadly. The man with impeccable decorating taste, the man drowning in seething rage, returns the picture frame to its enshrined spot and refocuses on his computer.

A couple of mouse clicks and the printer comes to life, inciting Toby to aggression. The cat leaps down ready to annihilate the evil white *squirrel* as it slinks out of its plastic *nest*. Josh relocates the hyperactive feline and retrieves the printout.

"Honestly, Toby, it's just a machine. So much rage for a nine-pound cat. Maybe you should see my shrink too." Josh smirks, congratulating himself for his wry wit.

Turning off the light, Josh exits with Toby at his heel. He stops in the kitchen to fill his travel coffee mug. Bending to pet the fur ball weaving through his legs, he instructs:

"Ok, Buddy, off to work. Don't sleep too long.

***

Loud banging echoes down the peaceful street of what was once a thriving and wealthy Suburbia. The decimation of America's economy has not been kind to this neighborhood.

Unfortunately, this is not the only neighborhood still bearing the indents left on America's stout neck as Time's icy fingers choked out her once proud life. Nor are the myriads of abandoned homes that pop up on the face of America like a bad acne outbreak the only evidence of a catastrophe. The most powerful country in history is on life support, battling back the impending flatline...

The banging ends as a smashed doorknob hits a dirty floor with a metallic clunk. A second later, the front door is kicked open, sending up an explosion of dust. Josh, hammer in hand, enters the impressive foyer and stops to get his bearings. Seeing the living room to his left, he passes under the large archway and rips down the drapes from the front picture window. Rays of light cut a swath through the disturbed layer of dust creating prominent sunbeam trails that reflect off a large wall mirror hanging above the couch.

Ignoring nature's ghostly laser-light show, Josh reenters the foyer to continue his tour of the first floor, ripping down curtains as he goes. Two more people enter—Walt, a seasoned man on the friendly side of middle age; the other is Braxton, a freshman at George Washington University home on winter break, looking to make some extra cash.

"Dude! What is that nasty stank?!" whines Braxton.

"That's the smell of foreclosure, Kid. You'll get used to it," Walt says, trying to offer solace to his nephew.

Josh likes Walt as much as he likes anybody. Walt's been with him since the beginning of his property preservation business. Property preservation is just a fancy name for maintaining foreclosed homes. But no matter what uppity title you give it, the facts are the same: Josh is making a small fortune off people's misfortune.

"In this case, it's also the smell of death," Josh calls out from the kitchen.

"Whatcha' find, Boss?" Walt asks as he joins

Josh. Braxton follows.

"That is straight-up disgusting!" Braxton protests as he covers his mouth and nose.

Laying in the middle of the floor is a decaying dog. Josh snaps his wrist, unfolding a construction trash bag. He holds it out to Braxton.

"Ready for your initiation?" Josh asks.

Braxton glares at Josh like he was crazy. "Are you serious?!"

Walt playfully slaps Braxton on the back. "Comes with the job. Better put on your gloves."

Determined not to throw up, Braxton gingerly maneuvers the canine into the bag.

"No need to be gentle. He's not getting any deader," Josh mocks and Walt laughs.

Once the bag contains one dead dog, Braxton struggles to lift it. "He must weigh fifty pounds!"

"I'd say fifty-five if you count all the maggots." Josh delights in his newbie-hazing.

"Please, you're gonna make me puke. Where do you want it?"

"In the front seat of my truck. Where do you think?! The dumpster!" Josh says.

Having endured fraternity hazing, Braxton knows not to show weakness. He strives to hold the full-sized "doggie bag" at arm's length as he marches out the front door. Josh and Walt watch him heave the carcass into the roll-off dumpster parked in the driveway.

"You promised you'd play nice," Walt reminds Josh. "He's a good kid."

"I'm just riding him to see if he can hack it."

"Fine, just ease up, please. I'm gonna hear it from my sister if he comes home crying."

Josh sighs as he offers a defeated "whatever you say" nod at Walt.

"Nicely done," Josh praises Braxton as he re-enters. "You good?"

Braxton offers a sheepish smile as he nods.

"Good." Josh shoulders Braxton as he walks past him and into the bowels of the house. And what a house it is. It's a large, six-bedroom, five-bath Colonial with all the amenities a well-to-do family could ever want. Each room is furnished to the hilt. And not just any old furniture would do, no sir. By the looks of things, the lady of the house would've had a coronary if there was one piece from something so gauche as Macy's or, heaven forbid, Value City.

His compadres, distracted by the spoils scattered throughout, have left him to discover the booty on his own. Eventually, his quest takes him to the second floor where he finds the husband's study, assuming the name on the certificates, degrees, and awards is correct. The man of the house was an orthopedic surgeon. Apparently, he got his Ph.D. from Harvard Medical School. Citations from Johns Hopkins, Sibley Memorial Hospital, and Inova Fairfax Hospital all speak to his greatness.

Completing his cursory search of the second floor, he ascends to the third. It is completely devoted to a cavernous study. Filled with wonder and awe, he enters the colossal room and takes it all in.

The study, clearly the wife's, was spared no expense. Everything from the pristine hardwood floor to the spiral staircase leading to a loft overlooking the entire room screams success.

Growing accustomed to the monstrosity, the numerous hanging plaques spread throughout suddenly *appear* to him. He responds with a big smile. On the wall behind the Pergola executive desk is a large degree stating that she graduated from Yale Law School. He imagines there was good-natured bantering between her and her husband over graduating from rival Ivy League schools. Walt and Braxton enter the wife's lair.

Braxton whistles as he scans the room. Josh turns to see the college boy's gaping mouth hanging down by his knees. He is entranced by the bookshelves housing the copious amount of legal books dispersed all over both floors.

"This is insane!" Braxton exclaims. "There must be over five hundred pounds of books up there. Not to mention the metric ton down here. My back is killing me just looking at it all!"

On his way to a window, Walt lands a drive-by punch on his nephew's arm.

"Thanks, Uncle Walt. That's helpful," Braxton complains as he rubs his arm.

"Watch and learn, Kid," Walt instructs as he opens the window. He then grabs a stack of books, marches back to the open window, and blindly heaves them into the great blue yonder. A second later, a loud *BONG!* greets their ears.

Smiling, Braxton joins Walt and peers out the window. Seeing that the books landed in the giant dumpster (narrowly missing Old Yeller— R.I.P.) Braxton leans back in and laughs.

"Right on! Work smarter, not harder," Braxton praises his uncle's resourcefulness.

Walt winks. "Momma didn't raise no fool."

"We get rid of everything, right?" Braxton verifies.

"Everything not nailed down," Walt confirms.

"It blows my mind nobody wants this stuff," Braxton remarks.

"The bank doesn't care what we do with it, just so long as it's all gone," Josh says. "And as far as what we do, we keep it simple. It starts with me and then Walt. If neither of us wants something, then it's yours. Otherwise, it all goes to the dump."

"Sweet." Braxton is digging the unexpected job perks.

"Let's check out the basement and then get started," Josh instructs, leading the way.

Finding the basement door closed, Josh opens it and flips on the lights. Descending the stairs, they discover a finished basement with a wall-hanging one-hundred-inch 8K TV in front of a theater seating sofa.

"Oh, man!" Braxton exclaims. "Does anybody want the TV? My frat house would love it!"

"Nope," answers Josh. That's one.

"Have two at home," states Walt. That's two.

DING! DING! DING! Braxton is the grand prize winner. He walks over to admire his major award.

Just then, a weak meow emanates from a bunch of boxes in the corner. Josh immediately investigates. A small tiger-striped cat emerges from the boxes. Josh bends over to comfort the little feline.

"And sometimes we find LIVE animals," Walt deadpans as he inspects the rooms off to the side.

"I can't believe it IS still alive," Braxton exclaims.

"Probably wouldn't be in another couple of days," shouts Walt from inside the utility room. "Its automatic food dish and water bowl are nearly empty."

"Braxton, do me a favor. Run up and grab my water jug from the truck," requests Josh.

"There's a bathroom right here," Braxton replies. He turns on the sink faucet, but nothing comes out.

"Water's turned off. Just grab it please."

Braxton complies.

"What are you gonna do with it?" asks Walt.

"Well, I guess Toby has a new playmate."

"Who?" Walt asks. He's never been to Josh's house.

"The other abandoned cat I found."

"Josh, you're gonna turn into a crazy bachelor if you're not careful."

Josh doesn't respond because Walt doesn't have a clue. Josh WOULD be a crazy bachelor if NOT for Toby and now his new sister. Cats keep him tethered to sanity, always have and always will.

Braxton returns and hands over the jug. Josh walks into the utility room with his new cat in tow and fills her dish. She greedily laps up the cool refreshment.

"Aww, poor little kitty. You were so thirsty," Josh coos as he pets her. After some getting-to-know-you-time passes, Josh stands to instruct the troops.

"We're not getting to the basement today, so I'll keep her down here and take her home when I leave." Saying nothing more, Josh heads toward the stairs.

"Can I get my TV now since we're already down here?" Braxton calls after Josh.

"Yeah, that's fine. Don't step on my cat."

"I won't," Braxton promises as he stares at his new TV. His furrowed brow tells Walt he's bitten off more than he can chew.

"Want some help?" Walt asks.

"Yes, please."

"Good thing you rode with me in my truck. I'm guessing that's bigger than your entire Kia."

"Pretty close," Braxton agrees.

Josh leaves the uncle/nephew team to it while he heads upstairs and out to his truck. There, he grabs his tools and a box of doorknobs and deadbolts. The first order of business, change all the existing hardware.

As he approaches the front door, Walt and Braxton exit, hoofing out the beast. Josh steps aside giving them room. Once clear, he starts on the door knob. A few minutes later, the duo returns.

"Start in the living room?" Walt asks.

"Sure," Josh responds and Walt obeys. He returns a few seconds later.

"Here you go."

Josh turns to see Walt holding a large Bible.

"Oh, nice. Let me see." Josh takes the Bible and reverently flips through the pages. "Mmm, uh huh. Nice, very nice. I have just the place for this."

Josh steps outside and unceremoniously flings the Bible like a Frisbee toward the dumpster. As it soars through the air, the pages flap as though trying to take flight. In anticlimactic fashion, the Bible bounces off the inside wall of the dumpster.

"Three points," Josh announces, satisfied and smiling.

"Whatcha do that for?!" Braxton condemns. "That's bad luck!"

Josh scrunches his face and rolls his eyes. "Please."

"Josh believes that all Christian homes contain the three B's—Booze, Babes, and Bibles," Walt informs. "He's unstable in his tyrannical certainty."

"Mock if you want, but you know I'm right."

"Whatever you say, Boss."

"I know what I'm talking about," Josh mutters as he heads to the back door.

A few hours later, the trio is on the second floor ready to knock out the bedrooms. Working in tandem, they silently haul armfuls of clothes, boxes, toys, furniture—the very things that make a home—down the stairs. Never diverting, they head to the dumpster, relinquish their payload, and march back upstairs for more like worker ants.

Eventually, the kids' bedrooms are empty leaving just two rooms—the master bedroom and the husband's study. The master bedroom is tackled next. Second verse same as the first: items are removed, items are kept, and items are pitched. The job may seem like an assembly line, but it's not. Otherwise, Josh could never hack it: he gets bored easily. Every house is different; every house has its own story to tell. That's the beauty of this business and why Josh thrives at it. No house contains the same things as the previous ten; no room contains the same furniture; no drawers contain the same things as the drawer above or below it. The rush of the biz never wanes. It's always an adventure, and he never knows what he'll find next. Case in point— the wife's bedside drawer.

Sliding out the top drawer, the telltale sound of pill bottles bouncing off each other greets his ears. He always reads pill bottles to see what the fam is poppin'.

"It seems the missus needed a little help from her friends," he announces while gathering the bottles and reading them off. "Xanax, Adderall, and to cap off the array of harsh drugs, Ambien. Probably to offset the speed."

"You'd be doing me a solid if you tossed the Adderall. Wicked stuff," Braxton confesses. "I got hooked on it my first semester. Made pulling all-nighters a lot easier."

Josh's respect for the youngin just shot up ten points. "No worries. I got you." Josh chucks the bottles into a garbage bag—minus the Ambien, which he pockets unnoticed: maybe they'll help stave off the dreams—and marches into the master bathroom.

Opening the medicine cabinet, he whispers to himself, "What do we have hidden in here?"

He discovers the usual embarrassing items that you'd never admit you're using and/or applying. He does, however, see two things of great interest: a full bottle of OxyContin and a full bottle of Vicodin, both maximum dosages. These little joy-inducers are the husband's.

*Probably threw his back out from too much golf,* Josh muses.

Looking in the mirror to make sure no one's watching, Josh stuffs the bottles in the same pocket as the Ambien.

"I guess his prescription pad isn't just for her," he whispers.

After bagging up the rest of the bathroom, he exits to find the master bedroom all but emptied. Any evidence of a husband and wife's life being lived is now a distant memory. All that remains is the king-sized bed, where love was made, and dreams were dreamed.

"What time is it?" Josh asks his employees as they return.

Braxton checks his phone. "Almost two."

"Perfect. We have an hour to empty the

husband's study. The truck's coming at three to take the dumpster. Drag out the bed and then meet me in there," Josh instructs as he heads outside.

"Way ahead of ya," Walt promises as he motions to Braxton to get to the other side.

Josh tosses his full bag into the dumpster on the way to his truck. There, he sticks his illegal pharmacy into the center console. Feeling smug by his subterfuge, he grabs another trash bag and heads back inside. Trudging up the stairs for the thirty-six-zillionth time, he promises himself relief will come tonight. Good thing, his arthritic knees and achy back are barking today. Oh, who's he kidding? He just wants to get high.

Entering the study, he begins emptying the massive desk. His workers join him. Progressing through the desk drawers, he arrives at the last one. And wouldn't you know it, it's locked.

"Here we go fellas," he announces.

"Locked drawer," Walt says. He's seen this enough times to know the score.

"Yep. And when the drawer's locked, you're about to be shocked." Josh knows how lame his little ditty is and wishes it sounded cooler. Wordplay is not his jam. But what is his jam is thinking outside the box. He removes a flathead screwdriver from his pocket and fiddles with the drawer. After some effort, the stubborn drawer gives up the goods...eventually, they always do.

Probing through the attempted buried treasure, a smile lights up his face. "As always, I'm right! Booze, babes, and bibles."

One hand holds a stack of adult magazines, the other, an unopened bottle of Jack Daniels' Bourbon. "The hat-trick is complete."

"Fine, I concede," Walt concurs.

"Ol' Jack here is too young to be tossed. I'll give him a good home," Josh says, smirking. "The smut, however, can go out with the rest of the trash." He sticks the magazines into his trash bag.

With the excitement dying down, Braxton returns to taking down the Bible verse picture frames. "Kinda hypocritical," he comments.

"Right. *Christian* and *hypocrite* are bosom buddies," Josh sneers.

From the window, Walt notices the truck arriving for the dumpster. "Guy's here."

"He's early," Josh complains. "I'll run down and stall him and then come help with the desk."

Ten minutes later, the truck leaves with the dumpster. Still standing in the driveway, the three watch the truck lumber away.

"It's amazing to me," Braxton says, pondering. "A lifetime of this family's memories and belongings were tossed into a filthy dumpster and carted off to the dump where they'll rot and be forgotten. Kinda depressing."

"Trust me, Nephew. You grow callous after you've thrown away enough family photo albums and little kid's refrigerator drawings."

"I found one of those papers stamped with newborn baby footprints that the hospital sends home with you," Braxton remarks, obviously emotionally drained.

"I promise, it gets easier. Desensitization

is a welcome friend," Josh says, attempting to comfort. Josh pulls out his phone to check the time. "I guess it's good he came early. I have an appointment and stopping home to drop off a cat was unexpected. You can take off. Back here tomorrow at eight. Sorry to make you work on the weekend."

"No worries, Boss," Walt assures as he and Braxton gather up their booty and take off. Josh heads to the basement to collect his new pet.

*\*\**

It's four o'clock. In all its sublime grandeur, the afternoon sun bestows its gracious vitamin D upon the scurrying inhabitants of the nation's capital.

Peering out the seventh-story window of a medical building, Josh watches those scurrying folk and wonders how many know what he knows…and for those who do, do they care? The reminder of the burden he carries erupts in his stomach and fans his smoldering bitterness. He didn't ask for this, nor does he want it. Just another example of God's cruelty, and why Josh hates Him and all who name His Name.

"Am I getting paid to play Dr. Mario World today or are we gonna get something done?" A voice drops into the silence and scatters it.

Josh turns to regard the voice. Behind him is a woman dressed in no-nonsense attire, sitting in a large leather armchair, legs daintily crossed. This is Dr. Susan Andrews, Josh's psychiatrist. He sees that she's holding up her phone, obviously drawing his attention to it.

"I don't mind," Susan promises. "My global ranking is high, but gotta keep playing if I want it to stay there."

"Dr. Mario World? Really?" Josh asks, bemused by her wittiness.

"What can I say? I'm good at handing out pills." Her million-dollar smile breaks across her attractive face.

Her comeback creates his own smile while also resurrecting last night's dreams. He sits on the couch. "Speaking of pills, what are you giving me?"

"Why? Are you having adverse side effects?" she asks as she swaps out her phone for her notepad from the end table.

"I guess. I don't sleep much these days, so I'm assuming it's the pills."

"That can be an unfortunate side effect," she confirms.

"But here's the thing, when I do fall asleep, I have nightmares."

"About what?"

"Are we interpreting my dreams now?"

"Sure, why not? Let's see what happens."

"Okay," he says, unconvinced. "They're all about the end of the world."

"That's nothing new, especially in this day and age. I thought you were gonna challenge me?"

"Alright, fine, take last night's dream for example. It was about a sickly deer but if it was anything like previous nights, men would've shown up and started shooting each other over something as asinine as a bottle of olive oil. That little ditty's a reoccurring dream."

"Oh, well, *that's* a new one." She takes a moment to find a different path in the conversation. "Let me ask you this—why have we been meeting for a month?"

"Because I had...a moment," Josh responds with a *duh, you know this* tone.

"A moment? I don't think breaking into a church, ripping up some Bibles, and spray painting hate speech all over the sanctuary walls can be considered a moment. Was spelling your name in urine on the pulpit considered folk art?"

"I get it. Not my FINEST moment," he concedes, not wanting to relive what put him in jail and then the mental hospital. "What's your point?"

"My point is you had a mental breakdown."

"Nooo, I was drunk."

"Noooo," she counters, one-upping him with an extra *o*. "Drunk is running around naked till the cops taze you and put you in the drunk tank. This was something else. In my mind it was premeditated, possibly vengeful."

"I guarantee it was, but what d'ya expect? My life was thrown into an upheaval. Everything I believed in and lived for was a sham."

"I understand, and it's terrible, but what I expect is for you to come to grips with what you did. If you leave the trauma undealt with, it could manifest in other ways."

"Like what?"

"Expressions of violence towards others."

"I could never hurt anybody. It's not in me. Case in point: even though many have suggested it, I don't bring a gun to work. I don't even own one. I hate 'em. I don't care how dangerous my job can be. Why risk somebody getting hurt?"

"Fine. That's admirable. And I believe *you believe* you don't wanna hurt anybody, but it'd be foolish to ignore your decision to vandalize a church."

Josh says nothing. He knows what she's implying.

"We both know you're not fond of Christians."

"Hatred is closer to the mark," he replies.

"Exactly. I believe you attacking a church was an indirect attack on Christians. I also believe you'll decide your attack wasn't satisfying enough. That, in time, your hatred will drive you to act violently against Christians themselves."

Sensing the room's heavy air, Josh decides stretching his legs is in order. He heads to her large bookshelf.

"Why shouldn't I hate them?" he asks, scanning the books. "Look at all they've done. Frankly, I'm surprised you don't hate them too."

"I may not be their number one fan, but I won't let them control me either. You're giving too much significance to an insignificant religion."

"They're not as insignificant as you think," he says, continuing his journey down the bookshelf.

"Alright, out with it Josh," she prompts.

"What?"

"You're not telling me something. What happened at work?"

"Nothing really. Same house as the rest."

"Tell me about it."

"Okay, here goes," he says with a *it's your funeral* tone. "I swear there is no difference between a Christian's house and a NON's house."

Now that he's started, the hatred and bias smolder even more. His anger rises and is accompanied by the sharp right turn on his *voice volume knob*. He adds pacing to the show.

"They have the same vices, only the NONs have no qualms about them. They lay it out there for all the world to see and don't care what anybody thinks. I respect that. What I cannot abide is these deceptive, self-righteous hypocrites who, on the surface, present this immaculate image, but in reality, they're hiding the same despicable sins that they are oh so quick to cluck their tongues at when the pastor is within earshot or some other equally sanctimonious Christian!" Amazingly, he said all that in one breath.

"Like a beautiful and ornate coffin holding a rotting corpse," Susan interjects, perceiving the *temperature* needing to come way down.

Taken aback by her unusual response, he stops pacing and stares at her.

"I think Jesus said that about the Pharisees." Seeing his expression, she explains. "I went to Sunday School when I was a kid."

"I don't think that applies, but I understand what you're saying."

Shrugging her shoulders, she twirls her index finger, encouraging him to keep his rambling jalopy moving. Her comment slowed his roll, calming him down.

"Anyway, among the backdrop of displayed Bibles and obnoxious 'I can do all things through Christ' nonsense pictures, I find porn and a bottle of Jack Daniels. Of course, they were tucked out of sight from the weekly Bible studies."

"You didn't keep the booze, did you?"

The briefest moment passes. "No."

*Liar, liar pants on fire...*

She's not buying it.

"That's good because liquor doesn't play nice with your meds, or your COURT-APPOINTED alcohol treatment."

"Relax. It's on the express train to the dump," he assures, sensing her skepticism. Wanting to escape her searching spotlight he turns back to the bookshelf.

"There it is! I thought I saw this the other day," he exclaims.

"What?" she asks, baffled by his sudden *Aha!* response.

He slides out a book and presents it to her.

"Nietzsche? What about him?" Susan asks.

"I find it interesting that you have this. Dare I say kismet, even?"

"Kismet?"

"Sunday's word of the day. Been trying to buff up my vocabulary. It means fate or destiny."

"I know what it means. Why is my having a Nietzsche book kismet?

"When I was still in the laughing academy..." he sees her disapproving expression. "Excuse me—THE PSYCHIATRIC HOSPITAL," he busts out his best snooty deportment voice. "The shrink I was seeing had the same book and suggested I read it. I did...voraciously." He sees her quizzical eyebrow. "Tuesday's word," he says easily.

"Josh, I'm glad you've decided to become a pretentious snob, but WHAT IS YOUR POINT?" She enunciates and drags out the last four words to display her growing vexation.

He flips through the pages and lands on the desired one. "Listen to Nietzsche's thoughts about Christians. 'I call Christianity the one great curse, the one great intrinsic depravity, the one great instinct of revenge, for which no means are venomous enough, or secret, subterranean and small enough – I call it the one immortal blemish upon the human race.'"

He claps the book shut. "That was from a century and a half ago. If he saw it then..."

He doesn't finish his sentence; the implication is obvious. Instead, he returns the book and then himself to the couch. The noxious air of arrogance swirls around him as he sinks defiantly into the couch and props his right foot on his left knee. He has taken the position of intellectual superiority.

Smiling, Doctor Andrews sets her notepad and pen on the table. She scoots forward and sits up straight. She is regaining the posture of power and dominance.

"Allow me to interject Sunday's word into this discussion. Do you know how Nietzsche's life ended?" Seeing the concerned look of impending defeat on his face, she continues. "He died as a sad, pathetic shell of a man. He lost his mind and ended up in a mental institution. A commentator, George Bataille, is quoted as saying this about the egotistical hater of Christians: 'Man incarnate must also go mad.' As you said, kismet."

Shifting uncomfortably on the couch, the worthy, but defeated combatant returns to his rightful posture—humility.

"Why do you have his book then?" he asks sullenly.

"Because he's a fantastic study on the power of the intellect and the repercussions it can have on the mind. Plus, he's required reading."

Desiring to change the subject and mend broken bridges (she's the only one he cares to talk to), he decides to be transparent…just a tad.

"I found a left-behind cat today."

"Another one? Are you keeping it?"

"I think so. That is if Toby says it's okay."

"You really do love cats, don't you?"

"Yeah, I do."

"Why?"

"Because they give me peace. Elizabeth was a huge cat person. Before her, I could take them or leave them. Now, because of them, it's like she's still with me, as though they replaced her or something." Unsure what else to say, he stops—chit-chat would only cheapen her.

Seeing the shadow of melancholy breaking over the horizon of his psyche, she joins him on the couch.

"Josh, I don't pretend to know what you're feeling, but it's good that you can talk about your wife. It's cliché but time really does heal. You just need to give *time* time to work."

This seemingly comforts him.

"Now, as far as your disdain for Christians, let it go. Stop giving them preeminence over your life. Only you can change you; so, do *you,* and forget everybody else." She nudges him with her elbow. "See you next week?"

Ventilating a heavy sigh, he nods and stands. As he walks to the door, she calls after him. "Remember, no Baileys in your coffee."

Stopping with his hand on the doorknob, he looks back at her.

"I drink my coffee black." And with that, a wink and the door closing behind him are the images he leaves her with.

*** 

Night has fallen. Josh paces his living room while clutching the neck of the rescued Jack Daniels bottle like a mountain climber clutching a sideways-growing tree after slipping. Just as the tree prevents the climber from certain death, so too does the bottle keep Josh from the chasm of his tortured mind where hateful demons lie in wait.

Exhausted, he plops into his recliner and plunks the bottle on the end table next to the found painkillers. Being the main event of the night, Josh snatches both pill bottles, thumbs off the childproof caps, and knocks out two each into his hand. After returning the pill bottles, he grabs good ol' Jack. He flashes an expectant smile before tossing the four pills into his mouth and chasing them with a tidal wave of bourbon.

Sinking into his recliner, he awaits the rush. To pass the time, he flips on the TV and stares at the flickering images. Scanning his bachelor pad, it'd be hard to judge it as a typical burnout's house. He's new to this crazy scene but is quickly becoming an expert, sad to say. Four months ago, he took his first drink—when his world stopped turning.

Ever since he's worked hard to destroy all that he was. Before, he was never hateful; on the contrary, he strived to be a good neighbor. If you asked what drove him, he'd look you square in the eye and swear to the purity of his heart. It's amazing what's revealed when the chips are down...

In his current condition, time is a relative thing. He's unaware that thirty minutes ticked away; until that is, he noticed the FDA-approved heroin kicking in. And boy oh boy has it ever! Weightlessness engulfs him. A big stupid grin lights up his flushed face; gales of laughter explode in the living room. He's watching his two felines, who fast became BFFs, tear through the house chasing each other.

Wanting to join in the revelry, he takes a giant swig and stands up...a little too quickly. The room spins. He's dangerously close to falling. Wisely, he sits back down and waits for the *teacup ride* to halt its "fun." Regaining his equilibrium, he slowly gets back to his feet, waiting to see if nausea blindsides him again. Nope, all systems are a go...and so must he—his kidneys demand he evicts some of this poison.

Stumbling down the hallway, the cats dart in front of him, nearly tripping him up. Leaning against the wall, he laughs as he watches them disappear around the corner.

"Oh, to be a cat! Not a care in the world," he sloppily declares.

Having breached the bathroom, he goes about his business. While breaking the world record for longest bathroom break, the cats continue their tomfoolery in the living room. Part of their racetrack is the couch where the Blu-Ray remote lies. A paw tramples on it, activating the player. A second later, a video starts playing—Josh's wedding video.

In the bathroom, Josh hears his wife reciting her wedding vows. Stunned, he holds his breath and listens to her voice resound down the hallway. Finishing up and flushing, he reenters the living room. The excitable creatures blast by again, startling him.

Fearing imminent blackout, he drops into the recliner like a sack of potatoes. He leans forward and cups his face in his hands, attempting to stabilize the room. He listens to the TV. Mercifully, the room slows to a crawl. Feeling confident, he looks at the TV. He cannot remember the last time he watched this or why it's even in the player. Did his wife pop it in? He settles back and watches, absorbing every detail.

Two hours pass. And in that time, Josh relived his wedding and much of the reception. Along the way, he also knocked back most of the whiskey. His stomach suddenly informs him that the party is over. Time for everybody to leave.

Josh narrowly makes it to the bathroom before evacuating his stomach's entirety. Once the unpleasantness concludes, he staggers into the kitchen. Removing filtered water from the fridge, he pours himself a glass and shuffles back to his recliner.

The hazing experience brought on by the inevitable crash hits him hard. He feels like he's trapped between two worlds—and in a way, he is. Coming down from his foray into nirvana, his mind begins its familiar dance of despair and sadness. Though dealing with this daily, which is why he escapes nightly, tonight there is a burdensome side effect—shame.

The video now shows guests recording personal messages to the bride and groom. At this point—barely holding onto consciousness— he's not listening; that is until he hears a familiar voice talking directly to him. Josh hangs on every word.

"Joshua, my love. I am thrilled to finally call myself, Mrs. Mendel. Always know that no matter what life throws at us, no matter what comes around the bend, I will always love you. So promise me, never let the cruelties of time and age dampen our love. And above all, never give up on us."

Overcome by sorrow, Josh clicks off the TV. Sitting there, languishing in the tyranny of sudden silence, he's aware of the room's emptiness. He's alone; his furry companions are in a different part of the house, recouping from their hullaballoo. His fading gaze unconsciously shifts to the end table.

Next to the Jack Daniels and the painkillers sits a lone medicine bottle he'd forgotten about—the Ambien. He stares piercingly at the circular, *plastic ticket* to never-never land. The longer he stares, the more the darkness overshadows him. The accusing demons that relentlessly plague him will not be lulled into submission. Suddenly, everything becomes crystal clear. A maleficent peace washes over him. He cannot stand one more day in this wretched existence. More to the point—he won't.

With almost no persuasion, as though he's a marionette being controlled by a devious puppet master, he grabs the Ambien bottle and empties it into his hand. Staring at the mound of pills—well over twenty-five—he knows he's about to cross the threshold of no turning back: he knows, and he must. Time moves forward; and in that time, babies are born, and people die. Is he going to join the latter?

With his right hand holding the slumber pills, his left hand reaches for the glass of water.

Suspended at chest level, his two hands meet. Combined, they create a silent assassin. He takes a final breath, gathering the courage to commit this abhorrent sin. A tear trickles down his cheek as his right hand approaches the open chamber door to eternity.

Suddenly, the new, still-unnamed kitten leaps into his lap, head-butting his right hand. In the blink of an eye, a series of lifesaving occurrences transpire: the pills fly into the air, and the water spills in his lap. The shock of a cat jumping on him—who's now disappeared after the unexpected bath—and the cold water soaking through his shorts, startles him dangerously close to a heart attack.

He jumps to his feet. That did it. The substances, mixed with the physical shock and sprinkled with the sudden rush to his feet, create a recipe for immediate blackout.

Falling forward, his forehead connects with the corner of his coffee table. In the morning, he will greet a nasty gash and an ugly bruise: small price to breathe another day.

# CHAPTER TWO

T hough the words— "exquisite", "ornate", and "awesome"— could justifiably be used to describe the sights and sounds Vincente Basile experiences, they'd still miss the mark. For all of man's sad attempts at bringing down the Almighty's heavenly abode, the Vatican puts forth the noblest effort.

Currently, in St. Peter's Basilica, Vincente saunters through the splendor, hardly breathing within its hallowed walls. He moseys from one breathtaking work of art to the next. From the elegant marble floors' precisely carved features to the awe-inspiring handcrafted sectional tiles that inundate the archways and ceiling, nothing was spared in the making of this devout venue. It is a testament to man's ingenuity and pious commitment to the veneration of its holy saints.

Intermingling with the other meandering tourists, he finds himself standing in front of St. Peter's Baldachin, the Baroque canopy constructed above the original pope's tomb.

He ascends the marble steps to the altar where history's popes have officiated high Mass. Standing under the canopy, his eyes trace the spiraling columns. Hand-crafted ivy, interspersed with clinging cherubim, circles the mesmerizing columns. His eyes continue their scrutiny until they land on the center of the canopy's underside. There he sees something so overpowering that he drops to his knees and bows his head.

Vincente is bowing before an image drawn by the Barberini family. It is a dove surrounded by a radiant sunburst. This is their representation of the Holy Spirit. As he kneels, a phenomenon hits the scene, causing multiple tourists to stop and gawk.

Crepuscular rays of light pierce through the windows in Michelangelo's Dome and spotlight the servant kneeling at the altar. It's as though he's receiving the Spirit through Barberini's dove descending upon him. He lifts his head, allowing the rays to light his face. Somebody from the crowd speaks, making the moment even more powerful.

"'This is my beloved son, in whom I am well pleased,'" quotes a man walking towards the Baldachin.

The crowd reverently parts for him. The man dressed entirely in red robes stops at the steps and bids Vincente to join him.

"Saint Matthew three-seventeen," Vincente adds as he obeys the waiting man.

"Hello, my son, I am Cardinal Romando. I have been instructed to retrieve you." The cardinal extends his hand. Vincente receives it.

"Hi, I'm Vincente Basile."

The cardinal smiles pleasantly; obviously, he knows this. He leads Vincente through the crowd of people witnessing the exchange.

The more devout cross themselves before bowing their head. Those not on a pilgrimage snap pictures with their phones. Despite the differences, nobody speaks.

Once outside, standing in St. Peter's Square, the cardinal stops the journey.

"Are you up for a jaunt? We can take a golf cart, but I enjoy walking across the Square when it's warm."

"I'd prefer the walk as well."

Still wearing the gracious smile, the cardinal points: "Wonderful. We are walking to that building. It is the Palace of Sant Uffizio, which, thankfully, was changed to Congregation for the Doctrine of the Faith. Still a mouthful but a lot easier than trying to pronounce Sant Uffizio."

Allowing himself to be led, Vincente marches along with the cardinal. As they go, birds take flight, and throngs of tourists stroll by. The duo is unnoticed. Neither the oblivious birds nor the self-absorbed tourists know who walks among them.

*** 

Vincente Basile and Cardinal Romando enter the Congregation building and continue the brisk pace. Arriving at a door, the cardinal opens it, ushering Vincente into a beautiful room. It is an immense library, housing centuries-old records of church history and its ever-expanding doctrines. Sitting at one of the many large tables is an engrossed young man staring at an open laptop.

Arriving, the two men startle the slouching laptop user. Sitting up quickly and removing his earbuds, he hastily closes his laptop, but not before Vincente sees the screen.

Standing over the young man, the cardinal notices the scattered chaos of empty energy drink cans and crumpled candy wrappers. Seeing the cardinal's disapproving scrutiny, the young man gathers his mess. Unsure where to stow the offenses, he chooses his backpack. Standing, he wipes his right hand on his pants and offers it for shaking.

"Sorry about that. Lost track of time. Hi, I'm Aaron D'Angelo."

Vincente smiles, excepting his hand, "Hello. I'm Vincente Basile. American?"

"Born and raised," Aaron confirms.

"Well, I'll leave you to it," Cardinal Romando says, eyebrow cocked in condescending disapproval. Turning on his heel, he strolls away, hands cupped against the small of his back.

Rolling his eyes, Aaron watches the pious cardinal walk away.

"That's why I escaped the church as soon as I turned eighteen. Can't stand the arrogant, holier-than-thou, hypocritical attitude of priests. And nuns! Don't get me started! My knuckles are still screwed up. I'm no longer convinced there even is a God. I know, can I be any more clichéd? But the Church has soured me to the whole deity concept."

Seeing Vincente's bemused smile, Aaron

freezes his rambling diatribe. "Excuse me! I wasn't thinking."

"No worries, my friend. I'm not a fan of the Hierarchy either," Vincente soothes. "As far as there being a God, there is…believe me. His fingerprints are everywhere; you just need to free yourself from the biblical ONLY view of God and search for Him with an open mind."

Sensing the uncomfortableness, Vincente changes the subject. "D'Angelo: How many generations has your family been in the States?"

"Both sets of grandparents came over on the boat. Pure blood. No mutts in my family."

"Family is very important to Italians. I know it all too well. Are your grandparents still alive?"

"Just my dad's dad, who refuses to go. His pride won't allow it. He's one stubborn Itie." Aaron states with obvious admiration. Vincente picks up on it.

"Sounds like you love your grandfather."

Aaron nods in total agreement. "My insatiable desire to succeed was gifted by him. He's an old-school Italian who knows the importance of being well-educated. His parents were raised under the tyranny of Mussolini. Vowing to take full advantage of the freedom his parents never had, he lost himself in learning everything he could. He believes there is no limit to the human mind or its capacity to retain knowledge; it is only because of man's laziness do many never achieve their full potential. I bought into that thinking early on and followed his example, which pleased him immensely. He forever preaches to me that an erudite man is a liberated man. He has a lot of little sayings, but that's his favorite."

Vincente delights in Aaron's gift for gab, even if it borderlines on rambling. "So with all this knowledge, where did the desire to be a journalist come from?"

"Hey! I'm the one who's supposed to be writing your story!" Aaron jokes.

"Please forgive me. I'd rather get to know people than talk about myself."

"Well, if we don't talk about you at some point, then the Vatican wasted their money bringing me over here. And we all know the Vatican is barely scraping by," states Aaron—ever the master of sarcasm.

"To answer your question, my love for the written word came from my father. I started writing silly short stories when I was nine. Though I don't necessarily want to be a journalist, he always insisted I not poo-poo it. He felt it could be a stepping stone for getting my work read as it was for him. My pops was a struggling freelance journalist whose ship came in when he wrote a piece on the trial of Anthony Cavallo, the most famous wise guy in Brooklyn at the time."

"Wise guy, huh?"

"Yeah, you know—mafia, Goodfellas, the mob," Aaron fiddles with his nose, sniffing exaggeratingly like a third-base coach signaling for the batter to bunt.

"Wise guys," Aaron says, providing a terrible Sopranos' accent.

Vincente smirks: "Yes, I'm familiar with the term."

"So anyway, he showed his piece to the *New York Times* and they bought it. It ended up being the lead article, right above the fold. He was respected and in demand for the rest of his life. As much as I love my grandfather, I love my dad even more. Miss him just as much..." Aaron drifts off. Obviously, the heartache still sears.

"I'm sorry for your loss, Aaron," Vincente says.

"Thanks. Even though he's been gone for a while, it's easy to remember him. He left quite an impression on the journalist world."

"But you don't want to be a part of that world?"

"Not even a little. Don't get me wrong, I'm grateful for my last name and the doors it's opened. It's because of that name I'm even here. When *The Times* found out the son of the great Stephano D'Angelo was an up-and-coming writer, they sold me to The Church, convincing them to give me the exclusive."

"I'm sure your work stands on its merit."

"So they tell me. Some of my articles were picked up by other newspapers and websites... eh." Aaron shrugs his shoulders as if to say *whatever, it's a paycheck.* "I graduated from NYU with a creative writing degree, so penning pithy articles doesn't exactly blow my hair back. But my dad cut his teeth interviewing a once famous old man, so who am I to refuse interviewing a soon-to-be-famous young man."

"What do you want to write, Aaron?"

Without a beat, Aaron responds. "Novels. Grand, sweeping stories that capture the reader and care not that they've been so. The power of the written word to create an expansive world from nothing more than a simple idea is exhilarating. The thrill of setting my muse loose in an unknown world to reveal what I didn't see previously is without comparison. Have you ever played a real-time strategy video game where you capture territory and control it?"

"I've never played *a* video game, but I certainly understand capturing and controlling territory."

"Sorry, I'm a bit of a gamer. My gaming drives my grandfather nuts. My response is that playing games to temporarily escape reality is not the worst thing in the world; I could be doing drugs. I say this because it's second in importance to him. 'Never, under any circumstances, do you ever do drugs, Aaron D'Angelo!' Since I've never touched a drug, even when I was at NYU, I remind him of this when he's on me about video games. It's a cheap tactic, and I'm not necessarily proud of it, but I love gaming."

"You're an interesting character, Aaron," Vincente affirms.

"Thanks, but nobody's writing an article about me. It's you the people are clamoring for."

"I'm not sure anybody is clamoring for me, either."

"Well, maybe not yet, but they will be. You're doing something that's never been done. It's man's nature to be inspired by greatness. Humanity needs to worship something, anything."

"While I appreciate what you're saying, I don't want to be worshipped."

"I understand, but that doesn't change the human condition. Man is forever looking for the next shining star; it's been that way throughout history, and history always repeats itself. Whether that star is worthy of wishing upon or not, well, only time will tell."

"Aaron, you are obviously gifted and well-read, even if you do spend too much time playing video games," Vincente jokes.

Aaron smiles. He always enjoys a good roast, even when he's the main course. "Thank my grandfather and my father for the former, and blame my generation for the latter. Well, anyhoo, I don't mean to cut off your probing, because heaven knows I enjoy a good probing, but we should probably get at this."

Vincente smiles. He allowed himself to be subjugated up to this point, but now it's time to take the reins. He notices a secluded alcove containing a plush couch and a welcoming armchair. Bright, piercing sunlight from the window wall behind the couch adds to the tranquility.

Pointing, Vincente proposes: "I think we'd be more comfortable over there."

Aaron looks at the suggested locale and

nods in agreement. Gathering up his gear, he trails after Vincente.

Arriving, Vincente situates himself in the armchair while Aaron plops on the couch and re-sets up shop. First order of business—plugging in his laptop and situating it on the coffee table. After opening it, he's immediately grateful for the screen's antiglare filter: the sun is brutally bright. Next, he lays out a legal pad and some pens. Lastly, he retrieves two lapel mics and attaches one to his shirt.

"If you don't mind, I'd like to record all this." Seeing Vincente's acquiescence, Aaron continues. "These are Bluetooth mics. They record what we say to a voice recorder app. May I attach this to your shirt?"

"Be my guest." To make it easier for Aaron to *wire* him, Vincente unbuttons the top two buttons. As Aaron enters Vincente's personal boundary, he notices the gold chain/strange amulet combo dangling against Vincente's black T-shirt.

"That's a striking necklace," Aaron comments. Captured by its elegance, Aaron remains awkwardly close to Vincente. "What is it?"

Vincente lifts the necklace so Aaron can get a better look. "You've never heard of the Italian Horn?"

"I guess my Italianess only stretches so far. What's its significance?"

"It protects against Malocchio. My grandmother insisted that my father wore it. She was very superstitious. Its only value to me is that it was my father's."

A peculiar moment of ogling passes before Aaron shakes his head. "Sorry, zoned out there for a second." He attaches the mic and exists Vincente's intimate zone.

Embarrassed, Aaron makes a beeline for the couch. He desperately wants to plant some clock ticks between the present and his strange behavior. Situating his pad and pen, he centers his mind, ready to chronicle this fascinating character's life story.

"We're a couple of decades into what has already been an eventful century, not to mention, millennium. Some are calling it the most momentous century in the history of modern man, and yet you somehow stand out from the congestion. Even more astounding...you're only twenty-nine." Aaron falls silent, waiting for his response.

"I'm sorry. I didn't hear a question."

"Vincente Basile, you are about to accomplish something that's never been done. Tomorrow, Pope Andel Vassallo will confirm you as a saint. You will be the only person ever canonized while still alive."

Vincente lowers his head. "I am humbled by the undeserved honor."

"How is this possible? How did you ascend to sainthood?"

Vincente quietly ponders this inquiry. "Aaron, it's a long story."

"That's why I'm here. Let's get crackin."

Again, Vincente is not hasty to answer. His attention is drawn away by the splendor projected on the window wall behind Aaron. Reflecting on the immense world of people hustling about the courtyard, he remains silent for one more beat. He absentmindedly pinches and twists the chain on his necklace, making the horn spin. Like watching a hypnotist's watch, Aaron is again enchanted by the necklace. The sun glistening off the pure gold helps arrest his attention. Vincente knows precisely what he's doing.

"It is a story that ends with forgiveness and redemption. But first..." Closing his eyes, Vincente allows his mind's eye to roll its movie reel. "It is one of loss and sorrow, of pain and betrayal, and garbage; I can still smell the garbage..."

***

A new day dawns. Though it may be a new twenty-four hours, the adage applies, "Same stuff, different day." L.M. Montgomery has a saying in one of her beloved books, "Tomorrow is a new day, with no mistakes in it." Surely, she didn't have Naples, Italy, in mind when she penned those words. Naples, Florida, perhaps, but definitely not Naples, Italy, because the Naples, Italy, Vinny Basile grew up in is anything but mistake-free. Rather, it is a cesspool of degradation and corruption. To make things worse, every day adds more mistakes on top of the previous day's indiscretions. It's a hopeless avalanche of inhumanity that Naples' poor citizens cannot dig out from.

Nineteen-year-old Vinny (impossibly beautiful and spilling over with charisma—his six-foot-two, muscular frame is imposing. In the world of breeding and heritage, he is a thoroughbred, an Italian Stallion if you will) exits his dilapidated apartment tower and makes his way through the mountains of trash the city will not remove. The stench, though once potent, is now nothing more than a faint smell: just white noise for the olfactory senses.

Emaciated dogs nose through the piles of trash looking for something edible. Stray cats scatter as the denizens of Trash Town, as it's become known, trudge through the waist-high walled pathway of months-old refuse.

Taking the path of dirty diapers, rotting food, decaying carcasses, et al, Vinny spies a mother struggling to push a stroller over the bumps, coming his way. Since the trail is only a single lane, Vinny climbs out of the way, making room for mother and child to pass. Passing, she offers a paltry nod of gratitude. Unoffended, Vinny climbs down and continues his journey.

Having left the peaks of Trash Town, Vinny arrives in the business district of Piazza Garibaldi: a slightly more civilized ghetto. He walks the streets unafraid regardless of them being in one of Naples' worst neighborhoods. The suffocating chokehold the Camorra—the Italian mafia—has on this town is unbreakable, not even by the police. The city's most powerful mafia family is the Vescovi Family.

Vinny was born into this family. His father, Emiliano Basile, is the current underboss. After turning fourteen, Vinny became a muschilli, *little fly*, whose only purpose was running drugs and other courier-related assignments. Over time, the antiquated title was changed to Associates— same responsibilities, just a more ominous name.

In the Camorra hierarchy, the next tier after Associate is Soldier. Their job is using "the easy way" or "the hard way" to collect the Family's "donations." The donors' willingness is rarely considered. Often, a Berretta M9 has the last word: ruthless to be sure, but more merciful than a led pipe.

As far as Vinny is concerned, Soldier is not his future. He'll skip right over to Captain. This is irregular, but it helps when you're the apple of the man at the top's eye.

Bastiano Vescovi, the Family's don, is quite fond of Vinny Basile. Early in Vinny's life, Bastiano noticed a unique aura clung to him. It was something he'd never seen before and could not explain. Almost like, the largest battalion of guardian angels ever assembled was assigned to him. It terrified Bastiano but also awed him. Those who know him will swear—that's an atypical response; few ever grab Bastiano's attention, for better or for worse.

The day Emiliano made him Vinny's godfather was a singular moment in his life. Emiliano knew Bastiano could not have his own son. It was his way of honoring not only the Boss but also his close friend. In response, Bastiano swore a lifetime blood oath that he would honor his friend's gift. When Emiliano requested that Vinny never become a Soldier, (he still suffers from the ghosts of the men he's killed and doesn't want this pain for his son) Bastiano gave his word.

Vinny's grandmother worked to offset the world he was growing up in. Weekly, he was browbeaten into going to mass with her. His dad, who endured the same indignity as a child, encouraged Vinny to suck it up and go. He knew it'd make her happy and keep her off his son's back.

As with everything involving his dad, Vinny consented ONLY because he asked him to. However, he only endured this irritant till he was thirteen. After that, he could no longer abide the weekly harassment about his sins by a hypocritical priest doing only God knows what. The way Vinny saw it, if God knew but did nothing about it, what difference did it make if he was in church or not? It was all theater.

Church wasn't the only worthless institution Vinny abandoned at a young age. His school teachers discovered his extraordinary aptitude early on. They were floored by his otherworldly 280 IQ and wanted to see just how smart he was. They forced him into every advanced class. They assumed the stimulation was helping him, but really, it was crushing him. His spirit was deflated by the time he was a teenager. He was sick of feeling like a lab rat. So, he dropped out. He was the smartest person in the entire school—the entire continent really—so why continue going?

Vinny arrives at his morning destination—the house of his second-greatest love: Angelica Laconi. She's his angel and he never tires of romancing her with this play on words. Standing at the steps leading up to her parent's apartment, he reflects on how much nicer her place is compared to his own...

***

There is a well-worn mafia cliché about higher-ups being flush with Ducats, which Emiliano Basile most certainly is. He is forever trying to dole out money to his prized son, but Vinny respectfully refuses his benevolence. He's determined to amass his fortune on his laurels, or he will die trying. Emiliano admires this, so he respects his son's wishes.

However, Vinny's mother...that's a different story. His parents split up when he was fourteen. Wanting to be a good son, Vinny stayed with his mom. Though he loves his father deeply —he's his hero and idol, after all—he believes a son should take care of his mother no matter what. Vinny's mom will never be the apple of anybody's eye. She is the equivalent of a human hurricane, always threatening landfall and a swath of destruction.

To be fair, she shouldn't bear the full brunt of the blame; her childhood was an endless cycle of deviant behavior at the hands of vile men, including her father. It's impossible for a preteen girl not to be psychologically altered by the incessant incest wrought upon her tiny heart and mind. Mercifully, she did escape the humiliation and desecration, but it was too late: the damage was done.

Emiliano found her on the streets employing mankind's oldest profession. Though never one of her customers, he eventually fell in love with her. After convincing her *employer* to free her from his employment, (mafia soldiers do wield a lot of power) he married and rescued her from the back alleys and hour-rate hotel rooms.

Vinny arrived on the scene nine months after they were married. As most new moms know the first look into their baby's eyes activates a deeply engrained response. If the natural order of womanhood is obeyed, it overrules all other compulsions and addictions: she listened and obeyed. Admirably, she made the sacrifices to be a good mom and a loving wife. But those who battle the ghosts of the mind know how tricky mental illness can be. If the fences are not maintained and a guard not constantly at its post, the wolves of repressed memories will find the weak link and seize upon camp.

During the first eleven years of Vinny's life, she successfully managed her schizophrenia with proper medication and biweekly talk therapy, but, alas, old habits die hard...

Wearied by Lithium's nasty side effects, she decided to stop taking it. After three skipped days, her demons returned to their favorite puppet and trotted her back on stage. The shame of the exposure to all her old addictions was unprecedented. The most potent—her unquenched thirst for male acceptance. She chased it with reckless abandonment, indifferent to the repercussions.

Emiliano forgave her for the first couple of indiscretions; in his mind, he has so many sins to atone for. How can he not forgive her? But it was her fourth tryst that finally broke him. Though he didn't leave physically, he left emotionally.

For three miserable years, he endured her infidelity. Her psychosis convinced her that each new man drew her closer to filling the hole in her heart left by her despicable father. Her belief was one more, always just one more, and her heart would be repaired.

It was when her heroin addiction turned her into a violent lunatic that he decided it was time to leave. A man can only take so many objects thrown at him and so many knife disarmaments before he's had enough. His only other option was having her *clipped*, but he couldn't do that either. He did love her and wanted her to get better, but with each passing day, healing seemed less likely.

It was when Vinny stood his ground, insisting he stay with his mother rather than going with him, that Emiliano finally saw the solution. Because she was never violent towards Vinny, and since it was maternal love that squared her away the first time, he hoped lightning would strike twice. If Vinny could save her, then he was willing to sacrifice his son: it felt messianic to the lifelong Catholic. That was five years ago and the only difference between then and now: way more drugs and way more men...

***

Seeing her depressed man standing on the street, Angelica exits her apartment to join him. Snapping out of his retrospection, he looks at her, the only woman who knows and loves him.

Shortly after his dad moved out, Angelica rescued a confused fourteen-year-old boy from dejection and sorrow; she's still rescuing him five years later. She will never replace a mother's love, but she has replaced a piece of his heart stolen by a selfish junkie. He has no idea what he would do if he lost Angelica...he never wants to find out. She gifts him with a delicate kiss before leading him inside.

Later that evening, the star-crossed lovers exit her apartment. They've had a wonderful day together. Her parents adore him, always happy to have him in their home. A parting kiss is shared under a streetlamp's glow before Vinny begrudgingly heads home.

Thirty minutes later, he crosses the imaginary line into Thrash Town. A few more minutes and he's swinging open the front door to his filthy apartment building. As he ascends the stairs to his apartment, the sounds of ghetto life play their perverse nightly symphony. Instead of the winds section, there are screaming babies; domestic violence has the percussion section covered; and in place of the strings, there is only the strung out. Vinny hates it here. The environment is bad enough but the daily struggles of tending to his burnout mom...well, he's burned out. He can't keep it up much longer.

Arriving at his floor, he approaches his apartment. With the key in position, ready to unlock the door, it suddenly swings open. A scrawny, taller man is leaving. The stranger stops, clearly too high to be startled by Vinny's unexpected presence. Vinny glares up at the waste of space blocking his entrance.

Something in Vinny snaps. He's in no mood to deal with his mother's *johns* tonight. Fearlessly, Vinny steps into this dirtbag's personal space. Not backing down, the man complies with Vinny's Alpha Male contest—this cat's none too bright.

With measured movement, the clueless addict lifts his shirt, revealing a gun tucked in his waistband. His hard expression suggests he's not to be trifled with. Unaffected and unintimidated, Vinny looks past the roadblock and sees his mother slouched in her disgusting La-Z-Boy. She's unconscious; the needle dangling from her arm probably has something to do with it. Another man leaving and another night ending with her passed out. Vinny's seen this scene one too many times. Like his father, he's had enough.

One more moment of the showdown passes and then...if you blinked, you missed it. With unholy speed, Vinny snatches the flaunted gun and launches it upwards, right into the dude's nose. Head flying back, nose spurting like a geyser, he staggers backward. Vinny grabs the guy's shirt and drags him down the hallway toward the stairwell door. With rage-fueled stamina, Vinny slams the guy into the panic door. In the stairwell, Vinny tosses him down the stairs and continues doing so till he reaches the first floor. At the bottom, Vinny drags the unconscious deadweight outside and tosses him into the sanitation nightmare.

A minute later, Vinny enters the apartment, locking the door behind him. The Incredible Hulk subsides; mild-mannered Bruce Banner returns. All he wants to do is escape to his bedroom and call it a night. But he knows he needs to attend to his pitiful mother first. Plucking her limp body from her La-Z-Boy, he carries her into her bedroom, lays her on her bed, and draws the sheets over her.

Walking back into the living room to close up shop for the night, he spies her cooking gear on the end table. Disgust and revulsion are not his responses but rather weariness. He knows the drugs are not the main problem but the by-product of issues she's refusing to deal with. That's about to change, whether she likes it or not.

Since he's already *flushed* the main problem, he flushes the by-product as well, down the toilet. Hypnotized by the swirling, powdery whirlpool, he watches until the tank refills the bowl. Realization wells up. The world he lives in is a toilet; he's tired of flushing it over and over and over. It's time to call it a night, both literally and figuratively. He enters his room, strips, and crawls into bed. His final act of this depressing night is turning out the light. In the morning, he will turn on the light to a new day and a new life. How will it play out? Well, he'll just have to see what tomorrow brings. Perhaps L.M. Montgomery will be right for once...

***

With the sun barely kissing the sky good morning, Vinny is rousted by an irate, out-of-control woman—dear ol' Ma. Despite weighing a paltry buck o' five, she yanks him to his feet and decks him. Though the pain is hardly noticeable, it's the rude awakening that irritates him the most. She swings again, but this time he catches the feeble punch and wrangles the screaming, thrashing lunatic against him, pinning her arms to her side. When she calms, he releases her. She marches him into the bathroom and holds up the empty baggie. A silent stare-down ensues. Leaning against the doorframe, Vinny doesn't flinch, nor show any regret. Seeing his resolute staunchness, there's only one thing her irrational mind comes up with.

Brushing past him, she marches back into his room, opens his window, and begins tossing out all his stuff. Sighing in deep sorrow, Vinny accepts this is the grand finale of the screwed-up opera. He knew today would be pivotal, but her tossing him out on the street was a surprise.

Vinny heads for the front door. Seeing his

retreat, she tosses random projectiles at him. Grimy dishes and empty liquor bottles smash against the wall all around him. Moldy food and rancid alcohol splash on him, but nothing life-threatening. Opening the door, he exits but stops at the threshold to give her one final look. He's hoping she'll see his distraught eyes and change her mind. She sees them; another barrage of ceramic artillery is her response. He closes the door as a plate smashes against it.

Standing at the closed door, a tear slides down his cheek. He loves his mother, even though she no longer resembles one. Kissing his fingers, he touches the door and says goodbye. He will never see her again.

*** 

Twelve months have passed since Vinny escaped Trash Town, and during that time, he, and Angelica were married and moved into a house outside the city. Vinny was also promoted to Captain, bringing with it a massive uptick in disposable income. It suits him; he wishes he chased it sooner.

Not long after becoming Captain, news of his mother's death reached Vinny's ears. She was discovered lying in a gutter; she'd choked to death on her own vomit. An autopsy showed she would've died within the hour anyway. Her untamed *horse* finally trampled her. He went to her funeral and paid his respects. He was the only one there. A fitting end to a sad life.

Vinny's new life, however, is anything but

sad. The whirlwind of success that captured him, and altered him is unlike anything he ever could've imagined. Life is so radically different, it's hard to remember how bad it used to be. His relationship with his father is restored and stronger than ever. Finally getting to work with him keeps Vinny in constant euphoria. He never wants to go back to life without Dad. He never wants to go back to poverty. His life is perfect. Heaven help the one who tries to take it...

A few months ago, a ruthless capo dei capi in the LCN—La Cosa Nostra, Sicily's mafia syndicate—began warring with the rest of the country, attempting to wipe out Sicily's other Families. Eventually, he did. But, as with all bloodthirsty tyrants, he desired more power. Controlling the *football* was gratifying, but it wasn't enough: he wanted the *woman's boot* as well.

Sicily's own Alexander the Great did breach Italy's shores and work his way north, successfully subduing the entire lower half. All the Families rolled over like sleeping cows at the shoving hands of the mighty don. Rome was next, but first, he needed to deal with Naples, which was proving harder than he expected. The ancient city's First Family was nearly impossible to infiltrate...nearly.

The invading LCN bided their time, waiting for a Judas to offer their contemptible services. But which Judas would it be? Would it be the one willing to do their own kissing, or the one who sends a rat in sheep's clothing to do it for them? As it turned out, it was the second Judas, and their chosen rat was an *empty suit*—one who isn't mobbed up but willing to do anything to be initiated into a Family.

***

A clandestine man, head engulfed in the hood of his sweatshirt, sits in a shut-off Fiat several street parking spots away and on the opposite side from a quaint bistro. The car's clock changes to 11:00. The hooded man has been sitting, waiting, for over ten minutes. Late last night, he received intel that a brunch involving two high-value members of the Vescovi organization would be taking place the following morning. He's been waiting for a phone call like this for some time, the opportunity to prove himself. If his plan's successful, it'll strike a major blow to the Family. Hoodie can feel his finger being pricked right now...

Having parked so the bistro's patio is seen in his driver-side mirror, Hoodie watches the first of the two-member brunch sitting at an outside table, his back to the front wall of the bistro, sipping his double espresso. With each passing second, Hoodie's anxiety draws closer to full-blown hysteria. The clock now reports 11:07. Member number two is late.

*What's the holdup?* Hoodie's inner voice bemoans.

The tardiness infuriates him. It's preventing him from doing this nasty business; it's holding him up from crawling back into his dank apartment and spending the rest of the day flying like a kite. On the way, he'd paid a quick visit to his *pharmacist* to get his *prescription* refilled. In retrospect, he should've swung by his hook's crib AFTER the job: his *meds* are burning a hole in his pocket. But, alas, NOT living in the moment is Hoodie's greatest weakness.

Unable to bear the pressure any longer, Hoodie digs out the small baggie from his pocket and lovingly gawks at it. Pretty Pink Powder's tantalizing siren song is only discernible to the hopelessly addicted; those who know her voice cannot resist her for long. Just a little taste and then he'd be straight.

After scanning for looky-loos, Hoodie ducks out of sight for a couple of snorts. As he sits back up, a car passes the driver's side, startling him. Holding his breath, he tracks the car as it parks two spots up from him. His eyes stay glued to the car, hoping member number two steps out. Wish fulfilled.

Through his windshield, Hoodie watches Vinny Basile exit, key-fobbing the lock as he walks. Hearing the horn honk, stage fright seizes Hoodie—time to break a leg.

Seeing another car coming but not wanting to wait, Vinny walks toward Hoodie's car. He'll cross when the coast is clear. Several feet from Hoodie's car, Vinny ignores all that isn't preventing him from getting to the bistro. If Hoodie played it cool, the powerful wise guy never would've noticed him. Pity. Hoodie looking down, stretching his hood further down his face, and spastically pinching his nose caught Vinny's attention.

Vinny stares into the windshield, then shifts his focus to the driver-side window as he crosses the street. Continuing his trek, he keeps his head craned towards the queer figure. Hoodie holds his breath, anxiety reaching dangerous levels. Thankfully, Vinny's attention is snagged by the crying out of his name. Hoodie releases a shaky breath as Vinny regards his brunch companion waving him over.

Vinny's street crossing ends in his father's loving arms. Stepping back, but still within arm's reach, he acquiesces to his hair being ruffled. With the pleasantries seen to, Underboss Basile sits, motioning for his son to join him.

Watching the father/son reunion play out, Hoodie repeatedly wakes and sleeps his cell as he reflects on the golden opportunity that's fallen in his lap...

After getting the call last night, Hoodie snuck out into the blackness and onto the bistro's patio where he planted a small Semtex bomb inside one of the planters. He was proud of his little bomb; he'd invested many stressful hours creating it.

For those who know Hoodie, the idea of him building a Semtex bomb is ludicrous. This is because the only associations he has are of the *doing drugs with* or *buying drugs from* variety. There's nobody in his life interested in getting to know him, that is until he met the Vescovi Judas: this person was deeply interested in him.

They learned his childhood dream was to be an electrical engineer and that fiddling with electronics and circuit boards was his passion. Convincing Hoodie to make a bomb strong enough to blow a hole in the Vescovi organization was Judas' role in this unfolding tragedy. If successful, the LCN making him a made man was Hoodie's reward.

The opportunity excited him, but there was a problem—he'd never made a bomb before. Sure, he's cobbled together a few alarm clocks over the years, but a bomb was a whole different animal. Getting shocked by an improperly grounded wire was a minor nuisance; getting blown up, a major bummer. So he consulted the ultimate source for higher learning—YouTube...

Snapping back to reality (his *meds* are experts at encouraging him to chase dreams and shadows), Hoodie panics as he gains his bearings. Disorientation shackles him. After a time, realization triggers his waking mind. Low on courage, Hoodie helps himself to another snort.

Back on the job, Hoodie confirms the Basile duo are still on the patio. However, they're wrapping up. Waking his cell (i.e., the detonator), he finds the bomb's attached cellphone's number and readies himself to spring his offspring onto the unsuspecting Basiles. His trembling thumb hangs ominously over the SEND button. Once he pushes the green button, nothing will be the same. He closes his eyes, takes a deep breath, and...

An uneventful moment passes. Not hearing an earth-shattering blast, Hoodie opens his eyes to see birds still pecking at the crumbs on the patio; passerbyes still passing by; and most discouragingly, Father and Son Basile still intact.

Flabbergasted, Hoodie rakes his tweaked-out brain, trying to understand what went wrong. He followed YouTube's instructions to the letter. No time to resolve this conundrum now, his marks have paid their bill and are standing to leave. Hysteria sets in. This will be his only shot at the big time. He cannot and will not fade into obscurity. His final act will not be ODing in some arbitrary crack house.

Only one idea blooms. Starting the car, he maneuvers out of his parking space. Death was supposed to come from an electronically ignited two-pound plastic explosive; now, death from an electronically ignited four-hundred-pound combustion engine will have to do.

As Vinny and Dad hug, Hoodie picks up speed. Looking over Vinny's shoulder, Dad spots the approaching Fiat, barreling toward them. Without a second thought, he pushes his prized son out of the way and takes all of it.

Vinny stumbles backward, tripping over a table. His dad's sacrifice is a success. The heat-seeking missile misses Vinny, but sadly finds one of its intended targets. The car slams into Emiliano, crushing him against the bistro's front wall.

Hoodie looks out the cracked windshield to see Senior Basile pinned between the car and the building; his top half lies face down on the hood. Sprawled out on the patio, next to the Fiat's passenger's side, Vinny stares, mouth agape.

Hoodie stumbles out of his car and skedaddles. Vinny watches, too stunned to give chase. Just before Hoodie disappears down an alley, he looks back at Vinny. Even from this distance, Vinny spots the diamond-shaped, quarter-sized birthmark on Hoodie's left cheekbone.

Time slows to a crawl. All around him, people scurry as they perform a soundless one-act play. Vinny tries to work through the absurdity but is distracted by something odd lying next to an overturned planter. He crawls to it—a small bomb. Picking it up, he examines it with quizzical fascination. Comprehension dawns: he and his father were green-lit, but by who?

Now's not the time for riddle-solving—his father calls for him. Vinny obeys. His dad's eyes are barely open, but they stare with extreme urgency. His gaze bores through Vinny's heart. The pain...incalculable; the anguish...without equal.

Feebly motioning with his balled-up left hand, his father beckons him near. Vinny has been fighting back tears, but now so close to his dad, the dam breaks loose. Amidst the deluge, Vinny offers a beggar's hand and accepts his father's fist with gratitude. Emiliano transfers something into Vinny's hand and, with the same hand, closes Vinny's shut before he can see it. Encasing his son's clasped hand in his own, he pulls him close. Trying to block out the pandemonium all around him, Vinny fights to hear his father's dying words. Undeterred by death's rattle ringing in his ears, Emiliano's diction is impeccable—*I am so proud of you, Son. I love you.*

With that, his hand falls off Vinny's and collapses onto the hood. Vinny weeps. Eventually, he reigns in his emotions and recaptures his legendary self-control. Slowly opening his hand, he recognizes an object he's long admired; an item that conjures up deeply abiding memories from his childhood. With shaky, bloody hands, Vinny reaches around his neck and connects a tiny clasp. Delicately, he holds out his father's golden, Italian horn necklace and stares at it.

He begins to comprehend the enormity of his father entrusting him with his treasure. The final ceremony of passing on a legacy is not lost on Vinny. No, he understands the gravity all too well. Seemingly, his entire young life has led up to this one moment, a brief respite from a tragedy that will forever define him. Vinny kisses the elegant horn and rests it against his chest. It'll remain there till he dies.

\*\*\*

Later that evening, after a few hours at the hospital and then a few more at the police station for debriefing, Vinny is freed to head home. He desperately needs Angelica's comfort. But first, he needs an Uber to take him to his car, still at the bistro.

A half-hour later, Vinny is home. However, he remains in his car, giving his emotions time to subside. Staring blankly at the garage door, his left eye catches movement. Now focusing on the front of his house, he sees Angelica peering through the drawn curtains. She's looking at him, and judging by her expression, something is amiss. Quickly, she draws back, leaving the curtains to sway by her sudden absence.

Vinny walks briskly to the front door. As he approaches, he sees hectic, jarring activity through the door's frosted privacy window. Whatever's happening, Angelica is agitated. Inserting the door key while still peering through the frosted window, his eyes see two separate movements: somebody else is inside. So far, this night is not playing out the way he envisioned it.

Adrenaline levels spiking, Vinny swings open the door and rushes in. With a clear view down the front hallway, Vinny spots the intruder climbing through an open back window. With nimble speed, Vinny charges the halfway-through-the-window burglar.

Vinny latches onto the man's belt, and with a powerful yank, the intruder is back inside. Stumbling backward, the cat burglar trips over the various debris scattered everywhere. For the first time, Vinny notices the mess dotting the landscape of what is no longer his safe abode.

Vinny lunges at the intruder's midsection, tackling him to the floor. Saddling the intruder,

Vinny wails away. Even with raised, blocking arms, Vinny does significant damage, but it's not enough…he wants to destroy this man. The pent-up rage needs to be liberated.

Vinny pries the intruder's arms away from his face with his left hand while cocking back his right fist, ready to land a knock-out punch. However, Vinny's *fight* is suddenly doused by bewilderment. The intruder turned his head to the right, bracing for the incoming four-knuckled missile. Vinny works through the reality of the diamond-shaped, quarter-sized birthmark now staring up at him.

*Obviously, he's here to finish the job and take out Angelica for good measure…Angelica!*

The reminder of his better half births a new reality—*I haven't seen or heard her since busting through the door. Where is she?*

His sixth sense answers for him. Turning to peer over his left shoulder, Vinny's cheek welcomes a swinging blunt object manned by his darling wife.

Tumbling off the trespasser and rolling onto his back, Vinny lies motionless, subdued. He heroically pushes back against the darkness threatening to devour him. Dizzy birds flitter around his head, reminding him of childhood cartoons.

Bringing his deteriorating view into focus, he watches Angelica drop the large living room lamp. His mind tries to convince him this is all a colossal misunderstanding; that, in her panic she swung at him thinking he was the intruder.

Despite his brain's best efforts, the evidence is irrefutable. Angelica straddling and then squatting her five-foot-five frame down onto his stomach hushes his brain: she knows what she's doing and to whom.

She stares silently at him. After a moment, her uncaring, wicked eyes soften as she leans forward and plants a kiss on his forehead. She then cups both sides of his face in her soft, cruel hands and bores into his eyes. Silence encapsulates Vinny; partly due to the shocking reversal but also the concussion-induced ringing in his ears.

Her lips move, uttering something inaudible. He feels her warm breath billowing on his face. Not a hundred percent sure, but he believes her lips mouthed—*Nothing personal. Just business.*

With the unheard words spoken, her dour expression changes from all business to impending pleasure as a crooked smirk lines her face. While still straddling him, she sits up and, without looking, holds up her empty hand. Hoodie coolly fills it with a handgun. The exchange seems coordinated like they've planned this all out beforehand. With cold steel warmed by her damnable palm, she swings it toward Vinny, lining up the sights on the *SWAK* mark left on his forehead.

Pulling back the hammer, she tenses her muscles and begins the final step of creating a Vinny Basiless-world. However, she halts her actions for some unknown reason, leaving her trigger finger suspended between two polar opposite worlds. As her maniacal expression loosens so does the tensity around the pistol grip. She thumbs the hammer back to its resting position.

Pushing off his chest, she returns to her feet. Hoodie joins her at her side. Through hazy sight, Vinny's drooping eyelids catch what will be a lifelong, motivating memory before passing out: watching Angelica take her cold eyes off him, turning them to Hoodie, and pulling him in for a long, passionate kiss.

After breaking the lecherous kiss, Angelica takes Hoodie's hand and leads him out the front door. Vinny retrieves his phone with shaky hands and activates the "Emergency SOS" feature. Then, passes out.

***

During his second trip to the hospital that night, it was discovered Vinny suffered a minor concussion. Even though it wasn't too serious, the doctor felt it prudent to keep Vinny for a few days. But, in all reality, the doctor had no choice: Boss Vescovi "snapped his fingers."

Bastiano Vescovi was trapped in an emotional spin-cycle. He was heartbroken by the death of his lifelong friend and enraged by the hit put on the Family's administration. And at the same time, relieved Vinny was still alive. He had to stay that way, even if it meant Vinny enduring an extended hospital stay, guarded by Bastiano's two best soldiers. Time was needed to find the rat skulking about the Vescovi Family.

Once Vinny's blinding headache subsided, he told Bastiano's Soldiers who the rat was. Vinny entreated his godfather to let him use his soldiers to deal with the "problem." He conceded.

Angelica was staying at an upscale hotel just outside Naples. The LCN's don promised to send a couple of enforcers to get her, but when it was Vinny's Soldiers standing at her door, she knew she'd misjudged Bastiano Vescovi's reach. (The garbage man would later find the LCN muscle, each bearing a fresh forehead hole, buried in a dumpster.) Angelica assumed sliding a C-note into the greasy hand of the head of hotel security would buy his silence. She was wrong... dead wrong.

With the help of some effective, motivational techniques, the whole sordid affair spilled out of Angelica's treacherous mouth in heaping buckets...

The LCN was tailing her for a couple of weeks. Eventually, her daily schedule was made crystal clear. Every Tuesday morning was spent at the beauty salon getting dolled up. On Angelica's next appointment, an LCN mafioso *just happened to be there.* During her two-hour appointment, the incognito mafioso heard Angelica confess her disenchantment with "The Life" and all its trappings to her stylist.

The following day, the LCN don himself approached Angelica and promised her freedom —even threw in a big sack of scratch for good measure—if she'd do her best *Delilah,* and betray her *Samson.*

After some further pressing by Vinny's Soldiers (as in, with a pair of pliers pressing her various extremities), she rolled over on her accomplice like a car tire over a witless squirrel. She told them Hoodie's part in all this. Her nervous energy prompted her to tell of Hoodie's later confession of spacing out and almost missing the opportunity to kill Elder Basile. But when asked if she knew where he was holed up, she had no concrete answer, only that he sometimes hung around the docks on the south side of Naples. Of course, the LCN don reneged on his agreement with Hoodie. With no protection, Hoodie was left to fend for himself, as always.

After that, she had nothing more to offer. Her final moments in life were spent dying buckwheats, a quirky mafia term for dying verrrryyy painfully and verrryyy slowly. Mafia justice against Family betrayal is absolute and unwavering, no matter who you are.

Less than a week later, the Soldiers' dedicated reconnaissance discovered the hole Hoodie was crawling in and out of. It was indeed at the docks. Hoodie would be fitted with cement shoes soon enough.

When Vinny was told of Hoodie's location, he put two restrictions on his Soldiers: one—they were to leave the filthy rat for him, and two— they could never tell Boss Vescovi he was the one who whacked Hoodie. They weren't down with the second one, but Vinny promised he'd take the heat. It was a small price to pay to have peace with his father's murder.

\*\*\*

After leaving the hospital, Vinny wasted no time. He drove to Hoodie's derelict warehouse that afternoon. Vengeance needed meting out.

Parked down the street, Vinny watches Hoodie crawl through a hole in the plywood boarding up the front entrance. Harassed by the morning sun, Hoodie pulls his hood over his grimy head and crams his hands into his kangaroo pouch before ambling down the seedy streets.

Mystified by Hoodie's unexpected appearance—his original plan was to ferret him out, put two behind the ear, and leave him to add his stench to the former fish warehouse—Vinny follows the nitwit on foot. Surely, he knows there's a price on his head. If he does then whatever he's doing must be worth the risk.

Striving to stay hidden in the building's shadows, Vinny prowls like a cat through the brush. Eventually, his prey exits time's forgotten wharf and enters a livelier area. His pace does not slacken. Whatever's at the finish line, it holds absolute sway over Hoodie.

Several blocks later, the *tape* is finally broken. Hoodie stops at the base of some steps, leading up to a mysterious building. In like manner, Vinny eases up and blends in with a crowd of people. Hoodie scans his surroundings, checking to see if he's being watched. Peering through the crowd, Vinny studies his mark, waiting for its guard to drop.

Seemingly satisfied, Hoodie bounds up the steps and enters the building. Furrowing his brow, unsure what building this is, Vinny leaves the gaggle and strides over to the steps. Staring at the building, Vinny struggles to accept what his eyes see. Of all places, why would his father's murderer be in THIS place? The place Hoodie slunk into...a Roman Catholic cathedral.

Vinny labors through the turn of events. The thought of entering a church after so long infuses him with cloying infuriation. He fusses to himself about the injustice of it all. Eventually, he sighs, shaking his head. There's no getting around it, if justice is to be done, then he must walk up these steps. Because, obviously, The Almighty's not gonna do it.

\*\*\*

Vinny slides in through the cathedral door. Standing in the vestibule, he gathers his bearings. He sees two closed doors made mostly of glass, closing off the sanctuary. Through the glass, he watches Hoodie approach the votive candles. Examining the rest of the sanctuary, Vinny sees that aside from Hoodie, it's empty.

Assured that only God and His saints will witness the next few minutes, Vinny slaps his game face on. Ready for action, Vinny watches Hoodie de-hood, lights a *prayer deliverer,* and then crosses himself before kneeling.

Vinny smirks as an irreverent thought pops in his head—*I hope that candle doesn't mind pulling double duty; I'll be hitching his soul to his final prayer...*

Slipping off his shoes for maximum stealthiness, he enters, gliding down the aisle in whisper-quiet socked feet. As he slinks, he removes his Glock 20 and thumbs the safety switch.

Arriving, Vinny positions himself on Hoodie's left side and points his burner at the oh-so-damning, identifying evidence—his birthmark. With sadistic fascination, Vinny muses over the wasted prayers.

Foolishly allowing inactive seconds to fritter away, an egregious reality trolls Vinny's murderous intentions—Hoodie's humanity.

The flickering candlelight highlights the earnest intensity on Hoodie's emaciated face. Now that he's this close, Vinny does not see the face of a killer but rather the face of a pitiful drug addict. He knows this look well; his mother wore the same face.

Disrupted by the memory of his pathetic mother, Vinny lowers his gun. Panicked he'll lose his resolve, Vinny quickly conjures up the memory of his father, specifically the Fiat crushing him. The intentionality works. The memory of his father wheezing his final anguished breath chases away all thoughts of mercy. How can he let this vile waste of space live, while his father died unjustly? He can't. He won't.

Freed from the spell of antagonistic thoughts, Vinny opens his eyes and breathes slowly, cooly. Raising the gun, he re-sets his sights on the imminent dearly departed and thumbs back the hammer. The sound of the gun cocking pulls Hoodie out of his beseeching.

Peering at the gatekeeper of his eternity, resolve and acceptance broadcast from Hoodie's bloodshot, weary eyes. He's asked for forgiveness. No reason to keep purgatory waiting.

Seconds elapse as the silent standoff stretches. Not wanting to test fate any longer, Vinny applies steady pressure to the trigger. It's now or never. Suddenly...

An earsplitting explosion ERUPTS in the sanctuary, and at nearly the same time, half of Hoodie's head disappears. Vinny ducks below the front pew and seeks for the origin of the gunshot not his own. With gun pointing, clearing the room, he sees nothing until his eyes catch movement from the darkened balcony. There he sees a gunman with a Remington 700 pressed against his shoulder, peering through the scope.

The sniper pulls back the bolt, expelling a 7mm spent casing into a row of seats. After shouldering his weapon, he picks up the still-smoking shell and pockets it before descending the balcony stairs. Temporarily out of sight, he remerges in the vestibule.

Able to see him through the sanctuary glass doors, Vinny watches the sniper walk up to the front door and push it open. However, he doesn't exit, but stands there, thinking. Finally, arriving at some conclusion, he turns to stare at Vinny for a second or three before disappearing into the encroaching morning glory.

Vinny works through what's just happened.

He knows who the sniper was—one of Vescovi's personal hitmen who only gets activated when there's no room for error. Vinny may be a super genius, but he doesn't need to be to understand the situation—his godfather, THE Godfather, knew what he was planning.

Stunned by the reversal, Vinny turns his attention back to the lifeless body lying spread eagle in front of the candles. As he stands, Vinny notices the blatant religiosity assaulting him from every direction.

Its garishness is excessive and effective; being in the presence of all this holiness causes his soul to chastise him. He's overwhelmed by his unworthiness to be in such a place. The uncomfortableness intensifies the moment he spies the sanctuary's centerpiece—the immense crucifix hanging on the front wall.

Life is full of moments that weave through our earthly experience. Most are trivial; precious few are defining. For Vinny, this is a defining moment. What will he do? Wisely, he does the smart thing.

Dropping to his knees, Vinny bows before the One who died for his sins. Large tears stain his cheeks. Weeping, he looks up at his Savior. Gazing on the crucified Christ gives him the strength to rise and enter the world as a changed man.

Walking up the aisle, he stops at the holy water font and considers it. He knows it's not to be taken lightly, but at the same time, it feels like the most natural thing to do. At last, feeling confident, he wets his two fingers and clumsily makes the sign of the cross. The weirdness of the act quickly passes. Knowing his world was rearranged, and that certain things will never be the same again, he walks through the glass doors and into the vestibule. There remains one final obstacle between him and his new life—the closed exit doors.

Staring at the same doors that took in "Vinny" and who will now be dispatching "Vincente," his eyes are drawn to the inscription above; it says— "Exit To Serve." Considering this, he looks above the sanctuary doors and sees the inscription— "Enter To Worship." He smiles. He's done the latter, now he must do the former. He leans into the exit door. The blazing sun smacks him in the face. Squinting his newborn eyes, he bravely enters the world as a new man...God's man.

\*\*\*

Aaron's eyes are suddenly thrust into hand-to-hand combat with temporary sun blindness. Putting both hands over his closed eyes, he rubs them softly, coaxing them to open. To aid in his efforts, he leans forward and looks down, hoping to find an ally in the shadows painted on the floor. Eventually, the tide does turn, giving him an advantage over his combatant. With objects coming into focus, the first thing he sees is his sneakers set against the backdrop of a very old carpet. His eyes wander across the floor, identifying random things as they go; one of those being his crumpled legal pad. Though why it's there, he cannot say: must've slid off his lap when he leaned forward. The thrill of victory is short-lived, however. His vision may be restored, but a new challenger rises—disorientation.

*Where am I?!* He thinks to himself, panic setting in. He's not digging the disassociation. Thankfully, his angst doesn't last long before recollection subdues the pitiless bully.

*I remember where I am. I'm in the Saint Uffuzioi, or however you pronounce it,* he reassures himself as he looks up. He sees a smiling Vincente, watching him curiously. *And there's Vincente, sitting across from me, staring at me like a creeper...why is he staring at me? Oh, man! Did I fall asleep!?*

"You okay?" Vincente asks.

"I am. I think I may've zonked out though. Sorry about that," Aaron confesses.

"You've been with me the whole time," Vincente assures.

"I have? Okay good."

Though relieved, he's certain Vincente is being polite by letting him off the hook. He knows he drifted off for a minute or two. Wanting to further chase away the haziness of his ill-advised power nap, as well as the lingering embarrassment from said power nap, Aaron gathers his things. He snatches up his crumpled legal pad and smooths out the wrinkled pages. He's immediately assaulted by a disheartening truth—nothing's written down. Frantically, he flips through the pages hoping to find words... any words. Nope. Bupkis. Vincente notices his discomfiture.

"What's wrong?" he asks.

"I didn't write anything down," Aaron bemoans. "Luckily I recorded it."

"There you go," Vincente responds, soothingly.

"But you know what's strange?" Aaron asks as an epiphany alights. "I don't think I need notes or the recording. Your story is so incredible, I remember every word."

"And every one was true."

"I don't doubt it. What really blows my mind is your giftedness at storytelling. Before this afternoon, I always considered my dad the best storyteller I'd ever heard. But now, compared to you, he's about as engaging as a monotoned economics professor."

Vincente laughs. "Thanks."

"No, seriously. I felt like I was there, that you somehow took me back in time so I could witness and experience everything firsthand. Or maybe you dropped some acid in my water, and I hallucinated the whole thing. But I don't see a mysterious empty glass."

For comedic purposes, he looks around the table for the *smoking glass*. Even checks underneath his laptop. "Nope, nothing. Guess you're off the hook."

Vincente delights in the tomfoolery. "Maybe I hypnotized you," he suggests.

"Hey, yeah! Maybe! Except...TSK!" Aaron's laying the sarcasm on thick. "That's all nonsense. Might as well say you possessed me and showed me the whole story."

"Now *that's* absurd..." Vincente remarks, coolly. His tremendous eyes pierce Aaron's, holding them captive. The silent, knowing stare unnerves Aaron, sending him into a fit of fidgets.

"Relax, Aaron. I'm just messing with you."

Aaron laughs nervously. "Obviously," he says, not all that convincingly. His eyes drift to the laptop screen and sees that the recording app is still recording. He stops it. When he does, he's stunned by the recording length—7:13:39.

"We've been at this for over seven hours?!" Aaron exclaims.

"We were having fun. That's the rule," Vincente says, tongue in cheek.

"I'm sure, but I don't remember stopping once, not even for a bathroom break. You must be in agony. Come to think of it, why am I not in agony? I have the bladder of a three-year-old girl."

"We took a bathroom break a couple of hours ago."

"We did?! Why don't I remember that?" Aaron snaps his fingers and points an *Aha!* finger toward the ceiling. "That's right. Because you drugged me. It's all coming back now."

Vincente smiles pleasantly.

"Gonna have to pay attention to your sneakiness tomorrow," Aaron promises, still relying on his default routine of clowning around when he's nervous. "Speaking of...you good with closing up shop and starting again in the AM?"

"I am. Let's meet at seven-thirty. I'll buy breakfast."

"It's a date. Get some rest, soon-to-be Saint Vincente. Tomorrow's a big day."

"Sleep well, Aaron of Brooklyn."

***

Later that evening, back in his hotel room, Aaron discovers that the sound on his recording app cut off right after Vincente said, "I can still smell the garbage." and didn't pick back up until Vincente said, "You okay?" seven hours later. In between there is only static. He has no audio evidence that Vincente ever uttered a word the entire time.

Refusing to allow his overactive imagination to get the best of him, Aaron chooses to believe it was his old laptop failing him once again. He's been meaning to buy a new one and this latest incident seals its fate. He'll purchase a new one when he gets back to the States, but as far as tomorrow is concerned, he'll make do. After this assignment's over, he can let his mind run crazy with all that might've happened, but for now, all he wants to do is sleep. Never has he wanted it more…

# CHAPTER THREE

J osh begins his morning routine. Life's drudgery, ever the tedium of man's restless soul, sometimes does us a solid and throws in a welcomed change. Now, instead of one crazy cat to feed, he has two. After satisfying his ravenous little ones, he tends to his own ravenous need—his caffeine addiction.

As he sips, he watches his heart's-desires contentedly eat. Unable to resist any longer, he tables his coffee and squats down behind them. Resting on his haunches, he strokes their furry bodies.

"Can you believe it?" he remarks to the felines. "No future dystopian dreams last night. First time in over a week. My shrink will be so pleased."

He continues scratching; they continue scarfing. Perfect symbiosis.

"Speaking of, sorry, gotta wrap this up. Meeting with her soon, and I haven't figured out where I'm headed today."

His business booms. He only had one day off between the doctor's/lawyer's house before needing to start a new one. Though middle age looms, he prefers to stay busy, to stay active. Like an old stick-shift truck, it's harder to get moving from a dead stop.

Snatching his coffee, he heads to his office to begin planning out the day. He doesn't have peace for long—his little miscreants are done eating and looking for trouble.

The recent adoption, Scamp, leaps onto the desk and head butts Josh's mouse hand causing him to click on a link titled: *What REALLY happened to the world; expert explains with five irrefutable facts.* There is no shortage of "experts" on the subject these days.

Sufficiently irritated, he plops the vexatious creature on the ground and opens his contractor portal. Before any further mishaps, he clicks "print" and waits for today's work order to spit out.

Being a fast learner, Scamp joins Toby in the assault on the printer. After prying the printout away from the flurry of furry paws of fury, he walks down the hallway while glancing over the paper.

"Whose house is the lucky winner?" he mocks as he peruses the work order. He halts, eyes widening in dismay.

"Mike?"

\*\*\*

"I've been doing this business for three years. I've never been this fearful," Josh laments. This is not him at his melodramatic finest; he's genuinely concerned. "I'm glad we met here," he adds as an aside. "This is a nice change of scenery."

"I thought we should enjoy the warm weather. A sixty-degree day in January is rare,"

Susan explains.

"This is some wild weather. The weatherman says we might get a nasty thunderstorm tonight." It may sound like small talk, but really he's verbalizing his discomfort. He's not a fan of lightning or its bombastic brother.

Ever vigilant for her patient's clues and cues, especially Mr. Mendel, Susan watches him throw breadcrumbs at ducks. They are sitting on a park bench overlooking the Lincoln Memorial Reflecting Pool.

"What are you afraid you'll find?" Susan asks, getting the psychoanalysis ball rolling.

"He was my best friend. I'm afraid my perception of him will be shattered. That I'll discover he's like all the rest."

"Rest, who?"

"Christians!" His "duh! Who else?!" look is blatant. She knows what she's doing.

"Why would this affect you?"

"Because I looked up to him. Perfect marriage, perfect family." As these assumed truths assault his mind, he tosses the breadcrumbs with a little more gusto. "What if I discover he had secret vices, shameful vices, hidden away?"

"Nobody's perfect, Josh. This image you have of your friend is not healthy. He's only going to disappoint you."

"I know nobody's perfect...it's just that, well, he pretty much saved me."

"From what?"

"Crippling insecurity. Before Mike, I never had a close friend, even in school."

"That's sad," she's genuinely sympathetic. "Why not?"

"Kids are cruel. Bullying isn't exactly a twenty-first-century phenomenon you know."

"I am aware. I'm kinda in the business. Why were you bullied?"

"Because of my nationality, mostly. You know I'm a Jew, right?" Josh asks with his usual embarrassment.

"I do. You were picked on for being Jewish?"

"Yeah, but it wasn't just me, my whole family was tormented. When I was sixteen, my parents moved from Manhattan to Upstate. They were sick of the city and wanted to live in the country, so they bought a house in Ithaca. They didn't know Ithaca was full of anti-Semitics. Eventually, our house was tagged with swastikas. At school, I was regularly harassed and beaten up. I developed a lot of insecurities that still haunt me."

"I'm so sorry that happened to you. When did you move?"

"When our house burned down. Up to that point, my father refused to be chased out by inbred hillbillies. When my father made an insurance claim, his agent said there was no record of his policy. That was the last straw. My parents moved back home, sans yours truly."

"How come?"

"Because I spent my first ten years in Jerusalem. I'd grown accustomed to the

American way of life and didn't want to go back. Since I was eighteen and graduated, I was free to make my own decision, which was to move here. Not sure why, but I felt like Washington was beckoning me. Even after my mom died shortly after moving back home, I still felt like D.C. was where I was supposed to be."

"I'm sorry about your mom."

"Thanks. She's been gone a long time." The pitch in Josh's voice dips. Susan senses the importance of moving on.

"When did you meet Mike?"

"Several years after moving here. I met him at a park. He liked to play pickup basketball there and always invited the players to church. It was his outreach, his passion. On my first time playing there, afterward, he invited me. I went and immediately fell in love with the whole church scene. It was unlike anything I had ever experienced. I wanted what they had and would do anything to get it. Mike became my best friend, and eventually, I came out of my shell. Mike's wife was best friends with Elizabeth which led to them playing matchmaker for us. And we lived happily ever after until Elizabeth stopped living. All I have left are memories. This is why I'm worried about Mike's house destroying those memories. Understand?"

"I do. But it sounds like he was a decent guy."

"Exactly, he was."

"Then what's the problem?" Her curt reply indicates she's tired of his refusal to move on. Yes, therapists should always be patient with their hurting charges, but Josh is a different situation. He's too intelligent to have such a ridiculous crutch.

"If I do discover he had secret sins..." His voice drags off, unable to fathom the fallout.

With a barely concealed, contemptuous sneer, she quotes, "'Be sure your sins will find you out.' That was Sister Margaret Mary's favorite threat in Sunday school. It never worked."

Josh throws the last bread piece and heads to the nearest trash can to toss the empty bread bag. Hands in his pockets, feet shuffling, he returns to the bench where he sits and slouches like a moody teenager.

As he sulks, he stares out across the pond. He knows she's right. *Why can't I just let this hatred go?* he ponders.

Like a backdraft escaping when a door to a burning bedroom opens, the answer rushes at him.

*Because they lied to me! I did everything they told me to do and said everything they told me to say. But what do I have to show for it? They got what they were promised. I was abandoned!*

Susan spots the internal battle playing out across his flushed face and steps in.

"Josh, please stop obsessing. None of this will change your circumstances. This infatuation with the past, incessantly holding onto the trauma dumped on you...these things are destroying you."

She grabs his left forearm, taking his hand

out of his pocket. Clasping his hand in both of hers, she looks intently at him.

"I'm pretty sure this is frowned upon," he says, jokingly. For added effect, he looks down at her inappropriate PDA. Not amused by his usual attempt at burying seriousness underneath the guise of humor, she gently yanks on his arm. Getting the memo, he looks at her.

"What?" he semi-whines, uninterested in whatever trick she's going to shrink his head with next.

"I need you to pay attention. Are you listening?" Defeated, he nods as he shifts his body to face her. "Things change. Let it go."

"To this extent?"

"Yes. Sometimes that's how life shakes out."

Josh stands to his feet. "Can we walk?"

Without saying a word, she stands. Both join the bevy of leisurely strollers. They silently march in step, lost in their thoughts.

"Susan, I hear you, but I don't think I can just let it go. And I can't move on like nothing happened either."

"I'm not saying you have to act like nothing happened. You must accept the facts, but they don't have to define you. She's gone. Your friends are gone. You're all alone. Stop whining and move on."

He's amused by her candor. "That's some raw counseling."

"I grew up with four older brothers. Sometimes it's best to speak plainly. You need to understand you're not the first person whose life's been blown up, nor will you be the last. The streets are teeming with shattered lives and broken dreams. They have lost their way; they have forgotten how to live. They are this way because either nobody came alongside to help, or they shoved the helper off the path and ducked into a dark alley, both literally and metaphorically. There they stay, never dealing with their problems. I'm here, right now, on this path, by your side. Will you listen or will you shove me away?"

As though cued by an unseen stage director, a raving homeless man, donning a sandwich board bearing an unoriginal message, appears in front of them.

"Repent! The end is near!" the man bellows.

Sometimes, a single event can alter your future, changing your life forever. In the mysterious majesty of nature, a previously sown seed will lay dormant, protected beneath good soil, until it is moistened. That hidden seed cannot water itself; it relies on life-giving rain to soften the shell. Once adequate irrigation happens, new birth begins.

Ironically, crazy as this man is, his antics produce a light mist, moistening the *seed* deep in Josh's heart. At this indigent soul's grand entrance onto life's stage, a powerful electrical surge shocks Josh's insignificant seed, beginning regeneration.

They both stare at the wild-eyed hobo.

"My friend, the end IS here," Josh instructs the destitute, broken man.

"Are you the one whose coming was foretold?" Grasping at straws, this strange character is.

"Not even close." Josh leans in and slips some money into the man's breast pocket. While there, he whispers something only the man can hear. "Get something to eat and read a Bible. Your message is obsolete."

The duo continues their trek, leaving the doomsday prophet to elucidate some other unsuspecting passerby. Intrigued, Susan takes a stab at gaining clarity.

"What just happened? What did you tell him?"

"I told him to get something to eat."

"But you were so gentle. Why?"

"I don't know. Something outside of me, I guess."

"You mean the milk of human kindness? That's your conscience, and that's inside of you."

"Yeah...maybe."

"But shouldn't he make you mad?"

"Why?"

"Because he's pedaling Jesus nonsense," Susan exclaims, surprised by his passivity.

"He's confused and doesn't know any better."

"And you do?"

"I do now."

Susan hides her confusion. "You're gonna have to explain."

He falls silent, not sure if he's ready to give up the goods.

*Ah, why not? Nothing ventured nothing gained, I guess,* he tells himself.

"I'm gonna let you in on a little secret. I'm not mad at Christians per se. I'm mad because I was wrong, and I don't know why."

"Wrong about what? You just said you knew better. Which is it?"

"It's hard to explain. Basically, in a nutshell, I thought I was a Christian, but clearly, I'm not."

"Why do you say that?"

"Isn't it obvious? I'm still here."

"On your left!" This warning comes from behind them. Without slowing down (meanderers along these paths know well the unwritten rules), they step aside so a bicyclist can pass. "Thanks!" he yells as he races by.

"Well, I'm a Christian and I'm here, walking with you," she says matter-of-factly.

Josh regards her with pity. "I mean no disrespect, but, no, no you're not."

"If by Christian you mean an insignificant group of heretics and haters that evolution finally did away with, then you're right; I am not."

Intrigued by her explanation for mankind's greatest disappearing act, he presses further.

"You're attributing the disappearance of millions of people to natural selection?"

"Precisely."

Josh frowns. "That's a stretch."

"How else can you explain the last four months?"

"Well, if all the stories I've been hearing for the last few years are true, then they were yanked up to heaven."

"Please don't tell me you believe in an asinine rapture fairy tale," her progressive sensibilities challenge.

"I don't know. Maybe," he says, a little unsure.

She wrangles in her indignation and ushers psychiatrist Susan back onto the scene.

"Josh, think rationally and, above all, scientifically. There have always been doomsday prophets, like Crazy Joe back there, insisting the world is coming to an end."

"You're kidding me, right? Scientists have been warning us about the environment for years. How are they any different than Crazy Joe?"

"You answered your own question. Scientists are telling us this, not an unhoused person. We are being warned because we are the ones destroying the planet, not some made-up god."

"According to the Bible that made-up God destroyed everything in a worldwide flood," Josh challenges, though unsure why.

"Noah's Ark? Utter foolishness. There is no scientific evidence such an event ever happened."

"Yeah, you're right. All those fish fossils must've ended up in the Himalayas and the Sahara Desert because a band of radical right-wing creationists hid them there like Easter Eggs."

Offended, his sarcasm is fueled by her calling the Flood, foolish.

"Hey, if the shoe fits," she says, bluntly.

"Listen, I'm sorry if I offended you and I'll admit your point is tricky one, but there's always a rational explanation. Like all the people disappearing. Please, let me make my defense."

Susan gently cups his arm. Her face displays remorse and a desire to mend bridges. Josh regards her pleasant expression and slows his breathing. He nods in agreement."

"Thank you," she says. "Evolution removed the dinosaurs to pave the way for a better, more powerful species. Now, it's happened again. Evolution removed the abhorrent, mutant strain that is Born Agains so humans could progress into the next phase: the perfecting of post-modernism. The shackles imposed on us by religion and the concept of sin are broken. Man is free to ascend to higher thinking without superstition muddying up the waters. Now, the only true truth can reign."

"Which is?" Josh asks.

"Humanity will save itself, not some erratic made-up god."

"Seems stupid that millions of people throughout history have willingly given their lives for an erratic made-up god."

"Couldn't have said it better myself," she says, a dash of elitism seasoning her voice.

"I was being facetious. Some of the smartest people I've ever known disappeared. Maybe we're the stupid ones."

"You're defending Born Agains now?"

"I don't know what I'm doing. I'm very confused. One minute I hate God and His zealots and the next, I'm upset when somebody disrespects Him and them. But, I know this much —He's not made up."

Feeling he needs a timeout, he cautiously walks over to some frolicking squirrels. Removing a Ziploc bag of nuts from his pocket, he sits cross-legged. Holding out a handful of nuts, he makes little squirrel noises, beckoning them. His patience is rewarded. Soon, he has three squirrels hopping over and helping themselves to a free treat.

Watching the enchanting scene unfold, she walks over to the "Dr. Doolittle in the Park" reenactment and sits next to the good doctor. The hyperactive tree rodents all scatter at her arrival. Without saying a word, he takes her hand and drops in a few nuts. Being a smart individual, she understands she's to hold out her hand for the woodland creatures to sample. Eventually, two of the three regain their confidence and venture over to see what's on the buffet.

"Lately, I find myself here, feeding every creature that allows it. Human interaction has lost its allure. Animals are easy, demanding nothing from you." He stops talking, his pensiveness on full display. "I should probably stop delaying the inevitable and go full-on monastic."

Lost in the simple joy of feeding goofy squirrels while still listening, her sixth sense kicks in. "I feel like you're avoiding something."

Thankful for her perception, he confesses. "You're right, I am."

She waits for him to continue but could end up dying while waiting. "Spill it. What?"

He sighs deeply before taking the plunge. "Last Friday night, I tried killing myself."

"Excuse me?" Her look and tone transmit several emotions: anger, concern, disappointment, and...fear, surprisingly.

He focuses on the world of insects scurrying through the grass. Eventually, he notices her look that says *Ahh, more info, please!*

"That morning, in the house I was cleaning out, I found an unopened bottle of whisky, some Ambien, Vicodin, and Oxys."

Disapproval flashes across her face. Josh sees it.

"I promise, my attempt wasn't premeditated. The Percs bobbing in alcohol may have been but tossing in the sleeping beauties was unintentional. It just happened, or at least, almost happened."

She twirls her finger, prompting him to stop rambling and carry on. He obliges.

"Late in the night, my stomach had had enough and said the party was over. After it'd finished giving the partiers the ol' heave-ho, I got off my knees and staggered back into the living room. I had been watching my wedding video but forgot about it till after I slumped into my recliner. Suddenly, there she was, talking to me on the TV."

"Your wife." Not a question, but a confirmation she's listening.

Nodding, he continues. "Her voice was

more than I could take. At that moment, all rational thought ceased. The anguish was so intense I wanted it to stop. I wanted out."

As she works through this disturbing news, she involuntarily spaces out. Recognizing her dreadful faux pas, she snaps out of it.

"Are you back?" he asks when her far-off stare returns.

"Sorry about that. Punching back in." Trying to smooth things over with physical comedy, she mimes punching a timecard. "Ka-Chunk! Carry on."

Josh smiles, appreciating the levity. "Once she finished her message, and the cameraman went back to recording the festivities, I turned the TV off. It's amazing how loud silence can be. I can't explain what happened next exactly but it felt like something *other* wanted me dead. It's as though my mind made itself up without my involvement; that I had no say in the outcome. Does that make sense?"

"Not really," she confesses. "Our time is almost up so why don't you explain as we head to our cars? And Josh, speak plainly, please."

"Fair enough. For the first time that night, I noticed the Ambien...

*** 

Ten minutes later, they're in the parking lot and Josh is wrapping up his harrowing near-death experience.

"Scamp may have saved my life, but the nagging suspicion that something else was involved is tough to ignore."

"What do you think this *else* could be?"

"I'm not sure, but *it* wants me alive. Like, something needs to be done that only I can do... that I was destined to do."

"That's a slippery slope, Josh. Delusions of grandeur can quickly spin out of control. The least detrimental—disillusionment. The worst— trying to assassinate a political figure."

"I don't see me ever going to that extreme."

"Hopefully not, but the desire to feel important, the need to leave your mark on this world, can be an all-consuming quest with no finale. I'm not saying you're wrong. Maybe you will accomplish something extraordinary that'll earn you a paragraph in an eighth-grade American history textbook. But I would caution you to proceed very carefully."

Approaching Susan's Mercedes, the magic of passive entry disengages the driver-side lock. After opening the door and tossing in her purse, she turns back to him. There is a moment of awkward silence. Throwing caution to the wind, Susan embraces Josh. Her combativeness of the last twenty minutes has been tamed by Josh's anguish.

Startled, Josh is unsure what to do. Not wanting to offend her, he loosely wraps his arms around the middle of her back but does not pull her in. A Bible could easily be inserted between them; Sister Margaret Mary would approve.

When she finally breaks the awkward hug, Susan elegantly enters her car, straps in, and leaves without giving him another look.

Josh, confused by the electricity on the scene, tries to understand why things suddenly got weird. He doesn't get to think long—his cell rings. Retrieving the jingling iPhone, caller ID informs it's Walt.

"Yes, Walt." Josh is silent as he listens to Walt's response. "No, you're not interrupting anything important; strange perhaps, but not important." Again, silence. "That's fine. Have Braxton begin hauling out the stuff from Timothy's room while you change the locks." More silence and listening. "It's at the top of the stairs on the left, the one that looks like a ten-year-old boy's room." Josh walks to his car as he listens. "Because Timothy's father was my best friend. I'll be there in thirty."

*\*\**

Exiting the roll-off dumpster, Braxton treks back to the front door. Noticing Josh pulling up to the curb, he offers a quick wave before disappearing back into the house. Peering through the sliding glass back door, Braxton locates Walt: he is on his knees, changing the shed's lock. Braxton shuffles through the backyard to join his uncle. The kid's swing set is along his journey. Coming up to it, he spies an empty pair of child's shorts draped over one of the motionless swings and the rest of the outfit and sandals a few feet past the swing's amplitude. Braxton walks an exaggerated arch around the swing set as though it were haunted.

"Yeah, that's not creepy," he mumbles to himself. "Josh is here," he announces to his uncle.

"Okay, pick up the stuff in the yard and then start on the other kid's bedroom," Walt instructs.

Braxton, wanting to chew the fat, sticks around. "This has Christian-home stink to it."

"Obviously. We don't get too many 'sinner's homes' these days."

"Do you believe what people say?"

"Believe what?"

"You know, that this family," Braxton says, pointing his thumb over his shoulder at the house, "and all the rest were dragged up to heaven or whatever you call it?"

"I only know one thing—there are a lot of people no longer living in a lot of homes. Our job is to empty those homes and move on to the next. Leave the state of their souls to the priests. Also, watch what you say, please. This was Josh's best friend's house so I'm sure he's a little raw."

Back in the house, faintly hearing the backyard conversation, Josh walks up to the open kitchen window and watches them. He can see them, but they can't see him.

"Gotcha, Unks. I'm headed back in. We'll see how "Christian" this house is." Braxton forms finger air quotes. Seeing his uncle's disapproving glare, he backtracks. "It's the last comment, I swear."

Josh observes the gesture and hears the word, *Christian*. He understands Braxton's biases and doesn't blame him. He wonders about the title's validity. He hopes those quotation marks have disappeared by the end of the day.

***

Work progresses, and so far, everything is on the up and up. Each armful of his best friend's belongings being tossed into the disgusting container may intensify his heartache, but happily, they also soothe his anxious stomach. Being reacquainted with the family's decidedly unoffensive diversions goes a long way in putting his fears to rest. All is going swimmingly when suddenly a wave of resentment capsizes him. For some reason, he's livid with his friend.

He worked hard to make his home identical to Mike's; not necessarily to be like Mike, but because he assumed that's what he was supposed to do. He knows externals don't make you a Christian, but they should count for something... shouldn't they? Apparently not because he's still here, laboring over Mike's acquired possessions. He joins Walt and Braxton on the porch steps, taking five.

"Hey, boss," Walt greets. "All that's left is the small room at the back of the basement. We gonna knock it out today?"

The remaining room is Mike's office. Comprehension dawns in Josh's wearied brain. If there's anything unscrupulous, this room will be hiding it. Now that trepidation is back, his animosity is booted out the door. Without answering, he heads to Mike's office but stops at the threshold. He peers in and scans, deciding where to begin. His eyes land on a picture frame sitting on the bookshelf. Captivated, Josh enters to scoop up the frame and gaze into it.

The photo is of him and Mike posing, arms around each other's shoulders, standing outside the Holocaust Museum in D.C. They had just spent the morning passing out short booklets telling the story of Jesus. It was an outreach ministry their church conducted every month. His internal film projector flips on and splashes the 70MM memory against the screen of his third eye, whisking him away to that day.

*\*\*\**

For those who volunteered, the experience was an arduous one. Climbing into the trenches of human anguish is a wearisome affair. Many visitors exit with tear-stained faces; for others, a thousand-yard stare is all they can muster. Regardless of the emotion, all were wounded by the displayed atrocities, and it was the volunteers' job to offer hope.

Some felt their presence was inappropriate, but most appreciated the gesture. Those tender souls longed for solace in something, anything that could shed light into one of history's darkest nights. Comfort was desperately needed, and they provided it.

Unsurprisingly, there were many Jewish visitors as well. Most graciously refused the outstretched booklet; others ignored the volunteers altogether. Thankfully, none were hostile; that is until Josh handed the booklet to an older Orthodox Jew.

Perusing the material, his rage smoldered. Eventually, he boiled over.

"How dare you hand me this offensive material!" the Jewish octogenarian screamed, his face inches from Josh's, who remained calm.

Stepping back, the man shredded the booklet. "This is what I think of your false Messiah!" He threw the confetti into Josh's face before spitting at his feet and storming off.

Having witnessed the exchange, Mike walked up to Josh and draped a comforting arm around his shoulders. At that moment, another volunteer walked up to them.

"That's perfect! Look towards me. I wanna get a picture."

Feeling better, Josh drapes his arm over Mike's shoulders and faces the cellphone-wielding woman. And just like that, the picture that is now in Josh's hands was created.

\*\*\*

"Whatcha looking at, Boss?"

Josh snaps out of his reminiscing as Walt and Braxton enter.

"Man, that's a lot of Bibles," Braxton remarks before Josh has time to answer.

He's looking at the shelf dedicated to all of Mike's Bibles, which there were indeed a lot of. Josh smiles at the memory Braxton unearthed. He said the same thing the first time he came into Mike's office. Mike answered that you could never have too many translations.

"I guess you can check off that *B*," Braxton

confirms. "Let's see if the other two are in here."

Walt fires a warning look at his nephew, instructing him to *mind his mouth*. Braxton's return look declares—*Message received*. Josh ignores Braxton's comment as he slides the picture frame into his back pocket. Its new home will be on his desk.

"I'm gonna start cleaning the upstairs while you two empty this room," Josh informs as he exits, heading for the basement stairs. Frustratingly, he doesn't make it halfway before Braxton calls out.

"Oh yeah! *B's* two and three coming up!"

Josh stops dead in his tracks. So close, but oh so far.

"What are you talking about?" Walt asks gruffly as Josh reappears to see Braxton standing at Mike's seven-drawered desk.

"Well, the desk drawers are locked," Braxton contests. "Isn't the saying, 'Locked drawers always bring shocks,' or something like that?"

Josh heaves a heavy sigh. "Yep. You're right."

The hankering look in the young fella's eyes is hard to miss. If Braxton doesn't break into the secret vault soon, he's gonna pop.

"Go ahead, Kid. Crack 'er open," Josh concedes, determined to embrace whatever appears.

Like a kid opening a Christmas present, Braxton dives in. His limited imagination concludes that if he pulls on the drawer's handle hard enough, it'll slide out. This yields no results.

He puts more *OOMPH!* into it. Still nothing. He employs this strategy on all the drawers with the same result: none of them budge. Braxton is noticeably discouraged.

Walt hands him a pry bar. Braxton takes the pry bar, touches it to his forehead, and offers a *thank you* salute with it. He then jams it into the top right-side drawer and pries at it. Walt again steps in, taps him on the shoulder, and holds out his hand. Braxton understands his uncle wants the pry bar back. He obeys. Walt waves his empty hand at him, instructing him to slide down to the end of the desk. Again, Braxton obeys. Walt jams the pry bar into the center drawer, and after a few expert jimmies, the center drawer's lock is broken. But before he pulls it out, he grabs the drawer handle Braxton was previously working on and says—

"Abracadabra!" With little effort, he melodramatically slides open both drawers simultaneously.

Not quite finished with his antics, Walt flamboyantly waves his hand over the drawers like Bob Barker's Beauties presenting a new car.

"TA-DA!" he exclaims as he pulls out all the drawers.

Amused by his uncle's unexpected showmanship, Braxton rolls his eyes. "Fine, fine, you're a genius and I'm a moron."

"Carry on," Walt instructs as he slaps his nephew on the back and moves out of the way. Josh also enjoyed Walt's shenanigans immensely. He's never seen this side of him before.

With great anticipation, Braxton pulls out the first drawer only to find nothing but an open package of printer paper. Spirits undampened, he moves down to the next drawer. Sadly, this one yields no booty either, only a lone accordion file. A disillusionment cloud blows in, yet Braxton presses on. The bottom right drawer is next. This drawer is a little more interesting. Here he finds a stack of neatly folded, crisp newspapers. He plops them on the desk.

"This is kinda cool," Braxton remarks.

"Yeah, Mike was a news junkie," Josh explains. "He liked to collect the most relevant front-page stories for The Times and The Post."

"I am too," Braxton confesses as he digs through the mixed stack of New York Times and Washington Post, reading the various generation-defining headlines—9/11, the Challenger explosion, JFK assassination, moon landing, and...

"Wow, it's been a year already?" Braxton asks as he pulls out one specific NYT and looks at the date. He opens it and peruses the pages. Josh catches a glimpse of the held-up front page: it's Aaron D'Angelo's article on Vincente Basile becoming the first living saint.

"A lot's happened since then," Braxton says from behind the opened newspaper. "If your friend was still here, he'd probably have one about Grayson Young's civil war breaking out on the West Coast."

Braxton closes the newspaper and refolds it. He sees Josh and Walt staring at him. "Oh, man! Sorry, Josh. I wasn't think—"

"No worries," Josh assures, cutting him off. "You're right, he probably would."

"Is it all right if I keep these?" Braxton asks. "Printed newspapers are basically extinct. That makes these even cooler."

"Be my guest," Josh confirms. "I'm headed back upstairs."

Walt waves as Braxton returns to his quest for the final two *B's*. The center drawer is next in line. Sliding it out, he rummages through the various pens and pencils. Hoping to find the only *B* that could be concealed under the drawer caddy—certainly, the missus would never look there—he lifts the plastic compartmentalizer for an expectant peak. Much to his chagrin, no scandalous viewing material. But...

"What's this?" Braxton asks, mainly to himself.

"What did you say?" Walt queries.

Braxton is too entranced to answer.

"Josh, wait!" Braxton commands his retreating boss. This time, Josh makes it halfway up the stairs before, once again, returning to the starting blocks. At this point, he might as well stay down here.

Returning, Josh asks with a hint of snippiness. "Yes, Braxton?"

Braxton simply holds out a sealed envelope. Josh accepts it with curiosity. The letters written on the Mead envelope boggle his mind. This is what they form:

Joshua Mendelsburg

2107 Oakwood St.

Temple Hills, MD 20748

That's his name and his address, but why is it here? It even includes a return label and stamp.

"That's you, right?" Braxton asks.

"Yeah, it's me."

"I found it under the plastic compartment thingy. I thought your last name was Mendel?"

"It is. I shortened it."

"Why?"

"Because I don't want people knowing I'm Jewish."

"You are? Why not?"

"What are you, five?" Walt condemns his nephew. "Stop asking questions and mind your business."

"Sorry, I didn't mean to offend you. I was just surprised."

Josh waves a *forget-about-it* hand as he continues staring at the envelope, trying to comprehend its existence. *Why didn't he mail it?* he thinks.

"Well, ya gonna open it?"

Josh looks at Braxton and sees that Walt too is standing by with an anticipating look.

***

Josh stands upright, having just fed his two tiny meat-eaters. His eyes catch the still-sealed envelope lying on his kitchen counter. He's not sure why he's hesitant to open it. He knows his fear is irrational, but he can't shake the feeling that whatever's inside, his life will change forever. He's not sure his heart can take another upheaval.

A new voice adds its two cents. *Maybe what's inside will have a positive outcome. Maybe your life will be changed for the better.* This voice is persuasive, adding some peace to Josh's off-the-rails foreboding.

Loud beeping fills the kitchen. Snapping out of his trance, Josh slides a piping hot, previously frozen, pizza out from the oven and onto a cutting board. Taking a pizza wheel to it and then sliding the newly created eight slices onto his plate, he completes the preparation by slathering them with ranch dressing.

His wife hated pizza and likewise hated it when he cooked frozen pizzas. She insisted the house smelled like pizza the rest of the night. He couldn't understand how somebody didn't like pizza?! He used to kid her, "Was pizza forbidden in your hippie commune?" This usually earned him a love punch on the arm. He misses being a battered husband...

By now, the enigmatic envelope is forgotten. The anticipation of pizza temporarily retards all cognitive dissension. Grabbing a soda from the fridge and scooping up his plate, he journeys to his much-loved recliner and turned-on giant TV, where he remains for a considerable amount of time.

As that considerable time ticks by, Josh occasionally steals glances at the envelope. Why is he equally drawn to it and repulsed by it? On a couple of occasions, he almost stormed over to either open it or destroy it: anything to silence its tyranny. What stopped him was his go-to excuse—not wanting to disrupt the two furballs sleeping on his lap. That excuse is about to be voided.

Suddenly, an explosion of light and drumfire rattles the house. In a flash, two tiny heart attacks befall the fur balls who scurry off elsewhere.

Josh too is startled by the atmospheric violence. Unfortunately, classic adolescent fears of thunder continue to dog his adult years. To calm himself, he says:

"Easy there, Josh, it's only a storm. There's nothing to fear. It has no power over you." Composure is eventually restored. He cranks the TV volume, determined to weather the thunderstorm.

Unaffected by the feeble incantations of mortal man, the talisman ratchets up the onslaught. As rapid-fire lightning strikes and ensuing thunderous claps ravage the inhabitants of 2107 Oakwood Street, the modern-day calamity awaits to play its part. Finally, it happens: the power goes out.

Sitting in the dark, completely undone by the "shock and awe", his mind registers the silence in between the crackling thunder booms. No gadgets fill the air with their ruckus, save for the grandfather clock's peaceful *tick-tocking*. Truthfully, it's not peaceful at all; it's terrifying. Being alone with only the sound of mankind's most unyielding adversary—the methodical passing of one's life—unsettles him.

Unable to take the maddening darkness a second longer, he heads to the kitchen to find the grill lighter. Success. Thumbing the safety and triggering the ignitor, he is gifted with a comforting glow.

Now somewhat at ease, he turns to confront the desolateness of his once peaceful refuge. But all he sees is that cursed envelope lying ominously a few feet away.

Sick of the wretched thing, he snatches it up. He's either gonna open it or destroy it, right... now! Mesmerized by the flickering flame, the desire to turn the envelope into ash overtakes him.

He extends the flame toward the envelope, ready to free himself. But, to no one's surprise, the oft-vilified Deus Ex Machina awakes from its dormancy. The flame extinguishes mere centimeters from the flammable papyrus. Undaunted, he clicks the trigger again...and again and again and again—no more fluid.

"Fine, I get it. I'm not supposed to destroy it," he announces to the silent room. "But now I have no light to see."

Blazing lightning explodes, illuminating the entire room. Josh's attention is arrested by his cell on the end table. He should've used the flashlight app to begin with, but his terrified mind wasn't thinking clearly.

With no more delay, he, and the envelope root themselves to the recliner. With a couple of taps, a bright light glows from the bottom of his cell. He removes two tri-folded pages from the envelope and wrist-snaps them flat. The moment of truth arrives, his eyes fall onto the penned letter. He reads...

Dear Josh,

I feel very silly writing you this letter, even more so in cursive. But I wanted to make it difficult for myself so that I would focus on what I was writing. I'm sure you're curious why I even wrote this letter rather than just talking to you. Well, like my cursive excuse, I want to choose my words carefully.

Josh, I love you like a brother, but sometimes brothers have to say tough things, even hurtful things when it's for their good. I heard this saying once, and I think it applies now: "Which is better—a doctor not telling his patient they have cancer because it will be upsetting or telling them so that something can be done before it's too late?" Josh, you have cancer, and I know the cure. Not in the medical sense but in the spiritual sense.

I've felt this for some time, but how do you tell a friend he has cancer? The answer dawned on me one day—tell him plainly and lovingly. Based on what I see in your life, backed up by what the Bible says, I don't believe you are a true Christian. I know, judge not lest ye be judged, but trust me, I did some serious soul-searching before I wrote this. Part of the blame lies with me. I just assumed you were, but never asked.

Josh, if you were to die today, I truly believe you would go to hell, not heaven. Harsh, right?

But remember my cancer analogy? I've known you for years, and I've watched how you live your life. Outside of Elizabeth, I know you better than anybody else. I know that only God knows your heart, yet I feel that He has prompted me to confront you with all this.

I don't want to Bible-thump you; I know how much you love that! However, the biggest reason why I don't think you are a true believer is because I have never seen true change. It's obvious that church Josh is all for show. It's just religious liturgy. Always in church, always volunteering, always feeding the homeless, singing the songs nice and loud, but none of that proves salvation. On Sunday, you say all the buzzwords and show great emotion. You do a good job convincing people that you walk with God and that you're His own. The problem is, they don't see you the rest of the week as I do.

I want to ask some tough questions. Do you agree with God's assessment of your sin? Are you in harmony with Jesus and ALL His teachings? Are you sensitive to the Holy Spirit's leading? Unless you are, saying you walk with God is self-delusion, and it's that deception that will damn your soul.

I see no true thirsting or hungering for righteousness. Not just me, but Liz as well. On the same day I decided it was time to confront you, Liz told Anna that she was concerned too. It couldn't be a coincidence. Had to be providence.

I admit, I've been hesitating to mail this to you. Even slapped on a stamp and return address label so that it was ready to go. So why didn't I send it sooner? I don't know. I guess I didn't feel like it was the right time. Maybe God is preparing you to hear these hard things with the right attitude and a ready heart.

I do know this, many, many seeds have been planted in your mind, so here's one more. Maybe this seed will be the one that takes root.

Repent of your sins, forsake them, and ask Jesus to save you before it's too late. I've never quite known how to say this, but I think all the traditions and rituals you've been taught have convinced you that the good works you are doing will earn you your salvation. That's just not true. Only He can save you, not your good works. Don't wait any longer. Do it now. I know you've heard this before, but I included a link explaining how to become a true Christian. Maybe now you're ready to submit and obey. Love you, my friend.

www.majestic-media.com/nasb.htm

Josh stares off into space as he ponders what he's read. He decides to read it again, slower this time. Curious about the link, he enters his office and sits at his desk. After opening his laptop, he connects to his cellphone's Wi-Fi hotspot.

He types in the web address and is greeted by a colorful website. He's surprised the address links to a legitimate website: Mike's not exactly tech-savvy. He enlisted his ten-year-old to teach him the internet and relies on him still to help him navigate the information superhighway... well, he did four months ago.

Taking a deep breath—he gets the feeling this will be sufficiently heavy—Josh clicks on the first page and reads...

*** 

Several minutes later his laptop closes, revealing a box of tissues on his desk. Gratefully, he yanks out a couple and wipes his eyes and nose: he's a blubbering mess. Collecting himself, he's gripped by a powerful thought: everything he's read makes perfect sense, and more than that, he believes it.

"Why couldn't I see this before?" he wonders out loud. "It was in front of me the whole time. Why did it take me so long to understand?"

What Josh doesn't know yet, but will soon, is that God is never late, nor is He early. He's always right on time.

The power comes back on, saturating his house in electricity. The irony is not lost on Josh. Just as the lights have brightened his house, so has comprehension's light shone brightly in his darkened mind. Gratitude floods his soul. He drops to his knees and buries his face in the carpet. In brokenness and humility, Josh prays to the God of the universe. At that moment, in the mere twinkle of the eye, resurrection takes place.

When Josh fell to his knees, he fell as a vile sinner, a hater of God headed to hell; but when he stands to his feet, he will stand as a redeemed, forgiven, lover of God, a true child now headed to heaven. Reflecting on all that's happened, he's aware of the absence of the burden he's carried his whole life. In its place is peace and calm; he feels like a new person.

He also notices something utterly foreign—he's starving. Not in the sense of needing food to fuel his body, but rather food to fuel his soul. Like a minutes-old newborn needing nourishment, he needs to feed on the Word of God. For the first time, he WANTS to read the Bible. He climbs back into his chair and rolls into his desk knee hole.

Not exactly sure where to begin, he decides to Google the answer. He types, "Where is a good place to start reading the Bible" into the search field. Google returns several thousand hits; he clicks on the first one. A website opens. The first thing that greets him is a "Verse for the Day" banner at the top of the page. It reads—

"For if you keep silent at this time, relief and deliverance will rise for the Jews from another place, but you and your father's house will perish. And who knows whether you have not come to the kingdom for such a time as this?" – Esther 4:14

Not sure what to make of that verse or if it even applies to him (he does know two things: that's the Old Testament and he's not about to start there!) he reads the site's directions further. The website does confirm not to start in the Old Testament, but rather the book of Mark, then John, and then First Peter.

"Okay. Whatever you say."

However, a problem arises, halting his resolution—he hasn't the foggiest idea where his Bible is.

He puzzles over where he last saw it. Eventually, its whereabouts alight upon his brain. Without hesitation, he heads for the spare bedroom. Finding the door closed (it's always closed because it's now a catchall for his desultory and sundry found spoils and he'd rather not witness this fact: plus, he'd never see his cats again should they get in) he leans his shoulder into the door and pushes against the chaos.

The swinging door plows enough out of the way to peer in. His heart sinks. How did he let it get this bad? The disarray threatens to swallow the room. If Elizabeth were still here, she'd have one colossal yard sale, posthaste.

Knowing that diving in was the only way to find his Bible, he looks behind the door to see what's stopping it from opening wide. What he sees makes the expedition rather anticlimactic. A precariously stacked pile of miscellany had toppled over. Atop the eyesore was his Bible, as though unearthed during an avalanche.

Grabbing it, he reseals the cordoned-off room and retreats to his living room where he re-plops into his recliner. It seems like a lifetime ago when he was here last, and in many ways, it was. That was a different life lounging in this chair; now a new one settles in, ready to begin anew.

Several minutes of his new life pass, and in that time, he's read the first chapter of Mark.

Surprisingly, (at least to him) he wants to read more. He never understood Christians droning on about Bible reading. It seemed so contrived, so phony. Nobody real could be that into Bible reading. Now, he thinks he has an inkling of what they're on about.

He turns the page, ready for chapter two—he's curious about what happens next. His mind drifts, also wondering what happens next for him...he has no idea.

# CHAPTER FOUR

I t's early and already the Vatican City bustles. Wanting to experience its many wonders, visitors teem across St. Peters Square hoping to catch a glimpse—and most crucially: the all-important footage for TikTok and their Instastories—of the morning sun reflecting off the ethereal buildings.

As though a drone hovered over the sightseers and picture-takers, Aaron D'Angelo zooms into focus. He's walking toward the Piazza San Pietro fountain; Vincente Basile is there, admiring the intricate carvings in the ancient fountain. Vincente had sent Aaron a text first thing, instructing him to meet him here.

Stopping behind Vincente, he stares unnoticed. He's thankful for the ten hours of sleep since last he saw this man; it's given his subconscious time to work through yesterday's kookiness. Even though he told himself, *don't go there!!* in the waning moments before sleep, his overactive imagination insisted he was taken back in time to witness Vincente's life. But now, his rested brain provides a better, more logical explanation. Vincente's uncanny ability to tell a story was simply the stirring stick that mixed Aaron's jet lag, thirty-six hours of wakefulness, and WAY too many energy drinks into the trippy cocktail he unwittingly *guzzled*. Still, something nags him, urging him not to take Vincente for granted. Watching Vincente seemingly glow in the morning sun convinces him to heed the warning.

"In a lifetime, I don't think I could ever fully appreciate all of the Vatican's beauty," Vincente says blindly into the morning air.

"Yep, pretty stunning," Aaron agrees, unsure how Vincente knew he was there.

"Ready for a hearty breakfast?"

"Beyond ready."

"Wonderful. Up for a morning hike? I know a delightful café a few blocks away."

"I grew up in The Big Apple, remember? These are genuine New York strong legs," Aaron brags as he smacks his quads.

Vincente smiles, amused by Aaron's braggadocio. "Alright then, let's put those legs to work."

Ten minutes later they arrive at the promised café and are greeted by an attractive Italian woman.

"Morning gentleman," she welcomes. "Two?"

"Yes, please," Aaron confirms. "Can we have a table close to an outlet? I imagine we'll be here for a while. You don't mind, do you?"

She flashes a heart-melting smile. "Of course not, follow me."

They obey as she leads them to an out-of-the-way corner table, next to a large window. She hands them menus as they sit.

"What can I get started for you?"

"Coffee and you might wanna ask Juan Valdez to keep grinding those coffee beans because we're gonna be drinking a metric ton." Aaron immediately regrets the lame joke. He just ain't no good at flirting, especially with overly attractive women. Amazingly, the joke earned him a smile and sincere laugh, followed by a shoulder squeeze and trailing fingers down his arm as she walked away. His heart skips as perspiration dampens his back.

Vincente delights in the spectacle. "It appears your forehead is glistening."

Aaron wipes his forehead with the cloth napkin. "Yeah well, my pits got the worst of it. Hope it doesn't soak through my shirt."

Wanting to erase his embarrassment, Aaron plugs in his laptop and opens it. With a few finger taps and mouse swishes, he's logged in and connected to the Wi-Fi. Word is opened next where he types this on the blank page—
*I will be video recording myself to see if anything strange happens while I continue this interview.*
After saving and closing out of Word, he opens up his video-capture program. Confident he's prepared for any shenanigans, he looks up at a coffee-sipping, patiently-waiting Vincente. Confused, Aaron sees his coffee was delivered as well. Must've been too distracted to see the beauty stop by. Just as well, probably would've said something stupid.

"Are you ready to order?" Vincente asks.

"In a bit." Aaron hands the Bluetooth mic to

Vincente.

"I thought you were hungry?" Vincente remarks as he "mics" himself up.

"I am, but it can wait. I wanna get started."

"Whatever you say. You're the boss."

Being as inconspicuous as possible, Aaron hits RECORD on his video-capture program. Once his mug appears and a counter ticking away the recording seconds, he minimizes the program and readies his pad for notes. Hopefully, there'll be some this time.

"I can't think of a clever segue or fancy movie transition shot, so I'll just pick up where we left off. One of Boss Vescovi's hitmen stopped you from killing your father's murderer, and this turn of events led to your remarkable conversion. What happened next?"

"I was called in."

"I don't follow."

"Vescovi wanted me to present myself. When a made man is called in, it's never a good thing. Some are simply straightened out, but most times they're coming in to face the music, trunk music that is."

"Trunk music?"

"As in the sound a dead body makes as it rots in a car trunk."

"Ahhh," Aaron says, raising his eyebrows. "Such a lovely image. Obviously you didn't end up in a trunk. Did you go into hiding?"

Vincente leans forward, looking intently at Aaron. "My friend, nobody runs from the mob. Eventually, you'll be found and wished they offed you from the beginning. Deserters are not looked on kindly. Any Soldati worth his salt is an expert at torture."

Aaron considers this unpleasant reality. "So, you're still in then?"

"No, I'm a free man."

"How did that happen? I thought you guys took a blood oath or something."

"We do, and typically, the only way out is death. Unless—"

"Unless you're the Godfather's godson," Aaron interrupts. "Sorry for cutting you off."

"You're fine, and you're wrong. What I was going to say was: unless the Godfather is supremely superstitious. Bastiano Vescovi owes his longevity to never disobeying his gut. He told me he had no choice. He said, and I quote—'God told me to let you go or He'll ice me.'"

"I'm sorry. What now?"

"Vescovi claims God told him in a dream that he was a dead man if he didn't free me."

"Fascinating. I don't recall my elderly Sunday School teacher talking about *God icing* someone," Aaron jokes.

Aaron's quip plants a fresh smile on Vincente's face. He's growing quite fond of the young man...

"Bastiano is an old-school Catholic. The idea of a 'fire and brimstone' God is still alive and well in his mind. He wasn't about to tempt fate. He knew the only way to keep his promise to my dad and to keep himself alive was to free me."

"The promise of never letting you kill

someone?" Aaron clarifies, recalling yesterday's story.

"Exactly. As loyal as my Soldiers were to me, wisely, they were more loyal to the Boss. It turns out that while I was following my father's murderer, Vescovi's man was following me."

"Did you want out?"

"At that point, yes. Although I thought getting out was getting whacked, which I was okay with. My father was right; the dreams were relentless. When I closed my eyes, all I saw was that man's hollowed-out face, and I didn't pull the trigger. I can't imagine the guilt if I had. I was willing to die if that's what it took to keep me from killing somebody."

Just then, their waitress reappears, infusing the ugly moment with breathtaking beauty. She stops with her hip pressed into Aaron's shoulder. Her perfume enshrouds him in its intoxicating web. He's not sure how much more his heart can handle.

"Ok, gentleman, you've chatted long enough. Let's get some food in you."

Vincente announces, "I'll have the Italian brunch torte."

"Excellent choice, sir. And how about you handsome?"

This catches Aaron off guard, paralyzing him and stealing his tongue. She hip-checks him, attempting to snap him out of it. He blindly fumbles through the menu.

"Have the artichoke quiche," she instructs. "It's my favorite."

He mindlessly nods approval. Resting her hand on his shoulder for support, she leans forward to take Vincente's menu and nestles it under her arm. With her now free right hand —her ultra-soft left hand still resting on his shoulder—she holds it out waiting for Aaron to give up his menu. As he does, he looks up at her. That did it. He immediately drowns in her prismatic green eyes. Her cheek flexes slightly as a soft smile crests. With a sultry wink and a delicate shoulder squeeze, she heads to the kitchen.

"Do you even know what you ordered?" Vincente inquires, charmed by the scene.

"No idea. Some artichoke thing. I don't even like artichokes, but how could I say no? Did you see the way she looked at me?"

"Aaron, a blind man could've seen it. You should ask her out."

"What's the point? I leave tomorrow. It would only be a fling."

"Maybe, but it would be a lifelong memorable fling. The kind of memory you tell your kids when their mother isn't around."

Aaron smiles at the idea. "But when would I have time? I'll be at the ceremony tonight."

"You have all afternoon. Ask her to coffee. I'll be interviewing with the pope, so you'll be free."

"But what if she says no?"

Vincente grabs Aaron's forearm. Aaron looks into his dark eyes. Have they always been this dark? They seem darker than usual, almost midnight black. Is he hypnotizing him right now?

"Aaron, I promise. She'll say yes. Trust me."

And with Vincente's pep talk completed, he lets go of Aaron's arm. Like waking from a short nap, Aaron blinks his eyes and shakes his head. He looks down at the arm Vincente was holding. It's blazing hot, as though on fire. Looking back up, he notices Vincente's eyes are back to their normal muted brown. *Is that possible? Did his eyes just change?*

"All this reminds me of a question I need to ask," Aaron starts, wanting to move along quickly. "Have you forgiven Angelica?"

"Well, God forgave me, so how could I not forgive her? That doesn't mean I've forgotten, or all is well. I allowed the two most important women in my life, my mother and Angelica, to break parts of me that'll never be repaired. I will never allow for a third."

"Does this mean you took a vow of celibacy?"

Vincente smiles at Aaron's reporter-like curiosity, inappropriate though it may be. "Well, I'm not a priest, so..."

"I read ya." Aaron pretends to write as he says, "STILL...A...PLAYER." This earns another smirking snort from Vincente.

Speaking of...Aaron notices the vision of beauty gliding towards them, holding their breakfast. After matching the plates with their corresponding owners, she offers a smile before departing.

Vincente crosses himself and says a quick prayer before digging in. Aaron, however, pokes at his food like it's a dastardly offense to his sensibilities. Feeling brave, he forks a meager portion into his mouth and waits for the retching. Relieved, it seems his stomach will not be rejecting this exotic food. Love truly does conquer all.

"Before we continue, I think there's potential for a full biography here," Aaron announces.

"If you say so. Tell you what, I'll let you write it should there be a call for one. Deal?"

"Deal. Certainly gives me more to sink my teeth into."

In between food-related teeth-sinking, Aaron slides his laptop next to his plate, slightly left of center. Wiping his mouth and hands, he retrieves his notepad, ready to get to work.

"I foresee a question entering the reader's mind."

"Did I have a hard time adjusting to life outside the mafia?"

"Exactly! How did you know?"

"Intuition, I suppose. To answer your future readers, yes and no."

"Thanks for clearing that up. Details, my good man. The insatiable reader demands details."

Smiling, he intends to oblige him. Aaron is unaware that Vincente knows this rule and is employing it on him at this very moment. Aaron took the bait—hook, line, and sinker.

"Most difficult was letting go of the warfare mindset. I didn't touch on this before, but my father was a master strategist. I grew up watching him conquer his enemies and widen the Family's borders. It dawned on me I had the same mindset. Sun Tzu's *Art of War* was gospel for my father, so it was for me too. It was the Bible before *the* Bible became THE Bible. Make sense?"

Aaron nods. "What about the *no*? What was easy to let go of?"

"The politics...though I didn't let that go, but rather I used it to my advantage. As a boy, I took the old dictums, *one hand washes the other,* and *you scratch my back, and I'll scratch yours*, to heart."

"So basically, you learned to manipulate people?"

"I wouldn't express it that way, but yes, in a certain sense. Let me explain it differently. I left people wanting more. I made sure I was always memorable to everyone I talked to. You never know when that quick exchange will work in your favor."

"Yeah, it still sounds narcissistic to me."

"When I was still in, yes, it was completely self-centered. When I got out and started my missionary work, I used it to help the less fortunate. In the mafia, I spent a lot of time glad-handing the local merchants. I also held court with elected and appointed officials. My personality and my connections got a lot accomplished. Those were formative experiences in my early years, and I leaned on them. While my father made an impact using brute strength, I won people over with mutual respect."

"Sounds like you read *How to Win Friends and Influence People*."

"Many times, my friend. Dale Carnegie was a brilliant man."

"How did you incorporate this talent into your missionary work?"

"Simply put, I gave people in Third-World countries hope. During my time hobnobbing with the Naples government, I learned one universal truth about people in power—they'll do whatever it takes to stay there. Every dictator, every president, every supreme leader, regardless of the language they speak or the land they hail from, are all deeply egocentric."

"I can understand the opportunities in your hometown, but how did you gain access to these foreign rulers?"

A mischievous smile flashes across Vincente's olive-skinned face. "A magician never reveals his secrets. No, the answer is quite dull; there is no great mystery to unravel here. I was in their country with foreign aid teams, so I was already in contact with government officials. Over time, usually in just a couple of weeks, my natural charm and winsome personality created the opportunity to talk to the powers that be. At that point, the difficult part was over; it was all downhill from there. I simply discovered what each ruler wanted. The human psyche is rather basic. Man is nothing more than an intelligent dog. Find the itch and apply the scratch. Before you know it, they're wagging their tail, willing to do whatever it takes to make you happy."

Aaron muses over this brilliant piece of wisdom. "You scratch behind their ears, and they do what?"

"Whatever I wanted them to do. Once I gave them what they wanted, I had control of their minds. Flattery, wealth, commendation—all are the Achilles Heel to the one enslaved by the allure of power. It is an implacable taskmaster."

"How could you possibly give them these things?"

"Ever heard the phrase, 'I know a guy who knows a guy'?"

Aaron nods.

"That's it. I used other powers from different countries to do my bidding and help me conquer the next power. Keep 'em fat and sassy, and they'll roll over for you."

"You would then use this to help the poor?"

"Of course. I didn't do any of this for my comfort; I did it for the betterment of others. I lived in the huts, in the metal-roof shanty towns. Everything I did was to raise people from the ashes of despair and help them stand on their own two feet."

"By manipulating rulers."

"CORRUPT rulers. Trust me, Aaron, once you see your first emaciated three-year-old, lying in their mother's arms, it changes you forever. When you see a ten-year-old boy carrying an AK-47, forced to fight because he was kidnapped in his sleep, it scars you in ways you never knew possible. Once you witness a starving family selling their twelve-year-old girl to the sex trade market, all so her family could eat that month, you will never sleep peacefully again. Yes, I did manipulate wicked rulers, but I saw it as the ends justifying the means."

Seeing the skepticism on Aaron's face Vincente continues. "It appears I'm getting ahead of myself."

"Yes, it appears so."

"Why don't I start from the beginning?"

"That would be swell."

"Finish your last bite, and I'll tell you."

Aaron dutifully forks his last bite and settles in for story time.

"If one is to change the world, he must start with his backyard. There was more than enough wrong with Naples. But where to begin? It didn't take much thought; all I had to do was look around. It was impossible to miss. The elephant in the room was the reprehensible mountains of..."

Vincente stops. He is suddenly alone. Yes, Aaron still sits across the table in body, but mind and spirit have vacated the premises. His glazed-over expression makes it obvious. It may be a blank look, but it's also imbued with wonderment. At this very moment, Aaron is re-experiencing Trash Town in all its grotesque glories.

Vincente catches the attention of their server and motions for her. When she arrives, he hands her both plates. She leaves without noticing Aaron's state. Vincente closes the laptop, which stops the video recording. Aaron thought he was being so clever, so sly; Vincente pulls the wool over people's eyes, not the other way around.

"Gonna have to rely on your memories. Enjoy the show."

\*\*\*

The rhythmic beeping sound of heavy machinery backing up interrupts the morning revelry of Naples' ghetto streets. Stupefied residents watch the hubbub from their front doors. What they witness must be a dream.

Sunlight reflects off the glass-encased cab of a large front loader, temporarily blinding the observers, as it moves with a purpose. The tenants of Trash Town watch the grated-cover bucket scoop up a full load and then secure it by closing its gruesome-looking, metal teeth. This outrageous scene looks like the giant beast ate the trash but was quickly besieged by the vileness. Racing to a waiting dump truck, it lifts its three-hundred-pound head over the truck bed's wall and vomits the wretchedness. Then it returns to the trash heap to continue this dismal undertaking. Though depressing, it makes short work of the mounds of months-old rubbish.

The stench is horrific, but the buzz of excitement rippling through the crowd is indisputable—this is a glorious day.

The noble road crew steadily works down the streets, ridding the residents of the bane of their existence. Overseeing all this is Vincente Basile. Standing a safe, breathable distance away, he confers with several foremen about the best way to dispose of this villainy and corruption.

Like a voice ushering from the heavens, Vincente speaks into Aaron's out-of-body experience, acting as a narrator.

"Mayor Ardovini's reign of terror came to an end. The stranglehold he had over Piazza Garibaldi was loosed. As corrupt politicians go, Ardovini was in a class all his own. To pay for his extravagant lifestyle, he helped himself to the town's treasury; none more gratuitously than the sanitation department. At first, it wasn't noticeable. A couple thousand here, a few thousand there. He assumed his embezzling went unnoticed, or nobody cared. In no time, the sanitation department was flat broke. Wanting to save face with the upper class, Mayor Ardovini moved enough funds from the welfare department back into the sanitation department to keep the garbage trucks running, at least in the prominent part of town. The rest is simple addition without subtraction. With nobody collecting garbage in the projects, the predicament passed the point of no return. I made one call."

Aaron's point of view shifts to a room in an abandoned building. A single lightbulb, swaying in the dusty air, hangs ominously over a slouching man shackled to a chair. His bloody face speaks to an old-fashioned working over. Two no-neck, tree-trunk-sized goons tower over him, cracking their blood-stained knuckles. Behind the two soldiers stands a captain ensuring everything is up to code: unfortunately for the sad sack, it's the Syndicate's code.

Boss Vescovi, accompanied by two of his soldiers, enters the room. The captain greets the Godfather with kisses on both cheeks. After the Mafioso customs are accomplished, the don approaches the prisoner and lifts his drooping head. Though the man's face is beaten to a pulp, his identity is obvious—Mayor Ardovini.

Again, Vincente's disembodied voice rings out. "Boss Vescovi took care of Mayor Ardovini personally. I didn't think violence should be included in the mayor's forced early retirement, but Vescovi felt other-wise. Ardovini had racked up a large tab with Vescovi bookies and couldn't repay; the boss saw it as a golden opportunity to kill two birds with one stone."

Boss Vescovi leans into Ardovini's ear and utters a few inaudible words before standing erect once again. Never taking his eyes off Ardovini, Vescovi's right-hand reaches back over his left shoulder. Without confusion or hesitation, the captain chambers a round and thumbs the safety before placing his gun in his boss's waiting hand. With no reluctance, the boss draws a bead right between Ardovini's eyes and pulls the trigger. Nobody blinked; nobody flinched. The entire sequence was without emotion. It was cold and calculated. It was all business. Without a second glance, he returns the smoking pistol to his captain and leaves.

"Boss Vescovi hasn't personally whacked anybody in years; nevertheless, he hadn't lost a step. Like riding a bicycle, I guess," Narrator Vincente informs.

Aaron's POV shifts again. He now sees clean, trash-free streets. There are even landscapers planting trees and mulching flower beds along the sidewalks. He watches dilapidated buildings demolished and new houses appear in the empty spaces.

"With the anti-champion of the people out of the way, new life was breathed into the city. The public housing authority tore down the projects and built new neighborhoods for low-income families," Narrator Vincente continues.

Like being on a virtual reality train, Aaron is taken on a tour across the revitalized city. The *mental light rail* stops at city hall where a large crowd witnesses the new mayor's swearing-in.

The mystical train stops at a new location. There, Aaron watches Vescovi and Vincente pass through the bustling streets. Vescovi greets everyone he comes upon. He also enters every single business: he clearly has an agenda. In each store, the same scene unfolds. The don's accountant hands him a large ledger. Vescovi flips to a specific page, tears it out, and hands it to the owner.

What happens next is a mirror reflection of every preceding store owner's enthused reaction —joyful tears. Tearing out the page was symbolic —the owner could now live pizzo-free, as in, no more paying protection money. Boss Vescovi initiated a handshake with the owner—which was unheard of—and then, without fail, the owner lavishly kissed his outstretched hand. After a tender cupping of the owner's tear-soaked cheek, the don headed to the next store to repeat the whole process.

"Having breached his seventh decade," Narrator Vincente's voice breaks in. "Vescovi felt the effects that seasoned men experience in their twilight years. Wanting to leave behind a legacy, he decided to set the city on a course to lasting vitality."

Aaron watches Vincente leave the procession unnoticed and head to a waiting metro bus. The digital destination banner informs it's headed to the airport. Vincente embarks on the bus but stops halfway up the steps. Turning, he glances back to see Vescovi being lovingly mauled by a new gaggle of villagers.

As Vincente watches the spectacle Vescovi's sixth sense kicks in. He turns to Vincente, ignoring the commotion all around him. In that moment, a lifetime of unspoken words passes between godfather and godson. Neither waved—the look said all that needed saying.

Vescovi turns back to his adorers, never again regarding Vincente. Understanding the moment is over, Vincente finishes his quest onto the bus. Once inside, the air pressure valve releases, the doors close, and a poignant metaphor for the closing of this chapter of Vincente's life is created.

"After helping fix my home," Narrator Vincente says over the bus's clamorous departure. "I was unclear about what came next. Several days spent in isolated meditation solved the mystery. One of the only pure things my mother ever taught me was how to meditate effectively. Before succumbing to a life of drugs, she looked to transcendentalism to manage her mental health. Though much of the philosophy felt hokey to me, the power of meditation stuck. During those days of meditation, God sent me a messenger. I obeyed the message. Wonderfully and unexpectedly, that messenger stayed. He's with me all the time, giving me information. Because of him, I always know what I'm supposed to do. Because of him, I now have a direct line to the Divine. "

*\*\**

Suddenly, Aaron is sucked backward, like going in the opposite direction of a Sci-Fi movie spaceship in warp speed. The rushing sensation of being pulled backward culminates in an incandescent blast, giving Aaron flash blindness. Hearing a piano but not seeing it, Aaron waits for the over-saturation of his retinas to subside.

When the flash blindness abates, his eyes are assaulted by Somalia's midday sun. As they adjust and focus, he now sees the ivories being tickled firsthand, and wonder of all wonders, the masterful tickler is Vincente Basile. This doesn't surprise Aaron. The more he learns of Vincente's indescribable genius, the more he's certain there's nothing he can't do if only he sits down to do it. In this case, he sits at a piano, playing accompaniment to a small group of Somalians as they sing an old gospel hymn, at least he thinks it's a hymn. Unsurprisingly, Aaron doesn't speak Somali, yet he's certain he recognizes the tune. He's sung plenty of old sacred melodies as a kid and this sounds like "The Old Rugged Cross."

The song ends, and Vincente swivels to address the worshippers. This he does in their native tongue. Big surprise; why wouldn't he speak perfect Somali?

Thankfully, Narrator Vincente also speaks. "I'm sure this vignette raises some questions. Rosetta Stone and piano lessons as a child. Not to be pretentious, but I can speak thirteen languages fluently. I've always picked up languages easily. Because of this, I discovered speech is the key to unlocking someone's mind. It's easier to gain their trust if you speak their language. And once you have their trust, real change takes place."

Aaron watches Vincente step up to a lectern and begin speaking. Sitting cross-legged in the dirt, all are grateful for the pavilion sheltering them from the sun; Vincente includes this thanksgiving in his prayer.

"My messenger instructed me to join a catholic missions team. Somalia was the first stop. Somalians have no reason to believe in a brighter future, so any comfort we provided was gratefully accepted. We didn't have a priest with us, so I led Mass. The team put up no resistance —my gift for capturing a crowd's attention was obvious. It was the first time I took advantage of an empty platform. It wouldn't be the last."

Aaron's view goes black. When sight is restored, he sees they are now in a stately conference room, the kind of room where politicians shake hands and sign intimidatingly large documents.

At the front of the room is a round table, big enough to seat six men. The men are broken up into three groups, two to a group, filling the top half of the table. There is one group on the right and one on the left, with the final group in the middle. The bottom of the table is empty so that spectators can witness the proceedings. The witnesses are made up of reporters, dignitaries, and cameramen. The event is broadcast on the Internet and all the major news networks.

Those at the table wear earbuds that translate each other's words into their language. Aaron doesn't have one of these fangled earbuds, so Narrator Vincente chimes in.

"I am sitting next to the president of Somalia. The Kenyan president and his advisor are on my right, the Ethiopian president and his advisor are on my left. Earning the Somalian president's trust brought all this to fruition. Word of my growing popularity among his people found its way into his ear. Fearing I was creating unrest and that revolution would erupt, he had me arrested and brought to him. Because I spoke Somali, I convinced him I was not a threat but rather an ally, one that could help him fix his nation's problems. He told me what his two biggest headaches were: a fractured government, and pirates and warlords."

At the table, Vincente moderates. After much back-and-forth between the three African countries, documents are signed, and hands are shaken. Hardy applause resounds among the witnesses. The cheering onlookers stand to their feet, giving more intensity to their boisterous clapping. The six men also rise and bask in the admiration.

"As I built trust with the Somalian president, I convinced him to reach out to Ethiopia and Kenya," Narrator Vincente says.

"After making introductions for me, I went to work creating an advantageous plan for everybody. Somalia has vast amounts of uranium along with substantial reserves of oil and copper. In exchange for instituting trade agreements with their two neighbors, Kenya and Ethiopia agreed to help Somalia form a sustainable government and establish peace by crushing the pirates and warlords. Wanting to further sweeten the deal for Ethiopia and Kenya, I orchestrated extra benefits for both countries. Kenya would send teachers to Ethiopia to address its illiteracy problems; Ethiopia would share its successful gold excavating blueprint with Kenya. This would fix their archaic mining regulations. The icing on the cake for all three countries was agreeing to pool their military resources and abolish ISIS's suffocating death grip."

After several minutes of question and answer time tick away, the three presidents and their advisors exit. The witnesses follow suit. All that Aaron is left with is an empty, eerily quiet room. Vincente's disembodied voice pipes in once again—

"I'm sure your eyes are glazed over by the tedious foreign affairs. I don't blame you. However, these cumbersome details are essential to the story. I am building the groundwork for an effective payoff. Without the foundation, the conclusion will not seem as wondrous. Trust me, stay with it. Trudging through the dregs of monotony will be worth it in the end. This was not the last table I presided over."

Like a movie technique of a bygone era, Aaron's POV is altered by a transitional wipe. The *wipe* reveals a new table, housing five men, one being Vincente, who appears frozen in time. There are also twice as many reporters and witnesses present. Word traveled quickly.

The scene adds a new twist: Aaron is also sitting at the table, though away from the five frozen men; and Narrator Vincente suddenly appears as though beamed there. He walks around the table and peers over each man's motionless shoulders, including his younger self's. Aaron watches, struck by the bizarreness of this latest mind trip.

Narrator Vincente speaks: "After Somalia, my missionary work took me to Port-au-Prince, Haiti to help with the latest massive earth-quake. Believe it or not, this one was far worse than the 2010 earthquake. Though all faiths and world relief organizations were there, I became the face and voice of the tragedy. It wasn't long before word tickled the right ears once again."

Narrator Vincente disappears, which activates the room. Aaron watches the scene play out from his vantage point. Vincente speaks into Aaron's exhausted mind, continuing the narration.

"The two men seated on either side of me are the Congolese president and the Haitian president, accompanied by their aid. Long the struggle has been between these two countries. The pursuit of a sustainable free trade agreement has been at the forefront of their international relations, but sadly, always just out of reach. Both are among the poorest countries in the world and desperately need a pact between both nations. It's been stated that the task of freeing the DRC from a tortuous history of conflict and instability and introducing democracy, peace, stability, progress, and prosperity is theirs alone. Sometimes a gentle prodding is all that's needed. Hearing what I did with Somalia, Kenya, and Ethiopia; the Congolese president was willing to come back to the table with Haiti. His only stipulation was that I mediate; I agreed without hesitation. Something extraordinary was happening and I was at the front of it."

As both presidents sign the trade agreement, Narrator Vincente puts the capper on the scene.

"My eminence and influence were taking shape; my astonishing wisdom and understanding were in extreme demand. Many leaders pleaded with me to visit their countries and replicate the same success. The most prominent of all the requests came from Iraq. After a sleepless night wrestling with my messenger, I boarded a plane the next day."

***

The term *boots on the ground* is a familiar saying in this world of never-ending conflict, but in this instance, it's *Italian loafers on the ground.* While *boots* represent dominance and authority through military might, these *Italian loafers* carry a more powerful and history-altering force. The saying "the pen is mightier than the sword" is true only if the one wielding the pen wields it with supremacy and authority.

Jacked into a new environment in this fast-moving altered reality, Aaron watches Vincente being escorted by heavily armed soldiers up the steps to the Iraqi parliament building in Erbil. Just a few hours south of Baghdad, the new parliament complex is finishing up the final touches of its history-defining construction. After long battles about what the building should look like, an agreement was reached. Now all that's left is for peace to come to this Shiite-controlled country.

Narrator Vincente speaks: "My sleepless night was born out of my concerns with Iraq. This ancient land carries so much history, both good and bad. But during that arduous night, my messenger insisted I believe him, that Iraq was key to how everything played out. That in a few short years, it would become the center of the world. Hearing this, I quit resisting and believed. I was smitten with intrigue. I spent the night meditating, receiving all the pertinent details."

The armed procession stops just inside the conference hall. Vincente is then led to his assigned seat by an awaiting attendant.

"First thing my messenger told me was that Iraq needed the violence to stop. The Sunnis and the Shiites have been at each other's throats for nearly a millennium and a half, and in that time, very little headway was made. How do you stop two boys fighting on the playground? Separate them, and that's what I did. The biggest problem for the Sunni was they had no true leader. Rectifying that was paramount."

The parliament speaker takes the stage, inviting Vincente to the podium. Aaron suddenly finds himself standing next to Vincente, giving him a view of the conference hall. Speech class was always Aaron's most difficult class. His stage fright is no joke. Even though nobody can see Aaron, the room's hundreds of eyes wreck him. Thankfully, Vincente begins his speech, easing Aaron's anxiety. Of course, it's in perfect Arabic.

Narrator Vincente summarizes his speech: "I recommended a worthy Muslim to lead the Sunnis. During my time in Somalia, I met a well-respected Imam, a Sunni from Kirkuk wrestling with his faith. Because of the endless warring over the minutia, he was disillusioned with Islam. While in Somalia, he completed advanced schooling and became a Mufti. Wanting to serve

Allah, but not by killing his fellow countrymen, he longed for an opportunity to make a difference. When my messenger led me to Iraq, he also prompted me to convince this man to present himself to the Sunni as their possible leader. Because of the news coverage, you already know the outcome; the Sunni embraced him as their leader. He then convinced the Shiites to put down their guns and pick up the olive branch. Iraq finally knew peace. The event you're witnessing is the process of divvying up the land between the two warring boys. They were now separated and living peacefully. This success earned me eternal devotion from the Iraqi people. In their eyes, I was now just below Muhammad."

As with all of Vincente's stops, media is present. Wanting the perfect shot of this historical moment, the platoon of reporters rush to the podium like enemy soldiers rushing a foxhole. The camera's rapid-fire flashing adds to the disorienting feel, like from an automatic rifle's muzzle flash. The brightness overwhelms Aaron, forcing his eyes shut. While the flashes caught in his retinas assault his frayed psyche, Aaron hears Vincente's voice slither into his mind.

"A whisper was on the wind; it grew stronger every day, reaching more and more nations. The message was clear. It couldn't be ignored...World peace is here, and it was in my hands."

\*\*\*

No longer experiencing light flashes, Aaron slowly opens his eyes. Discovering he's back in the café, sitting across from Vincente, threatens to undo him—he's sickeningly disoriented. The assignment has lost its appeal. He wishes he could just get on the next plane. Where to? He cares not, just so long as it ain't here.

*How long was I out this time?* he wonders. He looks down at what should be an open laptop. Seeing that it's closed crumbles his heart. Something worse than the realization of another failed recording dawns.

*Why does my mind feel molested? Why do I feel...empty?*

*Don't deny it, just accept it...*

Startled, Aaron looks up at a coffee-sipping, pompously smirking Vincente.

"Did you say something?" Aaron asks.

"Sure. I said, 'World peace is here, and it was in my hands.'"

"No, after that."

Vincente smiles his insidious smile before taking another sip. "No, my friend. Not a thing."

"Never mind. I must be hearing things."

"Perhaps."

Again with that arrogant smile. Aaron doesn't know what he wants more: to smack that grin deep into left field or fall prostrate at Vincente's feet.

Desiring to change the subject, Aaron returns to the interview. "How are you certain you can bring world peace?"

"Trust me, my dear Aaron (Aaron's heart

tightens at hearing the implied possession), it's inevitable."

Aaron's inner turmoil escalates. How he both loathes and loves this phenomenon sitting in front of him. "Don't you think you're being a smidge presumptuous?"

Vincente smiles as though he's explaining the mysteries of the universe to an inquisitive child. "It's already been accomplished. Time just needs to catch up with destiny."

"But time isn't linear."

"With all due respect to Kurt Godel, his attestation is incorrect. Time is linear, just as Newton and Aristotle proclaim. However, I'm willing to concede that if I am wrong and Godel is right, that time is circular, it's not true for me. I am history's exception to the rule."

And there's the straw. Aaron's nice-guy demeanor can no longer abide. He will implode if he doesn't denounce this narcissistic maniac.

"How you can be so arrogant?! It's nauseating."

Surprisingly, Vincente's customary smirk is MIA. Rather, a clamped, thin mouth presides.

"Confidence and arrogance are two different things. Experience and evidence are at play here. They are proof of the legitimacy of God's revealed message to me. Stop and think about all I've told you."

Aaron says nothing. Vincente continues swaying.

"Many have heralded me as the Messiah. I think that's going a tad far, but similar to Jesus, I am doing something extraordinary. Think about it...Jesus only had three years to effect change and look what He accomplished. According to my messenger, my work is just beginning. Imagine what I get done!"

All of Aaron's dander incitement defuses. The ensuing mental crash leaves him drained. Gone is the satiating righteous indignation; in attendance is crippling diffidence. Maybe he's the one with the wrong attitude. Maybe Vincente really is the world's savior.

"You look spent," Vincente remarks, stating the obvious.

"I am. These last couple of days with you have been taxing." Aaron recognizes how rude that sounded. He hastily dives on his fumble. "Sorry, I just mean that..."

Vincente holds up his hand to stop Aaron's backtracking. "It's okay. I took no offense. Why don't you go get some rest?"

Aaron looks at the time on his cell—three minutes shy of high noon. He begins stowing away his mobile worksite. "Thanks, I think I will. What are you going to do?"

"I have an hour before I meet His Holiness. I think I'll grab a sandwich, take it back to the square, and people-watch. I love it; people fascinate me. I try to imagine what their lives are like, if they're happy with how it's turned out."

Aaron curses himself for asking Vincente about his immediate agenda. He was just following proper social protocols. His mind can no longer bear Vincente Basile's brand of genius.

However, despite himself, he thinks he'll hear more.

"How?"

"By getting in their head and seeing through their eyes. 'The eye is the window of the soul; the intellect and the will are discovered there,' says Hiram Powers. All humans want the same thing."

"Which is?" *UGHH!! Shut up, Aaron D'Angelo! Why can't I stop? Because I'm drawn to him...just like everybody else.*

Aaron's flagellating reverie aside, he hasn't begun to piece together the conundrum that is Vincente Basile. Soon, Aaron will realize that one way or another, everybody falls under his spell.

"To love, to be loved. Security. Prosperity. But more than these...peace. Peace with their family, peace in their job, peace with themselves, world peace."

Vincente's mind drifts off. After a moment, he notices Aaron is standing, stuffed backpack slung over his shoulder, expectantly but still respectfully staring at him.

"Go, my friend. I release you. Get some rest."

Not wanting to look a gift horse in the mouth, Aaron smiles politely and turns to leave. He suddenly stops in mid-scoot and turns back.

"I forgot to ask. Whatever happened to the invading La Cosa Nostra?"

Vincente smiles. "It was stopped by a one-hundred-and-ten-pound woman. But that's a story for another time. Maybe for your book."

Aaron must be drained because not even

something as intriguing as this is enough to stay his fleeing foot. "Alright. Sounds like a good one. I'll hold you to it."

"Not to worry. There'll be plenty of time. Go."

Aaron's not sure what that means, nor does he care. Rest...he needs rest. He flashes a perplexed smile before heading for the door where he's swallowed by the incoming lunch crowd.

***

Pope Andel Vassallo enters an opulent chamber where a small group of people wait patiently. Intermixed among the expectant are two cameras and their cameramen. All conversation ceases, and an awed *hush* grips the room.

Vincente, who moments prior was sitting in an elegant armchair, stands to his feet and approaches the pope. Wanting to show respect, he grasps his hand and bows, attempting to kiss the Piscatory Ring. At this, a most unusual event transpires: Pope Andel jerks his hand away as though a leper grabbed it. Then, in an act of extraordinary obeisance, the pope clutches both of Vincente's arms and raises him to his feet. While this may not be an especially noble gesture for most popes, for *this* pope, however, it's stupefying. A precedent was just established.

"You will bow to no one, least of all me," Pope Andel reprimands. "In truth, it is I that should bow to kiss your hand. Come, my friend,"

Pope Andel instructs as he guides Vincente back to his chair. "Let's talk briefly before the cameras roll."

Vincente returns to his still-warm chair. His Holiness sits in the chair next to him. For all the meetings Vincente's had with dignitaries in the last couple of years, he knows this is the most important. Not long ago, his messenger informed him that Christ's earthly representation would join him, acting as a helpmate.

"How are you enjoying your stay?" Pope Vassallo inquires.

"Very well. Thank you. Rome is breathtaking."

"Agreed. I never grow weary of it."

Just then, the interviewer for the Holy See's Press Office enters the scene and sits across from the power couple. Apparently, the time for pleasantries is sufficient.

"If you'll pardon me, gentlemen," the reporter begs in his thick Italian accent. "We need to start the interview."

"Carry on, Giovanni," the pope instructs. He sees this hackneyed little man more than he'd care to, but constant, insipid interviews are part of the job. A pope's work is never done.

"Thank you, Holy Father. Ready fellas?" Giovanni questions the cameramen. They respond with a thumbs up. Three seconds later, the interview begins.

"Good evening, I'm Giovanni Abano, official reporter for the Holy See's Press Office. By the time this airs, history will have already been made. This morning, my guest rose from his slumber as an ordinary man, but tonight, he will retire as an extraordinary man. After today, Vincente Basile will be the first living individual to fall asleep as a saint. Your Holiness, you are no stranger to making history yourself. When the white smoke floated up to the heavens, a Greek pope, you, were elected. By now, we have all been blessed with the telling of your biography, but at this unprecedented event, please do us the honor of regaling us with it once again. Why was your election significant?"

"Thank you, Giovanni, I am delighted to. As you've stated, my story has been well publicized, so I will recapitulate only the salient points. The Greeks are a proud people with some of the richest history. Sadly, however, the sheen of her once proud majesty has been worn dull. As a boy, I was saddened by my grandfather's broken heart. The Greece of today no longer resembled the Greece of his noble stories. He was once proud to be Greek, but by the end, he only knew shame. I wanted to do what I could to make him proud, but I had no idea how. Then one day fate stepped in, or rather, stepped *off*...the plane that is. Pope John Paul the Second visited Greece. That pivotal moment was my answer. After doing some research, I discovered that there hasn't been a Greek pope since the sixteenth century! I was shocked. That needed to change, and I was determined to be the one to do it. We all know how that turned out."

"And this is why Vincente Basile's

accomplishments resonated with you, correct?"

"Correct. His astonishing attainments reached my ears, causing me to sit up and take notice. I wasn't the only one, either. Inquiry from almost all the dioceses broke through my periphery. All wanted to know who this man was. With each new success, I knew he could no longer be ignored; he needed to be acknowledged."

"And till now, outside of the Catholic hierarchy, few knew who he was," Giovanni continues filling in the blanks. Vincente remains silent. "Vincente, you are about to become a household name. Are you ready?"

Finally, the man of the hour speaks. "I am. I believe my whole life has led up to this moment."

"That's good, because after tonight, millions of people, dare I say billions, will be clamoring for Vincente Basile," Giovanni informs.

Vincente simply smiles a smile that barely conceals his escalating narcissistic infatuation. He knows they will, and he welcomes it.

"Case in point, I hear an aspiring writer has your exclusive?"

"That's correct. His name is Aaron D'Angelo..."

***

The whirring melody of a disengaging mechanical lock fills the empty hotel room. The heavy metal door swings open and spews a worn-out Aaron into the quiet, average-looking room. He cares not that it is average; he cares only that the door locks and the bed has a pillow: if only it were his own...

Flopping on said bed and head plunging into the aforementioned pillow, Aaron stares at the ceiling trying to chase away the images of all the other heads that've laid on this same pillow. He's a functioning germaphobe: watching all those Dateline hotel investigations was not wise. Nevertheless, he powers through the case of the skeeves and thinks about all that's happened today. He's witnessed history while being a part of it. Frankly, he doesn't give a flying rip about any of it. All he wants is to turn on the TV and watch something asinine—SportsCenter will do.

Looking at his bedside clock, he sees that it's just after 8:00 p.m. Perfect, the day's happenings in the sports world will have just begun. He snatches up the remote and fires an invisible infrared beam at the TV. The blank screen is immediately filled with Vincente's smug mug. The promise of escape alludes him. Precious TV betrays him.

The channel is reporting the boisterous festivities. The news camera shows thousands of adoring worshippers giving hearty approval to the newly sainted Vincente. Then it pans up to Vincente, standing high above the throng, peering out from the pope's balcony. To the delight of all, Vincente waves at the frenzied sea of spectators. Even though he knew exactly where he was standing, Aaron could never spot himself. The crowd is shoulder to shoulder.

He changes the channel only to be

dismayed by the new channel showing the event. Changed it again, same thing. One more try, same outcome.

"Come on! I just wanna watch some fool get dunked on!" he yells at the inanimate object.

Having learned from his mistakes, he slides out the bedside table's drawer. Inside he finds the channel list and consults it for ESPN's corresponding number. Punching in the digits, he is mercifully greeted by a commentator narrating today's top ten plays. Aaron sighs in relief as he sinks deeper into the pillow. Eight minutes into decompressing, he's aware of the five-pound bags of sand attached to his eyelids: they refuse to stay open. Despite the two-hour afternoon nap, he's still soooo tired. Sick of the fight, he gives in and closes his eyes for a second...

Being led by SportsCenter's famous segue jingle, Aaron crawls out of the dark tunnel and back into the light. Assuming he dozed off for just a couple of winks, he looks at his bedside clock.

"Eleven!! "What the...?!" Aaron exclaims, confused by the unexplained disappearance of time.

Wanting to reorient himself, he sits up and scoots back against the headboard. In doing so, his right hand mashes the remote resting by his side. The channel changes and is now showing different images, ones Aaron hasn't seen yet. On the TV, Vincente lounges in a stately armchair next to Pope Andel while a man interviews them.

Aaron is drawn to this intimate encounter.

Truthfully, it's a less obnoxious display of Vincente's zealousness. But Aaron wants only to write a few thoughts in his journal, visit the john, turn off the lights, and wake up tomorrow ready to get on a plane and leave this la-la land in his rearview mirror. Strangely, he doesn't turn off the TV but rather turns the volume down to a whisper. He may be sick of hearing Vincente's voice, but for some reason, it's kinda soothing.

Aaron crawls out of bed, retrieving his laptop. Returning, he turns on the laptop and settles back, ready to record his thoughts. He drags the cursor over to the icon labeled, *Journal,* and double-clicks. A program opens up, ready to transcribe Aaron's dictation. He begins.

"Thirteenth of January from Rome, Italy. Thankfully, I have completed my interview with Vincente Basile. I can no longer bear his peccadillos and idiosyncrasies. I fear I have spent too long in his presence and thus, infected by his immense arrogance and intolerable hedonistic demeanor. Granted, he hides all this behind a veil of piety, but I'm confident he believes all his perceived grandiosity. Whether consciously or unconsciously, he sees himself as a Messiah, or worse yet, THE Christ. How many men throughout time have believed this and have gone on to perform atrocities on a scale of epic proportions? However, in my mind, what sets this man apart from all that has come before him is that I believe he can accomplish all that he says he will. Alas, I must be honest here. Am I being paranoid? Did he at any time indicate he wanted to commit evil? Everything he desires to accomplish is for the good of all mankind. Can I fault him for having lofty goals and delusions of grandeur? Is that really a bad thing? Is what he's saying diabolical or just misguided? The world desperately needs improvement, and he believes he's the answer to life's ills. But here's the rub, so did Hitler."

While he spoke, unbeknownst to him, the interview concluded and started over again. No longer speaking, he suddenly hears his name. Curiosity piqued, he turns the volume back up.

"That's quite the gift you've given him." The pope is now engaging Vincente. "It seems God is pleased with this young man."

"He is. And more than that, I'm pleased with him and want to bless him mightily."

Aaron involuntarily leans forward wanting to get closer to the TV...to him.

"If he's party to all that you'll soon accomplish," the pope begins, "The blessings will be immeasurable. I'm confident God will continue doing mighty things through you."

"I strive to remain humble in the face of it all."

"And I'm sure it'll be a struggle for your young biographer as well," Giovanni chimes in.

Vincente's eyes which were once looking straight ahead, now shift slightly to the right and directly into the camera. Another second of silence ticks off as Aaron holds his breath. Skin crawling, he's certain Vincente is looking *through* the camera...looking directly at him.

"Fame and fortune await him. Everything he's strived for, all his goals and aspirations, will now be realized. His life has been categorically reprogrammed. He will never be the same again."

Once those haunting words escape Vincente's lips, he turns his attention back to Giovanni and the interview switches gears.

"I hear your next plan of attack is Rome. What's your strategy for success here?"

"It will be the same blueprint as the others: one step at a time."

The TV becomes ambient noise as Aaron scoots back. He now wants as much distance between himself and Vincente as possible. In doing so, he knocks his cell off the bed and onto the floor. Aaron leans over and retrieves it. As he draws back, his head bonks the underside of the bedside drawer he failed to close earlier. Cursing under his breath, he rubs the tender spot as he looks into the drawer. His heart freezes. Aaron spots the staple in every hotel dresser drawer—a Gideon Bible. His mind panics as a pernicious thought sparks, igniting his superstitious Catholic upbringing.

"Did I just sell my soul?"

***

The Great Disappearance (so named by those who have no idea what the Rapture is) rocked the world eight months later but not before Saint Basile made good on his prognosticating: Rome was restored to her former glory. But just as Rome's inception was longer than a day, so too was her redemption.

Degradation was deeply entrenched in the warp and woof of the millennial-old city, but unlike Vincente's previous successes, Rome's salvation came from a strange source. Rome's biggest problem was drugs, which naturally led to all manner of crimes to get those drugs. Their unceasing siren song had reached deafening decibels inside the Eternal City's crumbling walls. So to silence their refrain, Vincente took away their voice by legalizing all drugs; more accurately he, along with Pope Andel's clout (which is and always will be key to Vincente's influence on the world), persuaded Rome's mayor to sign the bill.

For the naysayers and pearl-clutchers, this seemed counter-intuitive. This is because they'd have to admit that the decades of false teachings and the billions upon billions wasted on an unwinnable war have yielded diddly squat. Drug addiction is still an epidemic and, in some cases, worse than ever.

There is no shortage of literature heralding the positive results of legalized drugs. But because the world is determined to stick with a *loser*, the literature is swept under the rug.

But there was one country, wearied by their beloved society crumbling at their feet, that decided enough was enough. They were going to do something radical. Nearly three decades ago, Portugal became the first country to legalize all drugs, and based on continuous positive results, it's a rousing success. Vincente used this fact to push his agenda forward.

Those who care to take their heads out of the sand will see that drugs are never going away. Vincente used this truth to get Pope Andel in line with his thinking. He needed the pope's influence to convince Rome's mayor to sign onto such an audacious, risky scenario. Nobody wants to be remembered for a colossal failure should the whole thing go sideways.

Vincente understood the mayor's concern for his legacy, but he also knew that once he heard his plan, the mayor would be on board. He knew this because he knew what made the mayor tick. He's a gambleholic; his pulse beats in perfect rhythm to a high-stakes drum.

When before him, Vincente convinced the mayor that he wanted this action; that the high risk, high reward was simply too sweet to pass up. Sure, if the plan failed, his rep would be tainted forever. However, should it work, he'd be named among Rome's great rulers of old. That closed the deal: the mayor was all too happy to roll the dice.

It took less than two months for the soaring drug crisis to be downgraded to a minor nuisance. Because drugs were now regulated and bought out in the open, the previous strategies to obtain drugs were a thing of the past. With dark alley transactions moved into the buildings of those same alleys, the stigma and dirtiness disappeared. Interestingly, this psychological shift freed up the addict's mind to consider why they were taking drugs, to begin with. Any honest individual saw that the drugs were an escape from their problems. Now that the fear of being locked up was gone, the user felt empowered to get help for those problems. Because the money that once poured into a fruitless war now went to treatment programs, those honest individuals got top-notch care.

Another long-touted benefit from the "Legalize All Drugs" crowd was also realized: the taxes for the sale of drugs went to improving the city. Another of Rome's significant problems was its disintegrating infrastructure. The roads that bore up under the feet of history's mighty men were in desperate disrepair. With Rome's coffers bursting, and the streets cleansed of its broken vials and aids-infested needles, those streets were finally repaired. But more than just the streets were dealt with. The graffitied walls were repainted, and boarded-up buildings were remodeled; essentially everything requiring a "Re" was addressed. Rome became relevant again, but more than that, it became powerful once more.

It was the fairy book ending the autocratic empire deserved; it was the ending they needed most. But, alas, not everyone was rescued by a dashing prince atop a noble steed and whisked away to his kingdom where they'll live happily ever after. One specific individual rode off alone on an entirely different horse to an entirely different location where cambions lurk, waiting to feed on his forfeited soul.

\*\*\*

Vincente's other prediction came true:

Aaron did indeed make a few bucks, and he did become renowned. A week after his interview hit the newsstands, he was hired to write Vincente's full biography. He received a sizable advancement (he also sold the inevitable movie rights for his biography) and a swanky apartment in Rome. He needed to relocate because Vincente moved there.

Amazingly, Aaron was inundated with requests for interviews as well. Suddenly, he was the story of the moment; people wanted to know everything about the world's most famous man's biographer. But like many overnight successes, all this came with a hefty price tag. The sudden attention, combined with the sudden *coin*, short-circuited his brain and altered his life.

Aaron always had several harmless "addictive hats" that he'd slip on to tranquilize the brain-numbing doldrums—the hat of a gamer, a gym rat, a shopaholic, etc. They were innocuous diversions he thought nothing of. The problem was, a foul beast lurked in a dark valley, waiting for the right trigger, to crawl up to the light and savagely plunder him.

This is not uncommon for people with addictive personalities. They spend their lives ignoring the warning bells, deceiving themselves into thinking everything's copacetic—*No worries, Man, I got this.* They continue this foolish thinking until it's too late. Eventually, their beast will find that trigger and pull it...they never stop pulling.

When Aaron's trigger was pulled, his life

took on a dreamlike quality. Reality became a highway mirage—it was always just out of reach. He was numb and wanted, needed, to feel something. In a fit of panic, he clung to a different kind of fantasia, one that could be attained through smoke, or a hollowed-out pen case. He reasoned, *at least these new delusions left me alone*...until they didn't. On the island of Fool's Paradise, sooner or later, the Piper will collect, and he does not accept food stamps.

In short order, Aaron ascended to the heights of full-blown heroin addiction. His new lifestyle completely altered his personality. No longer was he Aaron D'Angelo—slinger of fastidious phraseology and scriber of the quick gag. Now he was Aaron D'Angelo—binger of insidious pharmacology and imbiber of sick scag.

As some well know, addiction is a cruel mistress. She's not satisfied with token offerings for very long. Her demanding cry is always, *MORE!!* In his quest to satisfy her, he jammed all his earnings into his veins. He was now flat broke and destitute. He was living with a querulous enchantress and had no money to appease her. He lost his apartment and was living on the streets. Thankfully, Vincente recognized his dire straits and rescued him. Aaron moved in to be Vincente's live-in personal assistant. Even though the biography was finished, Vincente still wanted to take care of his friend. He couldn't let him die in the streets.

Aaron should've run back home but was ashamed of his lifestyle. Because Aaron allowed his pride to run the show, he gave his future to Vincente. Instead of providing treatment, Vincente employed the old strategy of providing him with an endless supply of drugs hoping that Aaron would come to the end of himself. Vincente knows Aaron needs to make this decision on his own. Forcing somebody into rehab is rarely successful.

Aaron's concerns for shelter were addressed but a new problem arose—heroin no longer mollified him. His parasitic mistress demanded something new. He tried Theraflu—a heroin/fentanyl combo—as it was *the thing* in Rome. But he, along with Rome, discovered something newer and better. All were onboard—the Cray-Cray train, that is.

Cray-Cray, so named because you must be crazy if you're shooting it into your broken veins. It's a mix of heroin and Carfentanil, an elephant tranquilizer, and is a whopping ten thousand times more potent rush than morphine. Obviously, it's not meant for human consumption, sane humans anyway. Sure, people have ingested cat tranquilizers and horse tranquilizers for years but taking something meant for the largest living land mammal...utter lunacy.

Falling down the rabbit hole isn't just a line from a classic story, it is a perfect analogy for the journey the addict takes. The further Aaron fell, the harder it was to see. Disorientation and confusion captured him while the fear of being buried alive became more intoxicating than the drugs. The luster and thrill of the chase dimmed long ago; now the desperation to herd the creepy crawlies back into the shadows is all that drives him. It's why he continues to shoot.

Seven short months removed from the infamous interview, and Aaron's life has reached a critical state. Vincente's strategy of forcing drugs down Aaron's throat to save him (if that was truly his intention…jury's still out) backfired spectacularly. Aaron is now trapped in the "rabbit hole" with no way of escape. His cries for help came too late; nobody could hear him. Can he be saved or is he lost forever…?

# CHAPTER FIVE

S usan Andrews sits at her vanity and robotically applies her face for the day. Normally, she wouldn't go through this much trouble on a Saturday morning, but she received a most unusual phone call from a most unexpected source—Joshua Mendelsburg. So here she is, slathering on make-up, getting ready to meet him for coffee. She determined yesterday their therapy was at an impasse; her objectivity was compromised. For all her self-arguing to the contrary, she can't deny it—she's attracted to him. So why is she going? Something about inquisitiveness and felines…

While applying mascara, one of the many triggers for endless nights of crying catches her attention. She stares into and through the mirror, as though it were a portal to a different plane of consciousness. In the reflection, she spies a picture frame atop her dresser next to her TV (CNN is on, but the volume is low). The picture is a shirtless man, standing in front of the ocean, hamming it up for the camera.

As she zeros in on the picture, everything else goes out of focus. Unaccounted-for seconds pass while she relives an unseen tragedy. Judging by her glazed-over eyes, this experience is old hat; the unseen trauma has played on an endless loop for some time. Often the most effective psychiatrists are the most damaged.

Even though this is the eight-gagillionth time she's looked at the photo, it's odd that it feels like the first time. Is it because this is the first time since "it" happened that another man captured her affection? A BREAKING NEWS banner flashes across the bottom of her TV screen, stealing her concentration.

The photograph goes fuzzy as the TV comes into sharp focus. Swapping out her mascara wand with the TV remote, she spins around and turns the volume up.

"The one-year anniversary of Vincente Basile becoming Saint Vincente has passed. Two months ago, Saint Vincente was inaugurated, becoming World President Basile," the perky anchorwoman reports. "In his short thirty-nine years, he has embodied two history-defining moments: first living saint and first world ruler. Now he's on the cusp of making history once again. More than eighty years ago, Israel became a nation. This Thursday, January twenty-second, the adolescent nation will be given what they've long fought for—peace. At one o'clock p.m. Israel Daylight Time, World President Basile will bless their newly finished temple and sign the peace treaty between Israel and the rest of the world."

Hearing *one o'clock p.m.* prompts Susan to check the time. She's disheartened by the report. She's late. But is it for a very important date? She'll soon find out. Putting on the finishing touches, she grabs her purse and dashes out the door.

***

While Josh and Susan prepare for their rendezvous, Josh's father, Benson Mendelsburg, strolls around Jerusalem's Temple Mount with Chief Rabbi Eleazar Segal. Ben and Ele—as they've always called each other—have been best friends since their youth. But they are more than life-long friends; they are brothers in tragedy as well. Their wives died in the same suicide bomber's cowardly explosion. Their bond is eternal.

"Ben," Eleazar speaks into the silence that replaced the chitchat nearly two minutes ago. "I sense you have something important to tell me. But I have a lot to do before Thursday. Can we talk about it later?"

Benson does have something important to tell him—life and death in fact. "You know me too well. Yes, we can talk later."

"Very good, my friend. Until then." Eleazar heads toward Israel's now completed third and final temple.

"Wait, I do have a quick question," Benson yells, halting Eleazar. "I'm leaving a plane ticket for Josh at will call. I want him by my side. Can you get him into the courtyard?"

"That's a hot ticket, Ben."

"What good is being chief rabbi if you can't throw your weight around once in a while?"

Eleazar offers a smirk and an arched eyebrow. Without saying a word, he spins, continuing his pilgrimage to the temple.

Benson yells after him. "Is that a yes?"

Without looking, Eleazar yells back. "Have I ever let you down?"

Benson whispers, "No, no you have not."

***

As Susan approaches the entrance of a quaint coffee shop she sees Josh coming from the opposite direction. Like a choreographed play, they reach the door at the same time. Without slowing down, Josh opens the door, allowing her to walk right in. Heart fluttering at his chivalry, as though laying his white coat over a puddle, she smiles and walks in.

Moments later, with coffees in hand, they sink into inviting armchairs. After savoring their first sip, both settle in and enjoy the flush of being comfortably numb. Susan begins.

"Didn't I see you yesterday? The courts only require once a week you know."

"Yes, and I do. This isn't couch-lounging related."

"Or in your case, obsessive pacing," she teases, hoping he sees it as such.

His smile confirms and his twinkling eyes approve. "Exactly."

"So?" She's priming the pump. "What's up? You sounded a tad manic on the phone."

"I don't know how to say this, so I'll come right out and say it."

Without realizing it, she's holding her breath. She has this strange feeling—call it woman's intuition—her immediate future lies in what comes next.

"Last night, I met Jesus. I'm a Born Again now."

Trying to keep her composure, she simply stares at him. She feels light-headed, as though all the oxygen was sucked out of the room.

"I'm sorry, did you say you met Jesus?"

"I know it sounds crazy, especially coming from me, but it's true. He *is* real. He revealed Himself to me. I know what you're thinking, and I get it; but trust me, there was no alcohol or drugs involved. Nor was it because of an undigested bit of beef or a crumb of cheese." He waits to see if she appreciates his Scrooge impersonation. Her perturbed look says *no*.

Unsure what to do next, she sips her coffee. How can she be so stupid? She knew better than to let her heart go on autopilot, to give her feelings a seat at the table.

"I promise, my mind did not snap last night," Josh says, trying to overrule the awkwardness. "In fact, it's never been more lucid."

"I believe you, it's just...well, not what I expected you to say."

"What did you expect?"

"Nothing. Never mind. It doesn't matter anymore."

Josh continues his story, but she hears none of it. For her, the whole scene is silent. His mouth moves but no audible words come out. The uncomfortableness is unbearable. She must leave, immediately. She absentmindedly guzzles her coffee to the point of burning her tongue. Plopping her empty mug on the coffee table like she just won a college drinking game, she gathers up her purse and stands. Though in the middle of a sentence, Josh follows suit, perplexed.

Both head for the exit, knife-cutting tension shrouding them like London fog. Josh again opens the door for her, but this time it has no effect on her: the butterflies have died in the stomach juices of anxiety and embarrassment.

Now outside, the awkwardness still unrelenting, she heads for her car. Josh watches her walking, but then he sees her stopping. Her back remains to him while she dialogues internally. Concluding, she turns her head slightly, giving him a side view.

"You know what I thought you were going to say?"

He says nothing, only listens. Sometimes men aren't completely clueless.

She walks back to him. "I thought you were going to say you had feelings for me."

He remains silent, his expression communicating confusion.

"I hoped you were going to say that because *I* have feelings for you, pretty strong feelings. Before you called this morning, I made up my mind that you needed to see another therapist. I can no longer treat you objectively. But then you called, and my foolish heart usurped my brain."

Having bared her soul, she waits for a response; none comes.

"Please don't misinterpret my confusion,"

Susan says. "I'm happy you found peace with your higher power and are now comfortable with your spirituality. It's a big step towards your healing. It's just that…"

Not sure what else to say, she steps in and kisses him full on the lips. At least one firecracker explodes in her head before she breaks the seal. Heartbroken that she'll never experience a full-on Fourth of July spectacle, she gazes sadly into his eyes for a passing second. Turning on her heel, she heads to her car: this time for good; this time will be the last time. Unbeknownst to Josh, he will never see her again.

Minutes later, Josh enters his car and reflects on what happened. He has a nagging feeling he should have said more, but what? Like a carrier pigeon alighting on his mind, he has the answer. He doesn't yet understand this is prompting from the Holy Spirit. He only knows this sensation is something new…and he likes it.

He unpockets his phone, finds Susan's number, and begins a text. He attaches the link to the website that Mike gave him in his letter. He adds a couple of grateful words for her commitment and dedication, tells her he's sorry for how things turned out, and concludes by saying he will pray for her.

Satisfied with the text, he sends it. No sooner is the text sent, than a new one comes in. It's from his father, asking if they can FaceTime.

Josh responds—*I'll FaceTime you in an hour.* This is perfect; he was hoping to talk to his dad today anyway. Hopefully, he'll take his news better than Susan did.

***

An hour later Josh attempts to FaceTime his father. Two rings later, his dad's face fills his laptop; undoubtedly, he was waiting nearby.

"My boy, how are you?" His father seems especially chipper.

"I'm good, Dad. How are you doing?"

"I'm good too." Father/son conversation is always so stimulating. "How's business?"

"Busy. I may need to hire another person to keep up with it all."

His father moves closer to his screen and focuses. "Sounds like a good idea. You look drained."

"Oh, I just had coffee with Susan. It was rather strange."

"Susan, huh?" Benson plays both the meddling card and the doting card dexterously.

"My shrink, Dad," Josh says, cutting his dad off at the pass.

"Oh right, right. You're still seeing her?"

"Not anymore."

"What happened?"

"It's a long story. I'll fill you in later. So, what's going on?"

"Where to begin? I guess I'll start with the most pressing matter. I'm assuming you know what's happening here next week, right?"

"The Temple blessing? Of course. The news *finally* has something else to talk about."

"What does next week look like for you?"

"Busy. Swamped. Why?"

"It'd mean a lot if you were here. Uncle Ele pulled some strings and got you in the courtyard."

"I'd assume so. What good is being chief rabbi if you can't throw your weight around once in a while?" Like father like son. "Dad, I'm sorry. I can't. I just told you how busy I am."

"But it's important to me. Your crew can manage for a week. What good is owning a company if there are no perks?" This very specific goading must be a Mendel-men bit.

Josh works hard to hide his irritation. It was much easier talking to your parents before video chat. You could make all the annoyed faces you wanted, and they were never the wiser.

"I don't think I can get a ticket on such short notice," Josh says.

"Already taken care of. I left a round-trip ticket for you at will call. Your plane leaves Dulles at seven Monday morning."

Josh falls silent, knowing there's no way out of this.

"Get here, please," Benson pleads, his face matching his emotion.

"Alright, Dad, alright. I'll be there. When's the return flight?"

"Friday morning. I have something else to tell you, but I'm not sure how you'll take it."

Here we go. Josh knew there had to be more to this call.

"Like a Band-Aid, Dad. Just tell me."

"Joshua," Benson stares boldly. His eyes are

transfixed on Josh's: never once do they blink. "This morning, I became a follower of the one true Messiah, Jesus Christ."

Josh's heart jumps into the RED. Did he hear his father right?

"Are you serious?"

"I am." Benson's dauntlessness never wavers. He is prepared to go to war if need be.

"What time?"

Benson's thrown off by this random question. "It was just before four o'clock."

Josh's senses tingle. Is it possible they believed at the same time?

"You look perturbed, my boy. Shall I explain?'

"Yes, please do."

Benson complies: "In my trek through the Tanakh…you do remember what that is, right?"

"The complete Jewish scriptures." Josh smiles at his father's look of parental pride.

"Excellent. As is my habit of going through the Tanakh every two years, I arrived at Daniel nine on Wednesday. It talks about the destruction of Jerusalem and the temple, which Antiochus Epiphanes accomplished. And then, verse twenty-seven grabbed my attention."

"What did it say?"

"'He will make a firm covenant with the many.' In the entire Jewish history, nobody has made a covenant with us. But next week, Vincente Basile is. Daniel's prophecy is coming true. Problem is this is not good news. The rest of the verse says this person will destroy us because he's only deceiving us. I needed to know more. I Googled this verse, and a whole study about the end times came up. My curiosity was piqued, so I clicked on it. My intrigue grew even more when I saw it was written by a Jew. I looked up the verses he used. But then everything came to a screeching halt; he included verses from the New Testament. I'll be honest, if this didn't come from a Jew, I would have stopped right there."

"You obviously kept reading, or we wouldn't be having this conversation."

"I did. First Thessalonians four, seventeen. Wanna know what it says?"

"I already do. It says those who are still living will be caught up to the clouds."

"Exactly," Benson praises. His pleased look morphs into a bewildered look. "How did you know that?"

"I'll tell you in a minute. Keep going."

"Very well. I decided to read this verse in Hebrew, so I translated it. As soon as I translated 'caught up,' I was convinced I could no longer ignore the New Testament. It meant, 'to snatch away.' Only the most stubborn fool would deny this is talking about the Christians disappearing. That, and World President Basile, convinced me it was time I took a sincere look at this Jesus fellow. After I read through Matthew, Mark, Luke, and John I was convinced—Jesus Christ truly was the Messiah."

Josh can bear it no longer. He must tell his own good news. "I did the same thing last night!"

"You're kidding me?" Benson asks, clearly

stunned.

"No, that's why I asked you when. I think we became Christians at the same time."

"What convinced you? You hate Christians."

"My friend, Mike. I cleaned out his house yesterday. One of my guys found a letter to me that Mike was intending to mail but never did. In it, he confronted me with the truth, that I was heading to hell. He gave me a website telling me how to become a believer. I read it, repented of my sins, and put my trust in Jesus' death as payment for my sins."

The elder and the younger fall silent; they share a bonding moment like never before. Even though they are thousands of miles apart, the screen's thickness is all that separates the new "brothers."

"Son, whatever happens on Thursday, I want it happening to both of us. That "End Times" link suggested I read Revelation next; I have been most of the day. If I understand what Revelation is saying, the next seven years are gonna be a bumpy ride."

# CHAPTER SIX

4:00 a.m. rolls around quickly in the Holy Land; especially when twelve hours of work, along with the tedium of processing through security checkpoints, was just accomplished a mere four hours ago. But you'll never hear Jasim Nader, a Palestinian living in the never-a-dull-moment Jerusalem, complaining about the long days.

Lying there, caught in between slumber and arousal, he reflects on what's happened to get him to this day. This day, today, is a very big day— the biggest in his short thirty years of breathing. His half-asleep mental stroll through life's recent blessings continues...

Jasim rarely lost himself in the politics infesting this ancient land. Yes, being a Palestinian is burdensome, but it didn't need to be as bad as his people made it. He worked hard and had no time for drama. He desired only to keep his eyes on the prize: Jannah...Paradise.

Unsurprisingly, his *C'est la vie* attitude didn't sit well with most; his dearth of indignation and national pride infuriated his countrymen. But that's their problem. His peaceful attitude earned him goodwill with the Jews which he leveraged into landing the job of setting up the network for the new Temple.

*May Allah be praised!* He'd been looking for work suitable to his IT degree for over a year. His baba's favorite saying proved true—*neighborliness is more dynamic at opening doors than dynamite.* It certainly helped at the security checkpoints into the Jewish Quarter.

It seemed like every morning there was one hot-headed extremist who held everything up. What did this person think their being ruffed up by Israeli guards accomplished? In stark contrast, Jasim's affability earned him a hassle-free pass from the guards. If not for the whackos, he'd be through the checkpoints in under ten minutes. Yes, life was going swimmingly...until somebody jumped into Jasim's *pool* and muddied up the waters.

About four months ago Jasim, who grew lackadaisical in keeping his mental guard up, met somebody new at afternoon prayers. Their bond was immediate. Eventually, he met his new friend's other friends. In less than a month, the new friends' constant conditioning poisoned Jasim.

Going along to get along no longer appeals to him. Now, he's all about justice and retribution and, if Allah wills, becoming a vital cog in vengeance's machine. Jasim's name means "Great" and "Exceptional," and after tonight's Salat al-`Isha is prayed, his name will be accurate. But for that to happen, he must get out of bed...

Jasim is greeted by breakfast's savory smells as he walks into the kitchen. The clock strikes

6. He has just enough time to eat and get to work—today is not the day to be late. His five-year-old son and three-year-old daughter add their greeting with tremendous hugs. The trio sits down to a hearty breakfast; his wife sits, completing the foursome. Jasim gives honor to Allah before the family digs in...it's his last family meal.

***

0600. Ariella Segal sits at a conference table, one of ten facing a SMART board hanging in a conference room. She is the only woman in a room teaming with coffee-guzzling, testosterone-laced braggadocios: she'd have it no other way.

When she was fifteen, her mother died at the hands of a suicide bomber. This tragedy may've made her diamond tough, but diamonds are NOT her best friend. She'll never be a typical woman, much to the chagrin of her traditional father. Should Eleazar be blamed for his agitation? When you're Jerusalem's chief rabbi, you have a definitive image to uphold.

His tomboy only child has always been a burr in his saddle. She has a brilliant mind to go along with her pitch-perfect street smarts and common sense. Why she turned her required two-year military service into a career is beyond his comprehension. She could've easily been a physician, carrying a clipboard and wearing a white coat. Instead, she opted to be a soldier, carrying a CTAR-21 and wearing fatigues; well, when she's not undercover that is. That's when she's wearing a burka—the official undercover outfit. His daughter wearing the enemy's attire makes his skin crawl. Jews and Muslims are forced to cohabitate, separated only by brick and mortar. But dressing like them even if it is for Jerusalem's protection...appalling.

She knows her career choices irk her father, but she will not apologize. This is her calling, and she's worked hard to get here. The *tape* of Ariella Segal's back story rolls.

*\*\*\**

After her mother's death, she became obsessed with the military, specifically combat soldiers—more specifically, the special forces. However, up to that point, girls in combat roles were relegated to fluff detail. It was a total joke—might as well slap a pink bedazzled beret atop their pretty bowed heads and hand them a glittery rifle.

She was determined to break through the barriers segregating the two sexes. Seemingly moments after taking the oath, she waged war for her voice to be heard, but success refused to come—those barriers were titanium-strong. The armed forces bristle against change, but few are more steadfast than the Israel Defense Forces (IDF). On a few occasions, usually during her most discouraged moments, she considered tapping into her father's high standing. But she always came back to her senses: she couldn't live with herself if she caved. Relentless stubbornness...it was a gift from dear ol' dad.

Sometimes, fathers need to step in for their child's well-being, whether that child likes it or not. After two years of watching his daughter emotionally concuss herself from ramming her head into the gender barrier, he secretly *swung* his noble tassels of authority. He convinced the IDF to give her a shot at surviving the sixteen weeks of basic infantry training and then the ten weeks of advanced infantry training. Knowing how famously grueling the special forces training was, he was confident her ambition would dry up and she'd abandon the foolish crusade. He was wrong.

From day one, not wanting to give the doubters any ammunition, she insisted on not being treated differently. She wanted everything equal between her and the men, right down to bunking in the same barracks.

Her gumption and gung-ho were noble, but for most who enter SF training, all brashness takes a suicidal nosedive rather quickly. Typically, only 25 percent survive week one: it's not called Hell Week for grins and giggles. It's quite effective at weeding out pretenders.

But because she trained and thought of nothing else since she was fifteen, Hell Week was just another seven days with less sleep. With each week checked off the calendar, she continually separated herself from the pack; so much so, that she graduated in the top three of her class. On day one they were sixty-five strong; by the end, only eighteen still stood.

Eleazar couldn't resist being impressed with his blood's history-defining. She was the first female to graduate from Camp Mitkan Adam's twenty-six-week special forces training course.

The day after graduation, she shipped out for two months of advanced urban navigation and counter-terrorism training. This was followed by four months of learning Arab traditions and language. Lastly, she was to have one month of sniper and driving courses.

She was a marvel in all facets, especially the sniper course, which was where her true giftedness revealed itself. Her exceptionally steady hand and cool thinking under pressure made her a marksman of the highest order. She could hit a moving target with freakish accuracy. It didn't matter the circumstances; she rarely missed.

Once the advanced training was completed, Ariella realized her dream—becoming part of the elite Mista'arvim task force. Her life would never be the same again. From now on, anonymity was her life partner.

Because of Mista'arvim's highly sensitive nature, very little is known about this elite counter-terrorism unit. They are described as ghosts. One minute a riot swells; the next minute the rioters lie spread-eagle in the street, dead. For the scant eyewitnesses who *think* they *might* have seen something, all their reports are similar, making for great stories that night at the bar.

*It was like two, maybe three ghosts appeared*

*out of thin air, killed 'em, and then disappeared again. Never saw anything like it!*

Always without fail, there'd be at least one non-superstitious person who'd cry, *nonsense!* They'd smugly inform the storyteller and all who listened that ghosts don't exist. The smarty-pants party-poopers would then offer a reasonable explanation. Usually, something like, *Obviously, they were already there, mixed in with the crowd, looking like everybody else so they wouldn't be noticed.*

You're right. But you should stop talking now. They might be sitting at the table next to you…

***

Her commander enters the room, bringing the *backstory tape* to a halt. He takes his place at the podium, ready to begin the morning briefing. Grabbing the remote, he wakes the SMART board. The screensaver—a swimming *Thursday the 22nd*—disappears and is replaced by satellite images of the Temple Mount.

"Alright, ladies, eighty-six the patty-cake playing, and take a seat," Commander Goldhirsch commands. The nervous-energied buffoonery ceases. At that moment, Isaac, Ariella's partner, sits next to her. He's late. She gives him a questioning look. A shrug is his answer.

"No offense to you, Lieutenant Segal," the commander continues.

"Well, I am a lady, so none taken," she assures.

"That's not what I heard." A brilliant remark from a not-too-brilliant person in the back.

She doesn't look in the voice's direction; she knows the gaping maw it's coming from.

"I heard you were a man, but you know how rumors are."

Typical jeering from a room full of keyed-up males works its way around. Men always appreciate a good gibing at their compadres' expense, especially if it comes from a woman.

Rouge lights up his face. "If you say so." Whip-smart, he ain't.

"I don't recall; who drank who under the table last night?" She's got him on the ropes.

Her partner tags in for the three count. "And who 'fell asleep,'" Isaac asks, making air quotes, "Under that table because he got handsy?"

Still looking forward, Ariella presents her left fist to the back of the room. Her scrapped, dry-blood-encrusted knuckles imply she recently worked over a slab of meat. She now looks back at him.

"And I'm not left-handed."

He discreetly rubs his bruised jaw as his buddies playfully ruffle his hair. He's been bested, so he shuts up. In very little time, she's earned considerable respect from her peers. Never willing to admit it, nobody dares mess with her... the smart ones anyway. She may be at the tail end of the petite spectrum, but don't be fooled; she's an expert at turning her 125-pound frame into a lethal killing machine.

"Alright, stow it. We're staring at a stressful day," Commander Goldhirsch reclaims the room. "With the world president here, tensions will be high. A lot of religious promises are about to culminate. I have no doubt, somewhere an Ahab Firecracker is itching to meet his seventy-two virgins at our expense. But they'll have to wait. Nobody is blowing themselves up today."

Tension-induced laughter spills out into the room. When it subsides, he draws their attention to the SMART board and continues.

"Here is a list of the groups of two who'll be stationed at each gate helping the police check lanyard-carrying visitors. And these are the two-person groups who'll be patrolling the mount undercover. Be sure to grab a PET before you leave."

When Ariella sees her and Isaac's names on the patrol list, she fist-bumps her partner. There is nothing more boring than standing at a gate all day.

"There are many Muslims not exactly tickled about this treaty. I guarantee, war will continue to the final second. Stay sharp. Dismissed."

The elite warriors gather their stuff and file out. Commander Goldhirsch pulls Isaac and Ariella aside before they reach the door.

"I put you two on patrol because you're the best. History is trying to be made today. Keep your heads on a swivel."

\*\*\*

As is his custom, Benson was up at five, reading scripture. What isn't his custom is reading scripture from the Bible. Before Saturday morning, he's not sure if he's ever *held* a Bible, much less *read* one. Since Saturday, he's read through Revelation three times, and with each reading, he's more concerned. But, curiously, he's also more at peace. He took this peace with him as he left to meet Eleazar for a morning stroll.

"This is a lot to take in," Eleazar confides as they mosey around the Temple Mount. "Having a peace treaty signed and the temple ordained is one thing, but being made the first high priest in nearly two thousand years is more than I'm ready for."

"Why?" Benson presses. "The biggest difference between being chief rabbi and high priest is you'll be performing rites."

"Exactly. Who am I to handle the rites and sacrifices?"

"You're a descendant of Aaron; that's who you are."

"Because I'm a Levite that qualifies me to be the high priest?"

Benson leans in and playfully elbows Eleazar's arm. "Ah, yeah. Kind of a package deal."

"Better be careful: the IDF are on high alert today. They might see that as an act of aggression," Eleazar joshes his buddy.

"I'm sure your daughter won't snipe me."

"Never know. To my knowledge, she hasn't shot anybody in a few days." Eleazar continues the bantering volley. "Have they run into each other yet?"

"Not yet. Josh's been battling jet lag. I'm gonna suggest they meet up tonight."

"Does Halvar know Josh is in town?"

"I haven't spoken to Halvar in months. I think he's ignoring my calls. Have you tried?" Benson inquires.

"I stopped in his store a couple weeks ago. He was skittish and not too happy to see me. I have a bad feeling our old friend has fallen in with the wrong crowd."

"He always struggled with interpreting people's intentions, especially when money was involved. I'll stop in soon," Benson promises.

Silence falls, both mulling over their friend's mental weaknesses. After rounding the northwest corner, Eleazar divulges a shocking secret.

"I don't know what I believe anymore," he blurts out, perhaps inspired by Halvar's struggles. "The thinning of the Christian quarter and much of the world has created doubt. What if the Born Agains were right all along? I keep hearing the word *Rapture* whispered among the people. If there was to be a Rapture, why doesn't the Tanakh talk about it?"

Benson stays quiet. He knows this is a perfect segue to telling him about Saturday morning, but he doesn't want to interrupt him.

"Speaking of our scriptures, Isaiah fifty-three has always irritated me, but after *whatever* happened four months ago, I can no longer deny it's talking about Jesus. Have we been wrong this whole time?"

With a handful of yards from the southeast corner to go, where the *waiting-to-be-blessed* temple resides, Benson grabs Eleazar's arm and screeches their walk to a halt. He can no longer hold his tongue. Surprised, Eleazar looks expectantly at his old chum.

"Ele, I have to tell you something. The other day, I..."

Like a "jump-scare" from a lazily written horror movie, a young man suddenly yells as he races toward the two men.

"Rabbi Segal! Rabbi Segal!" The young man arrives, wheezing and out of breath. Muscle memory kicks in, causing him to trout out an asthma huffer and administer two quick puffs.

Eleazar rests his hand on the boy's heaving shoulder. "Easy. Catch your breath and then tell me."

Obeying, he slows his breathing before relaying the message. "Sir, there are last-minute details that need your attention immediately."

"Alright, young man, lead the way." He turns and looks apologetically at Benson. "I'm sorry, can we continue this tonight?"

Discouraged but smiling, Benson responds. "Of course, Rabbi Segal. Shalom and Kol Tuv."

Eleazar mouths *thank you* to his friend as he allows the asthmatic Shamash to lead the way. As Benson watches Eleazar depart, he's annoyed with himself for staying silent. Finishing the circuit around the Mount, he promises to himself and God that he'll never stay silent again when he knows he must speak.

The Mugrabi Gate—which is at the southwest corner—comes into view. Soon, he'll be descending the ramp and stopping at the Western Wall for prayer. He's done this hundreds, maybe thousands of times, but he has a feeling God will be listening for the first time.

Passing the Al Aqsa Mosque, he sees a crowd waiting in line at the gate to be part of the ceremony. Even though it doesn't start for another five hours, the witnesses want to get in early. As he watches each endure customs-like security screening, complete with passing through a metal detector before entrance, he notices one specific drama unfold.

A backpack-strapped man has a conversation with one security guard and then a confrontation with another—this one is paired with a bomb-sniffing dog—before he's finally allowed to pass. Once Backpack Man is inside the Mount, Benson watches the confronting guard leave the chaos, step just inside the Mount, and regard Backpack Man intensely. The scrutiny doesn't last long before he's distracted by a raucous, lanyard-less man at the gate. The guard returns to deal with it.

Head down and pedal to the metal, Backpack Man pursues the Al Aqsa Mosque like a defensive end lunging at the quarterback. In his carelessness, he almost plows into Benson. Fortunately, Benson was alert. He simply strafes to his left, avoiding being sacked.

As he passes, Backpack Man looks up

at Benson for a split second before looking back down and continuing his quest. In that brief interchange, Benson could read the man's emotions. His face was pale; his eyes conveyed both deviousness and nauseousness.

Benson tracks the suspicious man. It's now his turn to either heed or reject the foreboding circling his mind. He chooses to obey by taking a step toward the retreating man.

Backpack Man arrives at the Mosque and swings open the doors. Just before disappearing inside, he shoots a cursory look at Benson, who is now even more determined to investigate. After all, the mantra in this day and age is "See something, say something."

Disastrously, the debatable, dastardly deed is quickly forgotten as Benson's heroics are aborted by the sound of a familiar voice. He turns to greet the *off-camera* distraction. And just like that, the count is now 0 and 2. One more strike and everybody's out.

\*\*\*

Roughly sixty minutes ago, Josh exited a taxi and entered through Zion's gate. He's still a tad beat down by jet lag despite the excessive hours of sack-time in his old room, which feels weird because he never actually lived in that room. His mom insisted that when they moved back to Jerusalem, the guest room be turned into Josh's room, complete with his old childhood stuff. She wanted him to feel at home when he came to visit. His dad kept it that way to honor his fallen partner...

Regardless of the jet lag, he's ready to reacquaint himself with the Holy City: his father's excellent coffee helps.

Sipping from his father's travel mug, Josh ambles down the fifteen-hundred-year-old Cardo, breathing in the wondrous history. When it was first built, it functioned as the main thoroughfare through the old city. Its rather wide boundaries—the equivalent of a six-lane highway —allowed both residents and pilgrims to work their way through Byzantine Jerusalem.

Eventually, he enters the wide-open Western Wall Plaza where he's overwhelmed by the zealousness happening at the Wailing Wall. The mosaic of people all worshipping is as diverse and beautiful as an actual mosaic. Even though men and women are segregated at the wall, from a distance, the sea of humans creates a living canvas of pious supplication.

As Josh observes the controlled chaos, a backpacked man unintentionally bumps him as he fights through the thickening crowd. The Mugrabi Bridge is his pursuit. Josh responds to the bump by regarding the retreating individual.

Like becoming *it* in *tag*, the "red dot" of laser-precise attention gloms onto the bouncing backpack. Josh is left to reflect on what he sees.

*** 

Having fought through several gnarls of tourists, Jasim arrives at a long line of tourists at the bottom of the Mugrabi Bridge. He grumbles silently at the inconvenience. The longer he waits, the more his will is tested. He's not sure how much aggravation he can handle. He feels like he's about to explode.

Mercifully, he arrives at the checkpoint; only two more people ahead of him. Jasim musters his last ounce of patience as he watches the couple get scanned.

"WAIT! We're with them!" The boisterous demand comes from behind. Jasim is shoved in the back as the howler crashes toward the gate. Without warning, another person SHOULDERS him out of the way.

*Fuse* lit, burning towards a bundle of *TNT sticks*, Jasim's internal timer begins. He WHIPS around, ready to confront any further attackers. He finds none. However, he does see the man he ironically bumped earlier, staring intently at him. Jasim quickly turns back around, wondering if this man is on to him.

*How can he be? Is he undercover? Surely, there must be some Mista'arvim skulking about. Is he one of them?*

Deep in speculation, he doesn't hear security yelling at him—he's next. Snapping to, he refocuses and steps up to the checkpoint where he finds a friend and a possible foe: the added Mista'arvim soldier, eying him suspiciously. Jasim hands his backpack to his friend and steps through the metal detector. Of course, it goes off—he brought through his thirty-ounce metal coffee mug. He offers up his mug and an apologetic look before stepping through again. Success.

"Jasim, you look a million miles away," remarks his security friend as he returns the parted items to the one whom he *shoots the bull* with most every morning. "And that's a ridiculous amount of coffee. Feeling not so regular?" Guy banter remains the same no matter what country you're in.

"Classy. No, all systems are a go, but thanks for the concern. Caffeine is necessary to make today happen. It's a stressful one."

"Ah, yeah," his friend dramatically sweeps his hand, drawing attention to the boisterous scene. "I hadn't noticed. Heading in to put on the final touches?"

"And I'm already way behind. I need to connect one more file DNS to the ODBC driver before the WP signs the treaty. Wouldn't want him looking foolish if the registry file extension is corrupted."

A blank expression showcases across his friend's face. "I have no idea what you just said. For all I know you're setting up a bomb."

Jasim laughs. "Yeah, right!" He looks into the Mista'arvim's accusing eyes. *Does he know I'm making stuff up? Is he on to me?*

Jasim nods at the Special Forces statue. "What's with the jarhead and Lassie?"

The cop looks back at the large soldier. "The Mista'arvim and his loyal bomb dog? They're with me. A gift chaperone for the day. Truthfully, he's driving me crazy, as well as all these *suddenly Orthodox Jews.* I might be forced to start drinking heavily."

"You already do," Jasim reminds.

"And I'm still waiting for you to do it with me."

"You're gonna have to keep on waiting."

"Still holding to your silly sobriety vow?" the cop mocks.

"Till the end."

"Well, since you're obviously planting a bomb, you should join me here on the dark side for one beer before you go."

Still striving to hang onto his disarming smile, Jasim rolls his eyes as he heads inside.

The cop shouts at Jasim's retreating back: "Say *hi* to Allah for me when you get there!"

Looking over his shoulder, Jasim responds: "Say *hi* to Yahweh if you get there first!"

Genuinely smiling, Jasim turns just in time to avoid slamming into a hulking roadblock.

"There're no backpacks allowed today," the burly Mista'arvim soldier insists.

"It's just carrying my work laptop. I need it to wrap things up."

"Doesn't matter. Not allowed."

A silent showdown ensues. Finally, a mediator kibitzes the brewing duel from behind.

"I'm vetting him," informs Jasim's security friend.

"I don't care if he's your long-lost twin. I have my orders."

"Which are to assist me, not overrule me."

"Fine, if he has nothing to hide then he can present his backpack to the dog," the soldier says.

"I insist."

"Just do it, Jasim, so we can keep this line moving."

The cop hurls some good ol' stink-eye at the defiant soldier as Jasim unshoulders his backpack and allows the dog a once-over.

After the dog shows no alarm, the cop asks: "Satisfied? Good. Go, Jasim, you're fine."

Not wanting to tempt fate any further, Jasim hustles into the Temple Mount. The soldier pursues Jasim; his stony expression implies more inspection is needed. Several steps in, a fracas develops in the line, stealing his resolve. He gives one final glance to the backpack as it *floats* across the Mount. Confident regret is in his immediate future, he turns back around to address the brouhaha.

Wanting out of the Neanderthal's penetrating gaze, Jasim rushes headlong as though battling against hurricane gales. In his inattentive urgency, he almost obliterates an innocent bystander. Luckily, the victim was alert and deftly stepped aside.

Jasim looks at the perplexed older gentleman as he races past him. He hopes Allah will forgive his woeful disrespect of the sexagenarian. Just before entering the Al Aqsa Mosque, he shoots a final look at the man. He sees the previous man he's certain is tailing him, approaching the senior. Before the swinging doors close, he hears the man greet his father. Jasim knows that if he doesn't get it together, he'll lose his nerve. He needs some of The Koran's encouraging ayats, *stat.*

\*\*\*

The clock strikes noon, and by now the Temple Mount teems with hundreds of stimulated visitors waiting to see history unfold. Israel's temple hasn't had a successful past. The first two were destroyed by Israel's enemies and her people were either slaughtered or taken into captivity. But this time seems hopeful. Vincente Basile has been purposeful in restoring Israel and her temple. Perhaps, this temple will remain, and Israel can live in peace. Maybe, third time's the charm.

\*\*\*

Jasim—fidgety, edgy, and gnawing his fingers down to nubs—paces in front of a room's entrance where the finishing touches are being completed on his laptop.

"Jasim, you need to stop," Safeer, a serious-looking Muslim man, commands from inside the room. "You're driving us crazy."

"I'm sorry. If I don't keep moving, I'm gonna explode."

The two men stop their tinkering and look incredulously at him. Jasim, realizing his Freudian slip, becomes even more nervous as his pacing resumes at an intensified clip.

"Why don't you come sit down," Ghazi, the other bomb expert, instructs. "It's almost time to start recording."

Jasim takes a seat just inside the nefarious-looking room.

"How did you know they wouldn't check my laptop? All that guard had to do was turn it on. He would've known something was up."

"But he didn't," Safeer counters.

"But he could've."

"Jasim, we picked you because of your connection with the guards," Ghazi soothes. "We knew you could get through."

"And you promise my family will be taken care of?"

"We told you they would. Be still. No more questions. We are running out of time."

Jasim falls silent as he watches the meticulous work being done on the device that'll send him to Paradise. Safeer grabs Jasim's coffee mug and carefully unscrews the lid. Reaching into the now bone-cold coffee, he removes an air-tight bag of white powder —trimethylenetrinitramine: for the chemically challenged, RDX, a very powerful explosive.

With gentleness and respect, Safeer places the deadly substance on the table and slowly slices the bag open with his combat knife.

"Why are you being careful?" Jasim asks "You said it was stable."

"It is. It needs a detonator, but why tempt fate?"

Unable to watch the construction of his death—along with many infidels, Allah willing—any further he scans the room for a distraction. Mercifully, one enters the room. A man, carrying a camcorder/tripod combo and a laptop, walks in.

He sets up the camera in front of an Islamic flag hanging on a wall and then busies himself with the laptop.

As Jasim watches the cameraman perform his role in the unfolding drama, he's arrested by the sound of his laptop clicking shut—he's been dreading that sound. He sees his executioners stowing the laptop in his backpack.

Ghazi walks a small device over to Jasim, who, upon seeing his backpack now locked and loaded, goes numb and placid.

"Jasim, I need you to focus," he instructs, seeing that Jasim is staring into the nothingness. "This is a dead man switch. Releasing this safety lever allows the detonator switch to be pressed, which then arms the bomb. Taking your hand off the switch will then..."

Jasim's tranquil look remains. Ghazi leans directly into his line of sight. "Do you understand? I need you to acknowledge."

Jasim's eyes Ghazi eerily. His look resembles a desensitized killer.

"Yes." Short and sweet.

Skeptical, but having no other option, Ghazi looks at the cameraman who gives a thumbs up: the camera feed is ready and waiting.

"It's time. We only have three minutes until the Zuhr prayer."

Jasim stands, takes his mark in front of the camera, and awaits the go-ahead signal. His fifteen minutes of fame begin now...

\*\*\*

Ariella and Isaac, dressed in plain clothes, nonchalantly patrol the grounds like loss prevention officers scouting for shoplifters. Strolling, pretending they are experiencing the Temple Mount for the first time rather than the four billionth, their eyes remain peeled.

Meandering towards a bench under a tree, she sees two men: one is Benson, resting on the bench. She's unsure of the second—he's turned around, snapping pictures with his phone. Benson notices her.

Not wanting to blow her cover, she smiles at Benson and nothing more; he's not offended, he knows the score. When she's a couple of feet away, the second man turns abruptly.

"Dad!" Josh's name-dropping halts Ariella. "This is more..." He stops talking when his gaze locks onto Ariella's already locked-on gaze. "Beautiful than I remember..."

The two stare at each other as though admiring a Rembrandt. The ogling lasts unnaturally long. Should the whole world suddenly go pitch black, the electricity crackling between them would flash the area with sparkling light. It's as though the attraction was preordained and now coming to fruition.

Isaac breaks up the uncomfortable goggling. "Honey, let's make our way up front. The world president is about to speak."

Not saying a word, Ariella allows Isaac to take her arm and guide her away: she couldn't have done it herself.

At a loss for words, Josh watches his

childhood friend, now a bewitching woman, steadily walk away. Smirking, Benson rests a hand on Josh's shoulder.

"Was that Ariella Segal?! She's all grown up," Josh says, hardly believing his eyes.

"She has. And she's quite attractive, wouldn't you say?" Benson's leading question is hard to miss. He may not be a very young man, but he knows what love is.

Descending from cloud nine, Josh blows off the insinuation like a ten-year-old boy hexing away the cooties. "Nice try. I'm a married man."

"You were."

"But she's obviously with that guy."

"No, she's not."

"Then why did he call her 'honey'?"

"Because that's her partner. She's undercover."

"Undercover? What does she do?" Josh asks, his budding infatuation tough to miss.

Benson knows he has a live one. "More than most."

***

As Josh works through unexpected feelings, Isaac interrogates his partner's unconventional reaction.

"What was that all about?"

"I don't know what you're talking about."

"Are you serious? I was about to tell you two to get a room."

"Don't be vulgar."

"Vulgar?! Your dumpster mouth would

make a Hell's Angel blush."

Snorting at his snappy retort, she puts up a smoke screen. "He's just a childhood friend. Haven't seen him in years."

Stopping at their predetermined advantage point in the middle of the crowd, she hopes her chicanery halts further rebuttals.

"Not your best deceptive efforts." Clearly, that's a no. "Man, I can't wait to tell Hannah that Ariella Segal, the avowed bachelorette, likes a boy! She'll absolutely plotz!"

"Tell your wife whatever you want," she insists, rolling her eyes.

The crowd erupts: Vincente exits the temple and takes his place at a microphoned lectern. The partners cease their bantering and transform into the lethal killers they are: it's all business from now on.

Vincente, basking in the glorious glow of adoration, holds up his hands to silence the assembly. Once the adulation subsides to a dull roar, his amplified voice booms across the Mount.

"I humbly admit to lacking the eloquence needed for such a profound moment."

While Vincente speaks, Jasim swims through the sardine-packed multitude. His destination: hugging proximity to the WP.

Vincente continues. "Israel has been fraught with despair and destruction for a long time. Her enemies have sought nothing less than absolute extermination. And yet, despite millennia of taking the world's best shots, She still stands. She is a testament to the indomitable human spirit to survive against all odds."

Ariella and Isaac scan the crowd while pretending to hang on Vincente's every word. Their masquerade is unnecessary: the masses are enraptured by the silver-tongued speaker; nobody would've noticed them.

As Ariella scans, somebody bumps into her and is swallowed again by the crowd before she sees the person. Her PET, a small device that detects explosive ordinances, activates. She checks the device: sure enough, a bomb just walked by. She shows Isaac the flashing, vibrating device and points in the direction of the assumed threat. They follow.

Up ahead, they watch heads move to the side as an invisible individual carves through the throng. From the constant parting, they see the trail leads to the platform where the world president and the pope stand...right next to the chief rabbi.

*My father!* Ariella screams internally.

In the throes of her duty, Ariella forgot he was up there too. A tidal wave of red-hot desperation courses through her, threatening to send her into a frenzied panic. She grabs Isaac's arm and nods toward her father; he interprets her perfectly.

The two overlook civility and violently push through the crowd. Five knocked-over people and numerous irate damnations later, Isaac and Ariella are at the front. They comb the area for the bomber but can't find him. A few yards away, Vincente continues orating.

"Though undeserving to be part of such a momentous occasion, nevertheless, I accept the privilege given to me. It is with great honor that I, World President Vincente Basile, ordain your new temple where you will be free to once again worship your God."

As a raucous cheer goes up, the partners spot Jasim. Zeroing in like a tiger about to pounce, they remove their handguns and advance on the enemy. All the while, oblivious to his imminent demise, Vincente carries on.

"Along with your temple being restored, I also give you, peace."

Vincente and Eleazar lean over a small table, ready to sign the treaty. In the crowd, Isaac and Ariella's stalking brings them within feet of Jasim. They see him remove the dead man's detonator: both recognize what it is. They also catch his thumb releasing the safety and his hand depressing the switch. In seconds, he'll explode.

Suddenly, two events transpire, shattering the historic moment's tranquility: One—several people see Isaac and Ariella's drawn guns, and two—Jasim yells, "Allahu Akbar!"

At that, panic rips through the crowd as it disperses. Several people are trampled. Vincente, pen hovering over the document, looks out at the commotion.

Like many selfless soldiers who've dove on live grenades before, Isaac tackles Jasim, blanketing him with his body. It happened so fast. Ariella's unuttered, anguished cry remains stuck in her throat.

Jasim's hand releases the switch, turning himself and Isaac into a cloudburst of bone and flesh that rain on the terrified spectators. The explosion was sandwiched by the ground and Isaac, minimizing the blast radius to almost nil. Miraculously, only non-life-threatening injuries occurred. It's anybody's guess how many lives were saved.

Battling shock, ringing ears, and threatening tears, Ariella assesses the horror show from a kneeling position. On stage, she sees something almost as shocking as her partner being ripped apart like paper mâché— Vincente standing. Apparently, the carnage and his attempted assassination have no effect.

She watches Vincente unceremoniously wipe away a small pile of gore from the document, leaving a smear of red, and signing his name. She also sees her father stand tentatively, surveying the heinousness. Vincente hands the blood-stained pen to a shocked Eleazar. He signs, emotionlessly. Throughout history, peace treaties were signed with blood but seldom literally.

IDF swarms Vincente, Eleazar, and the pope and drags them inside the temple. Eleazar's ordination will have to wait till a more opportune time. Ariella is also swarmed by IDF. They lift her to her feet and guide her away.

Still drowning in shock, she stares at the bedlam. Whether it's the shock or her still-ringing ears, everything moves in hazy slow motion and discombobulated silence. She feels like she's watching a sensationalized disaster movie…if only that were the case.

With the numerous kills notched on her belt (twenty-three in all, but only sociopaths keep track), she's never had the faintest hint of PTSD. But after this, her mind will crack, and no amount of psychological Gorilla Glue can repair it. The worst scars are always on the inside.

***

A TV screen goes blank, leaving two wearied viewers to the silence of their thoughts. Josh and Benson just sat through the first twenty minutes of the ten o'clock news; unsurprisingly, the day's events dominated those minutes. In that time, they relived the attempted assassination ad infinitum; mercifully, the footage was tame, judging by today's standards.

The doorbell rings, snapping the dispirited duo out of their trance. Benson snubs his protesting joints as he fights to get off the sofa.

"Relax, Dad. I'll get it," Josh commands.

Josh bounds from the La-Z-Boy and heads for the front door. Opening it, he's startled by the visitor. Ariella, with an unambiguous brown-paper-bagged bottle in hand, sways slightly under the exterior light. Josh regards her with equal parts relating and revulsion: two weeks ago, the roles would be reversed. Her puffy, bloodshot eyes disclose recent weeping. Benson joins his son to see the sad sight.

"Evening, Ariella," the senior greets.

Slurring, but not quite sloppy, she responds. "Hello, Mr. Mendelsburg. Sorry for the late hour."

"No need to apologize. Would you like to come in?"

Josh interprets her pleading look. "We're gonna walk, Dad. Don't wait up."

Benson leans it to kiss her forehead, tasting the salty alcohol sweat she's secreting.

"I'm praying for you," he assures her.

She offers a faint smile before trudging down the front walk.

Josh shoulders his dad. His dad entreats him. "Be careful. She's vulnerable."

"I will. See you tomorrow." Josh catches up with Ariella, who's waiting in the street.

"Up for a walk?" she asks.

"Certainly not a drive," he jokes.

"You're hilarious." She smirks as she leads the way. "Sacher Park's not too far."

"Sacher Park? Man, haven't thought of that place in forever."

"Not surprising, you've been gone forever. A lot's changed."

"Is that patch of woods still there?"

"Where we made a fort? Nope, been replaced by a skate park."

"Skate park?!"

"Yep, the potheads need somewhere to hang out," she quips as she takes a head-back chug of whatever's in that bag.

"Shame on those stoners. They should be more sociably acceptable like the drunks." The dripping sarcasm is palpable.

Her tomboy self springs into action with a drunken, flirtatious punch to his bicep. Awkwardness blooms as the night air crackles with magnetism. They walk in silence.

Ariella offers Josh her hooch. "I hate drinking alone."

Josh holds up his hand. "No thanks, just went on the wagon."

"You picked a bad time to take the pledge. Me, I drink way too much." Flaunting her *devil-may-care* attitude, she guzzles the last bit before launching the empty bottle into the night sky. A moment later, the bottle smashing and the responsive dog barking, pierces the witching hour's stillness.

She sees his disapproval. "I know, not setting a good example."

Josh shrugs. "They're your streets."

"Yeah, home sweet home, I guess."

Breaching the park entrance, they continue down the streetlamp-lined pathway in silence. It'd almost be romantic if not for one of them being sloshed. Up ahead, Josh sees a large thimble-shaped object hanging from an oriental-looking canopy.

"What's that?" he asks, pointing.

"That's a Bonshō. It was built after you moved away. Come on, it makes a fantastic sound."

The pathway leading to the shrine inclines slightly, giving the feeling of climbing a mountain to find enlightenment. Josh sees that the structure is on a foot-tall platform. He activates the flashlight on his phone and steps up. Bathing the magnificent bell in light, engraved inscriptions become apparent. He reads one of them out loud.

"'Pray for the peace of Jerusalem; serene will be those who love you.'"

"Well, peace is here. Let's bong this gong!" Ariella exclaims.

She unsnaps a concealed holster and removes a four-inch cylinder. With a powerful hammer swing, she drives the bottom of the cylinder into the bell, creating a resonant sound.

"Let freedom ring," she remarks, dully.

They listen to the echo fade away.

"What is that?" Josh is referring to the "bonger" in her hand.

With a forceful flick of her wrist, the device transforms into a two-foot-long beatdown stick. "Why, this is Extendo, my tactical baton."

"Cool," he remarks. "I could use one of those at my job."

She drives the baton into one of the canopy's pillars, collapsing the shaft back into itself, and hands it to him. Having seen enough action movies, he needs no instruction. With one try, he creates his own billy-stick. Taking it for a spin, he gives it a mighty swing. He senses the raw power...major testosterone turn-on.

"What do you do?" she asks.

"I'm a property preservationist."

"As in foreclosed homes?"

"Exactly. I run into my fair share of crazies,"

he says as he collapses it against the same pillar before handing it back to her.

"Keep it. I've got more than one."

"Thanks, but I'll never get it past TSA. I'm certain some overworked woman would beat me with it for even trying."

She smiles as awkward silence descends once again. She tugs on his sleeve as she heads down the pathway. He joins her.

A hundred yards later, growing more accustomed to the comfortable silence, their stiff gait softens; they no longer walk like jittery robots in need of a good greasing. At one point, their swinging hands inadvertently touch, igniting a blazing-hot sensation for both of them. They look at each other and say sorry at the same time.

"Jinx! Buy me a Coke," she yells, initiating the old children's game.

"Fine, but no Jack included." He continues playing fast and loose with the wino jokes.

A snort escapes on the coattails of her laugh. Embarrassment overtakes her, turning her sunbaked cheeks rosy-red. She looks down, wanting to escape those piercing brown eyes. The warrior princess is turning into a Disney princess.

*What's wrong with me? I've never felt this way before...about anyone,* she wonders privately.

When looking up again, she spies nearby swings. Thankful for the diversion, she nods in their direction. Josh gets the hint.

Arriving, they occupy parallel swings and

launch off. Pumping themselves ever higher, their pointing toes threaten to touch the shimmering stars. Euphoria seizes them as they delight in each other's company. It's as though life never separated the childhood best friends.

Once their legs grow tired, gravity kicks in, dragging them back down to earth. As their motion turns to a faint swaying, Ariella's e-motion takes its place. Caution is thrown to the wind.

"I had a crush on you when we were kids," she confesses.

"Really?! I never noticed," he remarks genuinely.

"That's because boys are stupid...until they become men, that is."

Enjoying the direction the conversation takes, Josh probes. "Oh? When's that?"

"Thirty-seven."

Their swings now barely moving, he looks at her. Her face is spotlit by the soft moonlight. Her beauty may not have been evident at ten, but it's indisputable now.

"Sweet! Been a man for a few years now. And here I thought my bar mitzvah did the job."

"Yeah...no, sorry to burst your bubble."

He playfully snaps his fingers. "Tsk. Bummer."

"I heard you were married. Where is she?"

"Gone," he replies.

"Where?"

He nods his head upwards. She catches his meaning.

"Ah, one of those, huh?"

"One of those, who?" he asks, smirking.

"You know, Jesus nuts."

He laughs good-naturedly. "I'm one of those Jesus nuts now."

She backtracks. "Really?! Sorry, I didn't mean to be rude."

"No worries. I once had the same attitude."

A thought dawns. "Then why are you still here?"

"Because I became a Jesus nut *after* they all disappeared. Better late than never, I suppose."

"If you say so," she says, flippantly. The wind vamooses from her previously smitten sail.

"Look, I get it. After Elizabeth disappeared, I hated God. I was convinced He did not, *could not*, exist. But then..."

She cuts him off. "He doesn't exist."

"Really? Have you looked up recently?" He points at the mind-blowing celestial firmament.

She looks up, considering. The reflection is all she needs to send her into a tizzy. She lands on her feet while pushing the swing behind her. She leaves the swing's amplitude just before getting bumped on its return. Josh snatches the penduluming swing, steadying it. He watches her pace back and forth like she is a pendulum.

"Alright, I'll play your little, *God-is-not-dead* game. Tell me, if He *is* alive, why did He allow my partner to get blown into a million pieces? Hmm? Any answers? No? Didn't think so."

Josh says nothing, allowing her to rant.

"Tonight, I had to look his wife in the eyes

and tell her Isaac is dead. I looked at his three kids and told them Daddy's never coming home again. My own heart is broken, but I had to put that aside and comfort a devastated family. If God was a good God, then why—"

Josh cuts her off. "No, we're not going there. Asking, 'Where is God in all this?' is clichéd and futile. I know because it was my daily refrain with no answer. Eventually, I'd had enough of the deafening silence, and chose to get blackout drunk every night. I'd never had so much as a glass of wine before but was now determined to erase a lifetime of sobriety in four months. My madness caught up with me quickly. Two Fridays ago, I tried killing myself."

She stops pacing and returns to her swing. His story softened her rage.

"I may be drunk, but not drunk enough to see ghosts. What happened?"

"An abandoned kitten saved me."

"Come again."

"I found a kitten in one of the houses and took her home. Later that night, she stopped me from swallowing twenty-five Ambiens."

Wanting to lighten things up, she opts for some levity. "So you swallowed the cat instead?"

Her ill-timed, not especially funny joke dies on stage.

"Sorry. Bad joke," she says, seeing his objection.

"I was sitting in my La-Z-Boy, wallowing in misery as I watched my wedding video. Unwilling to carry on, I poured the pills into my hand when she jumped into my lap. I leapt to my feet and immediately blacked out. I didn't wake up till the next morning."

Not sure what to say, she begins swinging. Josh follows suit. After a few passes, Ariella speaks.

"That's an amazing story, and I don't mean to be insensitive, but how does that apply?"

"God has a purpose for everything. He used an insignificant cat to keep me alive. Why? I don't know. Why did He allow your partner to die? I have no idea, but this much I can tell you—there is a reason."

"How can you be so sure?"

"Because the Bible says so. The Bible is our primary source to knowing who God is and how to have a relationship with Him."

She hates to admit it, but she's intrigued. She'd never heard anyone talk like this before, certainly not the rabbis.

"A relationship? With God? How is that possible?"

"That's a loaded question. Do you really want to hear?"

"I don't know why but, yeah. I do."

Josh smiles and shrugs. "Okay. First, by admitting we are sinners and that our sins offend a holy God, and because of this, we deserve hell. Second, repent of those sins. And finally, believe and trust that Jesus *is* God and that He took the punishment for our sins by dying on the cross. We must believe that ONLY Christ's death can make us right with God. All of this is a free gift,

Ariella. None of our good works, traditions, or rituals will do it. There is no other way to have a relationship with God."

She looks out into the distance. That's some serious heaviness he laid on her, and she's laboring to hold it. Of course, it doesn't help that she's fading fast. Josh recognizes the blank look. Unpocketing his phone, he requests an Uber. After receiving his confirmation, he leaves the swing and holds out a hand to her.

"Come on, I requested an Uber. He'll be at the entrance in fifteen."

Offering no argument, she accepts his hand and stands to her feet. Once standing, she doesn't release his hand right away. She looks into his eyes and feels an overpowering urge take hold of her: she must kiss him or go mad. Slowly and purposefully, she pulls him in close. Josh wisely douses her fire by gently releasing her hand and setting off toward the entrance. Coming to Ariella realizes what almost happened; she's grateful he doesn't see her embarrassment. She quickly catches up with him. They walk the rest of the way in silence.

Fifteen minutes later, they arrive at the entrance and finish at the waiting Uber.

"May I have your number?" Josh clumsily asks. He's nervous.

Ariella recognizes his nerves, helping her feel better about her blunder. "Give me your phone."

He obliges. She thumbs in her number and sends herself a text.

"There, now I have your number, too," she responds as she returns his phone.

"Thanks. I'm gonna send you a link that I want you to look at later. Okay?"

She presents a flirtatious, *Yes, Sir!* salute before opening the cab door. She moves to step in but stops. Still empowered by her waning inebriation, she turns back, grabs his hand, and pulls him in for a quick but passionate kiss on the lips. This time, he doesn't stop her.

Lowering herself off her tippy toes, she enters the car and buzzes the window down. Josh closes the door behind her; his hand remains where the window once was. She rests her hand on his and gazes up at him. No words are spoken. Josh steps back as the cab leaves. He watches after her; she never looks back. Oh, the mysterious ways of women; they always leave men wanting more.

*\*\*\**

It's two p.m. the following day. Ariella cautiously peeks out from underneath her pillow; unrelenting sunlight invades her room making everything ablaze. She swears the sun resides exclusively in her room.

Grunting under the harsh conditions, she plucks her phone from atop the nightstand and wakes it. Squinting, she stares at her wallpaper, trying to make sense of the time—1423 hours! She hasn't slept in this late since she was a teen.

"Thank God I'm not working today," she mumbles.

She gingerly props herself up on her three pillows and checks her texts. She sees one from Josh. Opening it, she reads to find out that he had a nice time last night, that he's praying for her, and that he wants her to check out the attached link. Having nothing better to do—other than dying in the clutches of this horrendous hangover, that is—she thumbs it. What opens is the same website Mike had Josh read. She rolls her eyes, sighs, and begins reading...

Thirty minutes later, a weeping Ariella waits for her call to connect to Josh's phone. After four rings, she gets his voicemail greeting. What she doesn't know is his phone is on airplane mode because, well, he's on an airplane. He never told her he was taking the first flight out. She didn't get to say goodbye.

A minute or so later, she ends the call, hoping he understands her hungover-induced rambling voicemail. It will be a while before she hears back from him...if ever.

*\*\**

Six thousand miles away, it's pushing towards eight o'clock on a brisk Washington D.C. morning. With coffee in one hand and phone in the other, Susan exits Starbucks to make the daily three-block trek to her office building. She finds "Josh" in her contacts and places the call.

Separated by the Atlantic, both Ariella and Susan simultaneously call Josh. Unlike Ariella, however, Susan is not surprised by his voicemail greeting; she figured he'd still be in the air. It's better this way; she has difficult stuff to say and would rather not do it *live*.

"Hi, it's Susan. I've been thinking a lot this week about our coffee date...well, not a date per se, more like a rendezvous. No, that sounds even worse. Sorry, I'm nervous, which is a new sensation for me. (She sighs deeply.) I just wanted to explain where I'm coming from and why my feelings for you are such a big deal. My mom died when I was eleven and it completely broke me. I was raised by my dad and four older brothers. They instilled in me an attitude of detachment, to handle things logically more than emotionally. So when I met my husband, it was very difficult for me to give him my heart..."

She is interrupted by Miss Robot. Susan has reached her message length and has four options. She picks number four—continue recording.

"Sorry, had to get permission from our future AI overlords to keep talking. As I was saying, I did not give myself willingly; it was his patience and love that wore down my resistance. I couldn't help but fall hopelessly in love with him. His being killed in a random mugging sent me spiraling into such a deep depression that it was over a year before I returned to work. You don't know this, but it was you that pulled me out, well your arrest anyway."

Once again, she's interrupted; and once again, she chooses option four.

"Again, sorry. Moving along. It's serendipitous. The prosecutor for your case happens to be friends with my brother. They were having drinks one night when you came up in the conversation. Tired of seeing me waste away, my brother convinced him to convince the judge to mandate you get your court-appointed therapy from me. I had no choice; I had to return to work. You were my first patient. You saved me."

The obnoxious robot femme interrupts anew. This time, when given the four options, she wrestles with the choice of erasing the whole thing and hanging up. But she can't do that. It all needed to be said. Besides, she has one more thing to say. Four is pushed a final time.

"One last thing. As far as the Jesus stuff, I hope I didn't offend you. I'm sorry if I did. I was embarrassed by my misunderstanding, and I took it out on you. You see, I've hated God ever since my mom died and it ramped up even more after my husband. However, I'm at a place in my life where I'm willing to open the door and let God in, except it must be on my terms not His. So, when you get back, we can talk some more if you'd like. I'll admit, you've made me curious. I've never heard religion explained that way before."

As she crosses the final intersection to her office building, her eyes catch a strange phenomenon screaming across the minutes-old 8:00 a.m. blue sky.

"What's that?" she questions absentmindedly into Josh's still recording voicemail. She cranes her neck to look while shielding her eyes against the sun. Whatever it is, it's coming in hot.

Others are now stopping and taking notice,

talking amongst themselves. It looks like a fighter jet, but they're in a no-fly zone. Suddenly, three more show up on the horizon.

Susan, phone still recording her message, watches as the first UFO begins its rapid descent. From her vantage point, its landing zone appears to be the Capital Building. Seconds later, her eyes widen in abject terror as the infamous image that's haunted all of humanity's dreams for the last seventy years rears its ugly head—the dreaded mushroom cloud rising to the sky. She, along with her fellow gawkers, spend their final moments gaping at the tidal wave of destruction rushing towards them.

# CHAPTER SEVEN

President Campbell hangs up the phone and looks at his wife who stirs from her once uninterrupted slumber. Interrupted snoozing comes with the job of being First Lady; she's used to it by now. Since moving into the White House, she's gotten less sleep than she did as a mother of a newborn.

"What time is it?" she asks.

"A little after six-thirty," he responds, apologetically. "I'm needed downstairs, immediately."

"The library?"

"No, *downstairs,* downstairs."

"Nathan, what's happening?"

"Sorry, I can't tell you...not yet."

She regards him with a look of fear and dread. His unusually long morning kiss does nothing to calm her; his especially worse-than-normal morning breath adds to her *red-alert* status. Either halitosis is setting in, or he's drowning in stomach-churning anxiety. His eyes say it's the latter: he's terrified, and now, so is she...

\*\*\*

At 0713 hours, President Campbell, now in ultra-secure Mount Weather, disembarks the shuttle train and enters Command Ops—a large room dedicated to saving the country, with an equally large oval table situated so that all seated around it can view the video screens on the walls —to find it standing at attention.

"Sit," he commands before directing his gaze at the still-standing, imposing Marine. "General Ramirez, how did seven nuclear Air Force bases get hacked? We have safeguards to prevent this kind of thing."

"With respect, Mr. President, no system is completely unhackable."

"I understand that, but these are systems controlling hundreds of nuclear weapons. They should be the closest to unhackable."

"Yes sir. They have the most powerful protections in place, but there is always a back door."

Campbell furrows his brow as he rubs his throbbing temples. "Fine. Can we kick them out?"

General Ramirez swallows, attempting to moisten his parched throat. "No, Sir, we cannot."

"Why not?"

"Because we've been locked out."

"How can we be locked out of our system?!" President Campbell bellows.

"Mr. President, this is Shreyas Modi, our Senior Network Administrator," the general informs. "He'll explain the situation further."

"Alright, Shreyas, make this easy for me."

"Yes sir. In a nutshell, the people who did this activated their own script, which is preventing us from taking control again."

"They hacked us? Why can't we hack them back?"

"Our best people are working on it, but it will take time. Whoever did this had plenty of time, probably years, to find a way in."

"We don't have time. We need them out. Now!"

President Campbell trades hollering for reflective pacing. His advisors allow him time. Arriving at a functional repose, he speaks again.

"General, who did this?"

"We're not a hundred percent sure, but we believe it's domestic."

"Our people did this?"

"Yes, but we believe they have outside help," the general adds.

"Who?"

Acting as the ultimate omen, an aid speaks. "Mr. President, President Kartashov requests a video conference with you."

"Put him through," Campbell commands.

The haggard face of Pavel Kartashov, Russia's president, fills the video screens.

"Pavel, are you somehow involved in this?"

"Involved in what?" the Russian president asks.

"Don't be coy."

"Are you referring to the security systems that keep America from becoming a bloody stain on history's highway being hacked? Maybe."

President Campbell breathes, gathering his bearings. "Pavel, please, tell me what's going on."

"Simply put, you let some apples go bad."

"What are you implying? That Americans are attacking their own country?"

"Is it really that surprising? You've allowed a civil war to smolder instead of stomping it out. You chose to coddle this asinine cancel culture instead of spanking them. You let homegrown terrorists run rampant through your streets. How many more spoiled children need to burn down a city before you take off your belt?"

President Campbell says nothing because there's nothing to say—President Kartashov's right. Kartashov continues his berating.

"Nathan, you and your administration are fools. Dissent has festered for a long time, but because you're too consumed with healing the world you've ignored the cancer growing within your own borders. So, to answer your question, yes, Russia is involved but only as support. Your people are the ones running the show."

"Who's responsible?" President Campbell asks. Truthfully, he knows already. The assumed anarchist's mug and voice have dominated social media for well over a year.

Pavel says nothing. The screen splits, giving one half to a new, twenty-something face—Grayson Young, this generation's Guy Fawkes. Campbell's assumption was spot on.

"The great Nathan Campbell! Only took shoving a bunch of nukes down your throat before you deigned to take my call," Grayson Young crows.

"The White House doesn't do business with terrorists," Campbell counters.

"Strange, it does if money fills the coffers and the rooms house the right people."

"You're misinformed, Grayson."

"If telling yourself that helps you sleep at night, then so be it. But the truth is, I, along with other interested parties, DID put you and your people in power. The problem is, we've seen no return on our investment. Racism continues. The economic divide is still as wide as the Grand Canyon. Equality for all is no closer than before you took office."

"Grayson, dealing with injustice is not a quick fix. It'll take time."

"Time? Let me tell ya, you've just run out. You promised change but you've changed nothing. Everything is the same. We bought your bill of goods. It's time to return it."

"What does that mean, Grayson?" President Campbell asks, seeing every eye on him. All the eyes belong to sensible people; they know what it means.

"It's time America gets a hard reboot. And it falls to me to push the giant red *reset* button Russia has so graciously handed to me."

"Pavel, are you really breaking all peace treaties to help this lunatic?" Nathan asks the smirking Russian president.

"Unquestionably. As the old saying goes, *the enemy of my enemy is my friend.* You may've ignored Grayson Young's booming voice, but we didn't. We've watched his ascension into power and influence with great interest. Russia has the best hackers in the world, so it was no bother lending him some. With America more divided than ever before, we saw it as the perfect time to do what we've always wanted to do."

"Destroy her," Grayson chimes in.

"The rest of the world may embrace peace," President Kartashov continues the beat down like a well-choreographed fight scene. "But old grudges die hard. Russia cannot live in peace if America continues breathing."

Nathan Campbell, the man many hoped would REunite the United States, stares quietly at the two men on the screen. He is defeated and he knows it. "What do you want me to do?"

"Die," Grayson Young says. Simply put by the man holding the *end of the world* button.

"You do understand you're violating the World President's wishes?" Nathan throws out a feeble punch. It misses spectacularly.

"I do and I do not care," Pavel Kartashov avows.

"You're willing to kill millions of innocent people just to get me? Who's the real enemy here?" POTUS: still swinging, still missing.

"Natural selection. Only those meant to die, will die. We're done here. I'm giving you..." Grayson stops to flourishingly wake his smartwatch. "Thirty-three minutes to get your affairs in order. After that, its bombs away. In case you're wondering, we have a nuke designated for Mount Weather. Yes, we know where you are. Let's see how impenetrable your little hidey-hole is."

After flashing devious smirks, Grayson

Young and President Kartashov's faces disappear, returning all the screens to black. President Campbell turns to General Ramirez.

"General put us up to DEFCON five. Get my family down to the PEOC. I suggest you all contact your loved ones." Short and concise, exactly what is needed. However, nobody moves. All are frozen, gripped by fear. The silence in the self-contained war room is thunderous. All know there is no stopping the attack. America is a sitting duck. In thirty minutes, the Home of the Brave becomes a cautionary tale. Only a miracle can save her now.

A shaken female voice pulverizes the stillness. "Mr. President, I think we should pray."

Nathan regards her. Campbell is not the religious type, but there are no atheists in foxholes.

"You're right," Nathan concurs, however, that's as far as it goes. Silence returns. General Ramirez, a lifelong catholic, clears his throat.

"If it's okay, may I lead it?"

President Campbell says nothing, only bows his head. The rest follow suit. The general begins.

"Merciful God..."

# CHAPTER EIGHT

J osh stares out the window, his patience reservoir now empty. The flight home has been tedious. Looking at the landscape unscrolling beneath him, he does his best to breathe. In less than ten minutes, he'll be in D.C.'s airspace.

Wanting to pass the time at a more favorable rate, he leaps back into his *mind-canoe* and drifts lazily down the placid, faraway creek of pensiveness. Even though he's sorted through the last twenty-four hours with a fine-tooth comb, he decides *what the hey? One more round of daydreaming won't hurt.*

Gazing through the clouds, his mind's eye unconsciously replays the queasy scene of two men violently coming apart. Cringing, Josh quickly switches out this *memory reel* and threads in a new one. This one is of him and Ariella walking through the park under the streetlights.

His tightened stomach muscles relax while his heart flutters at the romance playing in his mind. Engaged in the voyeurism of his memories, his pulse quickens as he witnesses the night stroll crescendoing next to the idling taxi—he knows a soft kiss will soon be his.

While Josh wallows in his private oasis the atmosphere in the cockpit is wholly different.

The captain, concern radiating from the seasoned sky jockey's eyes, listens to his headset. "Understood, Dulles. 227 out."

The captain flips a switch, ending the call.

"What is it?" the copilot asks. His captain's *just seen a ghost* look is hard to miss.

"America…" the captain begins but pauses, perhaps hoping it's all a dream. "Is under attack."

"Which part?" Asks the third member of the crew.

Taking a beat, the captain simply says: "All of it."

Dumbfounded, the other two stare as the captain flips the cabin switch and begins talking.

"Good morning, ladies and gentlemen," the captain's calm voice fills the cabin's stale air. "I've been informed that Dulles Airport is in emergency shutdown protocol. We will be circling and landing in London. I know everybody is weary, but we will do our best to continue making the flight as enjoyable as possible. Thank you."

An anguished moan rings out. Having to be buried alive in this flying coffin for another however many hours is more than the threadbare 350 souls can stomach. Immediately, the passengers harass the flight attendants, demanding an explanation. Subduing their own dispiritedness, the stewards of the air work to conciliate the disgruntled wayfarers.

Josh's middle-seat mate peppers him with questions. "Why do we have to cross the ocean again?" the elderly woman demands. "Can't we just land at the next closest airport?"

Josh wonders that himself but says nothing. The octogenarian continues her raving.

"This is outrageous! Wait till I give this airline a piece of my mind! And they wonder why they're struggling to stay in business. IT'S OUTRAGEOUS!"

"Do we even have enough fuel to get to London?" Thankfully, the old lady's aisle seat mate takes up the mantel of chief bellyacher, freeing Josh to mull over this predicament.

Hoping to secure a smidge of serenity, Josh turns his attention back to the tranquil clouds. Catching a glimpse of the tiny world below him, he watches home sweet home scurry past him, running in the opposite direction.

He heaves a sigh. *Maybe I should pray,* he considers and so does.

While Josh seeks help from the Captain of his soul, the lead flight attendant seeks help from the captain of this 777. Once allowed in the cockpit, she entreats the crew for answers.

"The passengers are restless. Frankly, we all are. What's going on?"

They stare at her gravely. The captain speaks: "I'll turn the TVs on. That should settle everybody down."

She stays glued to her spot, staring a hole through the captain. She knows something's up.

"Please. Go," the captain pleads. "I'll give you more information when I have it. Thank you."

Seeing that's all she's getting the lead flight

attendant exits the cockpit and beelines to the cabin intercom microphone. Her veteran voice addresses the passengers.

"Ladies and gentlemen, I've spoken to the captain, and he will be turning on everybody's TVs. Please return to your seats. We will bring the food carts out in just a minute. Thank you."

The promise of visual distraction does the trick. Everybody settles in as their personal TVs blink to life. Andy Griffith's black-and-white face fills the tiny screens, whisking the passengers away to Mayberry and its simpler times. Everybody slips on their disposable headphones, allowing Andy's mellow southern drawl to chill them out.

However, they're only allowed a few minutes of escapism before being yanked out of Mayberry and piledriven back into reality. A flash of light erupts from the left side of the plane tearing away everybody's attention.

Josh whips his head towards his window and stares aghast at the mushroom cloud sprouting from his hometown. Seconds later, he's bushwhacked by his fellow passengers who've rushed his window to witness the nefariousness. Shocked by the breach of his personal space, he disentangles himself from the chaos and stands in the aisle. Looking around, he notices that all the left-side windows are teeming with bent-over gawkers like a line of people peering through holes in a wooden fence trying to catch a free show.

Another flash ignites on the right side

of the plane, drawing its own spectators. Unbelievably, another nuclear warhead explodes, this time in the southern outskirts of D.C., Josh's part of the city. This reality hits him: his house was most likely consumed, all inhabitants included. Tears well up in his eyes as he comforts himself with the assurance that Toby and Scamp never felt a thing.

*They were snuggled up together on the couch, sleeping the day away*, he muses.

He's not allowed to mourn for long. The effects of the blasts send shock waves through the sky and slam into Flight 227. The plane dips and dives as the flight crew wrestles with the controls.

The turbulence is extreme. Anguished screams for mercy circulate as the plane struggles to stay tethered to the invisible strings keeping it in the air. Eventually, the engines can take it no longer. All power ceases, sending the plane into a nosedive. She fought the good fight but has nothing left. Josh prays...fervently.

# CHAPTER NINE

Exquisite music meanders through a long, elegant hall, bidding all stragglers to come and drink from its cleansing springs. Its epicenter is no mystery for the inhabitants of this courtly palace; in fact, this particular piece is one of the tenants' favorites.

Two men pursue the music with utter abandonment like treasure hunters tracking an inestimable antiquity. As they maneuver through the hallway, dimly lit only by sporadic wall sconces, "Moonlight Sonata's" immortal mora entrenches further into their souls. It's as though an angel fingers the keys.

Arriving at the end of the great hall, the two men breach a dark spacious room—its only contents: a grand piano and sheer curtains dancing in the invading breeze through open patio doors. The moon's soft glow spotlights the mysterious maestro hunched over the ethereal piano. The two men remain respectfully quiet as the sonata runs its course. When the final note escapes into the night air, the unseen pianist speaks.

"This isn't a coincidence. I'm confident Beethoven intended his masterpiece to be played by moonlight." The man pivots on the bench, revealing himself to the men.

"You may go, Tamir," Vincente instructs, Tamir obeys, leaving President Kartashov alone with the world president. "Follow me, Pavel."

The two men walk through the wispy, ghostly curtains and embrace the beguiling night. Vincente walks up to the terrace's railing and leans against it, allowing the bright moon to bathe his face.

"I don't know what it is about the moon in this part of the world. It seems more splendorous with the Arabian Desert as its canvas."

President Kartashov stands a few feet away and observes the man with unparalleled power. This whole cover-of-night meeting unnerves him. A guilty conscious has a way of doing that…

"Pavel, my friend," he says without looking at him. "Join me and see what I see." He turns his head sideways and regards him with his right eye. "Please."

Arm hairs bristling, Pavel does as he's told. Looking out, he sees the splendor of Vincente's kingdom, but also construction, now ceased for the night, dotting the landscape of this vast estate.

"It was nice of Saddam to leave behind such wonders. Of all his palaces, I like this one the best. Although, his decorating style leaves much to be desired. All this Arabian Nights decor is so gauche. But I do love the gardens. Remarkable, aren't they?"

Pavel gives the lauded courtyard a cursory look.

"No, you need to stand on the ledge and lean

out to get the full effect."

Pavel cautiously steps up onto the half-a-foot-high ledge and leans out. His torso hangs over the railing. Vincente amiably rests his hand on the small of Pavel's back.

"See, what did I tell you? Breathtaking."

Feeling Vincente's friendly, almost comforting hand on his back, loosens him up. Pavel truly enjoys what he sees. Just below him, a beautiful fountain serenades the lush gardens with its tranquil bubbling. Reveling in his heightened senses, he forgets his surroundings. He forgets that he is leaning precariously over a railing with nothing between him and a concrete walkway but thirty-five feet of gravity. And most of all, he forgets he's keeping company with history's most powerful man whom he's just defied and most likely knows it. Yes, all this escapes his mind until he's abruptly rushing toward the concrete walkway below.

The second-long flight ends with the most unbelievable pain screaming through his entire body. Lying there, marinating in his moon-reflecting blood, Pavel agonizes over his options. The previously delighted-in, babbling fountain —which he narrowly missed bouncing off of— wreaks havoc with his concentration. Naturally, his Amygdala triggers fight-or-flight; this is wasted energy: his body can do neither.

*How many bones are broken?* Pavel puzzles, striving to hold onto consciousness. *I wonder if I can reach into my pocket and get my phone.* Happily, he discovers the necessary bones for phone extraction are intact. Sadly, however, he discovers his phone is MIA.

*Where is it?!* his inner thoughts panic.

From a few feet away, his phone responds. Looking towards the jingle, he sees the glowing face beckoning for him to talk to it. Oh, how he wishes he could, but it's out of reach. Regardless, his still working left arm tries. The phone stops jingling. The silence covers Pavel in a smothering blanket of dread; how will he get out of this?

"It's true what they say—you Russkies are tough as nails. How are you still alive?"

Pavel ceases his striving and watches Vincente approach. After a few more yards, Vincente arrives at the crumpled mess on his precious path. Pavel's phone starts ringing again. Vincente snatches it up, cancels the call, and turns off the phone.

"Let's have no more distractions, shall we."

He gets on his hunches and dips his finger in Pavel's blood. Like a small child enjoying his finger paints, Vincente draws red stick figures on Pavel's white dress shirt.

"Do you know why you're in this predicament? You must."

Pavel tries to speak but cannot; his jaw is shattered. Seeing no movement, only blood dribbling down his chin, Vincente pats him reassuringly on the head.

"There, there, no need to answer, I'll tell you. You can't possibly believe I wouldn't find out about your involvement in America's attack. I had great plans for her but you took that from me."

Tears fill Pavel's blood-red eyes. Hopelessness drowns him as he watches Vincente pad over to a pallet of large sandstones. There Vincente stands, examining each stone, seemingly deciding which one will do. Finding it, Pavel watches Vincente grunt under the weight as he trudges it over to him.

Arriving, Vincente parks the one-hundred-pound-plus stone on the fountain's retaining wall and bends over to catch his breath. Once his breathing slows, Vincente straightens up, leans against the fountain, rests his forearm on the carried sandstone, and sets his fingers to drumming. Pavel's attention is drawn to Vincente's fingers. Vincente knows what he's doing: like a cat toying with a mouse...

"Trying to have me killed is one thing," Vincente says. Pavel immediately tries to speak, to defend himself.

"Stop," Vincente soothes. "It's okay. Don't waste energy lying. Truthfully, I respect it. Shows initiative. Makes me homesick in a way. But what I don't respect is you not respecting yourself. Be a man. Step into the streets and face me."

Pavel scrunches his face in confusion.

"Pavel, when did Russia become so weak and desperate? When did the Motherland become a cheap prostitute, willing to crawl into bed with whomever? Partnering with a flaccid cream puff like Grayson Young, whom I will deal with later, is pathetic. However, I get it: not a lot of give and take needed."

Vincente stops, taking a moment to

consider his next clichéd bad guy monologue.

"But your alignment with Iran is coming back to bite you. I know your partnership was inevitable. You've been flirting for years. But you've given Iran's ne'er-do-well cousins a seat at the table. Didn't your mom warn you about bad apples? Clearly not, because for the last several years, Russia's made some very poor decisions. I know your history is replete with cold, calculating aggression. Maybe this is just par for the course. But is finally getting revenge on America worth it? Your recklessness put a bull's eye squarely on Mother Russia's back."

Vincente takes a breather, again pausing his theatrical haranguing.

"I guess I understand. Undealt with revenge is a tough pill to swallow. Eye for an eye and all that. Nonetheless, order must be restored. I have already put the Muslim World's annihilation into motion. But not just Muslims, millions of Russians as well. You get to die knowing that."

Vincente talks himself out and eyes the sandstone distastefully. Not because he's thinking twice, but rather, he's not hip to picking it back up. Still, justice must be done. Summoning the spirit of a gym rat, he jerks the heavy stone off the wall and hovers it over Pavel's face.

Pavel's eyes widen; he knows his life will soon be squashed. He reaches out with his left hand, pleading for mercy. It does not affect Vincente.

"Unlike the tired saying, this *is* personal."

With that final quip, he lifts the rock to his chest and drops it. Pavel's head cracks open like an egg, spilling yoke in every direction. Seeing the mess oozing towards his Italian loafers, Vincente nimbly steps out of harm's way.

"Figures. Tweaked my back," Vincente says as he heads for his palace's entrance, twisting his back along the way.

In the shadows, he sees a cigarette cherry brighten—a clandestine individual is smoking. "I have what you're looking for," Vincente informs the shrouded smoker.

A desiccated, trembling Aaron steps into the moonlight. His right hand holds his cigarette as he drags on it while his left hand obsessively itches—more like digs—into his right elbow pit. One could almost see the imaginary scurrying bugs. He eyes Vincente with the voracity of an emaciated dog waiting for scraps from his master's table.

"But first you need to do something for me."

"Can I get a little now?" Aaron inquires, borderline begging.

"No, not till you're done."

Aaron invades Vincente's space, intoxicating him with his putridness. Unfazed by Aaron's power move, Vincente snatches the cigarette from Aaron's shaky hand and pulls on it. After reveling in the nicotine buzz, Vincente slowly exhales through his nostrils, —looking very much like a dragon—places the cig in Aaron's chapped lips, and gently nudges him back a few feet.

"Please! I need it," Aaron beseeches like a whining child.

"It's not my fault you can't parcel it out."

"But you did this to me!"

"I did nothing you didn't already want. I just gave you a push."

"Yeah, right over the edge," Aaron laments.

Seeing Vincente's emotionless gaze, Aaron knows he has no choice. If he's to be *fed,* he must earn it.

"Fine, whataya want me to do?"

Vincente points at the bloody mess. Having watched the whole thing, Aaron doesn't need to look. Vincente hands over Pavel's phone

"Use this to record yourself digging out and crushing his R-Chip. Then, for the love of god, scrape him off my veranda. When you're done, leave the phone in my office."

"And then?"

"That's it. Your meds will be waiting for you in your room."

Aaron's heart leaps. He's now ambitious. "Where do I put him?"

"Toss him in there," Vincente says, nodding at a construction dumpster.

Aaron locates President Kartashov's waiting hearse. There will be no motorcade for the Russian president as he's delivered to his final resting place—the local dump.

A sticky wicket suddenly makes itself known. Aaron turns back to see Vincente heading inside. He calls after him.

"I'm sure his phone is password protected."

Vincente stops. He looks at the motionless fright and then at Aaron. "His password is right there," he says matter-of-factly. "Wipe the blood off first." Vincente resumes his quest. Comprehension dawns on Aaron's burned-out brain.

As he walks, Vincente yells into the night air. "Turn off the password, unless you wanna bring his thumb with you." With that final sage advice, Vincente disappears inside. Aaron's eyes flicker with a spirited—*aha!*

Arriving at his waiting assignment, Aaron grabs one of Pavel's thumbs, wipes the blood off on his drying, red-stick-familied white shirt, and presses it against the phone's sensor. Sure enough, the phone unlocks. Vincente's so smart. He turns off the password before he forgets. With the incidentals out of the way, he finally gets cracking.

With a concerted effort, he flips the rock off Pavel's at-one-time face. Realizing he doesn't have a proper forehead-digging tool, he hunts for a suitable substitute. He doesn't need to look far. On his right, a garden trowel pokes out from freshly dropped topsoil. He unearths the trowel and without a second thought, not even for conscience's sake, he jams it into the corpse's forehead. With his left hand, he records with Pavel's phone. How macabre can you get?

With all the skill and care of a back-alley surgeon, he works to exhume the tiny chip. Even though this is a nasty business, he shows no emotion or revulsion. For the addicted, there's no boundary they won't cross for their fix...Aaron knows this intimately; he's crossed them all.

After a few jabs and scoops, Aaron surfaces the chip. He drops the crimson-stained trowel on the concrete path, its soft metal *clang* exacerbating the moment's grotesqueness, and plucks the chip from the roughly hewn hole. Holding it between his thumb and index finger, he stares at the flashing red light muted by Kartashov's translucent blood before crushing it. Step one—check. On to step two.

Grasping both arms, he lugs the disfigured body backward like he's dragging a heavy trash bag to the tree lawn. On the journey, he spies the wide bloody trail broad-brushing the walkway.

"Somebody'll have to hose this off," he mutters. "And it won't be me. I've done my job."

Arriving at the dumpster, he swings open the heavy gate, heaves the body in, and unnecessarily covers it with debris. It's unnecessary because Vincente didn't require it, but being a paranoid junkie, concealment is habit.

Closing the gate and latching it shut, he shoots some cautionary glances looking for witnesses. Satisfied the coast is clear, he darts back into the palace, making a beeline for Vincente's office. The sooner he completes his task, the sooner he can make his *soup*.

Ten minutes later, Aaron crashes through his door, scrambles over to his bedside table, and locates his reward. True to his word, Vincente did leave him a tiny Ziploc baggie. He plops on his disgusting bed, and with quivering hands, he performs the universal heroin-addict ritual of preparing a spike.

With a flick, a prick, a pull, and a push, Aaron leans back and melts into his filthy pillow as the rush overtakes him. Within seconds, he nods and drifts away, galloping off on a stately white horse, gleefully racing atop a glorious rainbow, arching across a twinkling starry sky. As magical as this sounds, it's paltry compared to the first time. Aaron accepted long ago that he'll never again achieve that first high's rapture. At this point, he's just grateful neither he nor his horse is dead...yet. Nobody can ride *the horse* forever. Sooner or later, the rainbow will end. Sooner or later, the sudden drop off into the abyss, both physically and spiritually, will come.

***

While Aaron escapes *on* his white horse, Vincente escapes *from* his white horse. He's allowed world peace to run free, but that *horse* has run its course. It's time to take it out back and shoot it, and its rider...

Whatever happened to him in that Catholic Church all those years ago either had no lasting effect or was never real, to begin with. Emotions are powerful, capable of convincing those enslaved by them that what they are experiencing is real, even if there is no proof to back it up.

Vincente is far removed from that young man who felt *something*. His actions speak to that reality. The person who walked out of that church is the same person who walked in. No change took place, despite the good vibes in the moment.

Vincente is not the only one along history's wide, dusty road who's fallen victim to self-deceit. One day, with Jesus standing between them and the entrance to the visible glories of Heaven, millions will be shocked when He hands down the alarming verdict and punishment—*I never knew you. Depart from me, you evildoers!*

With that, the ultimate Judge of character will justly cast them into total darkness, where they will serve out their eternal sentence, tormented by the brief heavenly vision. It could have been there's, but they chose the passing joys of this life over the lasting, true joys of eternal life in God's presence. And Vincente, along with the other untold millions, will have nobody to blame but themselves, forever...

Taking the scenic route to his office, Vincente thumbs out a text to Benito Falco, his top guy. When Benito was still "cleaning" for the mob, his nickname was The Falcon. Vincente convinced his godfather to release him, and several other wise guys, into his service. Like falcons, Benito was calculated, lethal, and struck so fast, his prey never saw him coming. Even though "the life" is behind him now, his no-nonsense sensibilities still come in handy.

*Be in my office in 5*, Vincente texts. Benito will get there before him; this is his plan. He wants Benito to wait for him. It's all mind games. He always maintains total mental domination over his men, which isn't that hard. Keeping his cattle in line isn't exactly a crucible for the super genius. However, like a good rancher, Vincente is not an unreasonable taskmaster.

For simplification and fluidity, Vincente has his men live in the palace on a rotation—one week in, two weeks out. He keeps this schedule because, as Edwin Locke's theory proves, happy men are productive men and it all starts at home. If Husband's not home often, then Wife's not happy. This naturally gives birth to: *if mama ain't happy, then ain't nobody happy.* Vincente has no time for drama. He has a world to conquer and a very short time to do it in.

Because he has no need nor desire for family, Vincente abhors depending on weak-minded men to accomplish his machinations. But, as supremely powerful as he is, he's still just one man. He can only be in one place at a time. So, because these men are necessary, he obeys the dynamics of this absurd human institution.

As designed, Vincente enters his office to see Benito standing next to a chair, waiting for his boss's arrival.

"Benny, sit," Vincente instructs as he heads for his desk.

"Thank you, Mr. World President. That little dope-fiend of yours was here a few minutes ago," Benito informs.

Vincente reaches his chair, plants himself, and fiddles with the delivered phone, opening the text app. He does not respond, nor does he bother to look at Benito.

"I have forthcoming importunate affairs to attend to, so I'll make this quick. President Kartashov is dead," he says as though reading the classifieds, or more fittingly, the obituary.

Shocked, Benito remarks. "Really, how?"

Vincente looks up and regards Benito with an, *are you serious?* expression. "I killed him." He reverts to composing his text.

"Oh, okay. Should I wake Pope Vassallo?"

"For what purpose?"

"For counsel."

With head still angled down, Vincente's eyes flutter up and bore into Benito's, piercing them with invisible daggers.

"Listen and understand because I will not repeat it. I do not, nor will I ever, need his or anybody else's counsel. I have need only of my own." He sustains the staring contest till Benito wisely taps out. Sensibly, Benito says nothing more on the matter.

Having completed his occupation, Vincente, smiling exuberantly, slides the phone across his desk. "Push play."

Benito retrieves the phone and does as he's told. He watches the roughly minute-long clip. Confusion lights up his face.

"Is this who I think—"

"Russia's former president? Yes. Best of all, that's his phone."

Benito watches it again. He's no stranger to dead bodies, mostly because he made them that way, but this video gashes even his sadistic callousness. Not knowing what to say, he simply asks, "Why?"

"Because I'm starting a war."

Again, still not sure what to say, Benito repeats his previous sentence with more perplexity. "Why?!"

Vincente reflects on Benito's understandable consternation. Even though he doesn't need to explain his reasonings, sometimes it's smart to allow people in your inner circle a peek.

"The goal," Vincente begins. "Is to incite the Muslims to attack me. And when they do, in the world's eyes, Muslims will be the guilty ones. They will believe this because that's what their screens will tell them. Society's programmed minds will interpret the endless news reports and public opinions as just another hostile act from a people with a long history of not keeping their word. Eventually, the world's leaders will look to me to do something. I'll gladly oblige. I will convince the wearied, frustrated leaders that retaliation is necessary; that we must strike back even harder or they will never stop."

"But you're in Iraq!" Benito exclaims. "You're in one of the most powerful Muslim countries in the world."

"Exactly, and it will be their devotion that tips the scales. Trust me. Iraqis would sooner turn their backs on the rest of the Muslim World before turning their backs on me."

"Is this because the Palestinians tried to assassinate you?"

"Benito, you and I grew up on the same

streets. You know the rules. You know eye for an eye. But I assure you vengeance is not the driving force. Let me be clear. I do not care one whit about any of the Muslims or their pettiness. All I care about is the Jews, specifically, their prostration. Once my counterattack runs its course, the Jews will be ecstatic. They'll see that I eradicated their forever enemy. And because of this, they will gratefully give themselves to me."

Benito mulls over what he's just heard. He's confused as to why Vincente needs the Jews' reverence so badly.

If Benito was a better student of world history, he'd see the pattern that's been laid out since nearly the beginning of time. Tyrants of old have always made it a priority to subjugate the Jews. But all attempts have failed because all have used the same worn-out strategies—aggression and tyranny. Vincente is doing something novel —he's using love and respect.

"Whataya gonna do with this?" Benito asks.

"Send it to Sanjar Rouhani," Vincente says plainly.

Vincente has no trouble interpreting Benito's incredulous look. "Is there a problem?"

"I mean no disrespect, Mr. World President, but you do understand Pavel's R-Chip will show he was here? President Rouhani will know you did this."

Vincente flashes a sly grin. "I certainly hope so. Get my jet prepped. I'm headed to Israel tomorrow morning."

***

The Radio Frequency Identification Chip, better known to a world obsessed with equality and the worship of science as the R-Chip, came into prominence because Greece's progressive youth refused to stop throwing temper tantrums. Determined to abolish all free and unfettered markets, they would not rest until a computer-driven, currency-less society rose from the ashes of their once proud country. Rarely does a spoiled child getting their way bring about something positive; in this instance, it did.

The concept of implanting a radio-frequency ID chip into a human is nothing new. For years, fanatics have allowed an electronic microchip the size of a grain of rice to be inserted into their bodies. Problem was, it produced subpar results. Yes, an end-user with the R-Chip in their hand could walk up to a door and unlock it without breaking stride. This was admittedly cool and satisfyingly sci-fi'y. But for more complex applications, the tech bogged down, dropped out completely, or was wholly impotent. Support for the revolutionary tech was waning.

It took a desperate scientist, kooky from being awake for seventy-plus hours and running out of government funding, to solve the riddle. He hypothesized that the brain's ability to transmit and receive complex sensory signals was what was needed. The hand just wasn't a suitable location. He was right. The method he used to discover this...cutting open his forehead, jamming in a microchip, and suturing himself shut.

Passing out from pain and exertion, the mad scientist awoke the next morning and discovered his EUREKA! moment. His irrational behavior produced all the desired outcomes for the fledgling technology. His work and pride were saved. Necessity truly is the mother of invention.

Hearing of the success, Greece became the first country to adopt the technology. A few years before Vincente's sainting, every Greek citizen traded in their physical ID for a digital one.

The R-Chip contained a new virtual file for that person. A social security number was no longer needed. Every detail about that individual —race, gender, preferred pronouns, religious affiliation, blood type, et cetera—was collected on the R-Chip and connected to the cloud.

But the young Greeks wanted more than just a new form of ID. They wanted a serious overhaul to the outdated currency system as well. The new technology's potential made it possible for them to ditch all unsanitary paper money and cumbersome plastic cards and hitch their wagons to a tiny silicone RFID Chip. The timing was perfect because digital currency was finally perfected. The implanted R-Chip became their digital wallet. Nothing could be bought without the R-Chip first being scanned.

The only backlash came from the location of the R-Chip. Many balked at having to dip their heads to be scanned. However, one bright wag pointed out—'For years we've dipped our heads to a digital thermometer before entering a building;

why not do it to buy something?' *Point taken...no further complaints.*

The rest of the world, however, was not ready to abandon their traditional way of life. Physical IDs and folding money were still desired. But one instance was universally accepted—all the world's top leaders received an R-Chip, not for monetary purposes, but for safety reasons.

By far the biggest selling point for the use of human-implanted R-Chips was GPS. Should an end user get lost, or, heaven forbid, kidnapped, GPS located the person immediately. Pet owners have depended on GPS microchips to find their lost pets for years. This was delicious irony for the libertarians. The world's most powerful bureaucrats now have something in common with a toy poodle. And right now, a very important poodle has gone missing.

***

The world's top brass's R-Chips (and by extension, their bearers) are monitored 24/7 in a high-level security control room. Thirty minutes ago, the three-man team assigned to President Kartashov sprung into action. The Russian president's Chip initiated a distress alert, signaling immediate danger...

The value of the R-Chip's GPS feature is inarguable, but it only scratched the surface. Like a blank canvas before a gifted painter, the technology's potential was nearly limitless. Those who held preventive medicine in high regard immediately saw the benefits of having a full-time health monitor inside the human body. Something capable of detecting and registering irregularities 24/7 needed to be researched and advanced.

Similar to the belief that a car can reach the 300-mile mark if preventive maintenance is adhered to, ongoing research suggests people can reach age 150 if preventive medicine is followed. Many believed the R-Chip was the missing piece to making this dream a reality.

Advancements came quickly as the technology was researched across the world. Discoveries were made, patents were registered and eventually, a powerful R-Chip straight from the Sci-Fi world of Star Trek landed on planet Earth. And like all new life-saving opportunities, Earth's MVPs got first dibs...

The emergency protocol manual for handling cardiac events is administered by Pavel Kartashov's team leader. The other two complete the instructions dictated to them.

Distracted by the sudden excitement in the otherwise dull night shift, the remaining techs look away from their hibernating charges and focus on the welcomed rumpus. Long ago, the red-eyed, bored sentinels of the powerful elite accepted that their dark, stuffy cave will never be known as the Romper Room. Nine nights out of ten, nothing ever happens; and even then, the one lively night is usually due to indigestion or a nightmare.

The first step is to call Pavel's phone. Like a malfunctioning Life Alert bracelet, R-Chips can sometimes register false alarms. Most times a simple phone call ends the emergency. In this instance, it's not a false alarm. Pavel really has fallen and can't get up.

The first assistant hangs up the phone. "It's been over thirty minutes and he's still not answering."

"That makes four attempts. The cutoff is three in thirty," the second assistant reminds the team leader.

While the team leader mulls over the situation, without warning, Kartashov's R-Chip goes offline. This means one of two things: either the Chip's battery died, or Kartashov did. At that, all second-guessing ceases; he *must* call the Iranian president, which is unfortunate— it's 1:30 a.m. Sanjar Rouhani has many traits; patience and mercy are neither of them. The two assistants, along with the rest of the room, observe President Kartashov's lead guardian, waiting to see what he does.

Fending off a panic attack, he sets up a video call. As he waits, so do his lungs. Finally, one of Sanjar's secret service agents answers.

"This is agent 1127, head lead for President Kartashov. In compliance with security surveillance protocol 51 dash 332, I request a confab with the acting Iranian president."

"Agent 1127, you do realize he's asleep?" informs the secret service agent. He too is not keen on waking the temperamental president.

"Yes, I am aware. I have a code red, I repeat, code red."

Knowing his job, and possibly his life, is on the line if he doesn't follow protocol, the special agent switches the feed to Sanjar's bedroom laptop. After several tense moments, Agent 1127's computer screen is filled with a groggy irate Iranian face.

Having received a SITREP from the secret service agent, Sanjar is up to speed, though this doesn't lessen his annoyance.

"Kartashov better be lying in his own blood."

"I apologize, Mr. President. I assure you; I would not be bothering you if I didn't first follow protocol to the letter."

"Fine, carry on."

"Yes, Sir. At approximately 0100 hours, President Kartashov's R-Chip initiated a distress alert. I and the other two members of my team commenced with performing the proper course of action as established by—"

"I know the guidelines. I helped write them. Get to the details."

"My apologies, Sir. At 0130 hours, President Kartashov's R-Chip went offline."

Sanjar quietly scans his room: he needs to process all this. After a reflective moment, he looks back at the computer. "Where is he?"

"His last known location was Baghdad…in World President Basile's palace."

"Not possible. I would've known he was going there."

"With all due respect, Sir, his location was verified shortly after 0030 hours."

"It doesn't make sense. Why would he—"

President Rouhani is interrupted by his phone vibrating on the bedside table. Without excusing himself, he walks over to inspect. Sanjar sees he's gotten a text from Kartashov. He returns to the computer and holds out the phone.

"I knew it was a mistake. He just sent me a text."

Sanjar opens the text and reads the words; they trouble him deeply. While seething in blind anger, he notices the video clip and thumbs the *Play* icon. Like water dumped onto a campfire, all the oxygen is snuffed out of his fury, and in its place...stupefaction.

Sanjar slams his laptop shut without a goodbye. Agent 1127 sits quietly, staring at the recently returned desktop image. A distressing question crawls up his spinal cord and burrows into his consciousness—

*Did I just start World War III?*

# CHAPTER TEN

J osh disembarks a small turboprop plane at rest on the apron. It's been a week of tedium since flight 227's fly-by-wire system engaged and pulled his plane out of its nosedive. Once the pilots righted the "ship" they landed the battered bird in London where Josh has been holed up waiting for a flight back to Israel. Eventually the prepositional phrase, *in the right place at the right time,* actuated, granting him entrance into this glorified puddle-jumper. Statistically, it was bound to happen. He refused to leave the airport till his *standby status* transformed into *wave bye-bye* status. The trope ensued just in time too: bathing in the bathroom sink and sleeping in the airport had become rather vexatious.

Though free of the horrors of living in a provisional airport hostel, he's not out of the proverbial woods yet. Riding the escalator down to Ben Gurion's baggage claim area, he's assaulted by the insanity happening at the luggage carousels. To be sure, this airport is always hopping but the craziness is on a whole nother level.

Sighing heavily, he stakes his claim next to the correct carousel. Watching for his luggage, he strives to remain calm in the face of constant shoving and elbowing by his traveling companions. Since his life was forever altered by the Truth, by and large, his anger is restrained. But now and then the *caged beast* breaks free to wreak havoc. Seconds before the *monster* picks the lock, his suitcase mercifully appears—close call.

Snatching it off the conveyor belt, he flees the anarchy in search of a power outlet. His phone needs some juice.

Like sailors lured to the uninhabited Starbuck Island by a mythical *siren*—which the Starbucks' logo is based on—Josh is beguiled by the promise of pleasure and satisfaction the second he sees Seattle's world-famous sign hovering like a beacon. Cutting a swath through the sea of humanity's choppy waters, he harks back to the last seven days...

On hour one of his 168-hour "vacation" at Heathrow Airport, he discovered his phone's battery was dead. His next discovery was remembering that the charger was in his suitcase along with all his belongings. Suddenly, his mind went into shock as that hit home. All that he owned could easily fit in a 23x22-inch suitcase. This final discovery accomplished the hat-trick of sadness for him.

Knowing there'd be time to mourn later, he purposed to wrap his mind around his predicament. Not sure how long he'd be here and when, if ever, he'd see his suitcase again, he thought it wise to forage for necessities: the most salient—a phone charger. Oh sure, underwear was important—he eventually bought an overpriced pack from John Lewis: the store, not some random guy—but he needed his phone if he was to keep his belfry bats at bay.

But, alas, there'd be no charger for him; EVERY SINGLE STORE was sold out. Everybody seemed to have the same priority as him. His reminiscing concludes when a woman hollers...

"Finally!" the bored-out-of-her-mind barista exclaims. "You're the first customer in two hours."

Josh, having crossed the threshold to nirvana, scans the barren Starbucks. Maybe the world is coming to an end.

"Really?! Where is everybody?" Josh inquires.

"I think they're too worried about missing their connecting flights that a shot of epinephrine is the last thing on their minds," informs the *desperately needing to exercise her loquaciousness* twenty-something.

"Yeah, well, I'm not going anywhere anytime soon," he assures the resuscitated Gen Z'er. "I'm gonna plug in my phone and run to the bathroom before I order. Can you watch my phone please?"

"No worries. Nobody cares about your phone, I promise. No offense."

He smiles at her cheeky candor as he springs his imprisoned cord from its Samsonite jailer. With a sigh of relief, he plugs his phone into the wall. He holds up his index finger, assuring the antsy-for-action coffee sorceress that he'll order in a New York minute.

Five New York minutes later, he approaches the counter and, like all Starbucks lifers, flawlessly recites his order. The symphony of milk being steamed and coffee being ground commences. Moments later, he returns to his phone with coffee in hand. The time he was gone was enough to resurrect his dead phone. His wallpaper banner informs him he has…

"Thirty-seven messages?!" he bellows, startling the girl. Not bothering to explain, he inserts his AirPods and catches up with the world.

The first message is Walt assuring him that he and Braxton have everything well in hand. Josh never assumed otherwise. He deletes the message, gladdened from hearing Walt's voice. However, his delight pulls a 180 when Walt's presumed fate dawns on him. Now saddened, he quickly moves on to the next message—Susan's.

Listening right to the point of impact, tears well up in his eyes as the message abruptly ends.

While Josh works through his emotions, Ariella works through the bustling airport crowds. A small break in the moving human wall affords her a view of Starbucks. She sees Josh. Relief floods her soul.

When she heard of America's extinction, her heart broke; not for America, but for this man who penetrated her walled-off emotions and birthed this alien feeling deep inside her. At first, she was annoyed by the insemination. But, she knew it'd be unfair to him and herself to abort the obvious conception. Whether she liked it or not, she was in love. So, from that moment on, she vowed that should this man be alive, she'd accept the spawned endearment. Staring at him, she finds this oath easy to keep.

Josh suddenly looks out the same window she's looking into. She holds her breath, certain he will notice her, but recognition never comes. He's staring into the distance, as though into a different reality where sorrow and pain do not exist.

Back inside, Josh digs out from the emotional avalanche and selects the next message. He hears Ariella's voice speaking his name. He listens intently as every word-accompanied breath blows away the dispirited clouds from his overcast mind.

"Josh, I read that website and I actually believe what it says," her message starts. "It's like a light turned on in my head. I did what it told me to do. Something happened to me; something I can't explain; something I have no words for except to say that relief and joy have washed over me. Please call back, so you can explain what happened. Call me...soon."

At the end of her message, there are only sunny skies. He closes his eyes and plays it again, just to be sure he heard it right. His findings—yes, she was transformed, just as he was...and he had a hand in it. This radical realization encapsulates his mind in awed silence. But the unbridled joy doesn't end there; a new and surprising thought alights: he is completely smitten with her, but how?

*I didn't fall in love with Elizabeth this quickly,* he reasons.

What he doesn't yet understand is that sovereign providence is afoot. Times are different. Everything has sped up. The final clock ticks and there is no allotted time in God's plan for dilly-dallying. It's obvious the day is ending, and the night is drawing nigh, which is to say—only a few years remain, so why wouldn't he be in love?

His sixth sense kicks in. Looking up, he sees Ariella standing in the doorway, watching him with ecstatic fascination. Absentmindedly plucking out his AirPods as he stands, he walks to her.

The barista watches them kiss. It drags on, clearly fueled by unbridled passion. After what seems an eternity, the coffologist watches the two separate. Feeling like a third wheel, she walks into the back to give them privacy.

Josh looks into Ariella's glistening eyes. Silence passes between them. He initiates the breaking of the encroaching awkwardness.

"I'm assuming my father told you I was coming in."

"That's why I'm here. If I'd known I'd be rewarded with passionate necking, I'd have gotten here sooner," she jokes as she punches his arm. "Not that I'm complaining, but I would've settled for some gas money."

"Necking? What, are we parking outside a sock hop?"

"Well, my dad did let me borrow his car…"

They fall silent again. "I was worried about you. Didn't you hear my messages?"

"I'm sorry, Ariella. My phone died and my suitcase along with the charger were in cargo. I couldn't get to it."

"Couldn't buy a charger?" Her police mind misses nothing.

"All sold out." Josh steps in and grabs both of her elbows. "But I just heard your first message."

Her eyes light up with delight. "I've been talking with your dad about it all week. You can't imagine how much I've learned, especially from the book of Revelation. I've already read through it three times."

"And you understand it?" Josh asks. He's tried to read it, but he can't get his head around it.

"Somewhat."

"Good. You can explain it to me. How about tonight? Over dinner."

A smirk reforms at his obvious attempt at getting a date. "Joshua Mendelsburg, I may be out of touch with the dating scene, but I'm pretty sure dinner is supposed to come *before* the goodnight kiss."

"I'm an adult. If I want my dessert first, who's gonna stop me?" The birdie smacking continues.

She mirthfully rolls her eyes. Finally, a worthy opponent to play *repartee-badminton* with, even if *the court* would be better suited in a Hallmark Christmas movie.

"Can't tonight. Working. How about tomorrow night? Besides, it'll give you time to spend with your dad. He's anxious to see you too."

"Alright, but if you stand me up because you're too busy cracking skulls, I'll be very disappointed."

"Yeah, can't do that anymore; hurts the perp's feelings." Smiling, she nods towards the door suggesting they *draw anchor* and leave Starbuck Island. "Come on. Let's get you home."

# CHAPTER ELEVEN

B enson Mendelsburg, freshly brewed coffee in hand, sits at his kitchen table with an open book lying before him. With each sip, clarity-enhancing caffeine surges through his excogitating brain, aiding him in his quest for morning nirvana. But, alas, he will not be achieving serenity *this* morning, and it matters not that he wants it now.

Two weeks ago, influenced by Daniel's once future prediction, he thought it wise to see what happens next. Thus, he began an immersive investigation into John's apocalyptic book *Revelation*. Much to his dismay, what he unearthed nearly turned his heart to stone.

Last night's disjointed, schizophrenic nightmares don't help the situation. The merciless spectacles were so indistinguishable from what he'd read in Revelation that he could not ignore their significance. This is why his hair has symbolically turned white; this is the culprit responsible for harshing his buzz.

As he reflects, man's willingness to remain in ignorance astounds him; it hurts his heart. Anyone could see that the Bible is true and can be trusted if only they would look with open, honest eyes.

*Ah, that's just it—they can't see—*he reminds

himself. *They are blind to its authority, content to spend their lifetime banging into the same philosophies and ideologies that have existed for centuries. Believing that the lies assaulting them from all angles will satisfy the longing in their souls. But, as Solomon said— "there's nothing new under the sun."*

His mind changes gears. He reminds himself that he too was like these poor souls. He too was once lost, following after foolish, empty things. That is until the Savior shone into his darkness and showed him the way out. Oh how he regrets the wasted years believing a lie, but he cannot live in the past. He has a job to do here in the present: telling the blind that *only* Jesus, not society, not psychology, not philosophy, can fill the tortuous void in their empty lives.

Josh shuffles into the kitchen. Last night's reunion was sweet and joyful; neither wanted to retire even after the little hand crossed twelve and was making a sprint towards one.

"Morning, Dad," he greets his father without looking at him. He heads to the sink and pours himself a glass of water from the tap. Leaning against the counter, Josh downs the whole glass in one committed gulp. Smacking his lips, he notices his woebegone father for the first time.

"Dad, you okay?"

Benson looks at his concerned son. "I'm just overwhelmed."

Josh sits at the table. "What's troubling you?"

"Last night's dreams, but also this," he says, sliding a book toward his son.

Josh retrieves the slid-book and rotates it right side up. "What happened in your dreams?"

Benson leans across the table and stabs a specific spot on the page with his finger. "Read." Josh obeys. "No, out loud. I want your ears to hear it as well."

"'The king will do as he desires. He will elevate himself and make the audacious claim that he is greater than all the gods. He will say horrendous things about the One who truly is God of gods. He will be successful in his exploits—but not forever—for the time of wrath must be fulfilled and what is decreed must be accomplished.'"

Josh investigates his father's steely glare. "Who is this talking about? Who's this king?"

Benson retrieves the book from his flummoxed son. "This is a study Bible, written by John MacArthur, complete with commentary," he informs.

"I know, Pops."

"Excellent. As I read through Daniel, which is what you just read from, I relied heavily on John's explanations. Impressed by his wealth of knowledge, I Googled him. Before being raptured with the rest, he was a pastor. I also discovered that his church's website archived all his recorded messages. Because he repeatedly referenced Revelation in his Daniel explanations, I listened to his messages on that book while reading along from his study Bible. Son, based on what I've heard and read, this wicked king has arrived."

"Okay, but *who's this king*?"

A beat passes while Benson looks back down at the table. Not for dramatic purposes—he's too old for such nonsense—but because he's about to make a very serious accusation.

"Vincente Basile."

Josh draws back from such a crazy notion. "As in *the* world president?!"

"I know how it sounds, believe me." Benson considers what to say next. Suddenly, his fortitude is invigorated as a *cartoon lightbulb* allegorically blinks above his head. "Follow me."

Benson leaves the kitchen. Josh remains, shaking his head in disbelief. Yet he does as he's told. A couple of minutes later, Josh enters an office to see his computer-genius father sitting at his desk, engrossed in typing and mouse-clicking his laptop into submission. Without taking his eyes off the *subservient information provider*, Benson points at the empty seat in front of his desk. Josh was not anticipating all the "excitement" this early in the morning. Nevertheless, he sits.

Eventually, Benson looks up, smiling triumphantly. "Listen to how John describes this king."

With a final mouse click, a digitized voice fills the room.

"He is the antichrist. He will have a fierce countenance. What does that mean? Countenance has to do with his face, his demeanor, his personality. He will be fierce. He will be strong. He will be vehement. He will be a class-one intimidator like the world has never seen. And he will understand riddles. He is a great problem solver. I think he will solve the problems of the world. At least they'll think he will. I think he'll be an incredible intellect."

The recording stops, allowing Josh to mull over what he's heard. "You think Vincente is *the* Antichrist?"

"I do and so does Ariella. Did she tell you what happened?"

"She did, and she says you've been helping her understand the Bible."

Benson snorts, smiling. "More like demanding my help! Her insatiable inquisitiveness has wearied me into submission. Now that I think about it, it's like I'm dealing with the adolescent version of you all over again. Which reminds me, she's been sleeping in your room. I'm assuming you don't mind."

The hormonal, adolescent analogy continues. The unexpected reveal that she's been sleeping in his bed does not elicit exasperation but elation. Oh yeah, he's got it bad for Goldilocks.

Josh nonchalantly asks: "How'd this happen?"

"She was staying here all day to study with me, then heading home for a nap before her shift began. After day three of this, I convinced her to just sleep in your old bedroom. But don't worry, I changed your sheets yesterday. I remember your, um, persnicketiness."

Josh knows he meant well, but he's

disappointed by Dad's attentiveness to his only child's eccentricities. Realizing he wants this woman's germs commingling with his leaves no room for debate. He decides to go for broke and speak it into existence.

"Dad, I gotta tell you something."

"I'm all ears, my boy."

"I think I'm in love with her."

Suddenly, a record scratches to silence, and all the newsroom phones and typewriters cease their clamoring.

"You don't say?" Benson responds coolly.

"I do say," Josh confirms, wise to his dad's meddling. "Her voicemail resurrected something I thought was long dead. I didn't think it was possible to love again, to feel, and yet I feel a strong connection to her that I never felt with Elizabeth. I know that sounds terrible, but I won't sugarcoat it either. I can't shake the suspicion that there's something specific only she and I are supposed to do; something that is outside of ourselves; something bigger than the trivial matters of life. Does that make sense? Because it barely makes sense to me."

Benson thoughtfully rubs his beard as he reflects. "Perhaps you've been brought here for such a time as this."

Josh's heart quickens at those words. He recalls them being the first thing he read on the night of his transformation. Benson sees his son's wheels turning.

"Then go to her," Benson insists. "Propose to her. Marry her."

"Ahhh, isn't that a tad premature? We barely know each other."

"You said you love her."

"I think so, but who knows? Everything is crazy right now. My country was destroyed a week ago. Who's to say I'm thinking clearly?"

"Who's to say you're *not* thinking clearly for the first time?"

"I don't follow."

"Josh, I truly believe God is orchestrating things differently than before the Rapture. The two-thousand-year-old question of 'when?' was answered. Now all that's left is for Earth's egg timer to tick off a few more years, and that'll be it. This version of humanity will be over."

"What are you talking about?"

"I'm talking about the end of this world and the beginning of the next. Let me explain."

"Yes, please do that, 'cause you're sounding like a loon."

"I don't doubt it. Simply put, time is short, like a little more than a handful of years left, short."

"How do you know?" Josh presses.

"Ironically, the Old Testament predicts it. I've read this passage many times, but I never understood it before. Do you remember the short phrase, 'but not forever' from the verse you read in Daniel?"

"Yeah."

"Good. Listen, because this gets confusing if you don't stay with me. I wouldn't understand either if not for John MacArthur's messages.

Daniel predicted there will be a final seventy weeks before Jesus comes, destroys the wicked, and sets up His kingdom. I'm not going to explain what all that means right now except for this part. Daniel refers to a week being seven years, as opposed to seven days. Get it?"

Josh gives a cautious nod.

"Okay. Hang in there. Don't get lost in the weeds. I promise it'll be worth it. Seventy times seven equals four hundred and ninety years. Simple math, right? Four hundred and eighty-three years, as in sixty-nine weeks, have already happened since the beginning of the rebuilding of Jerusalem after the Babylonians destroyed it till roughly the moment Jesus rode a donkey into Jerusalem during the final week of His life here on earth. Understand?"

"I think so."

"Excellent. So that leaves one week of the predicted seventy left. According to John MacArthur, and others I've read, the seventieth week, as in, humanity's final week of seven years, begins after the Rapture. There's no arguing the Rapture's happened. But John goes on to explain that even these final seven years will be split in half, separated by a very specific, life-altering event."

Josh's still half-asleep eyes glaze over. Benson notices. He loudly snaps his fingers in Josh's line of sight. His eyes come back.

"Sorry," Josh says, shaking his head and comically slapping his cheeks. "I'm back."

"I know this a lot, especially so early in the

morning."

"That and the easily distracted, digital life we live," Josh reminds his father. "You understand. Maybe your computer genius brain can whip up an animated educational video for me."

"I'll get right on that," Benson sarcastically promises.

"Perfect! But keep it under three minutes. That's all peoples' shriveled attention spans can handle," Josh says, lampooning inept society.

Benson smiles, shaking his head. "Nice to see your mother's wit lives on. ANYWAY..."

Josh shuts up and sits up. He's ready to focus.

"The first three and a half years of the final seven-year week will be eventful," Benson continues. "Some of it will be bad, but most of it will be incredible. Life will be better than it's ever been. The king Daniel refers to will have unprecedented success in reshaping the entire planet. He will usher humanity into the utopia it's long dreamt about. He will do so much good that mankind will easily believe he's the Messiah, whether they're religious or not. However, things will be different during the second half. Whatever event happens at the midway point will be so earth-shattering that the entire foundation will be shaken at her very core, literally."

"What do you mean?" Josh asks. "What happens?"

"In those final three and a half years, it will

be nonstop terror and horror like the world has never experienced. My dreams last night gave me a preview. I'm telling you there's no time to waste. This is why you need to tell Ariella how you feel and do what you believe God is calling you two to do. Because, if even half of my dreams are true, then all of hell's fury crouches at the door, and Vincente's about to let it in."

***

It's early afternoon. Josh, at his father's behest, is leaning over a large, well-lit glass display case. He's in a jeweler's store, and the display case displays jewelry, which seems reasonable. From what his uncouth eyes tell him, he's inspecting some exquisite bling, and he'd be right—none more exquisite in all of Jerusalem.

Normally, jewelry and Jews have no etymological commonality with each other. However, in this case, jewelry is synonymous with this Jew—Halvar Kellman, the third member of the Eleazar Segal/Benson Mendelsburg's childhood trio.

Knowing he'd get a fabulous deal on a fabulous ring, Benson sent Josh to his old friend's store. Plus, he could do some reconnaissance while there. Perhaps Halvar will confide in his pseudo-nephew.

While Josh peruses, Halvar returns to the showroom, busily polishing what assumingly is a special ring. Since it was in his private safe, the adage about assuming does not apply. Satisfied it's achieved maximum sheen, he hands the ring to Josh. As he takes it, Josh jokingly acts like the weight is outrageous—the diamond is massive. Halvar chuckles, appreciating Josh's levity.

"You were always funny, even as a boy, comes from your mom," the old jeweler informs the grown man standing before him. "'Funniest woman I've ever known,' your father used to say."

Josh smiles, remembering his dad's earlier comment. He's glad his mom keeps coming up. It's a tangible way to involve her in his plans. Sometimes, her absence is keenly felt. He still misses her...

"She was always good at finding the funny side of life even when life wasn't exactly a 'knee-slapper.' That was one of her favorite phrases."

"Knee-slapper? Yeah, she loved that one. She's been using that since high school." Halvar allows a moment of silence to pass. "Your mom would be overjoyed that you two've quit fooling around and obeyed fate. She always knew you'd eventually marry Ariella. We all did. Better late than never, I guess."

*Uncle* Halvar has no understanding of God's timing or providence. Frankly, neither does Josh, not really. But he knows enough to trust "The Plan." If Josh never married Elizabeth, then he may not have met The Christ. And to that end, neither would Ariella.

"All for a reason, Uncle Halvar. Jesus knows what he's doing."

Seeing that Halvar would prefer a gun to his head than discuss (gag...) JESUS, Josh graciously returns to the business at hand. "You were right;

this ring is perfect. I'll take it. I'm curious about what other treasures you got in that private stash of yours. Any antique jewelry?"

Relieved by the arrival of a new topic, Halvar dives onboard. "It just so happens that I do. None of it's for sale, but I'd be happy to make you jealous. Got some time to ogle my vendibles?"

All that's missing from Josh's bewildered look are a couple of flies buzzing around his head. Halvar smiles, delighting in his successful confounding. He retrieves a nearby desktop calendar and shows it to Josh. It's a "Word of the Day" calendar; *vendible* is today.

"Oh!" Josh responds. "I have one of those too. Yours must be more advanced."

"Has to be. The upstairs cobwebs appear faster than they used to," Halvar informs while pointing to his snowy dome. "Gotta stay ahead of the little buggers. You'll understand soon enough."

"Can't wait," Josh remarks with a wide grin.

"*Vendible* means merchandise that could be sold. I don't always find a way to fit the day's word into conversation, but today's was a no-brainer." His unintended quip delights him.

Josh playfully but respectfully rolls his eyes as he moves to join  *Uncle* Halvar behind the counter. But before he rams his hip into the counter swing gate, the front-door chime fills the store. Halvar stops in his tracks to examine the two newcomers planted just inside. Their appearance causes his merriment to go the way of the dodo bird.

Josh senses the sudden emotional barometer dip. He looks at the front door. The blazing sun through the glass doors silhouettes the arrivals, obscuring their features. Judging by Halvar's stone-cold expression, they're not a welcome sight.

"I'll have to show you another time. If you'll excuse me, these gentlemen and I have business to attend to." Halvar's gaze never leaves the two men.

Josh does not like this new development but respects his wishes. "Okay but let me pay. I'm planning on giving it to—"

"Take it," Halvar interrupts. "You can settle up with me later."

"Are you sure?" Josh's unease increases.

"Yes. I know where you live. Now go."

Josh remains glued to his *mark*; his *trouble's-a-brewing* radar spins wildly. Halvar regards Josh. His look is comforting but deadly serious. "It's okay. Go."

Convinced of his resoluteness, Josh heeds Halvar's command and heads for the door. As he approaches the twosome, he feels like he's stepped into a Francis Ford Coppola movie. The two men—more appropriately, goons—look like they just came from a mafia fantasy camp. But though they resemble caricatures, they're anything but cartoonish.

Believing the continued staring contest is hazardous to his health, Josh wisely aborts his gawking. When he arrives at the door, the two men refuse to move. After a tense showdown, the men finally relent and step aside. He passes through the parted sea and pushes on the door, reactivating the chime. Yet, he doesn't leave. Instead, he broods over two assumed outcomes. If he stays, he will not leave; if he leaves, Halvar will not stay...alive.

They turn their heads slightly, heeding the loiterer from the corner of their eyes. Josh gets the message and goes about his business.

Walking across the street, mentally kicking himself for leaving Halvar behind, he spies an older gentleman sitting on a bench, feeding some squirrely squirrels. Approaching the old man, he nods hello and continues home.

Once the young man exits his view, the bench-dwelling senior citizen returns to achieving sufficient senility. The squirrels appreciate his reestablished undivided attention.

And just like that, in a handful of minutes, the fifty-plus-year-old childhood trio will be reduced by one, leaving a duo to carry on the bond.

Later that evening, the news will relay the only eyewitness account of a beloved neighborhood merchant's senseless murder. The elderly man will report having seen what looked like two camera flashes come from inside the jewelry store. Then, two well-dressed men (one carrying a black briefcase), exit the building. Even though they walked past him, wisely (the oldest trout in the creek achieves that distinction by staying in the shadows), the elderly man never saw their faces.

When Josh briefs the PD on the men's specifications, it will be documented but ignored. The police know who the triggermen are; but more importantly, they know who their boss is, and they want nothing to do with him. They, too, want to become old trout.

# CHAPTER TWELVE

T horoughly engaged in their first official date, a relaxed Josh and Ariella lounge on a couch in the exquisite Rooftop Restaurant atop the Mamilla Hotel.

Basking in delicious food, splendid conversation, and elegant ambiance, the budding lovers live this perfect night to the fullest. Even though the view of the Old City from this open-air restaurant is beyond comparison, they only find attraction in the six feet of couch real estate they both share.

Feeling like she needs to *cleanse her palate*, Ariella gazes at the horizon's color explosion left by the setting sun. Josh, his attention captured (more like enraptured) by her walnut-brown hair being tussled by the warm breeze, keeps his focus solely on her.

*Was she always this beautiful?* Josh entreats the heavens. His continued admiration is arrested by her summer dress' spaghetti straps drawing colorful lines across her tanned shoulders. She turns back to him; he notices one of those straps shift slightly down her shoulder. Smiling brightly, she readjusts the strap while at the same time disentangling her runaway hair from her face.

Her piercing look stops his heart...could've

stopped a charging bull. All the energy drains from his limbs, but if he is to do what he plans to do, he needs to quit frittering the moment away.

A few tables away, a husband and a wife, engrossed in their goings-on, silently sip their wine while gazing out at Jerusalem's splendor. A unique movement is caught out of the corner of the wife's eye, drawing her attention away from the last vestiges of the day's setting sun.

Delighting in what she sees, she touches her husband's hand, stealing his attention as well. Picking up on her pointing, he turns to see Josh kneeling at Ariella's feet, holding out his hand, palming an open box.

He watches Ariella respond in typical female fashion—cupping her hands over her mouth while happy tears stream down her cheeks. He then sees her pull Josh off his knees to reward him with tear-soaked kisses.

With his heart buoyed, the husband turns back around to see a copious dollop of enchantment waiting for him. Similar tears are flowing freely from his wife's bewitching hazel eyes. She has ceased witnessing the germination of a new life and focuses on her man. At the same time, as though being guided by some mystical power cultivated over the years, they both stand and lean forward for their own kiss.

They enjoy their passion for a spell before sitting back down. The husband suddenly signs, *I still love you just as much.* A heart-swelling-induced smile creases as she too signs, *and I love you more.*

Long ago, this deaf couple learned the richness that comes from having a Deaf gain. Though they only experienced sound in the early years of childhood, they feel no sense of loss or anger. Rather, they feel deeply blessed with a knowledge the hearing will never know—the most powerful moments are the ones felt, not heard.

***

Five setting suns later finds Josh sitting on a secluded bench nearly finger-drumming bruises into his right knee. He's feeling anything but peace. To distract himself, he inspects the elegant arbor surrounding him and the bench. His inspection moves onto the glowing torches and robust rose bushes lining the seating area and extending along the many pathways. He's currently chilling in Jerusalem's gorgeous Wohl Rose Garden, doing his best to chill out. He's about to get married and for some reason this time around threatens to undo him.

Benson enters the area unseen from a path behind Josh. Even from a few yards away, his son's anxiety is palpable. Bensons joins him on the bench and envelopes Josh's fidgeting hand in his own, ending the unrhythmic drum solo.

"Why are you so nervous?" Benson presses.

"Because I'm not good enough for her," the words tumble from Josh's dry mouth. "It won't take her long to see it."

"Why do you say that?"

"She's so amazing and I'm so...I don't know

—insignificant," he says, shrugging his shoulders and mentally castigating his pitifulness. "She lives this exciting life, full of danger and intrigue. I throw away people's used Q-Tips and old magazines for a living."

"Not anymore. Technically, you're unemployed," Dad says.

"And homeless. Thanks for the reminder."

"Exactly. You'll be moving in with her and living off her salary."

"You're not helping, Dad."

"Actually, I am. I'm helping you think about things that are true. Why are you homeless and jobless?"

"Because America blew up," Josh answers Professor Dad.

"And Who allowed that?"

Josh recognizes the leading question and says nothing.

"God wiped your slate clean to make room for your next assignment."

"Which is?" Josh asks.

"For right now, providing security for Ariella. Josh, I've watched her grow up for much of her life. I may soon be her father-in-law but I was an uncle first. Yes, she's an extraordinary woman, but she's also a damaged, lonely woman who misses her mom and longs for stability. I've heard many stories from her dad, lamenting over the endless string of guys she's gone through."

"That also bothers me. Not that she's been with all these guys, but that I've only been with one woman. I'm a babe in the woods. On top of that, I feel guilty, like I'm cheating on Elizabeth."

"And that's why you're what she needs —boring but faithful Joshua Mendelsburg not shallow and amoral Don Juan. When she was with me for that week of studying, she asked a lot of questions about you."

This admission generates several rapid-fire beats from Josh's heavy heart. These are the goods he's longing to hear.

"Like what?" Josh presses.

"Random questions—your teenage years, your life in America, your marriage, whether you're happy or not. She doesn't know this but one evening, after she woke up from her pre-work nap, I walked past your bedroom. Your door was cracked open enough for me to see her looking through a box of your childhood mementos."

"Really?!" Josh enthuses. "How long was she looking?"

"For quite a while. I didn't want to embarrass her, so I walked away. Several minutes later, I returned ready to warn her about the time. When I stopped at the door, I saw she was now standing at your dresser, staring at your wedding picture. I could see her reflection in your dresser mirror. There was sadness in her eyes, maybe a little jealousy too."

"What could she be jealous of?" Josh snorts derision at such foolishness.

"Not being the reason for your happiness."

"What...How could you possibly know that?"

"Old eyes may go bad, but they see things young eyes don't see."

"I don't know, Dad. It feels too romance novel-y."

"Like you two getting married after only a week?"

Josh nods, smiling a defeated *that's a valid point* smile.

"I think she's always loved you. Years ago, Eleazar told me she was thrilled we were moving back to Jerusalem but was crushed that you stayed in America. Then her mom dying shortly after sealed her heart off for good. I think it's why she chose guys she felt no connection to. There was no chance of her heart breaking again."

"She did tell me in the park that she had a crush on me when we were kids," Josh admits. "But I passed it off as drunk talk."

"Don't you see? Aside from Christ, you are the missing piece to the puzzle of her life, the WD-40 that's greased the rusty hinges and swung wide the gate to her heart."

A bright smile lights up Josh's depressed complexion. He'd never heard his dad speak so poetically before. Who would've guessed the old man was a hopeless romantic?

"To add another layer, you're also the one who introduced her to Jesus in the first place. You've not only shown light into her desperate situation, but you've become a tool of healing for her broken heart. She can't help but have a powerful, undying love for you. You've given her everything. She's bonded to you for life."

Feeling overwhelmed, Josh stands and turns his back to his dad. Not out of disrespect, but because he needs to process all this alone. He gazes at the dazzling full moon who's graciously lent its charm to the proceedings. Benson meant well, but he doesn't realize how much pressure he's put on his son. Elizabeth understood well the trappings of being Mrs. Mendel. Josh's crippling insecurities are a lot to put on anyone's shoulders, let alone a wife's. Josh's self-hatred runs deep and takes up a lot of space in his fractured mind. It's hard for him to accept that somebody could see him in a light different from the one he uses.

Several reflective moments pass, but those moments are over. Josh feels the sleeve of his guayabera shirt being tugged—his father is trying to get his attention. Josh regards him. On his father's face is an enormous flashing grin and the kind of gawking typically reserved for the presence of royalty. Josh looks in the direction of his father's gaping. What he sees takes his breath away.

Ariella, wearing a simple but elegant summer wedding dress and holding a small bouquet of white roses, stands at the foot of the path, glowing in unbridled exquisiteness. Though there is no sound apart from the soft breeze rustling the many leaves, Josh swears he hears Pachelbel's Canon in D major. It's as though her stunning beauty were potent enough to pick up a violin and fiddle the composer's ethereal masterpiece.

Her elegance, the smell of her perfume

now wafting towards him, the full moon's bright beam seemingly spotlighting her and her alone: all these things boot the rabble-rousers at his private pity party out the door. He'll clean up their mess later. Right now, he just wants to marry this beautiful woman.

Eleazar joins the proceedings to walk his daughter the rest of the way. After entrusting her hand into Josh's, he takes his place under the arbor to begin the ceremony. Josh and Ariella square up in front of Eleazar. However, Josh sneaks one more peek at her; he can't help himself—he's hopelessly enchanted. Oblivious that Eleazar hasn't begun, Josh continues his leering. Ariella finally looks at him. A smile breaks across her face, inflaming Josh's heart further. She lovingly cups Josh's cheek, caressing it. Her warm hand is pure heaven on Josh's face. After a few more seconds pass, she gently turns his face forward so that he sees a smiling, waiting Eleazar.

"Now that Josh is joining us, we can begin," Eleazar jokes.

"Sorry," Josh says.

"It's alright, Son. I was the same way with her mother. Beauty runs deep in her family."

Ariella wipes away a stray, happy tear. She recognizes her dad's genius at finding a way to include her precious mother in the ceremony, as though she's now a part of her happy moment.

"Thank you, Dad," she whispers.

He smiles as the two share a silent moment of remembrance for their lost loved one.

"I'm confident Leah is watching too," Eleazar adds, wanting to include the missing Mendelsburg matriarch as well.

"Thank you, my old friend," Benson says, wiping his own tears.

Eleazar smiles once again before closing his eyes and entreating Yahweh to bless the ceremony.

Twenty minutes later...Both the Ketubah and the Sheva Brachot were recited, and the first kiss of their new union was lost to the sands of time. All that's left is for a glass to be shattered under Josh's mighty stomp and for *Mazel Tov!* to be shouted.

As it is stated, so it is done.

Benson and Eleazar impart blessings and congratulations on the newlyweds at the melody of crunching glass.

As anxious and excited as they are to whisk each other away to the marriage bed, they graciously spend time with their fathers. It is an important night for all four because soon any sense of normalcy will also be lost to the sands of time.

Yes, terrible things are coming; unfathomable atrocities that rush headlong with the ferocity of rabid dogs who only have a short window to ravage all humanity. And yes, humanity is directly responsible for Earth's coming doom, but not because of climate change or failure to save the bees. Rather it is because they refuse to acknowledge God for who He says He is.

But all this will commence in five days. Tonight, the two lovers will be allowed to drink their fill; and they will, right to the dregs.

# CHAPTER THIRTEEN

C reeping out of his hotel room, looking like he's leaving the scene of a crime, Vincente Basile approaches his security detail, standing by at the ready.

"I'm headed to the bar. I'm assuming you're coming with me?" Vincente asks his two secret service agents.

"If you don't mind, Mr. World President."

"I don't, but I want you out of sight. It's one-thirty. I'll be amazed if there's anybody in there to protect me from."

Minutes later, Vincente and his mini entourage enter the Oriental Bar. To Vincente's surprise, there is somebody here: a solitary man sitting at the bar, staring at his phone, and nursing a glass of something white. Regardless of the unexpected patron, Vincente still instructs his compadres to cool their heels away from the bar. Like a couple of coonhounds, the two obey the wordless *point* from their master and take a seat at the designated table.

Vincente walks up to the bar. "Mind if I join you?"

"Be my guest," Josh says, not looking up from his phone.

"Thanks."

The barkeep comes over, ready to serve.

"What can I get you, Mr. World President?"

At that sentence, Josh investigates the paranoid bar mirror. The reflection claims to be the most powerful man in the world, but he doesn't believe it. Surely, this must be a funhouse mirror. He swivels his barstool to the left. Yep, the mirror is vindicated: it truly *is* the World President sitting next to him.

"I will have a bourbon sour, my good man. And for my companion, he'll have what I can only assume is another White Russian."

Vincente turns to Josh for clarification. Josh is too dumbfounded to speak.

The bartender smiles: "That's straight milk."

"Really?!" Vincente responds. "Alright then, fill 'er up with your finest top-shelf cow juice."

"Very good, Sir."

Vincente now swivels toward Josh and offers a hand, attempting to draw him out of his trance.

"Hi. By your stupefied expression, I assume you know who I am. But just in case—Vincente Basile."

Josh blinks cartoonishly, realizing he's responding like a goof. He warmly accepts the age-old gentlemanly gesture. "Sorry, I wasn't expecting any visitors, especially the world president. Hello, Mr. World President. I'm Josh Mendel."

"Please, we're just two gentlemen enjoying a drink together. Call me, Vincente."

Josh nods obedience as he releases hands

with the all-sovereign ruler. Not wanting to show disrespect, he remains facing Vincente, giving him his undivided attention.

"How long have you been sitting here?" Vincente inquires. "Judging by your half-full glass of milk, not long." Vincente flashes his best ultra-mesmerizing smile.

"I know I look silly, but alcohol and I broke up a while ago. We were not soul-mates."

"I can respect that. I once gave up sugar for lent when I was a kid. I lasted for all of thirty minutes." Vincente jokes, looking to dull the edges off the seriousness. Just then, his requested drinks arrived. Vincente offers the booze supplier a *thank-you* nod.

"It's a powerful man who can recognize his demons and gain mastery over them. Here's to you, Josh Mendel." Vincente offers up his glass for Josh to clink. Josh obliges him.

With the *clink* warding off any calamitous spirits, the two men sip their newly blessed drinks.

"I'm sure you could've had milk delivered to your room," Vincente informs.

"I'm sure, but I wanted to stretch my legs. The milk was an afterthought when I saw the bar was open. I thought it closed at eleven."

"It does, but I asked them to open it for me. You must have timed it right."

"Seems so."

Silence descends as the two drinking buddies sip their drinks. Vincente, feeling the whiskey warming his tummy and flipping on his *yakkety-yak* switch, retrieves the conversation thread.

"How long have you been at the hotel?"

"First night. It's my honeymoon."

"Congratulations! Where's the bride?"

"Upstairs sleeping."

Vincente chummily nudges Josh. "Tired her out did ya? Sly dog."

"Yeah, I guess you can say that," Josh says, turning red. "Her snoring was keeping me up, so I snuck out."

Vincente smiles as he reflects on his own sneaky departure. "I can relate to that. I just left a room full of abominable snoring myself."

"Oh, I didn't know you remarried. The media never shows you with anybody."

"No, not married. Just a companion."

"Got it." Josh wisely reads the room and moves on. "This is my second marriage. My first wife disappeared with the rest."

"Married to a Born Again, huh? That must've been interesting."

"What was interesting was at the time, I thought I was one, too."

"But, obviously, you weren't."

"Right." He takes a deep breath and gathers some courage. "But I am now."

Feeling like a bad taste invades his mouth, Vincente chugs his drink and motions for another. It's a toss-up between whom he hates more: the loathsome Jews or the detestable Christians.

Sensing the uncomfortableness, Josh

reaches for his milk to gulp and to skedaddle. "Well, I should probably leave you to it."

Wanting to mend the *conversation bridge*, Vincente grabs Josh's glass-clenching hand, stopping him from drinking. "No, no, stay please."

For reasons he doesn't understand Vincente's drawn to this nobody, desiring to be in his company. There's a charm about him...

"I was just taken aback by your confession. I thought all the Born Agains disappeared at the Rapture or whatever the term is."

"Those who were before the Rapture, yes, but people are becoming Christians now too."

"Then why are you still here and not with the rest, wherever they are?"

"Good question. I have no idea."

Vincente falls silent, perplexed by this information. He'll store it away and deal with it later.

"I'm surprised you got a room," Vincente remarks. "They closed off floors four and five for security reasons. Something about my presence is making everybody jumpy."

"Really? I didn't know that. We're on the fourth floor. My new father-in-law is somewhat of a bigwig in Jerusalem. He must've pulled some strings for us."

"Who's your father-in-law?"

"Eleazar Segal."

"As in, High Priest Eleazar Segal?" Now it's Vincente's turn to be impressed. "Ariella Segal is the new missus?"

Josh is unsettled that the world president—and possibly the final antichrist—knows his wife. "You know her?"

"I do. It was her partner who saved me."

Josh's hypothalamus lowers its yellow threat level to blue, leaving him feeling foolish. Of course, he knows Ariella.

"Thank you, by the way," Josh randomly says.

"For what?"

"Refusing to let an attempted assassination stop you. It means a lot for my people."

"Oh, so you're a Born Again AND Jewish?"

"The nose didn't give it away?"

"It did, but I was being polite. I love the Jews." Amazing. He didn't even flinch... "That's why I signed. Armistice between the Jews and the Arabs is very important to me. If we are to have world peace, it must start with Earth's oldest siblings."

Vincente motions for round three. Lickety-split, another bourbon sour arrives. Vincente hoists the goblet glass and imbibes liberally.

"I was referring to the temple inauguration, not the peace treaty. True, lasting peace will only happen when the Messiah returns and sets up His Kingdom," Josh says boldly, matter-of-factly.

"But what if he's already here? There's a whisper blowing through Jerusalem's streets testifying that I'm the Messiah."

No longer concerned with showing respect, he swivels his stool back towards the bar mirror and downs the rest of his milk. His buttons are being pushed so he'd better bounce before it's too late. He may not be drinking, but his tongue is loosening up just the same.

"I see by your reaction you don't agree with the populace," Vincente says, sensing a verbal war marching in over the horizon. He loves a good debate, especially when it's centered around his favorite subject—Vincente Basile.

"Can you really ignore all that I've done? Jesus couldn't bring peace. He admitted his own impotence. He said he didn't bring peace but a sword. Yet not only did I bring peace, but I convinced everybody to put down their swords. So tell me, how am I not greater than he? How am I, not the Messiah?"

"Hate to rain on your one-man parade, but you're a fool. I've got better things to do than sit here and listen to your absurdity."

Oh Josh, Josh, Josh...

Josh gets up to leave, but Vincente stops him by dropping his left hand on Josh's left arm, pinning it to the bar. This sudden action activates Vincente's men, causing them to stand and advance. Vincente holds up his right hand, freezing them in their tracks. Josh returns to his seat, stares straight into the mirror, and prepares himself for the verbal beatdown his disrespect calls for...hopefully, that's all that's coming his way.

An amused sneer lights up Vincente's flushed face. He's not offended but rather captivated by this wee little man's brazenness. Nobody in his inner circle has the pluck to talk to him like this. He slides his barstool next to Josh, invading his intimate space. Once there, he rests his right hand on the back of Josh's stool and stares menacingly at Josh's left-sided cheek. Josh refuses to look at him, though you best believe he's spying on him in the mirror. He watches Vincente motion with his left hand for the barman to stop by for a visit.

"Johnnie Walker Black, neat."

Silently, the bartender obeys. While the whiskey is being poured, Vincente silently stares at Josh. When the tumbler arrives, Vincente retrieves it with his left hand, downs it with one *jerk,* and then returns the glass to the bar —all while never taking his boring eyes off his prey. Wiping his mouth and smacking his lips, he adds his left hand to Josh's stool and pulls it towards him, filling the bar with the sound of reverberating rubber dragging across a tile floor. Josh remains frozen as he finds himself next to the most powerful man on the planet, close enough to smell the recently gulped *oat soda,* close enough to feel his warm sour breath on his cheek. Josh, hardly breathing, waits out the obvious power move being perpetrated on him by the world president.

At last, Vincente speaks. "Joshua Mendel, I want you..." Josh finally turns to look him squarely in the eyes, "to work for me," Vincente finishes.

How can one man be this arrogant? How is it not obvious that Josh wants nothing to do with this wicked king, no matter how badly he needs a job? Yet, how does Josh tell him this without finding himself floating in the Dead Sea—dead? Well, Josh came this far, might as well keep the spunky train chugging along.

"Vincente Basile, that'll never happen. You may have the world under your thumb, but not me."

Somehow, Vincente finds more space to fill in as he scoots closer. Any closer and he'd be sitting in Josh's lap.

"Because I'm completely captivated by you," he says with a hint of slurring. "I'm gonna do you a favor. Not only am I *not* going to have those two men daily deliver a piece of your anatomy to your new bride, but I'm gonna save your life. Tomorrow, you and Mrs. Mendel need to relocate to a different country."

Knowing enough is enough, Josh pushes himself away from the bar, away from history's most unstoppable human force, and heads for the door. Vincente doesn't stop him, believing his warning has its intended purpose. However, just before Josh exits, curiosity gets the best of him.

"What's gonna happen?" he asks, half-turned towards the supreme ruler still sitting at the bar.

"Blind reprisal." Neither the words nor Vincente's expression carries any emotion.

# CHAPTER FOURTEEN

A s Eleazar Segal walks the posh hallway of the King David Hotel's sixth floor, his temporal lobe works overtime.

The world president has been back in Jerusalem for a week. His stated purpose—encouraging Israel after their strongest ally was wiped off the planet. For whatever reason, Eleazar cannot shake the foreboding weighing heavily on his mind. The loudest ruffian in his crowded brain is the one that asks—*how do you know Vincente didn't have a hand in America's fall?*

And that's what's troubling him—he doesn't. Something feels fishy about him suddenly coming back. His world speech could've been broadcast from Iraq, but Vincente insisted it be done from atop the new temple to show strength and the beginning of a new era.

This sounds great, and frankly, it's what the Jews have wanted for millennia, but Eleazar isn't buying it. His sechel— (a Yiddish word for their strong gift of intelligence, reason, and common sense) shouts a different message...

Eleazar has observed Vincente grow into his unparalleled power from the get-go. Throughout their eventful history, the Jews have warily watched the effect power has on brilliant men. They watch warily because, often, they find themselves in the crosshairs of these "Hitlers." However, this time is different; Vincente went out of his way to befriend Israel, not destroy her. And it's this divergent reality making Eleazar feel like a cat in a room full of rocking chairs. Which is to say—he's very nervous.

Arriving, he raps on Vincente's hotel suite door. A few moments pass before the door opens, revealing a shirtless, scrawny man. Revulsion washes over Eleazar. The black and blue marks painting Aaron's arms add to the abhorrence. The unbearable situation magnifies as Aaron remains motionless in the doorway. He looks like a crypt vomited him up; smells like it too.

"Who is it, Aaron?" An unseen Vincente's voice cuts through the noxious air.

Not taking his dead eyes off Eleazar's, he responds. "I don't know, some dude with stupid curls."

Vincente, looking spry and peppy despite last night's mini-bender (he downed three more shots after Josh left), appears behind Aaron. "Those are called payos. Go back to your room and do whatever you need to be functional." Without a single change in expression, Aaron does as he's told. "Please forgive my young associate. He's a simpleton."

"No need to apologize. I understand. True orthodoxy is an endangered way of life," Eleazar says, doing his best to hide his shame. "Your car is ready whenever you are."

"Very good. We have a few minutes, yes?"

"We do."

"Then please, come sit while we wait for my colleague to take his meds," Vincente instructs, heading to the living room. Eleazar follows.

On his way to the couch, he walks past the second bedroom's open door and stops. Inside, he sees Aaron sending a few pills bodysurfing on a tidal wave of bottled water down his throat. Aaron, wiping the excess water from his chin, looks coolly at the leering high priest.

*Medicine...I'll bet.* Eleazar's inner voice remarks. *I know a heroin addict when I see one.*

"Don't be troubled, High Priest Segal," Vincente reassures. "My young traveling companion threw his back out on the plane —severe turbulence...you understand. A local doctor was gracious enough to supply him with back pills to help him get by."

"It looks like he needs something to keep him upright."

"Exactly. Now please, sit. Let's discuss today's events. I trust everything is ready for Pope Andel's oration?"

"It is, Mr. World President." Eleazar joins Vincente in the living room and sits. "He will go live at ten o'clock promptly."

"And how are my requested safety precautions?"

"Active and in place," Eleazar vouches.

"Very good. I'd rather avoid the same thing that happened to me happening to Andel. He doesn't have the fortitude that I possess."

"That was an unfortunate event, and will not be repeated."

"If you've followed my instructions precisely, it won't."

A clothed, vastly more presentable Aaron enters the living room. "I'm ready, Vincente," Aaron announces, shocking Eleazar with his lack of decorum. Addressing the world president by his first name? The dynamic of this relationship's oddities continues.

"Do you have everything you need?" Vincente presses Aaron.

Eleazar witnesses two curious scenes play out. One, Aaron's shade-throwing look at Vincente's preposterous question, the kind a petulant teen throws at his non-hip father. And two, Vincente doesn't seem to notice. The modern-day *Felix* and *Oscar* makes Eleazar quite uncomfortable.

"Excellent. Well then, let's be off," Vincente instructs as the clock strikes 8:55 a.m.

# CHAPTER FIFTEEN

Thirty-four minutes of mankind's borrowed time has fallen into history's nearly over-flowing bucket since the threesome left King David's namesake. At thirty-four and a half minutes, one event is plucked from all the simultaneous events being orchestrated by the Master Conductor and takes front and center.

A clandestine, back-packed figure skulks through the interior of a large building. He moves with a purpose, seemingly on a mission of grave importance, towards the center of the building's layout. Just as his purpose is cryptic, so too is his identity. Like the breathless anticipation of a chasing spotlight finally revealing a scurrying prison escapee, so too does the desire for this scofflaw's identity hold sway.

Since all the lights are off, the only source of illumination comes from the sparse windows throughout. Each time the sneak walks through a rectangle of dust-infused light his identity is nearly revealed. But, frustratingly, the natural light is never enough. For as quickly as his face can be identified, it is blackened just as quickly. It's as if he knows he's being watched.

Even though the individual remains a mystery, luckily his location does not. He is in the Dome of the Rock as evidenced by the courtly pillars and exquisite Arabic ambiance filling the octagonal layout.

After a few unnecessary tiptoed strides across the carpeted floor (he has the whole place to himself), he arrives at a cage-like structure walling off an important site. *Important* is too weak a description; *esteemed* is far more appropriate. For, this section has a name; it even has a birth certificate.

It is called the Foundation Stone and it holds great significance for two different races, the Jews, and the Muslims, and for two completely different reasons.

The Muslims believe it was from this surface that Muhammad ascended to heaven in the Night Journey. The Jews believe it was where the Ark of the Covenant rested. But even more substantial than a floor that once held a sacred vessel, according to the Talmud, the Jews also believe it was from this rock that the world was created, hence the moniker—*Naval of the Earth*.

Whichever is true, it is indisputable that the two ancient people groups hold it to be a supremely sacred place: a place worth protecting at all costs. Because of this, the Foundation Stone becoming a *touchstone* for utter chaos and war is highly probable. You don't need to be Phi Beta Kappa to figure that out.

*\*\*\**

With a vertigo-inducing location hop, another of the simultaneous events of 9:34:30 a.m. now gets an opportunity to tell its story.

Pope Andel Vassallo is propped up on a transportable kneeler praying to the Blessed Virgin Mary. What exactly does a pope pray for anyway? In previous years it would've been world peace (he can check that one off...for now), the abolition of abortion, and quite possibly, piously reciting the prayer of St. Gertrude the Great—that's good for a thousand rescued souls from purgatory right there.

But now, all prayers are for himself. Prayer to not grow weary in well doing; prayer to handle wisely the power and responsibility afforded him; and most importantly, prayer for strength to exalt Vincente—that's his whole purpose, and the meaning of his name backs that up.

Throughout history, few have been more fittingly named than the current pope. Andel means "God's Messenger," and Vassallo means "Service to the King." Seeing as how Vincente means "Conquering," and Basile means "King," it's not a stretch to see why. Talk about being born under a sign—whether it's a bad sign or a good sign remains to be seen.

Back when the title, "Pope" was added to Andel Vassallo's name, his affinity for speaking to the masses increased exponentially. Ever since his ninth-grade speech class, where he discovered his proclivity for public speaking, he has religiously pursued the bottom side of a soapbox. Thankfully, he had the talent to harmonize with his desire. He was so good that every speech competition resulted in him walking home with the blue ribbon pinned to his Lacoste shirt.

However, all that changed when he became the world president's emissary. Despite his impressive accomplishments, he willingly abdicated being "Andel" in favor of embracing "Vassallo." Were a *tell-all* book to be written, Andel would confess that, initially, he feared his bombastic ego would protest playing second fiddle. But he quickly discovered it was an unnecessary preoccupation. The first time he heard Vincente speak, any chance of an impassioned insurrection was thoroughly squelched. Only a lowbred fool would deny that Vincente is the most gifted speaker to ever tickle mankind's yearning ears—Mrs. Vassallo didn't raise no fool.

Up until today, it's only been the world president addressing the New World. But now, Andel will get the opportunity to stretch his vocal cords once again. He's been tasked with warming up the world for Vincente's forthcoming, crucial speech: to woo them into wholly giving themselves to their world president; to be encouraged to believe that he will escort them into the next evolutionary phase; and to trust him to supply all their needs. The imminent inundation of infinite blessings and immense wealth will be unlike anything the world has ever seen. And it's all theirs if the price is right. To wit—eternal prostration to Vincente Basile's absolute sovereignty.

\*\*\*

As though a spiraling transition wipe and

theme music jingle from a '60s campy superhero TV show has happened, the opening *9:34:30 a.m.* incident continues its narrative...

The creeping slinker walks to the southeast angle of the Foundation Stone where he finds an ornate archway enticing him to pass underneath and stride down the ancient stairs to yet another holy location. This new place also has a name, a rather ominous-sounding name—*The Well of Souls.*

Before descending, he dislodges his phone from his pocket and ignites its flashlight. Good thing too, or he'd be using his phone as an actual phone to call for help. Standing at the bottom of the stairs, he scans the room. The floor is covered in ankle-murdering, face-plant-inducing chunks of debris and gaping holes. Clearly, excavating is going on in this small room, more accurately a cave. But it's not just any cave.

This historically and religiously important cave could be housing the most sought-after religious artifact in man's history—the Ark of the Covenant.

Cue historical flashback in *three...two... one...*

\*\*\*

It's been postulated by Jewish archeologists that the Mercy Seat (along with the rest of the gold-plated acacia box) was buried underground beneath the centuries of knees that have come to pray. Sadly, they were never allowed to test their theory; the stubborn Waqf (managers of Islamic property) are staunch in their refusal to play ball. They will not permit the Jews a peak.

To make matters worse, several years back, something happened that was so incogitable, so despicable, that it ignited a verbal holy war. What was the spark that set Jerusalem ablaze? New carpet was put down.

During the needed renovation to the Dome, the old carpet in the Well of the Souls was removed. This revealed previously undocumented, cryptic geometric patterns on the ancient tile. Without notifying the Jewish authorities about the discovery, they simply covered it back up with new carpet. And they would have gotten away with it too if it weren't for the meddling mole who leaked the inflammatory pictures of it being done.

Once those pics filled the Israeli scholar's peepers, chaos broke loose. Verbal cannonballs were lobbed over the port bow. The Jews accused the Muslims of going behind their backs and purposely using glue that would permanently damage the tile.

The Muslims played it off as only putting down new carpet. Nothing more, nothing less. To further show the Jew's maniacal paranoia, a lowly carpet layer demonstrated to a reporter that the glue comes right off as he rubbed his glue-encrusted fingers.

Ah yes, such is the joys and delights of living in Jerusalem. Never a dull moment. And to that point, Vincente Basile added another layer of controversy. This time, though, it's in the Jew's favor. As part of the treaty, the Jews were allowed to study the cave floor's patterns in exchange for Palestine receiving its long-sought-after two-state solution.

To the casual and uninformed observer (which there is no shortage of), it seemed the deal was one-sided. But that's only because they don't know Israel's history. Their dream for the rebuilt temple is finally realized. The Ark returning to its holy abode would be the "pièce de résistance." If they must give up some worthless war-torn territory to get it, so be it.

But, after all this time, who knows what they want? It all boils down to two embittered brothers trying to get a piece of the same pie. The problem is, in their eyes, their brother always gets the bigger piece, so the vicious, multi-millennial cycle continues.

Unsurprisingly, the Arabs are not content with their slice. They feel cheated out of what they think is owed to them. Throughout the Muslim Quarter, loud, boisterous complaining is heard at every corner and in every alley. Even though they agreed to the terms without a fight, it doesn't stop the disgust. They loathe the idea of the infinitesimal Jews getting their way. In their minds, the Jews are spoiled brats just like their favored *father.*

The hostility turned up a notch when the previously benign research turned malignant. Feeling they had enough evidence to warrant a more invasive study, the Jewish scholars took full advantage of their freedom by demoing the floor. Dedicated, around-the-clock excavation commenced as they dug, brushed, and documented. They were driven to find the Ark, or at the very least, a clue to its whereabouts.

Of course, this got Ishmael's sons' dander up. Believing they were hoodwinked, the Muslims attempted to intervene, but their plans were quickly foiled. Vincente, knowing it would come to this, stationed a small company of Israel's most seasoned IDF throughout the Temple Mount.

After the allotted seven days for further digging were completed, the Jews packed up their tools and closed shop. Sure, they could have requested more time, but why prolong it? There was nothing there, not even a clue. Despite their disheartenment, it wasn't a total loss. Many artifacts were found they believe date back to Solomon's time, maybe his father's. Plus, though they'll never admit it, they got to make a large mess in the Muslim's precious prayer nook. Should they feel inclined—though it wasn't part of the agreement—they'll clean up their mess... when they're good and ready.

Through all this, Vincente only feigned interest in the Jews' quest, and even less in the chaos he orchestrated. Unlike Hitler, he has no interest in the Ark or what it represents. Rather, he cares only about the dirt: more specifically, the shifting of it...

\*\*\*

Back to the present day and back to the

pope's provided *chapel*...the holy pontificate is lost in self-affirming meditation. So much so that he doesn't hear the soft rap at the door; nor does he hear the second, albeit louder interruption. Finally, the heavy wood door creeks open, allowing a self-effacing face to peer in.

"Please forgive my intrusion, Your Holiness," the timid bishop requests. "It's time."

Not waiting for a word of thanks (he'd have died there waiting), the bishop bows and closes the door. Pope Andel is not a *servant to the servants of God* as his predecessor referred to himself.

Crossing himself before rising to his feet, he piously shuffles through the door and past the apoplectic, bowing bishop. The pope may be humble before Vincente, but at all times, he reminds everybody else they are beneath him.

Once a suitable distance is achieved between them, the bishop reanimates and takes his felicitous place. He is required to always be three steps behind the supreme pontiff.

***

Back in the Well of Souls, the intrepid intruder targets each hole with his flashlight as if reciting *eeny, meeny, miny, moe*. Once his flashlight cone lands on the *winner*, he unshoulders his backpack and approaches the chosen hole.

He gently places his backpack on the cluttered floor and unzips it. Reaching in, he removes a black nondescript briefcase (the same one being carried out of Halvar's jewelry shop), carefully rests it on its back, and pops the two thumb locks. Continuing his reverence, he opens the case to reveal what looks like a pneumatic capsule at a bank's drive-thru, nestled in shock-absorbent foam.

He removes the tube and runs his flashlight over it, looking for something specific. Eventually, he finds what he's looking for— a basic switch. He flips it. Anticlimactically, no little red light comes on, not even a clichéd *deadman* metronome beeping.

After waiting for something, anything, to happen, he decides to flip the switch a few more times. But still no proof of life. Eventually, his inner voice speaks up:

*Your job is to flip the switch and drop it in a hole; making sure it works is not in your job description.*

Satisfied he's done his job, he returns the tube to its suitcase and lowers it into the hole. For good measure, he covers the hole with some nearby debris before waking his phone.

A couple of *thumb-prompts* later, the text screen is up. And just like that, the mystery man is revealed. In the glow of the screen light, the bloodshot eyes and sunken cheeks of Aaron D'Angelo are illuminated. He thumbs out a quick text. It reads—*good to go.*

***

While Aaron's text travels from one holy site to another, the soon-to-be-recognized prophet steps through a door leading out to the temple roof. Bracing against the brutal arid air, Pope Vassallo zeroes in on the waiting podium, and two cameras and beats feat towards them.

As he walks across the temple roof, he mentally thanks the Jews for adding a canopy: it helps mitigate the desert sun's tyranny. Even still, the canopy doesn't stop the blessed pontifex from murmuring about the torrid Middle East.

*Just one more day and you'll be home*, he assures himself.

Halfway across the roof, the pope detaches from his serf and completes his journey alone to a sitting, arms-folded Vincente. He notices Vincente is alone, which is peculiar.

"Where's Aaron?"

"He's around," Vincente backhands the air like he's shooing away a pesky fly.

Just then, Vincente's phone vibrates, signaling that Aaron's text arrived. He unpockets his phone, reads it, and smiles. After stowing his phone, he looks back up at *his* pope.

"Are you ready?"

"I am, Mr. World President."

"I hope so because, after this broadcast, nothing will ever be the same again. The world needs to be assured that all will be well."

"You can depend on me."

Vincente's iron gaze could've stopped a bullet. "Then get soothing."

Vincente shoots a nod past Andel who turns to see the producer holding up two fingers: they go live in two minutes. Andel nods understanding and heads to the lectern. As requested by Vincente, the Dome of the Rock serves as the broadcast's background. The sun reflecting off its gilded roof will purposefully catch the viewers' eyes. Vincente may want the world's ears tuned to Andel and then himself, but he wants their eyes glued to the sacred building...

Twelve minutes later, Andel is back in his seat, enjoying the afterglow of a finished speech.

Vincente whispers to him: "Couldn't have said it better myself."

Andel nods an appreciative thanks as he watches Vincente stand for his turn at the microphone. Wasting no time, Vincente launches into his exhortation. Suddenly, something so preposterous happens the viewers assume it to be a Hollywood camera trick. Behind their charismatic world president, a large but muffled blast erupts in the ground beneath the Dome of the Rock and swallows it whole.

The cloud of dust rushing across the empty courtyard envelopes the new temple, blinding the world to the broadcast and symbolically shrouding them in utter stupefaction. Did the most famous mosque collapse into what appears to be a man-made earthquake? Who would do such a thing? It took the Waqf all of three hours to figure out who.

# CHAPTER SIXTEEN

T wo days after the atrocity, leaders from the Muslim nations (minus Iraq, of course) gathered at an undisclosed location nestled securely in one of Afghanistan's mountain ranges. Lounging in a lush field of grass with a massive opium poppy field serving as the backdrop, they go about the business of planning retribution.

Since satellites no longer monitor these once felonious fields (Rome's "legalization of all drugs" success was applied to the rest of the world), this small conglomerate can meet safely without any concerns of being watched.

At first, they were willing to believe the Dome of the Rock tragedy was an earthquake. But, thanks to dumb luck, the truth eventually surfaced.

Once the dust settled—literally and figuratively—they began their investigation. First order of business: checking the footage from the many cameras stationed around the Temple Mount. Surprisingly, all were deactivated during Pope Andel's homily...all but one, that is.

Sure, the Waqf gave the contemptible Jewish scholars the run of the place, but they didn't do it without eyes on them. Before the *keys* to the *Well of Souls* were handed over, a camera was secretly installed in a dark corner. And it was this camera that caught Vincente Basile's pathetic manservant punching his own ticket.

So here they sit, chomping at the bit to exact revenge, refusing to consider that maybe their vitriol is directed at the wrong person. Rather than using sound judgment, they allow circumstance to be their evidence: albeit, damning evidence, but still.

Thankfully, among all the rage-possessed lunatics on the grass, there is one self-possessed nation unwilling to betray Vincente. They've been sitting in silent lucidity, but the moment to speak is now. They know if the madness continues, this nightmarish dream isn't over, it's just begun.

"How do we know Vincente Basile is behind this? There is no concrete evidence," Waseem Jumaa remarks. "Do we really want to go to war over a camera feed?"

The powerful rulers stop their enraged babbling and *shoot daggers* at the Jordanian King.

"Waseem," Yury Dubrovsky, Russia's interim president, says. "I'd be mindful about challenging us. It would be no trouble to slide to the east and visit your country as well."

"Forgive me, Mr. President. All I'm saying is that Vincente may've had no idea what his associate was doing. He's unstable and possibly acting on his own. It's no secret he enjoys the produce of that field," he says, pointing his thumb over his shoulder at the acres of poppies behind him.

"Have you forgotten President Kartashov?" President Sanjar Rouhani asks. "His R-Chip places him at Vincente's palace the night of his murder."

"That too is circumstantial, certainly nothing proving Vincente had anything to do with it."

"We have evidence his associate was involved in that too, which means Vincente was involved."

"What evidence?!" Waseem asks incredulously.

Yury "wakes up" his phone and thumbs a couple of swipes. "That junkie doesn't have two working brain cells to rub together. He couldn't have done this. Vincente's fingerprints are all over these barbarities." He hands the phone to Waseem. "Push play."

Waseem watches a grainy surveillance camera feed showing Aaron digging out Pavel's R-Chip. However, nothing is seen except Aaron's back. Also, the camera is several yards away, attached to a corner of Vincente's palace. Not exactly conclusive.

Waseem returns the phone. "Sorry, this is too convenient. How did you get this video?"

"In an encrypted email," Sanjar remarks with a tone of "case closed" certainty.

The Jordanian king looks around the circle and regards each leader's flushed face. *Are they really this foolish, this stupid?* His inner monologue puzzles.

Needing a break from the crazies, Waseem stands and wanders over to the edge of the poppy field. There he looks out at the vast terrain of green balls on sticks. He reflects on how they look like thousands of tiny beacons of freedom pointing defiantly upward, united as one. Inspired by the vista, he returns to his matted-down spot in the grass.

"Okay, let's say you're right...that the world president is behind it all, why? He knows we'd retaliate. Why would he provoke a war? He's too smart to be so foolish."

"Because that's his plan," Sanjar states. "He wants us emotionally unbalanced, to act without thinking. To rush into a war without counting the cost."

Waseem furrows his brow at the irony. "Isn't that precisely what we're doing?"

"It is, but we're completely rational," Yury counters.

Unwilling to hide his consternation any longer, Waseem responds. "Yes, we're all models of restraint. Again, why would he do this?"

"To wipe us out, or at least try to," Sanjar responds. "Vincente knows our nations are the only ones powerful enough to stop him from controlling the world."

"But he already does," Waseem declares. "We allowed it."

"And that's why we need to dethrone him," Yury adds. "No one man should have absolute power."

"We tried. We failed. And now he's even more powerful, more revered."

"Yes, his assassination attempt did not go

as planned," Sanjar admits. "But we will not fail this time."

"How can you be so sure? The world is enraptured with him. All will gladly take up arms to fight for him."

"Simple, we strike fast and hard. We have the upper hand because we have the element of surprise," Yury explains.

"Brothers, don't let your lust for autonomy lull you into false security. I assure you, your underestimating him will be our undoing."

"Waseem, I'm beginning to suspect that you, too, bow at his feet like the rest of the weak-minded rabble," Sanjar Rouhani hisses.

"Sanjar, let me be clear; you are a fool. Just because I respect him doesn't mean I love him."

If the Iranian president had feathers, they'd be ruffled. The last man to call him a fool found himself on the trash heap, sans head.

Emboldened, Waseem barrels forward into the abyss of impiety. "You're all fools if you believe he's not onto us already. If he is provoking war, then he's drawing us in to pick us off one by one. I'd be shocked if he wasn't already planning —"

Suddenly, Waseem's mouth stops moving because his neatly severed head lies silent in the middle of the pow-wow. His lifeless body crumples forward, spilling out a torrent of blood from his open neck like a tipped bottle of Merlot. Kamal Sattari, the Afghani president, stands over him with a blood-stained sword.

"I see you haven't lost your touch, Kamal,"

Sanjar remarks.

"My Taliban days still serve me well. When you've lopped off dozens of heads, you never lose the talent for it."

"Well, nonetheless, thank you," Sanjar expresses as he motions for two soldiers to remove the body. Without delay they obey.

Kamal scoops up Waseem's head nonchalantly as though picking up a fùtbol. Absentmindedly passing it back and forth between his hands, he paces around the inner circle as he reflects. Drunk on bloodlust, his mind flashbacks to his former g(l)ory days.

"The trick is to swing hard enough so that it only takes one to cut off the head. Or at least sever the spinal cord so he's paralyzed. I've made that mistake a few times, and let me tell you, it's not pleasant. Nobody wants to see a panicked man running around with his head half-attached."

Never being good at "reading the room," Kamal misses the revulsion on his peers' faces. Not so much from the story, but because each time Waseem's head smacks against Kamal's hands, blood and gore splash out.

Sanjar walks over to Kamal and stops him in mid-pace. Coming out of his self-hypnosis, Kamal regards Sanjar with confusion.

"Kamal," Sanjar says, resting his hand on his back. "He's gonna need that head, and we need to wrap this up."

Kamal looks to where Sanjar is motioning and sees a soldier standing a couple of yards away.

"Oh, excuse me. I lost myself." He underhand tosses Waseem's head to the waiting soldier. Thankfully, he caught it. If he fumbled the pass it might have landed in the Saudi Arabian king's lap, or worse, bounced off the Pakistani president's head.

Sanjar gently coaxes Kamal back to his spot in the grass as he continues the meeting.

"Brothers, a unique window of opportunity is opened for us, but it's closing quickly. We have good intel that Vincente is still in Jerusalem. If we attack now, we can kill two birds with one stone: that other bird being the Jewish populace."

"President Rouhani, that is an excellent idea, but there are many Muslims who will also be killed," Cawo Muktar, the Somalian president, advises.

"Thank you, President Muktar. You are right. This afternoon you will tell all of Jerusalem's Imams what's about to happen. You will also tell them what to say to their congregants if they want to survive."

"Which is?" President Muktar presses.

"At the end of Friday's Isha, they are not to go home; they are to leave the city. Early Saturday morning, judgment will fall."

"But what about the feeble and the elderly? How will they go?" President Muktar asks.

"If they cannot find help, then may the angels swing wide the gates."

"Sanjar, I fear there will be some who betray Islam and warn the Jewish authorities," Kamal warns as he wipes clean his saber.

Sanjar takes a beat. "May Allah strike them before they can."

"Mr. President, Friday is in two days." Kamal reminds. "How can we be ready by then?" Like a cat, he has the taste of blood and is ready for more.

"Several warships, loaded with Iskanders, are stationed in the Mediterranean, one hundred and fifty miles offshore," Yury Dubrovsky informs. "The moment I learned the Dome tragedy was an act of war, I placed them at the ready."

"President Dubrovsky, those missiles will never get past Israel's defense system. It's lauded for its securi..." Halil Sukkar, Syria's president, stops in mid-chide when he sees Yury's smirk.

"Like America, no system is completely secure. Comrade Sukkar, I assure you my missiles will find their mark."

# CHAPTER SEVENTEEN

T he Muslim nations weren't the only ones engaged in a secret meeting. Vincente (who's in Iraq, not Jerusalem; hopefully Iran didn't overpay for bogus intel) and his ten leaders are huddled up, albeit through a video conference call, to discuss provocative things.

"Gentlemen," Vincente begins, preparing himself to lay down *the heavy*. "At this very moment, the Muslim world is planning Jerusalem's annihilation."

Once his words are translated into their specific language by their computer's translator program, cries of indignation return at the outlandish announcement.

"What will we do to stop them?" Fynn Hoffmann, Germany's leader, demands.

"Nothing," Vincente replies.

"Please explain," Itsuo Shiraishi, Japan's leader, requests.

"I know this seems counterintuitive, but listen, and I'm confident you'll understand."

Vincente waits for the murmuring to die down because their understanding the big picture is vital to his New World. The Muslim's brazen betrayal must remain an aberration; he cannot afford to have the rest of his government mutinying either. Though he foreknew what the

Muslim World would do and that his ten will never betray him, still, he understands it's far easier to lead a dog when a leash isn't needed...

Vincente's messenger, battle-tested and proven, never ceases to amaze him. Somehow, with all the information transferred to him over the last few months, this strange, all-knowing voice keeps things fresh and Vincente on his toes.

At first, the message was simple. Like a boxer's trainer yelling encouragement from his corner, Vincente only heard the same sentiment —affirmation and positivity.

*You are the most important person to ever live. You will do things many hoped to do but failed to accomplish. You will fulfill humanity's hopes and dreams. You are what the world is longing for. You are the world's greatest desire...*etc, etc.

But on the night before his attempted assassination, the sentiment radically changed. For the first time, constant praise and exultation were absent. Suddenly, he heard about destruction and death, beginning with his own. He was assured the attempt would fail, but that wouldn't be the case for nearly a billion people. The day after his assassination attempt, he was to begin a multifaceted scenario to liberate society from an infuriating antagonizer.

Over time, the specifics of the different phases were given to him. The plan was incredible, but some of the finer points bewildered him. Some were painful to hear. But because so much time was spent stroking his overinflated ego, he chose to trust all will happen as his messenger predicted. For his faith, his messenger revealed the end result—a worldwide utopia with Vincente in the forefront, basking in the splendor.

The Muslim nations were the antagonizer. Dealing with them, however, required several moving parts. Killing President Kartashov was step one in shaking the *Muslim Tree*, but more was needed to send them into an all-out war. He must take an axe to that *tree* before they'd sacrifice good sense. Unwitting *axe-holders*, like Halvar Kellman, were crucial. Poor Halvar. His shady business dealings had finally come to collect.

Because of Vincente's unlimited access to the vast tunnel system weaving through the underworld, he was aware of Halvar's back-breaking debt to the wrong people. Taking advantage of Halvar's disadvantage, Vincente had the suitcase bomb delivered to the jewelry shop in exchange for Halvar's debts being zeroed out. Halvar didn't know what was being delivered. He only knew that a new life, one free from his debtor's prison shackles, was his payment. He gladly accepted. He didn't know two bullets were part of the package.

Halvar's axe-wielding role was a success, as evidenced by the impassioned Afghanistan summit. The next phase, which has been developing in the background, is the culmination of an ancient prophecy: a fully functioning one-world government.

The world has been trying to pull this

off for decades but the concept always lacked two vital components—the right leader and the right nations. World President Vincente Basile unquestioningly settles the right leader issue. And with his messenger's help, he's solved the right nations dilemma as well.

Early on, Vincente established a group of national leaders he refers to as The Ten. They are his cabinet. And through these ten, Vincente exercises his calling—building and leading a new world. And just as Homo sapiens are strongest when their feet and toes are healthy and functioning, so too is the New World as it stands on the foundation of The Ten. It is from this foundation that peace came.

But this situation is the toughest the fledgling organization has had to deal with. Ever since 1945, the world has tirelessly whipped back an encroaching World War III. Taking on the Muslim nations will undoubtedly bring it to pass. The fighting could stretch on for years, sending peace back to the Dark Ages.

Vincente knows this will not be the case. He knows the war will last less than twenty-four hours. He knows because his messenger told him. However, Vincente was warned that even though the conflict would be brief, the fallout would be unbelievable. He was told that more death would come in the following months than from the actual fighting. To help his frail humanity deal with sending millions to their grave, his messenger graced him with a clear analogy.

*It will be like scrubbing off dead skin so that*

*new skin can appear. Vincente, a new life and a new world will be humanity's rewards.*

Convinced and emboldened, Vincente ended his pre-assassination attempt night of mediation. Now, it's time to convince his ten. Good thing he's a master manipulator...

"Gentleman, a golden opportunity lies before us," Vincente continues.

"Which is?" Leif Olofsson, Sweden's leader, presses.

"To do what no one could ever do—wipe out the Muslim scourge, permanently."

An uncomfortable silence smothers The Ten. Speaking disparagingly of Islam was thoroughly bullied into extinction by the Old World's badgering *hall monitor*. Seeing that The Ten are stunned into silence, Vincente moves towards closing the deal.

"I understand this a tough pill to swallow, so allow me to crush it and mix it up in chocolate pudding. Islam will never stop coming; it will never stop chipping away at the fabric of society until it's reimagined into their vision—sovereign control under Sharia Law."

Vincente stops talking and allows what he said to percolate in their minds. In quiet reflection, each ruler reminisces over the decades of strife and aggravation Islam has brought to their respective country.

Matthew Chapman, the UK's PM, breaks the silence. "For far too long, I've watched the invasion of my great country by a people that don't care about our history or our laws. I've watched my predecessors be bullied into submission by progressive ideologies whose only goal was to restructure society and erase centuries of greatness and tradition. Up until now I, along with all of Britain, have been forced to stay silent and go with the flow. That ends right now. Mr. World President, you have all of the United Kingdom behind you. What can we do?"

Vincente smiles at England's fist-pumping rebellion. They are not the only ones. Other leaders, also sick of seeing their lands destroyed, join the rallying cry. However, mixed in with all the chest-beating and ballyhooing is one leader strangely out of place like the old Sesame Street game— "One of these things is not like the other." This oddity speaks.

"Mr. World President," Fadhil Khalaf, Iraq's ruler—the same man Vincente recommended to bring peace to the Sunnis and the Shiites— begins, "You know Iraq will follow you without question. You also know we have forsaken Muhammad and his doctrines, but there will be many innocents caught in the crossfire, those who think like Iraq, who care not about religion, but about surviving. May they be spared? If not, we trust you. Our reprobate brothers must be destroyed, and if some must sacrifice their lives, so be it."

The deafening silence is all that's heard across the live feed. The other nine, caught up in their outrage, forgot about their adopted brother. Fadhil is not offended by this. He understands how anomalistic his attitude is. He also understands that sometimes a family member must abandon a destructive family regardless of the consequences. Right is right, and Iraq's family is wrong. Besides, Iraq knows their identity is not in their race—it's in Vincente, their Redeemer. He reshaped their future and gave them hope. They are forever in his debt.

Vincente, not often impressed with anything other than himself, is overcome with pride for Fadhil. It takes a lot of guts to deny *blood*; takes even more to scream for *it*.

"My dear Fadhil, my brother, you make a reasonable request, and I'm happy to say I have a plan. Yes, sadly, there will be many martyrs, but there will also be many who will survive, and not just survive but thrive. For those who reject their old way of life and instead mirror Iraq's submissiveness, I will enrich their lives beyond all imagination. Not the surviving Muslims only, but the whole world as well. Men, let me be clear...for the next several months, life will hang in the balance for much of the world. But for those who let me lead them will find they've been led to the Promised Land."

Maurice Toussaint, France's ruler, speaks. "We accept the Muslim nations need to be dealt with. But please, explain your entire plan to us. What's going to happen? What are you about to do?"

Vincente smiles as he reflects. Everything has panned out exactly as his messenger foretold. Because of this, the stage is now set for the final showdown. The Muslim nations took the bait and walked into his trap. Vincente finally answers—

"Something spectacular..."

***

It's just like any other Friday. The reverberations from the Muezzin's melodious chanting soften and evanesce into Jerusalem's night air. The dogs cease their howling, thankful the clamoring air silences.

Five minutes have passed since the western sky's red light disappeared. The final Isha prayer in Al-Quds' current condition (Allah willing, by tomorrow morning, Jerusalem resembles a smoldering quarry) has been obeyed, and now Islam's devotees file out of the different mosques throughout Jerusalem.

In Muristan, a small section of the Christian Quarter, two IDF soldiers—Ariella Mendel and her new green-as-grass partner, Caleb Harel—leave a café. They shift their shoulder-strapped TAR-21s to their sides, freeing them to imbibe their brew. Ready to execute their duties, they saunter down the sidewalk sipping while keeping a watchful eye. A couple of buildings down and across the street, they see Muhammad's proselytes leaving the Mosque of Omar. Only they don't appear to just be leaving: they appear to be fleeing.

Ariella has watched Isha end enough times to know the habits of the departing faithful. Some nights, many will stop to visit and fellowship. On other nights there may be only a handful staying behind. Either way, without exception, there are always at least two but not tonight. Tonight, nobody looks at each other much less speak. Instead, with what looks like forced composure, everyone ambles down the same alleyway, albeit, at a purposeful clip. Ariella stops Caleb in mid-sip, causing him to spill a droplet or two.

"Did you see that?"

"See what?" Caleb asks, wiping the splotch of dribbled coffee off his cleaned and pressed BDU blouse.

"I don't know yet. Come on."

Not wanting to draw more attention from the café crowds than necessary—compared to the Jewish Quarter, the Christian Quarter is a veritable Mardi Gras on Friday nights—they move casually toward the Mosque. Within seconds, they arrive at the Muslim's escape route and peer down the alley. It's empty, save for the scampering shadows growing large against the cobblestone walls as they escape the streetlights' glow.

They look at each other before tossing their coffees in a receptacle and thumbing their weapon's safety to *red*. With adrenalin coursing through their veins, they break off into a full-on sprint.

Regardless of the two's prime conditioning, they cannot catch up to the runaways: paralyzing fear creates the best wings. After sixty solid seconds of *pedal to the metal*, they arrive at a still-as-night intersection where clichéd alley cats hiss and slink out of sight. Amazed that they've lost a foot race to a group of civilians—including women in constricting abayas dragging children by the hand—they puff hot billowing breath. Assessing the situation, they see four paths to choose from. However, none show any sign of being recently used.

"Ariella, what is going on?"

"I have no idea."

"Then why are we running after some peaceful Muslims? They haven't done anything."

"I know they haven't, but I've learned to trust my instincts, and they're screaming at me. Something's not right."

Her instincts transmit a new message. Heeding her *gut*, she presses her radio talk button.

"All units, is there any suspicious activity in your sector?" She depresses the button and waits for a reply. Within seconds, all reply with a resounding *yes.* They report seeing Muslims fleeing in the same direction—out, as in, out of Jerusalem. Not by car though...all are on foot. Once the chatter dies down, Ariella processes all that she's heard. Always one to think better on perpetually moving feet, she paces in circles.

Caleb stares blankly, contemplating. After a moment of pensive silence, he speaks, reverently. "I have a mental image that I can't shake."

Not at all interested, she half-heartedly probes: "Of what?"

"Terrified animals running from a raging forest fire."

While Ariella and Caleb stood in line for coffee, a parallel plot unfolded. On a jagged mountainside, a new-to-his-thirties Jew sits, back propped up against a sturdy tree and head staring down at a laptop. He's been sequestered in this area atop Mount Carmel for several hours. It's a solitary mountain patch overlooking the Mediterranean Sea. He'd spent the morning surfing before making his way up to this little slice of heaven, his favorite spot on the entire mountain.

When the weather is agreeable, this is his routine—surfing away the morning and writing away the afternoon. Several months ago, he began yanking his first novel from the clutches of his bored, restless soul. Mostly, the glorious struggle is rewarding, but, occasionally, his mind refuses to turn on the pump to his *creative juices vat*. Today was one of those days. Early on, these days wreaked havoc on his psyche. A looping diatribe would pummel his mind—*I'm a hack! I have no business writing! I'm just gonna quit!* But it was during a lucid afternoon that salvation came to his rescue: surfing and writing have a lot in common.

As someone who's surfed the temperamental Mediterranean Sea for years, he's learned stick-to-itiveness. He knew that no matter how much time is spent waiting for the lull to pass, he needs to stay ready because when the swell comes—it always does—he'll finally catch an epic wave. From that moment, it was up to him to stay in the pocket till it closes. That's exactly how writing is. The blank white screen may be torturous to stare at; but eventually, if he stays patient, the payoff of a sick inspirational pipeline will come. It's always worth enduring the flats of writing's briny deep.

The problem with these frustrating days is they usually throw everything out of whack. No matter: when things are clicking, the keyboard keys must stay clicking until his persnickety muse scurried back into the forest of his mind. Normally, refusing to close up shop and drive home was no big deal. However, the Sabbath is about to begin. The distant sound of the Muezzin's call to prayer clued him in. Time really got away from him today. Overwhelmed by panic, he leaps to his feet and haphazardly shoves everything into his backpack.

He is a Jew by race only; he obeys none of the laws and traditions he grew up with. But, to keep his parents happy, after completing his mandatory, three-year military stint, he begrudgingly became a twice-a-year Orthodox Jew: he observes Rosh Hashanah and Yom Kippur. As he's gotten older and less *stick it to the establishment*, he's replaced his youthful mantra with—*go along to get along*. There's no way he can get home before the Sabbath begins, but he needs to try. He can apologize to his neighbors and his parents later for "working" on the Sabbath.

With his backpack slung over his shoulder, he scrambles toward the path that will take him to his car. As he descends the matted-down trail through the tall grass, he unconsciously peers out at the sea. An audible gasp escapes his lips as he screeches to a halt. Frozen in place, his mind argues with his eyes. He must be hallucinating. There's no way four large destroyers float atop the Mediterranean all pointing at Israel. He stares, unwilling to move, hoping upon all hope that these warships are simply lost and are stopping to ask for directions.

Time crawls with nothing happening, until…something does. A lone, skinny red object emerges from one destroyer and screams across the dusky sky. Its destination is unmistakable…

***

Having heard her partner's macabre metaphor, Ariella stops her pacing and stares at the rookie. Not desensitized to the job yet, the terror in his eyes is apparent.

Despite her attention and emotions being arrested, she has no time to ponder the alarming analogy. An alien noise broadcasts in the distance like the muffled rumble of a thunderclap.

"What's that?!" a now frazzled Caleb asks.

"I'm not sure," Ariella answers as she walks toward the noise like a curious mosquito toward a *Zapper*. "It kinda sounds like…"

She doesn't need to answer because the answer is there. The ear-piercing answer screams overhead and rams into a building a couple of blocks away.

"GET DOWN!!" Ariella hollers while

grabbing the frozen, mouth-agape rookie and jerking him to the ground.

They wait, but not for long. The next buzzing is quick on the original's heels. This time they know where to look. They see a dragon-tailed UFO slam into another building, this time a few blocks down from the previous building.

As though a pump was primed, the night sky is inundated with flaming UFOs all headed for The City of David. How is this possible? David's Sling is supposed to stop the barrage of violence being leveled on Jerusalem. But somehow, these missiles are getting past the lauded defense system. The city is wide open, free of charge.

Another fiery projectile comes into view (how many does this make? She stopped counting at thirteen) and finds its mark a few yards away from their location. Large chunks of debris rain all around them. It's a miracle they're not *has-beens*. Explosion after earth-shattering explosion rocks the city. They need to move, but where? All over the city, *red flowers* bloom, and buildings topple. Anguished screams, heard briefly before the unleashed hell drowns them out, cover the city in a blanket of horror and woe. People are dying; lives are snuffed out in an instant; Ariella prays they go quickly; she prays the same for herself and her partner if it's to be so. A thought splashes the turbulent waters of her mind:

*My dad! Josh! Josh's dad! Are they okay?!*

Seeing that she's still clutching Caleb's arm,

she yanks it, drawing his attention. "There's nothing we can do. Get to your loved ones."

He nods as terrified tears stream down his cheeks. Not sure he understands, she slaps his young face, squashing the alligator tears and dispersing them like tires driving through a puddle. The light comes back into his eyes. He's now present and accounted for.

"Do you hear me?" she bellows. "Do you understand?"

"Yes!" he shouts back, fueled by fear, pain at the slap, and anger BECAUSE of the slap.

"Then go! Now!"

He hugs her. She hugs back. He's off in a flash. She watches him go, assuming at any second, she'll lose another partner. Perhaps it'll be him losing his first partner.

Ariella pulls out her phone and calls Josh. While waiting, she breaks off into a sprint only to stop again when he answers.

"Ariella!" he shouts. "Are you okay?!"

"I am. Are you?"

"For now. Where are you?"

"Staring at the rubble that used to be The Church of the Holy Sepulchre. I'm headed for my dad's. Are you still at yours?"

"I am. We're in—"

Ariella doesn't hear the rest of his sentence due to a missile colliding with a nearby building. Dropping instinctively to her hunches, she looks for an alternate route around the rubble that's just materialized. Her scouting stops when she notices a woman, whose lower half is pinned beneath concrete chunks, several meters away.

"I'll call you back when I can. Love you."

She hangs up and rushes to the woman. Arriving, she sees not a pinned woman, but rather a dead woman's torso. She's not affected by this ghastly sight; she's seen her fair share of gore. However, the split-in-two body fills her mind with images of her dad in the same situation. This shuts off her training and turns on her nurturing. She needs to get to him; nothing else is more important. She turns on her heels and darts down a different street.

***

Josh ends the call and turns to his dad. He is on the couch reading his Bible.

"I knew this was coming," Josh confesses as he paces the room. "And so did Ariella."

This unlikely confession snatches Benson's attention. "I don't understand. What are you talking about?"

"On the first night of our honeymoon, after Ariella fell asleep, I went for a stroll around the hotel. I couldn't stop my racing mind. After a while, I bumped into Vincente downstairs."

"Basile?!" Benson verifies, dumbfounded by the randomness.

"Yes. He too was staying at the King David Hotel. We got to talking. His arrogance was on full display. At one point, he insisted he was the coming Messiah. I was sick of the conversation but felt I couldn't leave. It was like he had a mental hold on me. I started getting mouthy with him. Not sure where my boldness came from. But instead of putting me in my place, he tells me to come work for him. My disrespectfulness continued. In a nutshell, I told him, fat chance. Then it got weirder. After assuring me he should have me killed for my sass, he warns me to get out of Jerusalem before it was too late."

"Despite you needing a job, you were right to refuse him. I'm proud of you. He's dangerous and his mind is twisted. Redeemed people have no business aligning themselves with him."

Josh flinches at the latest explosion. The missile strikes are inching ever closer.

"I suppose, but I should have listened and gotten us out of here. Ariella heard me walk back into the hotel room. I told her what happened. She said she'd be AWOL if she abandon her duty. That we'd have to trust God to protect us." He stops pacing and plops despondently on the couch next to his dad. "I should've been more assertive."

Josh grabs the remote and points it at the TV; but before he can push the power button, Benson rests his hand on Josh's outstretched arm. He turns to his dad. Benson says nothing. Tenderness shines on his face; it's all that's needed for Josh to get the hint. He allows his arm to be pulled down, remote removed, and placed out of reach. The time for *shoulda, coulda, woulda* is over.

Benson taps the couch, signaling for Josh to scoot closer. Josh obeys. Once in the requested location, Josh finds half a Bible in his lap and his father's arm around him—father is leading son to *living waters*.

While the world burns outside, inside, two men receive strength and courage. Suddenly, the *burning* hits close to home, actually *on* home: a missile strikes the apartment building... everything goes black. A handful of missiles later and Israel returns to her previous holy demeanor —silence.

***

Back on Mount Carmel, the thirty-something surfer/wannabee writer stands dumbfounded by what he's watching. The far-off sights and muffled sounds all speak to it being the Fourth of July; the problem is it's May and he's not in America. Ever since the first missile was tossed onto the *epicenter of the world*, he's remained in place, too petrified to move.

In the barely three minutes he's been watching, the realization of what's happening to his city stirs in him a sadness like he's never known. From here, it's impossible to be certain if any of those missiles landed on his parents' house. But judging by the dozens of smoke clouds wafting up from all over the city, they've hit close.

As he watched the uninterrupted swarm of missiles pummeling Jerusalem, breath barely escaped his lungs. With each missile strike, dismay threatens to overload his broken spirit. Was nobody coming to Israel's rescue? Abruptly, the answer came...

Without warning, hope took flight in the form of *flying red snakes* appearing from the Mediterranean's south. Their destination— the attacking warships. The ensuing eruption of resplendent red enflamed his hurting heart: somebody was returning fire!

Missile after missile launched straight up from the south, arched, and screamed furious rage as they crashed into the four destroyers. But they didn't just come from the south; suddenly, missiles were coming from the Sea's north as well, landing on the destroyers. Within seconds, the missiles synchronized into one cohesive attack, deluging the ships with their devastating payload. This counterattack lasted for only four minutes, which was a minute longer than needed: all the warships were smoking floating husks nine missiles ago.

In the distance, faint anguished cries rose in the eerie silence that descended upon this gruesome scene. Whether they came from the sea or Jerusalem, he knows not, but does the source matter?

Staring at the billowing smoke rising from two different sources, a thought forms in his creative mind, one he'll need to write down later:

*Underneath all clothes, insignia, or ceremonial dress lies the same human frailty—it is vulnerable, breakable, and severable. It matters not your station in life; pain is the great equalizer. When all are stripped bare of pretense, prejudices, and hatred, one commonality applies to us all—all bleed, all cry, and, eventually, all die...exactly the same.*

***

What the aspiring author witnessed was the outcome of three countries doing the hard work of handshakes and back-scratching to create a sustainable future for each. Because this effort was maintained for many years, these three countries could rescue an insignificant country (as many see it) and keep it breathing for another twenty-four hours.

In 1961, Great Britain granted independence to Cyprus, freeing them from their control. Once the *Treaty of Guarantee* was signed, their relationship warmed and remained so for the last several decades. As part of the treaty, Cyprus provided British Forces with two sovereign base areas, giving them a military presence throughout the island.

Little over a week ago, at Vincente's behest, the UK began landing C-130s busting at the seams with fully loaded MLRSs (Multiple Launch Rocket System) on the small island of Cyprus.

It is from this small armada, placed along the southern part of the island, that the covey of *suicide dragons* from the north came from. But what about the South? What's going on there? Well, this was a trickier setup requiring Deus Ex Machina to sort it all out.

DEUS EX MACHINA—Oh, how wrong it is to rely on a lazy and contrived plot device, but sometimes concrete solutions cannot come in neatly wrapped gifts. Sometimes they just need to be accepted like an ugly Christmas sweater from your gam-gam.

Egypt is the source of the southern bombardment, which is shocking. Egypt has been primarily a Muslim nation for the last fifteen hundred years. But it's only shocking to those unaware of Egypt's two consecutive heartbreaks by two allies interested more in progress than loyalty.

Iran and Egypt were once partners who labored to make their alliance work. The problem was they had an unhealthy partnership. They were that uncomfortable-to-be-around couple who always argued; always just one more bad fight away from breaking up. Eventually, they did break up, each stating irreconcilable differences.

Though saddened, Egypt was grateful for its union with Russia. It was a beautiful arrangement full of mutual respect and admiration. But all that changed the day Russia's eyes wandered and *fell in love* with Iran. Spun out by this betrayal, Egypt severed all ties with Russia.

But then there's Vincente. Could he be what he says he is? As a Muslim country, they're supposed to hate him too but they've always been oddballs in the Muslim World. They love Israel and see them as their little brothers.

Egypt and Israel go way back. Some of ancient history's wildest stories (a few that will be rebooted in the coming years) have played out between these two nations. The greatest Jew to ever live (in Israel's eyes anyway) was born in Egypt's sand-swept lands. As a boy, he was rescued from becoming an eventual crocodile breakfast by Egyptian royalty. It was the Jews who physically built the pyramids. It was in protecting the Jews that thousands of Egyptian soldiers drowned. Yes, there is much history, good and bad, between these two nations. Vincente displaying nothing but respect and loyalty to Israel has Egypt's attention. Great Britain piqued their curiosity even further.

After the secret meeting with Vincente's Ten, the UK reached out to Egypt. They relayed all that was happening, including Cyprus's involvement. Egypt loved the idea of joining forces with Cyprus, one of their strongest allies, to rescue their little brother. Felt poetic. Without a second thought, Egypt laid all its military divisions at Vincente's feet. He thanked them but requested only one division—their armored division.

This request revealed a spooky twist. Early in the twenty-first century, the US delivered their final batch of M270 MLRSs to Egypt before Lockheed Martin discontinued their production. How's that for providence...

Many years from now, historians will note that this counterattack resembled a scene from an old Wild West movie. Cowboys on horseback chasing powerless Indians on foot into a dead-end canyon. Once the cowboys have the Indians cornered, they'll discover too late that they were lured into a trap. At just the right moment, a great number of Indians appear on top of both canyon walls and pick off the cowboys: like shooting fish in a barrel.

But there's a second part to Vincente's brilliant scheme. Borrowing from another military strategy, while the Muslim world was distracted by the happenings in the Mediterranean, Vincente was stealthily moving an armada of submarines around *the back* to clean up the rest.

The submarines hail from four of The Ten. They are powerful nations, but more importantly...they are nuclear nations.

# CHAPTER EIGHTEEN

At an electronics store in Jerusalem's upscale outdoor Mamilla Mall, one TV nestled amongst shattered glass, crumbled drop ceiling, and various smashed electronic devices, faithfully broadcasts the news.

The only functioning fluorescent light fixture, freed from its metal interlocking splines, hangs by its wires and swings, intermixing flickering light with electrical sparks that pop and hiss. Amazingly, this electronics store's power is still on; maybe it's a case of electricity being *comradely* to its own; or perhaps personification is being used to bring normality to this unadulterated chaos. Even inanimate objects need to chip in during unprecedented crises.

The working TV, fallen from its normal eye-level perch and now leaning against a wall, is tuned to BBC World News. From a distance, a pair of eyes see the talking head and racing banners, but the included ears cannot hear what's being said. Zeroing in on the TV's uncivilized location, the unseen, low to the ground, entity—quite possibly a crawling, injured individual—labors toward the cavernous mess.

Along the way, a blur of scampering legs carrying panicked people darts across its view, momentarily blocking its path to the TV. More than once, the creeping individual is kicked and knocked over by the mass of people scurrying out of the devastated city. Nobody stops to help or apologize; they care only for their safety: panic brings out the worst.

Eventually, unbreakable determination wins the day. The crawling individual arrives, drops its bleeding snout, and scarfs up a half-eaten falafel lying in front of the TV. With pursued food quickly chewed, the scruffy dog scampers off before more flailing feet drive into its rib cage.

Though nobody stops to listen, the TV pumps out rapid-fire information just the same. But like the dog, nobody cares what's being said. Jerusalem's residents care only about surviving. Later they can take a breath and focus on what else happened while they were being bombed.

Even though Jerusalem lies in ruins, amazingly, the nice French lady isn't reporting it. Something more historic has happened, and this is what dominates the airwaves. At the time Cyprus and Egypt initiated their counterattack, nuclear warheads were launched from four locations. The anchorperson takes it from here.

"...India, France, China, and the UK are taking responsibility for the coordinated nuclear attack. What is known so far is that each country's fleet of submarines was already in place for military exercises. According to the statement given by Great Britain, when Jerusalem was attacked, orders were given for the submarines to immediately retaliate. Why these specific countries were targeted is yet to be known. We can tell you that, apart from Russia, the countries were primarily Muslim."

Off to the side, a graphic lists the specific countries that were attacked—Russia, Iran, Saudi Arabia, Syria, Turkey, all the 'Stan countries east of Iran, and several African countries.

"According to satellite imaging," the anchorperson continues, "the widespread destruction is unimaginable. Rough estimates of two hundred million dead are being reported. World President Basile will make a statement within the hour. For now, keep those who've lost loved ones both in Jerusalem and around the world in your thoughts."

Legs flash in front of the TV; they belong to Ariella Mendel. She is alive and headed towards her father's house, hoping to add him to the "still alive" list. He's not answering her calls. Refusing to mull over the "what ifs," she focuses on her training and compartmentalizes her anxiety: there's work to be done.

When she left the Church of the Holy Sepulchre, ideally, it should've only taken thirty minutes at a full sprint to get to her father's apartment in Katamon. But, she's not running on a polyurethane track. She's having to take unexpected detours around the endless path-blocking debris. Plus, being forced to run through the open-air Mamilla Mall didn't help. All the escaping, panicked people created a bottleneck, making it impossible to get through. Thankfully, improvisation is her strong suit along with rad parkour skills. She effortlessly carved through and over the various walls and obstacles as she escaped the mall.

Twelve minutes later, she arrives at her father's apartment building. She's overjoyed to see it standing, a small miracle considering several buildings in the neighborhood are not.

Her joy turns to annoyance when she sees him outside mingling with dazed and scared neighbors. She knows he's gifted with unyielding compassion and a servant's heart, but right now he should be in his apartment building's bomb shelter. *Parking* her out-of-control, emotional jalopy, she runs over and bear-hugs the stuffing out of him.

"Dad! Why are you outside?!"

"Instead of in my bunker, you mean?" Freeing himself from her hug, he holds her at arms' length and motions to all the trembling people. "Ariella, these people need me out here not in there." He points to a door presumably leading to the bunker.

"I've been calling you," she rebukes. "Why didn't you answer?"

"I'm sorry, Daughter, but I left that cursed distraction inside."

Ariella takes a deep breath and *whips* her badgering badger back into its burrow. "You're right. Have you heard from Josh or his dad?"

"I have not, but—" He pulls her away to speak privately. "Honey, I can't be certain, but I think I saw missile strikes close to Benson's neighborhood. Look around you. I doubt there are many blocks as lucky as this one."

She does look. Aside from small concrete chunks in the street, his block is untouched. The other buildings in the neighborhood, the same ones she ran past not more than five minutes ago, are now hollowed-out shells or are completely flattened. Catching her breath, reflecting, the likelihood of how many dying people she ran past dawns on her. Guilt wells up. She was trained to run *to* the injured, not past them. Her emotions —so tired, so frayed—spike, pronouncing damnation for her selfishness. Wanting to atone for her sins, she scans the street for somebody to help.

Seeing the raging, internal war in her eyes, Eleazar climbs into the *storm-tossed boat* with her.

"Honey, you did what you had to do."

Listening only to her blustering mental-drill-sergeant's voice, she ignores her dad and starts heading back the way she came. He grabs her arm and spins her around. He grasps both her shoulders, locking her into place. Though shackled, she still looks over her shoulder and down the *graveyard* she just ran through.

He gently touches her cheek and turns her head toward him. "Ariella, contrary to what you think, you are not Wonder Woman. You can't save everybody. Your priority is your husband and father-in-law."

At the mention of her husband, she switches from warrior mode to wife mode. The guilt of bulldozing over his emotions by not listening to his insistence they leave pummels her.

Not wanting her dad to witness her emotional breakdown, she looks at the ground. He lifts her chin and focuses her attention on his eyes—his loving, comforting eyes. Her own eyes drown her cheeks.

"There will be time to weep, but not now. Pull yourself together, soldier. Go."

He releases her and steps back. She remains motionless, unsure what to do—she's so tired.

She allows a few more seconds of bathing in his gentle but firm eyes before squaring herself away and tapping into her depleting reservoir of spare strength.

"Please go inside and get your phone. I'll call you when I find something out."

At that, she's off with a flash.

***

Close to twenty minutes later—she's running out of steam—she arrives at Benson's apartment. When she sees the building's condition, her heart catches in her throat: it's a pile of rubble. Refusing to fall apart, she wrangles in her emotions and looks for her man and his dad. But the more she calls out their names with no reply, the more the reins slip through her fingers. Heartbroken and exhausted, she wearily sits on a chunk of concrete and buries her face into her hands. The lamenting of one who's lost everything pierces the somber night. After a solid two minutes of gasping and weeping, a hand touches her shoulder.

Without opening her eyes—didn't need to, she knew it was Josh...somehow—she grabs his hand, pulls him down onto the rubble next to her, and lays her head on his shoulder. She's too tired for clichéd squealing and relieved sloppy kisses.

Josh drapes his arm around her and pulls her in close. Black smoke billows throughout the city, virtually covering the moon and darkening the sky. But for the newlyweds, they are nearly unaffected. They dwell safely in their newly formed cocoon, separated from the atrocities going on all around them.

Benson ambles over to the couple and unapologetically embraces the third-wheel role. He rests his hand on Ariella's head; she squeezes it.

"Is your dad okay?" Benson asks before taking a seat on a nearby concrete chunk.

"He is. In fact, his whole block seems okay. He was outside, comforting. I yelled at him for not being inside his bunker."

"Of course he was." Benson smiles at the image of his lifelong friend doing his *thing*.

"I assume you two were in yours?"

"Yes...we were the only ones," Benson says, his voice tinged with gray sadness.

"I'm sorry, Benson."

"It's okay. Nothing can be done. I'm telling myself the rest of my apartment neighbors are safe somewhere else. No sense in dwelling on something I don't know for sure."

She remembers to call her dad. She lifts

her head from Josh's shoulder and retrieves her phone.

"I told my dad I'd call him when I had info, if the cell towers are still standing that is." She sees five bars lit up on her screen. "Five bars. I guess they are."

With adrenaline escaping, leaving her shaky, she wills her hand to settle down and select Dad's number from her "Favorites." With the call request sent out, she squishes the phone to her ear and waits for him to answer. He does.

"Dad, they're both okay. Are you still okay?"

"Honey, you've been gone for twenty minutes. Stop worrying about me. Let's talk later; Vincente is about to address the world. Give my best to the Mendelsburg men. I love you."

She hangs up and regards them. "He says, hi," she informs. "He also said Vincente's about to address the world. I'm assuming the bunker TV isn't working."

Benson shakes his head. "We can watch it on your phone."

Shaking her head in an *Oh yeah! Duh!* fashion, she scoots Josh down the concrete chunk, so there's room for Benson to sit next to her. She opens the BBC News app and sees they are gearing up for Vincente's address. The countdown timer at the bottom of the screen informs that he will go live in three minutes and thirty-six seconds. They huddle close and stare at the 5.5-inch screen.

***

Deep in contemplation, Vincente sits, allowing the makeup crew to make him "camera-ready." Not that much work is required: Vincente Basile was born with an extra helping of comeliness. As limited as the "finishing touches" may be, like an athlete before a big game, Vincente is grateful for the opportunity to get his mind right. He knows the next several minutes are vital for his plan to move forward with minimal hiccups. He must convey to the world that though everything may look *out* of control, he is very much *in* control.

His pregame self-psyching is terminated by bright lights blasting him. His eyes shut out the intrusion. The hot, bright lights are a nuisance but it's the price to pay. He loves world-addressing. It's his favorite part of the job. Staring into a camera and speaking into a microphone is now his jam. He may not see his reflection in the lens, but he knows it's there, looking as stunning as ever. He loves fantasizing about his silky-smooth voice perforating the microphone. It's the most euphonic sound he's ever heard.

*How lucky the world is to have me as their president,* he muses.

Knowing his fake-humility shtick is needed, he locks up his promiscuous pomposity. Not that he needs extravagant focus to pull this off. He's performed this jive so many times that he's polished it to a glossy sheen. He needs only to shovel a wheelbarrow full of trite tropes—*we will rise up* and *because of this adversity, we will be a stronger, more unified world*...blah blah blah—

onto a malnourished world, and they will lap it up like ravenous dogs. Their unrefined, peasant ears live for a good tickling, and his knuckles have all been cracked.

His aim tonight is to borrow heavily from the speech he gave The Ten. However, he'll only relay details of the incredible transformation the world will soon experience and leave the gritty details of the counterattack on the editing room floor. Telling the scared populace that the UK's submarines were in the Baltic Sea, focused exclusively on Russia's western half is obviously ludicrous. As would telling them that France's submarines were tasked with bombing Turkey, Syria, and Saudi Arabia.

Certainly, their anxious hearts don't need to know that part of China's subs were in the Sea of Okhotsk where they attacked Russia's eastern half. Or that the rest were in the Indian Ocean joining India's subs to attack the 'Stan countries and the Muslim-controlled African countries. Yes, telling them all this would be preposterous.

What his people need to hear is his unwavering commitment to minister to and care for the innocent survivors of Russia's unprovoked attack. He will also tell them his plan to extend mercy to those who survived the necessary retaliation and will lay out the details of what that will look like. He knows that once his people hear his grandiose plan, it will take no effort to convince them to get on board. The resiliency of the human spirit is a powerful force, one not to be taken lightly. However, the real challenge will be in how he manages their emotions. If not guided wisely, that spirit can morph into a raging beast, eviscerating everything in its path. It takes a special kind of person to channel that raw energy into a force for good. Spoiler alert: Vincente is that kind of special person.

This will segue into the second part of his address. He'll give them more than hope of things returning to normal. If that's all he could do, he'd be no better than those who came before him. No, what he has planned for those who follow him will be unlike anything they've ever seen. No other human has ever accomplished what he's about to do. The gates to the Promised Land are being greased and will swing wide to the obedient very soon. And once they enter, misery and discontent will disappear. In its place—unparalleled prosperity and unending satisfaction.

This is what he told The Ten, and this is what he'll be telling the world, in five seconds. The pre-interview busy bees have buzzed out of sight; now all that is seen in the camera viewfinder is Vincente sitting at his desk. The five-second countdown ticks away and once again, he speaks to the world...his world.

# CHAPTER NINETEEN

A s though peering through the bloodshot eyes of an insomniac whose channel surfed through the night, gruesome scenes in the eastern half of the northern hemisphere play for those celestial bodies daring to watch. They are different *channels* with one thing in common—every scene resembles famous Black Death paintings come to life.

Sadly, these scenes are not reenactments from the 1300s; they are current-day events, five months after Vincente's nuclear retaliation. The only discernible differences between the 700-year-old images and this reiteration of mass death are the fashion differences and the absence of foul, fowl-like men attempting to heal the hordes of living death lying atop one other like a grotesque game of Twister. Plague doctors are superfluous because no cure exists.

The scenes are brutal, and stomach-churning. Those who can watch and not hide to discreetly vomit need to do some soul-searching.

Who can watch a crying infant lying in the street being gnawed on by a pack of rats—so... many...rats—and not be affected? Would they be invited to a dinner party? Unlikely.

Or, could one witness raving lunatics cannibalize a still-breathing human being and not yearn to self-lobotomize? Certainly, nobody you'd want babysitting your kids.

Is there anybody who can watch a panicked, dying person hack off his limbs in an attempt to stave off further infection, and not book an all-inclusive stay at the neighborhood asylum? Probably not.

Try as they might, even the most committed Pollyannas cannot sweep these scenes under the cosmic rug because this is what's happening in the nuked regions. Increasing instances of starvation, radiation poisoning, plague, and murder—along with a perverse grab bag of other calamities too abhorrent to name—stretch across the lands like ripples in a lake.

The body count is so extreme that it's past the point of effective management. Bulldozers are used to pile up corpses in out-of-the-way corners like snow in a mall parking lot. The stench, the maggots, the flies, and the roving packs of dogs hoping to snag a leg or two before they go bad are of such unspeakableness, it's cumbersome to describe. This plague of starvation, disease, and death is wiping out millions wholesale with little hope of stopping it.

Unsurprisingly, it didn't take long before those lands became uninhabitable. Up to this point, the world never experienced the long-prophesied nuclear holocaust. Humanity has only ever hypothesized the outcome. Those wallowing in the atrocities attest that all prognostications fell woefully short. Hell has opened and is swallowing everything whole.

Vincente knew this would happen, which is why he presented their escape plan in his world address five months ago. He instructed the survivors to come to either Iraq, Israel, or Rome. There they would find a revolutionary, universal system waiting for them at the door. But they had to enter with hat in hand. If they did, their hats would be filled with food, shelter, and medical help. If they did not...if they came with distrust and skepticism, refusing to get in step with what Vincente was doing, the door became a revolving one...

*\*\**

A door opens, giving Benson Mendel access to one of Vincente's numerous meeting rooms in one of his numerous mansions. Standing next to the door-opening servant, Benson's struck by the enormous half-shaded window consuming much of the wall directly in front of him. It frames Vincente's palatial gardens as though a living Georges Seurat painting hung on his wall. Two large armchairs face each other, with the giant window running parallel to them. Breathing deeply, Benson enters.

He's barely broken the threshold before the servant briskly closes the door, leaving Benson to stand awkwardly alone. Unsure what to do, he scans the vast empty room. The menial's reaction does not surprise Benson. He's certain that should he interview Vincente's staff, he'd find they're all on edge. He, too, falls into the "on edge" assembly. To say he's not thrilled with being here is a gross understatement. Every fiber of his being wishes he told Eleazar to beat feet down the street. But, like a nitwit, he fell prey to his impassioned insistence that he at least hears what the world president has to offer. He's staying with the high priest because he no longer has a home, so it's hard to tune him out. Hoping to shut up his well-meaning friend, he agreed to take the flight from Israel to Iraq on one of Vincente's private jets.

Standing before this man, the most wicked to ever live (should his interpretation of Revelation prove true), is not exactly where he'd like to be. Despite Eleazar's haranguing, his frayed emotions are the scoundrels responsible for befouling his better judgment. It was, after all, three days ago that the sky fell, killing untold millions. The previously described outcome of nuclear fallout hasn't happened yet, but Benson knows the heinousness is coming. He's seen the documentaries on Hiroshima and Nagasaki.

As adept at rolling with the punches as the human mind is, fear has a way of unbalancing even the most stalwart of mettle...of forcing one down a darkened path they'd never take in the normal light of day. But it's too late: he's here now. He's walked too far to retreat, so he presses on, willing to be buffeted for his countrymen. Israel was also nearly destroyed, so if he can stave off extermination then he must do it, even if it means sleeping with the enemy. He hopes his foolish delusions of grandeur don't cost him his soul.

"Did Leon abandon you?" a voice assaults the silence. Benson turns towards the source and sees Vincente entering from a separate door. "Well, you know, good help and all that. Might be time to train a monkey to replace him. Maybe then I'll finally get a decent Daiquiri."

Benson watches the sovereign ruler sashay over to a serving table set up against a wall. It holds a coffee carafe, along with a gang of exquisite decanters, all brimming and ready to rumble. Vincente clearly has a penchant for the strong stuff; no wussified booze will do.

"Until then, I'm left to my own devices I suppose," Vincente says, heaving a melodramatic, fake sigh as he gestures to the left armchair. "Sit. Please. Thank you for coming in. Eleazar speaks highly of your expertise and assures me it's second to none. He says your command of coding is interchangeable with your command of the English language. High praise from the high priest I should say."

"That's very kind of him, but I'm nothing special," Benson swears as he sits in the indicated armchair. "There are thousands of programmers just as good."

"That may be true, but none of them sit in front of the world president," Vincente promises. He palms the carafe, discovering it to be warm. "Nor will they be imbibing impeccable coffee. Thankfully, Leon can still do the one thing he's good at. Care to have your coffee Irished up?" Vincente inquires as he displays a bottle of his finest rum.

"No thank you. Unleaded coffee will do," Benson jokes, hoping to soften his discourteous rebuff.

"Oh, that's right. Eleazar did mention you were a Born Again. But you're a Jew. What must your parents think?"

"They've been dead for many years," Benson remarks, hip to Vincente's not-so-subtle disdainfulness.

"Just as well, I'm sure they'd disapprove of your decision." Vincente hands Benson his coffee before settling into the armchair on the right. "But I digress. You didn't come here to talk religion; you came here to help me save the world. Did Eleazar explain what I need from you?"

"Not in great detail." Benson sips his coffee in hopes of hiding his irritation. His continuing forward on this foolhardy path already wears on him. "Something about writing code."

"Precisely. I'm sure you're familiar with the success of Greece's RFID Chip technology."

"Yes. Brought the country back from the brink and fundamentally changed their society."

"Yes, it did, and that's what I'm going to do on a global scale."

"Which part?" Benson asks, growing apprehensive. He doesn't like where this conversation is headed.

"All of it. More."

"Mr. World President, those Chips were implanted...in human beings."

Vincente leans forward and shoots a

scornful look at Benson. "You're not one of *those* are you?"

"One of those *what*?" Benson's ire continues to rise.

"One of those conspiracy theory fruitcakes. I read the forums; I see the threads. I know what people are saying about me. But please, trust me, I am *not* the antichrist. I'm just a guy trying to save the world. Nothing more."

The mercury in Benson's thermometer dips. Maybe his imagination *is* running away with itself.

"Let me explain my plan, and then you can decide if you want to be a part of something extraordinary. Deal?"

Benson nods. "Okay."

"Good. Thank you." Vincente takes a healthy chug of his cooling coffee/rum mix and begins his presentation. "A business has different departments all committed to making the business successful. It has production, HR, marketing, product research, accounting, sales... you get the point. The world has endured a hard reboot; wouldn't you agree?"

Benson's nod communicates *that's a 10-4 good buddy.*

"Well then, it's time to start over by reformatting society's hard drive—"

*Is he patronizing me or relating to me with computer jargon?* Benson reflects. *Does he think I wouldn't understand his plan otherwise?*

Vincente continues:

"—turning the entire world into one large

syndicate made up of all the remaining countries. All cash flow generated from each country's myriad of businesses will be funneled back into the parent company, i.e., the world, and I will be its administrator."

"I'm sorry; did I hear you right? You want to turn the world into a business conglomerate? And you're going to run it?"

"Yes, on both accounts."

"But that would be a conflict of interest. How can you be world president and world CEO?"

Seeing Benson's consternated look Vincente changes tactics.

"Know what else I read in those forums, at least between the lines? The world is begging for somebody to unite them; to assure them all will be well; to provide a stable economy for their children and their children's children."

"And you believe you're the right man for the job?"

"I don't see anybody else answering the want ad."

Benson doesn't know what to say, so he says nothing. Vincente, never at a loss for words, leaps into the silence and scatters it.

"It's okay Benson, you don't have to understand it all, just trust that I do. My business will be separate from my government."

"Okay," Benson pledges unconvincingly. "So, what are you asking of me?"

"To help me create a monetary-free society."

"With RFID chips, correct?"

"Yes. Brick-and-mortar banks will be a thing of the past because every individual will be their own bank. But the chips will do more than abolish banks, they will also erase traditional IDs. A new identity will be given to every individual. This identity will be linked to every facet of the person's life and stored within the chip's code. No more driver's licenses. And speaking of driving, there won't be a need for car keys or any key for that matter. Everything in a person's day-to-day life that once required a key will now be programmed into their R-Chip."

"And I will be the one writing the code for all this?"

"Exactly." Vincente falls quiet for a handful of tick-tocks, pondering over a difficulty. "But for all the good, I'm struggling with one detail. Not because it's a bad idea, but because it grates against my philosophy."

Benson is intrigued. Self-doubt rising in this cock-sure man is a new development.

"My natural inclination leans toward capitalism. I strongly believe that a free market and minimal government intrusion are key to creating and sustaining a healthy society. We have decades of evidence confirming Socialism destroys society not improves it. However, with life evolving into a monetary-free existence, it's time to rethink how this new world should function so all may reach their full potential. I have a solution that will both fire up the anemic economy and allow my capitalistic sensibilities to sleep at night."

"Which is?" Benson presses.

"I call it communism-lite, as in, there will no longer be a traditional private sector, but the government won't be controlling things either. The world business conglomerate, as you put it, will be the one controlling all the businesses and making all the decisions. Do you want to hear more, or would you just rather hear what your role is?"

Along with his master's degree in software architecture, Benson also has a BA in business, so he understands the guts of business.

"I'll hear more."

"Excellent! But I'll only give a synopsis. Regardless of a person's background, everybody will be given a job, but it'll be based on their G.A.T score. Do I need to explain the G.A.T?"

"General Aptitude Test? No, you do not."

"Very good. From that score, a list of jobs will be generated for the individual to pick from. Because I want everybody to start on a level playing field, no matter what job they pick, everybody will have the same base salary. But this is where my communism-lite plan kicks in. There will be an incentive program at every company in every department. It'll be based on annual goals determined by the managers of those departments. Everyone who meets those goals will receive a bonus. This plan accomplishes two things: it allows the go-getters to apply themselves and earn more, while at the same time addressing the long-ballyhooed Income Inequality diatribe of the Old World. Everyone will be forced to take accountability for their effort or lack thereof. If their neighbor has nicer things than they do, they have nobody to blame but themselves. Yes, I'll provide every working individual with a car and a furnished house. But Bill driving his new luxury car to work because he had a lucrative year in bonuses may inspire Jim to strive for those bonuses next year. I'm providing an opportunity to earn more money and the mental blessings that come from achieving a desired goal through hard work. Personal self-worth is a vital component of the human experience. The Old World ignored that fact."

"That's not bad," Benson genuinely remarks as he reflects on the many dead-end jobs he's had throughout his life. "But what about supervisors and execs? Why would anybody wanna be brass if they make the same as everybody else?"

"Good question, to which I have an answer. To help curb feelings of exploitation, the goals get progressively more lucrative the higher up the ladder. But here's the other caveat to all this. There are only two ways to move up—one is to achieve a predetermined score on the G.A.T. From here the individual can take another test related to the specific higher position they are pursuing. If they achieve the required score on that test and desire to keep trying for an even higher position, they can take another test for the next tier, and so forth. Get the point?"

"I do. What's the second option?"

"Wait for the position to open through death or demotion. From there it will be like what

I just explained, only they'll be competing with the other hats thrown in the ring. The job will eventually go to the individual with the highest test score."

"What if people get the same score? Then what?"

"I'm still working out those details. Maybe they'll battle in the Thunderdome," Vincente says with sarcastic levity.

"I assume you're kidding."

Vincente doesn't answer, only smirks, and changes the subject. "There's one final detail and it'll sound harsh at first, but if you open your mind, I believe you'll see the wisdom in it."

"Go ahead," Benson says, his disquietude at an all-time high. His sixth sense has been rapping its icy knuckles on the back door of his mind ever since he entered this infernal room. He can no longer tune out the booming clatter. Something wicked this way comes...

"Yes, everybody is welcome to the benefits of my plan, but there are stipulations. Everything begins with the R-Chip. Without it, nobody will qualify. They won't even be able to buy food."

And with that, Benson's sixth sense kicks down the door and rushes in like a SEAL team breaching an insurgents' nest. Did Benson just hear Vincente bring Revelation 13 to life? Is Vincente introducing the long-prophesied "Mark of the Beast?" Benson cannot deny what he's heard. And because of this, there is no longer any doubt—Vincente truly is THE Antichrist.

Annoyed for not heeding his suspicions, he

searches for an escape. He knew coming here was a mistake. He knew this man could not be trusted. So why did he willingly walk right into his den?

Failing to hide his distress, Vincente sees the "look" flounce across Benson's troubled face. Ever the confident conniver, Vincente beckons Mr. Charisma to the stage like a perfectly coiffed televangelist beseeching the faithful for seed money. It's time for him to take over—both mentally and spiritually. But for it to work, he needs Benson off balance...

"Did your son tell you we met?" Vincente asks, setting the trap.

"He did. You were both staying in the same hotel."

"Exactly. I stumbled upon him in the restaurant. He was bellied up to the bar."

Benson's neurons misfire like jamming a moving car into reverse. *Why did Josh keep that detail from me?* Benson wonders.

"Was he drinking anything?" Benson asks.

Vincente notices the apprehension in Benson's voice—he's scared for his son, and this is exactly where Vincente wants him. He recalls Josh's confession to alcohol problems in the past, and like any good recovering alcoholic, step nine would be accomplished by now.

"A White Russian, I believe. Why, is this a problem?"

Benson says nothing because his mind is spiraling. He remembers the conversation he had with Josh before the ceremony. He was nervous and overwhelmed. Maybe the pressure was too much for him and he needed to get by with a little help from his old friend. Further unsettling Benson, he recalls a detail from Josh's story. He remembers Josh musing over why he was so bold. Well, mystery solved. Alcohol is the best "courage elixir" around.

Leaving Benson to stare out the partly shaded large window, Vincente beelines back to his bounty of booze. After filling a highballer with top shelf whisky, he activates an app on his phone. As the window's motorized shade ascends, Vincente's cresting, evil smile synchronizes with it. The sudden blazing Iraqi sun temporarily blinds Benson. With Benson's optics glitching, Vincente attacks the auditory next. A few more phone thumb-swipes later and barely audible music seeps into the room. It's soothing music, subliminal in nature.

"Your son is an extraordinary man," Vincente affirms as he returns to his chair. He'll continue his menticide from a place of coziness: for him, that is, not Benson. Benson is unaware that hooks are now embedded into his brain, pulling him in for the kill.

"He is," Benson confirms. "His mother would be proud of how he turned out." His son's disappointing *wagon-falling* lodges the unwarranted boast in his throat.

"Would be?" Vincente questions.

"She died over twenty years ago," Benson answers.

"I'm sorry. Was she sick?"

"No, she was hungry," Benson remarks caustically. "For much of the nineties, we were in the States. Eventually, America's ignorance drove us back to Israel. We'd been home for less than a month when Leah, my wife, took her life-long friend out for a slice of pizza."

Genuinely caught off guard by the direction of this story, Vincente has an *aha!* moment. "Your wife died in the Sbarro Massacre?"

"Yes, and so did Eliana Segal."

"As in…"

"Eleazar's wife."

"Eleazar never told me how his wife died," Vincente responds. "Then again, I never asked. So Josh and Ariella have known each other for a long time?"

"Since they were in diapers. The moms would be tickled to see their kids finally married. Concocting ways to get them together was their unapologetic mission in life."

Fascinated by this story, almost to the point of losing his grip on the *hooks*, Vincente resorts to the oldest trick in the hypnotist's playbook—shiny things.

Remembering his newly acquired ring from his morning *encounter*—another tribute from another tryst; they do love to show their appreciation for the pleasure of his company—he slides his right hand into his pocket and slips it on.

"Angelica, my wife, was murdered as well. I wear her ring in her honor."

Making a fist, he holds out his right hand to

show off the elegant, diamond-encrusted band.

"It's on your right hand," Benson points out.

"In my country, when a spouse dies, the living spouse wears the deceased spouse's wedding band on their right hand as a sign of mourning. It remains there until the grave, or when a new spouse replaces it with their own."

Vincente's masterful flimflam-flinging impresses even himself. It's total poppycock, of course, but he's hedging his bets on Benson knowing nothing about Italian culture.

"It's very beautiful," Benson remarks, unable to take his eyes off the breathtaking ring.

With his hand on his armrest, Vincente rotates the ring with his right thumb and prattles on. The sunlight pouring in from the massive window reflects off the spinning diamond ring, creating a swirling explosion of colors and sparkles.

Benson sees nothing and hears nothing. The flashing prismatic colors ensnare him, stealing all his mental facilities. He's like a trout mesmerized by a spinning, shiny lure. He feels strange, otherworldly. It's like he's being pulled out of himself, floating away on the wings of an out-of-body experience.

What's happened is he's been hypnotized. The words coming from Vincente are messages being planted in Benson's mind. To further flesh out the *hook* and *shiny lure* analogy, Benson is now caught and flopping on the banks of a quiet country stream. Vincente has total control.

"What do you say?" Vincente's words

descend into Benson's clouded mind.

"I'm sorry?"

Vincente approaches Benson and jerks his shoulder forcefully to arrest his attention. Benson, as though waking from an intense dream, blinks rapidly, struggling to come back from wherever he was. He looks up at Vincente who stares down at him waiting for an answer.

Suddenly, all reasoning for not helping this man flickers out of existence. So, when Vincente asks—

"Benson Mendel, will you help me help the world?"

—there is no hesitation.

"Mr. World President, count me in."

***

"There's no way this is the correct address," Josh says out loud. He's talking to Ariella on the car speaker. "I must have punched it in wrong, or the GPS is confused." He stares accusingly at the dashboard screen insisting that he's arrived at his destination.

"Where are you?" Ariella probes.

"In the Katamon neighborhood. I think I'm close to where your dad lives."

"That's a nice neighborhood."

"I can tell. I'm parked in front of a gorgeous apartment building," Josh says.

Just then, Josh hears his name being called out. Buzzing down the driver-side window, Josh searches for the yeller. His eyes catch movement from a third-story balcony—it's his dad waving wildly at him.

"I guess I'm at the right place. I see my dad waving at me."

"Love you. Let me know how it goes," Ariella requests.

"I will. Love you too." Josh disconnects and exits his car.

"Go to that side door," Benson yells as he points. "I'll buzz you in. Come up to the third floor. I'll meet you in the hallway."

Josh, feeling like he's sleepwalking, obeys. His dad called a little over an hour ago, telling him he has incredible news and that he needed to come to this address right away. The excitement in his voice was both intoxicating and disconcerting. He sounded hyper like he'd just guzzled three 5-hour Energy shots in rapid-fire succession.

Still a few yards from the door, Josh hears the buzzing electronic lock, signaling that the door is unlocked. Whatever his dad wants to tell him, he dares not waste a second.

An elevator door slides open. Josh exits into the third-floor hallway and is immediately accosted by his dad calling to him.

"Over here!"

Josh turns toward the excitable clamoring and sees his dad standing in front of an open apartment door, waving to him.

"Let's go! Get in here! I've got so much to tell you!"

Josh scrunches his face as he heads to his dad. His squirreliness is unsettling. While still in the hallway, Benson begins his story.

"You'll never guess where I've been!"

"Touring a laughing gas plant?" Josh jokes, trying to make sense of his dad's bizarre mania.

"Good one!" Benson praises as he closes the door behind Josh. "Come. Sit. Make yourself at home. I'll make us some coffee."

"Better make yours decaf, Dad."

"Another good one! Believe it or not, I've only had one cup today," Benson assures as he disappears into the updated kitchen.

Realizing his dad's hyperactivity can't be blamed on too much caffeine intensifies Josh's angst. He examines the elegant, furnished apartment, laboring to understand why his dad's here. He has a decent understanding of what Katamon apartments cost...his dad ain't got that kinda scratch.

Josh spots picture frames amongst various knickknacks and curios displayed on a shelf. He walks over to inspect. Grabbing one of the frames, he stares into it—the people's identities are a mystery.

"Dad, I don't understand what's going on. Who is this?"

Benson returns with two coffee mugs. He sees Josh displaying the picture frame. "Previous owners. The superintendent just gave me the keys a couple hours ago. Haven't had time to get rid of their stuff."

"That's not helping me. Where are these people?"

"Sadly, they died in the attack. Sit. I'll

explain everything."

"That would be nice," Josh says, taking the outstretched mug and sitting. "Because, no disrespect, you're acting like a fruitcake."

"I know. I'm sorry about that. Not feeling like myself. I'm having a hard time calming down. A lot's happened this morning."

"Why don't you start from the beginning," Josh suggests.

"Okay. For the past three days, Uncle Ele's been browbeating me to interview for an important job. This morning, I succumbed."

"Why? I thought you enjoyed retirement."

"I do, but this was a once-in-a-lifetime opportunity."

"To do what? Come on, Dad. Out with it."

Benson isn't quick to answer. He knows how ridiculous what he's about to say sounds.

"Help save the world." It's the first thing he's said quietly, almost reverently.

Josh raises a confused eyebrow. "Whaaattt...?"

Again, Benson is slow to answer. He takes a deep breath before letting the cat out of the bag.

"Vincente hired me to save the world."

The freed, agitated *cat* lands in Josh's lap and *shreds* him to pieces. There's no way he heard his dad correctly.

"I know what you're thinking but let me explain," Benson says, seeing the tumult in his son's eyes

"What's to explain?!" Josh yells, anger and disappointment sullying his voice. He can't help it. He's just heard that his father, the person he admires most in the world, sold his soul.

"Now hold on," Benson demands, catching his son's disrespect. "I'm still your father."

"Yes, you are. You're the same father who told me that redeemed people have no business aligning themselves with him."

"Yes, I did, but this is different."

"How?"

"Because he explained everything to me, and I agree with his vision completely."

Josh stands to pace the room. He does so love to pace when the atmosphere gets heavy…

"Son, I think I've earned the right for you to hear me out."

"Fine, Dad. I'm listening."

Seeing he does have Josh's attention despite the mindless pacing, Benson begins.

"You cannot deny the success Vincente's had. He's finally brought peace to the world and now he's going to cure society's ills. Son, he has the perfect plan to eradicate hunger, poverty, and homelessness. I don't want to bog you down with the details, so I'll just tell you my part in it. I'll be writing the code for the new radio frequency chips that'll be implanted into those who accept Vincente's plan. I received one of those chips this morning."

Benson shows the Band-Aid on the back of his hand. Josh's eyes widen.

"This is why I'm in this gorgeous apartment. And this is why I'll be making more money than I ever dared imagine."

"What about those who don't accept Vincente's plan?" Josh demands.

Benson is taken aback. If he did consider this possibility, it wasn't for long.

Josh marches over and forcefully grabs his dad's hand. "Dad, you sold your soul for a bag of magic beans!"

Offended, Benson rips his hand away. Josh continues his assault.

"You took the Mark. You aligned yourself with the Antichrist. You turned your back on the real Christ. You turned your back on me."

At the mention of "Christ" something explodes in Benson's subconscious. A faint light sparkles in his once muted eyes as though scales had fallen off. He's disoriented and nauseous. Not liking the accusing thoughts in his head, Benson attacks his son like a drug addict at an intervention.

"Who are you to preach at me? I know you were drinking with Vincente."

"What?!"

"He said you were drinking a White Russian."

"It was milk! You can ask the bartender if you don't believe me. Vincente knew it was milk. He lied, just as he's lying to you now!"

Hating the way he's talking to his son, but unable to stop the runaway train, Benson continues the assault.

"What am I supposed to do? Sit idly by and watch people die?"

"Dad, you signed up to be the executioner of

thousands."

"What are you talking about?"

"You know what happens to those who refuse the Antichrist's Mark."

This reality again smacks Benson in the face. But rather than deal with it, he walks over to his new front door and opens it. He looks pointedly at Josh.

"That's not my problem," he says, unwittingly taking an iron to his conscious and searing it. "Look at your own life and see what you're doing with it before you tell me how to live mine."

The stab to Josh's heart brings tears to his eyes like fresh blood from a knife wound.

"Dad. Please. Don't do this," Josh's cracking voice pleads.

Benson says nothing as he stands resolutely at his open door. Josh recognizes the hopeless situation, so he places his coffee mug on the kitchen counter next to Benson's phone. Just then, it dings, announcing that Vincente sent a text. Seeing Vincente's name appear on the screen ignites a blazing fire deep in Josh's stomach. No longer is he sad for his dad; now, he's just mad. He marches to the open door, wiping his eyes.

"Your master's whistling for you," Josh hisses as he enters the hallway. He never looks back.

Benson closes the door and retrieves his phone. He opens Vincente's text. It reads—

*I trust you're settling into your new digs. A service will pick you up tomorrow morning at 6.*

*Many long hours lie ahead but it'll be worth it. This is your purpose in life. The world is depending on you. I'm depending on you. Don't let us down.*

Benson reflects on the strange text. It was wordy, but they were all carefully chosen. The veiled threat was not lost on Benson. He's never felt more trapped in his entire life...

# CHAPTER TWENTY

I t's been a little more than two years since World President Vincente Basile gifted his children with the "pie in the sky" they long hungered for. In that time not only did he bring Herbert Hoover's promise of "a chicken in every pot" to fruition, but he did Herbie one better: all those pots were solid gold, figuratively, of course. The sudden wealth thrust upon every still functioning corner of the world was staggering. But before Vincente blessed the world, he set to rebuilding Jerusalem first.

It was determined that nearly one hundred missiles found their mark, toppling an unprecedented number of Jerusalem's buildings like a sadistic game of Jenga. Whole neighborhoods were wiped out. One hundred and fifty thousand plus people were blinked out of existence. Over a quarter of the Old City was fundamentally altered. Jerusalem hasn't looked this bad since the Babylonians stopped by for a visit back in the 500s B.C. Thankfully, this time the temple was still standing.

Seeing the golden opportunity to restructure (as anyone who lives there will tell you—real estate is a hot commodity), Vincente wasted no time in bringing Suburbia to the City of David. Since a third of the work was already accomplished—leveling the previous buildings— it was just a matter of hauling away the rubble and breaking ground.

To help expedite the process, Vincente brought in construction companies from all over the world. Like Post-WW1 America, in no time several brand-new, single-family home neighborhoods were constructed. For the sake of fairness, a housing lottery to get one of these new homes was enacted. There were outcries at the molesting of culture and history in the beginning, but when people realized they could have their own driveway and fenced-in backyard, much of the whining ended and the signing up for a chance at Suburbia began. Being able to live and breathe without being on top of each other was a fantasy hipster Jerusalemites refused to admit to lest they lose their "too cool for school" card.

Jerusalem was reborn, and so was the rest of the remaining world. But it was more than just the wealth, prosperity, and sudden shift in the quality of life that thrilled Vincente's children —though you'll never hear the kiddos complain about having a reliable car, a nice house, and a full bank account. It was the unending peace (the kind they dared not hope for, lest they have sorrow upon sorrow) that made their hearts sing the loudest.

Many of the people subsisting under Vincente's sovereign but gracious rule lived their former lives uncertain if they'd make it the three blocks to the market without getting blown up, or injured in crossfire. To be sure, a new Lexus was swell: but falling asleep to the melodic sounds of chirping crickets instead of the nearby rat-a-tat-tat of machine gun fire...ahhhh, this indeed was bliss.

However, all is not perfect for all; some are barely surviving. During Vincente's world address two years ago, an unexpected dichotomy birthed into existence. There were multiple others having a hard time ignoring what they were witnessing. At the conclusion of his world address, these *others* now knew what they were looking at. While most saw "The Good Life" shining brightly; the *others* saw "The Great Lie" snickering in the shadows.

Like the Mendels, these *others* had stumbled onto similar Bible-related websites written in the Old World. They could no longer deny that the Born Again, Jesus Freaks of the Old World were right. Driven to understand more clearly, they poured themselves into all things *Jesus*, to see if He is who He says He is. Eventually, many eyes were opened to the truth they'd always mocked.

Now believers and followers of Jesus Christ, they knew their allegiances needed to change. They understood that getting Vincente's R-Chip was off the table. He made it clear in his address: if you wanted his blessings, you had to follow his rules. This clearly didn't line up with what the God of the Bible says— "You shall have no other gods before Me..."

Unfortunately, these new converts discovered quickly what it meant to follow Jesus.

Because they refused the R-Chip, they were not only instantly impoverished but also the dregs of society. They were shunned and ousted by all those who accepted Vincente as their savior.

Struggling to accept their new station in life (some of these new believers were the movers and shakers of the Old World), Jesus' 2,000-year-old words became their rallying cry—

"In the world you will have tribulation. But take heart; I have overcome the world…"

Because prejudices are deeply engrained in fallen humanity, Vincente's faithful introduced two monikers into the New World's lexicon. They adopted the title, VP (Vincente's People) for themselves and named the fools who rejected Vincente, Anathemas—someone detested and accursed, deserving of excommunication and damnation. Apparently, *mean girls* are still alive and well.

There were many VPs who's lust for punishment wasn't satisfied with childish name calling. They wanted to kill, maim, and destroy all the vile wretches who didn't love Vincente and his world system as they did. Some things never change…

Uncontrolled violence broke out for a few days, creating many dead Anathemas before Vincente stopped it. However, he didn't curb the violence because he was a nice guy (he too wanted to join the throng and kill 'em all) but because his messenger told him to.

The day after his pivotal world address, Vincente's messenger informed him of a new coming war. But unlike the violent aggression against the Muslim world, for now, this war would be handled with patient passivity. The full-blown assault would come later.

***

The slow jogging hands of history's clock, ever in perpetual motion, always come back around to repeat itself. Because of Vincente's animus for the Anathemas, the treatment of these poor people is reminiscent of the Jews experiencing the psychological tactics of isolation and dehumanization during World War II.

His messenger's insistence on patience irked him at first but now a new mindset comforts him—toying with them like a cat with a mouse. Because the Anathemas believed the R-Chip was the asinine Mark of the Beast, he mandated they get a distinguishing mark burned into their hands. It was delicious irony; his cruel heart loved it.

The Mark he chose for these nitwits—an infinity sign—was purposeful. However, it was not the traditional-looking infinity sign; this one came with a specific message. The infinity sign was formed with a looped snake swallowing its own tail. It was to remind them that they are their own worst enemy, that it was their choice that brought on this curse, and that the consequences would never end, unless...

Oh, how he wished there was no exception clause. If he couldn't kill them outright, then watching them all die off was the next best thing. But there were some VPs not copasetic with his coldhearted ways. They didn't want the Anathemas suffering endlessly just because they made some bad choices. Like the ideals of the Old World, these VPs maintained their love of rehabilitation, for corporal punishment rather than capital punishment.

For a time, Vincente had no intention of altering his policy, but his messenger changed his thinking. Yes, Anathemas deserved no mercy, but by extending it, he'd not only be more favored by these bothersome VPs, but he'd also gain more followers by giving the Anathemas a redo.

Vincente instituted a "cooling-off period" for the Anathemas. If an Anathema saw the folly in their decision and wanted in on Vincente's kingdom, he'd allow it. But it came with a hefty price—50 percent less than what all the other VPs get.

Once the worldwide praise rolled in for his magnanimity, his ego pushed him to offer more graciousness: if after five years they still toed the line, they'd receive full benefits. That pushed him into the realm of deification, which is where his messenger wants him—all eyes on Vincente, none on his messenger's adversary.

Despite the exhaustless adoration, the World President was unsatisfied. The browbeating he took from the sanctimonious VPs didn't sit well. He knew he could only live with himself if he had the final word, or in this case, the final FOUR words.

The NHFA Law (No Help For Anathemas) was passed, making it illegal for VPs to lend aid to the Anathemas. Breaking it came with a stiff and unconditional punishment—the offending VP immediately became an Anathema. Threaten one's cushy life and, typically, ideals are quickly abandoned. Yes, that did it. Vincente could now look himself in the mirror. Supremacy was restored, at least with the VPs anyway: with the Anathemas…not so much.

Despite Vincente's clemency, not many Anathemas recanted. Most remained true to their decision; to remain faithful to their God. But for all their nobility, it did nothing to help them survive. The problem was obvious —they had little to no common sense about surviving in less-than-ideal conditions. They had zero street smarts and were clueless about scavenging the wastelands. If the wild animals and the lawless marauders who controlled the wastelands—those who refused Vincente's R-Chip for anarchist reasons, not religious ones— didn't kill them, then the desert finished them off. If the Anathemas were to survive and thrive in their role during this monumental time in history, then they needed their own leader. They needed their own hero. They needed their own savior…

# CHAPTER TWENTY-ONE

"**G**ood morning," Josh announces softly as he enters his and Ariella's bedroom, their inner sanctum.

All expressions of their love have played out in this room: emotionally, physically, and spiritually. It is their place of solitude, their place of safety. It was here, on an emotional night two-plus years ago when their lives were altered. They were talking through their options now that life was a sticky wicket for those refusing Vincente's new system.

Murder is still a capital offense in the New World. As it was in the Old, investigations are thorough and the punishment harsh...if the victim was a VP. But if an Anathema ended up in a dumpster with several new *body piercings*, or endured an agonizing death at the bottom of a cliff, or experienced a myriad of other sadistic forms of murder...eh, whataya gonna do? It's like this all over the world; for Jerusalem Anathemas, it's especially bad.

Some felt they'd fare better in the desert outside of Jerusalem's walls (they didn't), but most thought it wiser to stay INSIDE Jerusalem and hope for the best. If their home still stood Vincente allowed them to stay there. But since utilities are linked to the R-Chip they have no gas, water, or electricity. Once the shock of being *homeless* people with homes wore off, they settled in and went about persevering. Having shelter was only part of subsisting; they also needed sustenance which came mostly from dumpster diving and curb shopping.

The Old World was accustomed to the scrappers and garbage pickers that invaded their tree lawns every trash day. So, watching the Anathemas root through their trash cans wasn't a head-scratcher for the VPs. As long as the guttersnipes didn't leave a mess after they slinked onto the next house, the VPs shrugged their shoulders, rolled their eyes, and allowed the front curtains to swing closed once again.

For Josh and Ariella, this bothered them greatly. Technically, they too were Anathemas, but because their fathers play a significant role in Vincente's wicked world, he made an ill-advised exception for them. He gave them one of the new suburbia houses, a small food allowance— barely enough for the two of them, certainly not thousands—and their utilities worked. They even had cellphones and a pre-R-Chipped car that still used a standard key. Ariella saw this as no small thing.

"Clearly, God made us bulletproof for a reason," she stated on that aforementioned night. "We need to take advantage of it."

It was an excellent point with no further insight. It was just her train of thought click-clacking down the rails of her mind. Agreeing wholeheartedly, Josh hopped onto his wife's *train* and settled *down* next to her. They were given an inexplicable godsend, but where was God sending them? They lay in bed and held each other into the wee hours of the night as they prayed for revelation. But heaven was silent.

Exhausted by their fruitlessness, they decided to turn off their brains and doze off. A wise decision. Their answer lay dormant and could only be awoken when Josh fell asleep. In his sleep, he was treated to a dream more spectacular than all his previous dreams.

Ever since the Rapture, Josh has had several dreams come true. At first, this phenomenon was disconcerting, an unwelcome passenger accompanying him on his descent into madness. But when he became a Born Again and the rockiness of his life smoothed out, the dreams were no longer unsettling. They became a kind of heavenly talisman, a reminder that Someone far greater than himself was in control. And on that unique night, he was reminded of this reality once again. But this was only possible because God prepared Josh beforehand.

\*\*\*

His father's scathing *what are you doing with your life?* remark compelled Josh to spend the next few days searching for an answer to that fair question. He may be furious with his father's betrayal, but his rebuke hit hard nonetheless. His dad was right. He was doing nothing, good or bad, aside from growing moss on the sidelines. Eventually, through prayer and contemplation, he was led to the only dependable source of spiritual information to solve the riddle—the Bible.

*But where to start?* Josh mused. *The Bible is nearly two thousand pages long and time is short! We need answers yesterday, not six months from now.*

Choosing the most obvious conclusion, he read Revelation.

*Since we're living in the end of scripture,* Josh reasoned, *makes sense to start there.*

He read through it once shortly after his conversion. However, he didn't understand a word of it. Maybe this time would be different. He was wrong. Still had no answers. Discouragement set in. His mental enemies cued up their old chants—*Woe is Me; I'm a loser; I'm a failure; People are dying because I'm a waste of space...*

But God, who has uniquely gifted wives in this way, eventually used Ariella to rescue Josh from his shortcomings. God-approved, ordained marriage is powerful, and not to be trifled with. Woe to those who mistreat it...

On the morning before Josh's epiphanous dream, struggling with his thoughts, he brooded alone on the back patio. Ariella, buzzing through the house, enjoying domesticated life, joyfully sang as she tidied. Josh could hear her excellent singing voice through the screen door. She sang the same song over and over. It was a song she loved as a little girl. The words burrowed into Josh's mind and silenced his destructive imps.

"Start at the very beginning; a very good place to start!" Ariella impressively parroted Julie Andrews' famous song.

Laughing at the moment's preposterousness (especially since he's always hated that song), Josh entered the house, kissed Ariella passionately and appreciatively, grabbed his Bible, and returned to the patio. Opening to page one, he read out loud:

"'In the beginning, God created the heavens and the earth.'"

He spent the next few hours reading through Genesis. By the time he arrived at the book's extraordinary conclusion,—which is centered around a Jew named Joseph who was given the overwhelming task of saving thousands of his starving countrymen—he was ready for the forthcoming dream that would change everything.

***

In the dream, Josh stood in a long line up a hill, ending at a large silo. In the sun, holding a weaved basket and wearing a head covering, a cloth skirt, and sandals—as was everybody else—he had a hunch he was not in the 21$^{st}$ century anymore. He wasn't sure if he was even in Anno Domini. His assumptions were half correct; he wasn't in A.D., but he was in the two thousands... B.C., that is.

Time marched forward as did the line. Eventually, he could see a table positioned at the silo's entrance and one man sitting at it, facing the line of people. Behind him stood a small group of workers. Josh watched each person get called up to the table. First, the man behind the table spoke. Then the called person spoke. Lastly, the man at the table spoke a final time but only to the waiting workers behind him.

Josh couldn't hear what was being said by either party; but judging by the response the Man in Charge's words elicited, it was a question first, then an answer; and finally, instructions. With no confusion on the workers' part—this operation functioned with precision—they approached the silo, scooped out what appeared to be grain, and then transferred it into each called person's basket.

With a bow, excitable words, and a kiss on the MIC's hand, the receivers turned and followed the directions of another group of workers guiding them to the exit line.

When Josh's turn arrived, he approached the table and waited for the MIC to speak. A moment passed in silence. The MIC's broad smile implied that he was delighted to see Josh. He finally speaks.

"Josh, you know who I am, don't you?" the man asked.

With extraordinary illumination, Josh responded: "Yes. You are Joseph."

"I am. Do you understand what's happening? Do you understand what's being accomplished?"

"I do."

"Good, now go do it."

Immediately, an ultra-trippy transformation usurped his dream. Josh took over for Joseph. But instead of a silo's entrance behind him, it was his house's back door. Adding to the trippiness, a pristine darkness slowly cascaded over the sunny sky as though pinpoint white intermixed in dynamic black paint was dumped on the earth. Josh's work would happen only at night.

Some similarities to Joseph's role were included in Josh's dream. There is a line of people, although discreet and smaller, waiting to stand at Josh and Ariella's door. Josh has helpers behind him ready to divvy out food and supplies. There is also somebody guiding the people out a different way once their transportable coffers were filled.

When Josh awoke from this incredible dream, he shared it with his partner, his co-equal. They seized each other and gave license to their happy, fearful tears to flow freely. They knew how formidable their charge was, but they also knew God was with them. So, what could mere men do to stop it?

*** 

Their enterprise quickly grew to include dozens of like-minded, Godly anarchists all helping to save hundreds of starving Anathemas. The design is quite shrewd in its simplicity.

After the full-scale attack on Israel, Vincente established three other Israeli cities besides Jerusalem to act as safe havens for the displaced—Tel Aviv, Beersheba, and Haifa.

Since Josh and Ariella live in Jerusalem, they established their fledgling venture there first. Eventually, their brainchild invaded the other three cities but was tweaked to accommodate each location.

Taking advantage of the already established four sections of Jerusalem—the Christian, Jewish, Muslim, and Armenian Quarters—Josh and Ariella chose a specific house in each Quarter to be the centerpiece for their grandiose plan. The chosen house became a drop-off for the various items that would be distributed to the Anathemas once a week. The items were collected and delivered to these houses by two different couriers—Runners and Scavengers.

Runners (there were a total of nine—two assigned to a Quarter with one floater filling in as needed) each outfitted with heavy-duty hiking backpacks, collected food left in donation boxes. There were four boxes strategically placed in each Quarter. The boxes were standard-looking trash bins nonchalantly positioned next to the normal trash bins in an alley. The stamped district name on the faux trash bin was misspelled to help differentiate it from the others. Nihilist VPs (those disobeying Vincente's inhumane NHFA law) secretly left food in these bins—bought with their own money—to be picked up later.

The donation bins are emptied twice every day except on Saturdays. The Runner makes a circuit around the city, stopping at each bin while attempting to time it so that two hours separate each pickup. The reason for this is to provide ample time for dealing with unforeseen issues, donations to be made, and emptying their backpack if needed at the drop-off house. They start at 8:00 a.m. and try to be off the streets by 5:00 p.m.

The genius behind turning a trash bin into a donation box was Eric Warren, the Mendels' first convert and the one who helped set up the entire operation. Nobody batted an eye at seeing a VP tossing a garbage bag into a trash bin. And on the flip side, nobody paid attention to an Anathema filling up their backpack with trash from a trash bin.

The other courier, Scavengers (each Quarter had their own), were just what their name implied: individuals combing through abandoned houses looking for larger items that the Runners couldn't fit in their backpacks—clothes, blankets, etc.

Scavengers always traveled together in twos and always drove a fifteen-passenger van. They were exclusively able-bodied, converted VPs: *able-bodied* because scavenging was dangerous and rigorous, and *converted* VPs (many were abandoning Vincente's wicked world and believing in Jesus) because they have the R-Chip, allowing them to drive.

Tuesdays and Thursdays were "unloading" days for the Scavengers, assuming they found something to unload: not a lot left to scavenge. They'd pull their van into the drop-off house's attached garage, wait for the overhead door to close, and then unload. No matter how long it took, they always stayed for at least an hour. That way, should anybody notice a nondescript van pull into the garage and the overhead door close, they won't see the door open, and the van leave minutes later. That's a good way to get raided as drug dens from the Old World can attest to.

Distribution night was the culmination of the entire plan. Every Saturday night, once the Sabbath ended, one member from each Anathema household arrived at their Quarter's drop-off house. There they received the food and supplies they needed for the upcoming week free of charge.

In the first couple of months, there were many bumps along the way; sadly, some of those bumps were murdered accomplices. This did not dissuade the faithful; it emboldened them to fight the *system* even more passionately. But as with all productive crusades, foresight must be the horse that leads the earnest cart. Because of this proverb, many working parts and a dizzying number of checks and balances were put into place; security was now Josh and Ariella's top priority. They were determined to keep everybody involved ASAP—As Safe As Possible.

So far, all their safety measures have earned them an excellent OSHA Incident Rate. But if they want to keep it, Ariella needs to quit pining for more rest and get up and get dressed, because there's much that needs doing and no spare seconds for losing. In five days' time, both literally and figuratively, all hell will break loose...

Still standing in their bedroom doorway, Josh's attempt to restore his wife back to consciousness is interrupted by his *Basile Phone* vibrating in his pocket.

Toiling to dig it out as though scuffling with a rascally weasel running amok in his pocket, he frees his phone from the other contents. Seeing the caller ID, which irritates him for his wasted effort, he thumb-stabs the red *End* button with an animosity reserved for telemarketers.

"Ariella," Josh speaks again, already emotionally moved on from the unwanted call. "Love, it's eight-fifteen. Eric will be here soon."

He sits on the edge of the bed and rubs her back. Playing possum—she was awake long before he came in—she remains still and savors a little longer his gentle but strong caressing hand.

Content with his effort, she rolls over and looks up at him. With his right hand now free, he presses it into the bed on her left side and leans on it like a kickstand. His left hand brings up a previously hidden desert wildflower and sets it on her nightstand. She retrieves it and holds it under her nose.

As she looks into his piercing eyes, she reflects on all that's transpired. Before Josh, all relationships of the romantic variety never appealed to her. The military was her confidant, her lover, her soulmate. While her senior-year peers fussed over landing their prom date, Ariella fussed over getting her four-mile run time under twenty-six minutes.

But now she gets it. Love is pretty grand and she's glad it found her. When Josh was reintroduced into her life, everything went haywire. She willingly laid her soul bare and let him in. And to this day, after almost three years of marital bliss, the nervous exhilaration of being vulnerable has not waned one iota. She'd literally follow this man to the ends of the earth. And if it were not round, she'd gladly leap off the edge with him like buffalos following each other to their death—one love, one life, you get to share it as you carry each other...

Once those pre-approved seconds of staring into her beau's eyes expire, she cups both hands around his face and pulls him down for an amorous kiss; it is the kind of kiss that would've made The Great Bard himself swoon.

As the kiss lingers on—*Let's go you two! No time for anything more!*—she finally breaks the seal.

"Get a move on!" she annunciates, their faces only inches apart.

"Waiting on you, Lieutenant," he asseverates.

She smiles, plants one last quick one, exits her pillow-soft bed, and switches over to disciplined auto-pilot for her morning routine. She slides into her bathrobe, unplugs her charging cellphone, and drops it into her bathrobe pocket. One final task remains —rescuing Josh's thoughtful wildflower from a lonely death on her end table.

She marches into the kitchen and approaches a cupboard. Opening it, she retrieves an empty vase and fills it with water.

Josh heads toward a different region in the kitchen—the *Keurig District*, where he busies himself with filling up a mug. Oblivious to Josh's activities, Ariella finishes the day's initial task by dunking the flower and displaying the duo in the middle of their kitchen island.

Next, she heads to the Keurig where Josh is waiting, leaning against the counter. He stops her in mid-quest with an outstretched, coffee-grasping hand. He flashes an *I got your back* smirk as he quaffs his own coffee. She gratefully accepts his loving gesture and takes a sip. MMM, just the way she likes it, and it's in her fave coffee mug too. If he keeps this up, she'll be leading him back into their inner sanctum...

She backs up against the island and watches her husband sip quietly. She can tell his puzzler is puzzling through some puzzlement.

"What was it about?" she asks gently.

"What was *what* about?"

"Your dream. That's a desert flower," she says, pointing at the vase. "And it's fresh, which means you picked it this morning. Obviously, you took a walk to make sense of it."

"You know me too well."

"I may not have listened in the beginning, but I'm listening now."

When Josh first told her about his dreams and the subsequent early-morning desert walk to work through them, she discounted them as nothing more than paranoia. It was the revealed dream of his father joining Vincente the day before it came true that convinced her to reconsider. When he had his next dream, the Joseph dream, she was ready to believe. He hasn't had one since; so, if the lengthy span of nocturnal silence was broken, then it's message must be important.

"It was about this Saturday night," he answers.

"When the Sanhedrin publicly consecrate Vincente as their Messiah inside their newly resurrected temple," Ariella says, assuring him that she too floats along his stream of consciousness.

"They sure aren't wasting any time, are they? It's only been three months."

"The Sanhedrin was finally resurrected after five hundred years of failing. Do you blame them for wanting to take their shiny new assembly out for a spin?"

"But does that spin have to involve crowning a mad man their Messiah? Why is your dad going along with this?"

"He has no choice. His hands are tied."

"He's the high priest. Doesn't that count for something?"

"It does…one vote."

"There aren't others opposed to this foolishness?" Josh asks.

"Not enough. It's a majority vote. Vincente's been their man ever since he signed the treaty, so why does this little ceremony matter?"

"It doesn't, I guess. But even though my dream didn't show any specifics, I can tell you the mood wasn't heartwarming. They have no idea what they're getting themselves into."

"Of course, they don't. Josh, this Saturday marks three and a half years. The second half, the most terrifying three and a half years the world will ever know, is knocking on history's final door. I don't know exactly what's coming but I do know there's no stopping it. You know it too."

He does. "I do."

Josh's dreams and her father arouse her recollection.

"I know this isn't the most ideal time," she certifies, a touch of hesitation impregnating her voice. "But there's another more immediate matter I want to discuss."

"Yeaahh..." Josh answers cagily. Ariella being less than assertive is uncharacteristic. Typically, it's bulls on parade when it comes to her speaking her mind.

"Have you talked to your dad recently?"

"I have not. Why?" His tone implies he's not down with this line of questioning.

"He's been texting me because he can't get a hold of you."

"I know. I'm ignoring him."

"So, you are getting his texts and voicemails?"

"I am. In fact, he called me a few minutes ago. But as I just said, I don't wanna talk to him."

She brings her prized mug back up for a

hyperbolic sip before she responds. Josh watches her eyes narrow over the rim.

"Are you nine years old?" Ariella asks. Uh oh! Close the China shop doors! Here come the bulls! "Talk to your father. He needs you. He's not saying it, and I suspect it's because he's afraid the wrong people will hear, but I think the guilt is eating him alive."

"He should feel guilty! He's the reason why we do what we do."

"You weren't there with Vincente. You don't know the details."

"I don't need to know the details. He's always done the right thing no matter the consequences."

"Then maybe he was under compulsion. My father told me he's 'watched Vincente effortlessly get into people's heads, tweak their gears, and turn them into spineless pantywastes.' That's a direct quote."

Josh offers up a half-smirk. "I can't see your dad saying pantywastes."

Ariella returns the smile, grateful the mood is changing. She reaches to him with both hands. Putting his mug in the sink, he accepts her hands and allows himself to be towed into her embrace. She rests his head on her shoulder and strokes the back of it.

"I'm confident your dad withstood for as long as he could, but maybe his will wasn't strong enough. Stop whining and start shining."

Josh pulls away; a faint smile appears. "Catchy saying," he praises. "What does it mean?"

"It means shine the grace of Christ onto your dejected, backslidden father. Reach out to him. He needs you."

Her strong will and *butt kicking into gear* prowess are two of his favorite traits. Sometimes, however, usually when it's needed the most, it bugs him to no end. This is one of those times.

"Okay," he says.

Her face softens with a mixture of love and sympathy; she knows he's hurt, but she also knows he needs to suck it up. She offers a conciliatory kiss. He accepts before tending to the sink of dishes.

"It would also help to change your thinking about the situation," she suggests.

"How so?" Josh asks as he loads the dishwasher.

"Remember that God is behind the scenes whether we see Him or not. Clearly, God providentially used your father's sin to move us to fulfill His plans and purposes in our lives."

Focused on the dishes, Josh nods. "That's a good point."

"There's another side to this," she begins, handing him her empty mug. She returns to leaning against the island. "If your dad *is* feeling guilty, then that means he's under conviction. Maybe God will use your father's terrible sin for His glory and the Anathema's good."

"How can this be for anybody's good?" he asks, having loaded the final dish and closed the dishwasher. He puts his remaining frustrated energy into wiping down the counters.

"No idea," she admits, staring at his back as he cleans. "But God's ways are not our ways. Besides, I'm hearing things from my dad."

"What do you mean?" He stops wiping to look at her.

"Rumors about a rebel in Vincente's ranks."

"An anarchist in the Antichrist's administration? Ironic."

"Clever."

"And you think that's my dad?" Josh presses.

Pursed lips, raised eyebrows and a shrug are her answers. Just then, a soft *ding* sounds from inside her bathrobe pocket. Conceding to its Pavlovian beckoning, she retrieves her cell. Wringing out the rag and hanging it to dry, Josh joins her, his shoulder mashed against hers. They both stare at her phone.

A CCTV image showing a full view of their backyard displays on the screen. Because an intruder *broke* one of the strategically placed home perimeter surveillance sensors, a specific backyard camera linked to an app automatically activates. They watch a man skulk across the backyard, heading to their sliding glass door. They know it's Eric, but protocol needs to be followed.

Ariella's training and real-world experience have made her an expert in the art of clandestineness. She knows how to function in the shadows, to dwell in and among the populace while never raising an eyebrow. Also, her understanding of how terrorist organizations work, and their own virtuosic cunningness at staying undetected is useful to what they do.

Arriving at the door, Eric begins security check number one—rapping the secret knock confirming *all is clear* against the glass door. The rhythmic knocking infiltrates the silent kitchen ambiance.

Both remain propped up against the island. Security check number two must happen before they answer the door. This is accomplished using an app on her phone. She activates it.

A screen pops up showing a nondescript green button that simply says, "Begin." She selects it, which brings up a progress bar. Several seconds pass before a message pops up— "Security check complete. No threats present," as in, unrecognized R-Chips in the vicinity.

Josh enters the adjoining living room where he slides open the glass door, allowing Eric to come in.

"Good morning, Eric," Ariella wishes. "Coffee?"

"Good morning, Ariella. No thanks. I've had too much already."

"Is that even a thing?" Josh asks, tongue in cheek.

"It is when you have IBS and limited access to communal bathrooms," Eric sheepishly informs.

Borrowing a page from the chapter, "Her Darkest Period" in America's history book, the VPs have taken the infamous *Whites Only* bathroom policy and turned most of the public bathrooms into *VPs Only* bathrooms. There aren't many city bathrooms the Anathemas can use. The Runners know this all too well and plan accordingly.

His embarrassing *taxicab* confession doesn't faze them. Life is tough for the Anathemas. It's a wonder they're not all riddled with a myriad of diseases: cured, unidentified, and everything in between.

"Sorry to hear that, Eric," Ariella consoles.

"Eh, whatcha gonna do?" Eric says, shrugging as he approaches a door. Arriving, he swings it wide and flips a light switch; a set of descending stairs encased in a tunnel is illuminated. As he's done many times before, he descends into the depths of the Mendels' house, flipping switches as he goes. Each light illuminates a new room as he walks deeper into the Mendel's large, multi-roomed basement. Josh and Ariella follow the lights as though following a trail of breadcrumbs.

Eric finally arrives at his desired destination—a nondescript door. He swings it open, flips yet another switch, and reveals that his calculated pilgrimage has taken him to...the furnace room. For all the secrecy and deliberateness, this room is incredibly anticlimactic. But wait, there's more to this expedition. He advances toward the circuit breaker panel, karate-chopping the voluminous head-level cobwebs like a jungle adventurer machete-cutting the thick brush preventing his quest to an inestimable antiquity.

The basement's owners arrive at the furnace room entrance and watch Eric do his thing. Even if Ariella was the kind of homeowner that'd be bothered by cobwebs, she wouldn't mess with these: they are necessary to their survival and the survival of hundreds more.

Eric opens the panel and shuts off an unlabeled breaker inconspicuously mixed in with the rest. Nothing earth shattering happens, just the whirring *click!* of an electrical line lock disengaging. Something somewhere was deactivated.

Eric walks to the concrete block wall behind the hot water tank where something unusual is readily apparent—two vertical splits in the shape of a door are now outlined. Shockingly, the supposedly structurally sound basement wall is a ruse! It's nothing more than a masterfully painted fake wall, rivaling even the best of Wile E. Coyote's mountain tunnel paintings.

With a push, the unlocked door opens into a secret room. Stepping in, Eric turns on the lights. Several fluorescent bulbs flicker to life. With the room's contents now illuminated, Eric stares at the uniform rows of floor-to-ceiling metal shelves. At first glance, the room resembles a library, but instead of shelves of books, its shelves of food and supplies.

A shock-whistle escapes Eric's lips. "There's a lot more here than last time. What happened?"

He asks this as he checks on a jerry-rigged, whisper-quiet inverter generator sitting in a corner, padded for maximum silence. This is part of his drop-off routine. Good thing too because a simple test reveals something's wrong with it. Its whole purpose is to provide backup power to the breaker that powers the electrical line lock securing the stockroom's door. It automatically kicks on if the power goes out, keeping the clandestineness intact. Otherwise, their secret stockroom will be about as secretive as a giant "Eat at Joe's" neon sign. He's about to report the issue, but Ariella enters and makes an announcement of keen interest to Eric.

"Our Scavengers stumbled onto an untouched house. It was packed," Ariella informs, explaining the over abundance.

Eric regards Ariella, immediately forgetting about the generator. Ariella reads his gaping look loud and clear.

"Yes, Emily was here recently," she confirms.

"Oh, that's nice," Eric says, trying to be aloof. But really, he's *a fool* if he thinks he's fooling anyone.

"You can stop with the charade. We know," Josh confesses.

"Is it that obvious?" Eric asks, blushing like a schoolboy.

"Just a tad."

"Our question is, what are you waiting for?" Ariella adds.

"Waiting for what?" Eric asks.

"Popping the question," Josh says. "There's precious little time left. Stop wasting it."

"We're getting together this Friday, so who

knows," he announces with a twinkle in his eye.

"Keep us in the loop, Son," Josh jokes.

"Will do, Dad," Eric returns the *serve*. Eric checks his watch and reacts. "Oh man, I didn't realize what time it was. Where do you want last night's final pick up?" he asks, unslinging his backpack.

Ariella points. "There's an empty spot at the end of this row."

With *blinders* on, Eric disappears down the specified row, empties his pack, and turns to leave only to slam on the *brakes,* befuddled. He reappears at the front of the row.

"Where did all this olive oil come from?!"

"Amazing, huh?" Ariella remarks. "Your girl found them in that untouched house."

Eric shakes his head in astonishment as he follows the Mendels out. The generator never returns to his recollection. Perhaps he'll remember next time.

So what's with the *little girl screams* and near shock-induced heart attack? Why does olive oil garner headlining news? Simply put, it's now *THE* must-have commodity...

Throughout mankind's narrative, there have been specific natural resources highly sought after. At one point, it was salt; other times it was cedar and saffron. Now it's olives, specifically olive oil: its myriad benefits cannot be overstated.

Olive oil is more than just a healthier alternative to Crisco. It can also be a moisturizer for sunburns, substitute shaving cream, shampoo, makeup remover, and a hair loss preventative. And for those who don't have health care, i.e., the Anathemas, it can be an antibacterial and an anti-inflammatory. It even helps fight Alzheimer's disease, reduce the risk of diabetes, and prevent strokes.

Since the VPs have the best healthcare system ever devised, the only real reason they lust after olive oil is for its hygiene benefits. After the world was reset, the gaping hole in toiletry manufacturing has yet to be filled. Almost all the companies that produced toiletries were in America.

Because Grayson Young's America is now the most dangerous place on the planet, olive oil is the essential *medicine cabinet* staple. Until those factories are humming again (Vincente is hyper focused on making this happen), olive oil will remain in high demand. Vincente knows it's more cost effective to get existing factories back up rather than build new ones. He promises lucrative incentives to those who'll move to America and face the shocking brutality.

Though not as bad as the gas shortage in the seventies, the quest for olive oil has reached Black Friday levels of insanity. Like hunting for that "must have" toy of the season, many call different stores to see if a shipment came in and if not, when? Once people caught onto this strategy, everybody did it. This led to lines of anxious people wrapping around the store. Espying the impending anarchy, lawmakers passed an edict to limit households to three bottles a month to keep similar instances of the *Cabbage Patch Doll* and *Tickle Me Elmo* fistfights from happening over a fruit. Recognizing the boundary's fairness, VPs responded positively. For now, rioting was averted.

This is all well and good for the VPs, but what about the poor Anathemas? *Too bad; so sad,* is the VPs' common refrain. As generous as some VPs are, none are donating olive oil. If Anathemas ever get their hands on olive oil, it's because it was in a Scavenger's hands first...

Having just reentered the furnace room, Eric pushes his fingers into a specific section of the faux wall. The push reveals a hidden spring-touch latch, giving him something to grasp and pull the wall-door shut. With the door latch securely in the strike box, he switches the nameless breaker back on. A faint buzz fills the air, and the electrical line lock activates, resealing their booty room.

The final step is reestablishing secrecy by restocking the area with cobwebs. But how? Do they have a legion of trained spiders ready to spin out strands of icky-sticky silk, or possibly a friendly neighborhood spider "person" on retainer? No, they have a chemist who knows how to turn D-limonene and polystyrene into perfect-looking cobwebs.

*** 

Before the world went kablooey, Eric was an esteemed chemistry professor teaching at his alma mater: the Massachusetts Institute of Technology. Though the last thirteen years of introducing young minds to the world of interactions, reactions, and transformations was successful and rewarding, he wasn't always just a professor. The idiom, *those who can't, teach,* does not apply to him. In fact, his distinction was birthed during his time as an FBI chemist in their STEM division. His near OCD levels of attention to detail garnered him much praise and set him up for a successful career in the FBI.

Then why did he leave the Bureau and cleave to Academia? As he succinctly told his wife one exasperated evening—*because the courts are broken.* When this reality first rammed up against his idealistic mind, it inspired him to work harder at beating the system, determined not to buckle under its disheartening malfeasance.

But no matter how meticulous he was, cases were still thrown out for asinine technicalities. Knowing that dead-to-rights murderers and rapists were freed because incriminating evidence was mislabeled by a cop or a hotshot lawyer implanted doubt in a jury's mind, wrecked his psyche.

Finally, the inevitable happened—he lost his passion to see justice served. Seeing no reason to hang onto his positive disposition, he abandoned his horn-locking with Cynicism. When this happened, the writing on the wall was unavoidable: if he didn't retire from the FBI soon, his righteous indignation would open up a new career—professional worm feeder.

The particulars of how Eric joined Josh and

Ariella have become so commonplace in *The Story of Man* that it barely warrants unpacking. That's not because his story isn't unique or doesn't deserve the "full-scoop" treatment. History tells of many a person's neatly organized life-threads suddenly unraveling, forcing them to start from scratch, only to discover their new life is better than the one they lost. His CliffsNotes are as follows...

Eric was in Saudi Arabia guest lecturing at King Abdulaziz University. Like Josh's return flight back to America, Eric's plane was rerouted to Jerusalem because of the land of the brave becoming a wasteland. Learning of his wife and kid's deaths, Eric's life went into a vicious nosedive, eventually landing in front of Josh and Ariella, literally.

Broken and unwilling to carry on, he tossed himself off a three-story building and landed in front of Josh and Ariella *who just so happened* to be out for a mosey by moonlight. Miraculously—a lot of that happening these days—Eric earned only a sprained ankle and broken wrist. Josh and Ariella brought him to their home, mended his minor wounds, and introduced him to the One who could mend his most critical malady: his broken relationship with the God of the universe. In time his broken heart was mended too.

He's been committed ever since to improving the war effort in any way he can, even if *any way* translates into menial labor. In the Old World, his hard-earned Ph.D. opened lots of doors; but in the New World, those three letters can't even open a public bathroom door. However, not all his previous hard work was exiled to a bygone era; there is one other skill wrought in the cast-iron cauldron of sweat and toil that still takes him places—his fatigueless legs.

While in high school and then at the collegiate level, he excelled in track and field. And during his training at Quantico, his run times were near the top of his class. Tack on two finished Boston Marathons and you have an egghead that can run like the wind. And right now, this egghead needs to double-time it. There are garbage cans to pick through...

***

Before leaving the furnace room, he slides over a MgO ceiling tile and stands on his toes. Reaching in, he grabs an odd-looking DIY plastic bottle/air hose contraption and sprays a substance around the path to the secret stockroom. Magically, new cobwebs appear—it's like he was never here.

"Emily will be here any minute," Ariella reminds him. "We're just going to respray the area again."

"I know, but my fastidiousness won't let me leave otherwise."

"You mean your anal retentiveness," Josh says.

"Tomayto, tomahto," Eric responds.

But never mind Eric's psychoneurosis, the real confoundment is why the cloak and dagger? This elaborate security seems extreme. It's not like they're living through the USSR's Anti-Religious Campaign where at any moment, the KGB could barge in and beat them or worse... right?

Though they have no concrete evidence to justify their secrecy, nevertheless, they live life wisely and obey the established steps. Forget one and the whole thing could tumble like a house of cards.

Because of their concerted efforts, they've bought themselves and the Anathemas more time, but that time is running out. Soon, an *old-timey-prison's searchlight* will symbolically spend every moment looking for Anathemas. Soon, Death will pound on their door. Soon, the need to run for the rest of their days will be understood. Soon...

Eric returns the web-maker to the ceiling, slides the tile back, and heads upstairs. Josh and Ariella follow. The trio stops in the kitchen.

"I'll be in the Hochbergs Quarter till Thursday," Eric informs as he opens the fridge. "May I grab a couple waters, please?"

"Of course," Josh says.

Eric nods a silent *thanks*.

"Good," Ariella chimes in. "Because we haven't heard from them in two days. We're assuming they let their phones die and *conveniently* forgot to charge them."

"Well, the Silent Generation does like their silence. My grandparents were the same way. Refused to get cellphones," Eric says.

"Fine, but we need to communicate with

them, so please, respectfully encourage them to keep their phones charged."

"I'll tell them."

Just then, as if on cue, Ariella's cell emanates a soft *ding*. She inspects it. On the screen, the automated surveillance cameras show a passenger van idling in the driveway.

"Case in point. How can they keep track of things if their phones are dead? Kind of defeats the security protocol we've set up," Ariella says.

"I hear you, Ariella. I'll talk to them," Eric assures. This should have triggered the generator-memory but the realization of Emily being only a few yards away short-circuits his brain. His normally razor-sharp focus is clearly dulled by his smitteness. He approaches the glass door. Josh joins him and waits for Ariella's *go-ahead* nod before he releases Eric back into the wild.

She initiates the security program. While they wait for the program to finish its *digital frisking*, Eric mentally prepares himself to *push off the starter's blocks*.

After a moment, the *all's well* banner appears on her screen. Ariella nods. Eric offers a goodbye wave before stepping into the already sultry morning. Now in the backyard, Eric pauses to mull over his options. Normally, his routine is to immediately go through the fence's back gate and then lose himself in the street's morning hubbub. However, he decides to take a small detour to the front of the house and hide in the large shrub on the garage's corner instead. From his Peeping Tom nest, he sees the waiting van. But it's not the van he cares to see, it's the driver.

Through the bug-stained windshield, he catches sight of Emily. He cannot take his eyes off her nor does he want to. But, alas, he must. He has a solid hour hike through the twisty turns and winding alleys that eventually land him in the Hochbergs' Quarter.

In the van, waiting patiently for Ariella's security program to give her the "okie dokie," Emily senses she's being watched. She looks at the giant shrub, discovering her intuition was correct. There, peering from between the branches, she sees Eric's rapturous ogling. A subtle smile lifts the corners of her mouth causing her whole face to light up. Their eyes lock and remain for a short but thoroughly reveled in five *Mississippis*.

The garage door opens, breaking the tractor beam between the two amorous lovers. Agonizingly, she is pulled back to a reality that doesn't contain Eric. Returning her focus, she slowly enters the garage.

Eric continues his gaze unperturbed by the waning seconds allotted to staring; these are all he gets till Friday evening.

His eyes track her as she slowly passes. And just before she disappears, she sneaks one final glance his way. In that second, the entirety of history's love sonnets is *shouted* for all of heaven to hear.

Once the garage door closes, Eric sighs a sigh mingled with sadness and ecstasy before returning to the task at hand—being swallowed by the morning's hustle and bustle.

# CHAPTER TWENTY-TWO

$S$itting at his desk, staged in a moderately sized but ornate-to-the-hilt office, Benson sighs as his call goes to voicemail. His son is still refusing to talk to him. There is a knock at his door. Benson grants access.

"High Priest Segal is here, sir," Benson's assistant announces through the ajar door.

"Okay, thank you, Ethan," Benson says still looking at his phone.

His assistant clears his throat. "Forgive me, sir. It's Pietro."

Benson regards the twenty-something and shakes his head sheepishly. "Sorry. Please be patient with me. It usually takes me a few days to remember people's names."

"It's okay. Today's my first day, so you have some time," Pietro says with a good-natured smile.

"Thank you...PIETRO," Benson exaggerates the pronunciation to prove he'll make good on his pledge. "Please tell the high priest I'll be out in a couple minutes."

"Will do, Sir," Pietro vows as he steps back and closes the door.

Benson closes his laptop, hiding what was once a screen full of mind-numbingly boring source code. Since he only got as far as opening

UltraEdit, shutting it down was no real loss.

Still at his desk, Benson decides it'd be advantageous to him and Eleazar's weekly stroll if he remains a minute longer to get his head right: the unexpected flashbacks are tussling with his suffocating depression. The reminder of his original assistant dying two weeks ago—the one who correctly bore the name, Ethan—is more than he can handle at the moment. What's worse, Ethan's death is entirely his fault.

*\*\**

Ethan was by Benson's side from the very start. He was kind, caring, and always willing to help. After Benson and Josh had their falling out, Benson subconsciously made Ethan a kind of surrogate son. Ethan suspected this was the case but never let on.

Ethan was thrilled to help Benson rebuild the world. He was always willing to free up his boss from the day-to-day trivialities so he could focus on what really mattered. In this way, Ethan knew he played a pivotal role.

Ethan, the poster boy for all that Gen Z stands for, believed fully in Vincente's vision. He knew that everything his peers and their parents fought for was realized in the world president, that he would finally bring about lasting equality and social justice. Witnessing all that Vincente's done already, Ethan couldn't wait to see what came next. He was convinced that Vincente Basile is the one to usher mankind into the Promised Land. Until that is, he was *un*convinced by Truth. The One who does ultimately fulfill man's deepest longings already came and was coming again to finish what He started...oh so very soon.

This reality changed his heart and revealed to him that the only paradise Vincente was leading the world to is "Fool's Paradise." Ethan's response was immediate and extreme. The very next day, he graciously told Benson he had to quit. The only excuse he gave was that *staying would be a conflict of interest*. Day two was part two of his new life—removing the R-Chip.

Sadly, this misstep led to Ethan's death. Although, in the grand scheme of things, this misstep also altered Vincente's agenda: Providence doing its thing once again. Not fully understanding the ins and outs of his new life but knowing he had a mark linking him to Vincente, Ethan was desperate to scrub it off.

He knew going to the hospital was out of the question, so he went down a different route —as in, down a back alley. Back-alley medicine is nothing new. Scoundrels and scallywags, who can't have the traditional medical community tend to their improprieties, have chosen this method for ages.

Because the Anathemas have no access to medical help, some well-meaning brothers and sisters hung their shingles in a few still-standing abandoned buildings. Problem was, none of them had anything resembling a medical degree. The little knowledge they did have was from medical books and DVDs of old hospital TV shows.

Complications arose during Ethan's surgery, which was no surprise. These *surgeons* had no anesthesia, so they did the next best thing —getting their patients blind drunk. Ethan's heart stopped; and despite the *surgeon's* valiant efforts, he could not resuscitate him. Ethan died on the table and was abandoned. His *surgeon*, afraid of getting caught, skipped town, taking his shingle with him.

The second Ethan's heart went into V-fib, his R-Chip sent out a distress signal, which beeped on Benson's smartwatch. His smartwatch is linked to his office computer where the R-Chip monitoring program runs. In this program, Benson has a list of favorites that he personally monitors. Stuck in a meeting, Benson raced back to his office where he had full access to Ethan's R-Chip stats. By the time he arrived, Ethan's R-Chip was offline: he was dead. Because the R-Chip's GPS relayed Ethan's whereabouts, First Responders had no trouble finding him. His body lay cold on a heartless surgical table, a hole in his forehead, and the chip submerged in blood coagulating in a metal bowl. Benson broke. He lost a second son. But God...He used this to soften Benson's seared conscious.

Benson doesn't know the details that led to Ethan's unintentional suicide, but he didn't need to either. Rumors of VPs seeking to have their R-Chip removed began making their rounds. The reason was obvious—they'd become Born Agains.

It wasn't hard for Benson to connect the dots: Ethan had become a Born Again too. But what was hard for Benson was continuing to ignore the massive elephant in the room. VPs were becoming followers of Jesus Christ and were now desperately trying to free themselves from the evil he created. The solution was obvious— hack his own program. But this was riddled with peril. If Vincente heard of his treason, well... instant death was the best he could hope for.

His nail-biting caper consisted of three steps. Step one: Go through the backdoor. Thankfully, he learned over the years to install one in all his programs. Effortlessly, Benson crept in unawares and wrote a new code, allowing VPs to deactivate their R-Chip without being detected.

Step two: Write a new program that completely erases the existence of the R-Chip. Since each chip has a unique designation for its host, it wouldn't be hard for authorities to locate the traitorous end-user. Benson's currently making it possible for an R-Chip to never have existed. That's what he was about to work on when Pietro walked in.

The final step: Get the word to the masses. Obviously, he couldn't hang a sign outside his office that read—*Tired of Vincente's infernal chip? Then come on in! I'll erase it for you!* So, how will he make it happen? The same way everything gets done without Big Brother knowing—under his nose, i.e., underground.

This is why he's determined to talk to his son. Josh forgiving him for his arrant apostasy is only his secondary concern. His primary concern is that Anathemas are dying unnecessarily, and Benson believes that Josh is the key that will unlock Vincente's shackles. He believes this because, along with the rumors of R-Chips being removed, he's also hearing that Anathemas are being secretly cared for. He has no proof it's Josh and Ariella, but he intuitively knows it's them. Josh has their ears and Benson has the words...

***

Benson, now mentally attuned, steps into his waiting room. It's empty. Confused at first, he eventually notices Eleazar pacing the hallway, looking lost in tormented thought. Determined to rescue his bestest buddy from the murky mire, Benson *slaps* on a happy face. He turns to Pietro.

"Hold down the fort, please," he instructs his new assistant.

"I haven't turned the sofa cushions into one, yet. When I do, I'll hold it down," Pietro remarks, his smile sly and eye twinkling.

Benson offers an appreciative nod for his new ward's satirical humor as he enters the hallway. It helps add truth to his forced smile. Eleazar notices Benson approaching. He turns to greet him, a beaming smile on full display. His sudden demeanor change implies that he, too, is determined to be a friend in need.

"You look in better spirits today," Eleazar compliments.

"I'm getting there," Benson confirms. "And you look terrible. What's going on?"

Unoffended, Eleazar asks: "This giant goofy

grin didn't throw you off the scent?"

"Not in the slightest. I could sense your tension from my waiting room," he says, pointing backward for emphasis. "Out with it. Does that monkey on your back have a name?"

"Pesachya Chanin."

"Who?"

"What do you mean, who? The Nasi?" Eleazar says, hoping that's the only hint needed. Benson's blank look says, *more, please.* "He's the president of the Sanhedrin."

"Ohhhh, right." If Benson rolls his eyes any harder, they're liable to fall out. "Those guys."

"Honestly, Ben, do you pay attention to anything other than your computer screen?"

"Of course. Just not them."

Eleazar wants to argue, but truthfully, he's envious of Benson's laissez-faire attitude. After all, it *is* the Sanhedrin that's causing his angst.

"Come on, tell me while we walk. I'm all ears," Benson promises.

"Thank you. You mind walking me to the temple? I have a meeting at nine."

Benson looks at his watch and sees that it's eight-twenty-five. "Then we'd better get moseying."

*** 

Blaring horns, blistering heat, blinding sun-glares ricocheting off passing cars' windshields...it is these things that assault the *almost* elderly Jews as they step out of Benson's tall office building.

"It's already unbearable out here," Eleazar bemoans as he unbuttons his shirt's top two buttons.

"All week, Ele. Shed some of that religious garb, and you'll feel better. I'm sure the Sanhedrin won't mind you wearing a tank top and board shorts."

Eleazar lets out a *Yeah! As if!* snort at such a ridiculous notion as they cross the busy street. Once back on the sidewalk, they hang a right and an immediate left down a more *conducive to meaningful conversation* corridor.

They walk till the corridor spills out into the reservoir that is an outside mall. The busy street's cacophony is now in their six; in its place are the babbling sounds of laughter and excitable chatter. The retail lagoon is awash in bright lights, money-spending mood music, and dreamy consumers going from shop to shop, intoxicated by the enchantment of a nearly bottomless, virtual bank account.

At first, the sudden influx of disposable income was tough for the penny-pinchers and coupon-cutters of the Old World to handle. They'd spent their lives convincing themselves that the knock-off brands were just as good as the name brands. But now, they are born-again hedonists fully accustomed to the wealth and decadence Vincente provided. The former inner monologue, *do I really need this?* was replaced by, *can I really live without it?*

Since entering the sea of consumers, neither has spoken. This is wasted time, and somebody needs to speak, or else why are they enduring the "dog days" rather than being in the shade where a smart dog would be? Benson finally breaks the silence.

"What's weighing you down, Old Friend?"

Eleazar regards him; puffy bags of exhaustion protrude from beneath his aging eyes. If he's getting any sleep, it ain't much.

"My crisis of faith." The confession topples from his mouth like skeletons tumbling from a sprung-open closet door. "It's a relief to say that out loud."

"Then why haven't you?" Benson presses.

"Because I'm the high priest. I'm not allowed to have doubts."

"Well, that's erroneous," Benson says in a loving but rebuking tone. "You're still fallible, no matter what that costume represents."

Eleazar examines himself in a shop's large window. Staring, observing each accouterment, he assimilates the asininity of the whole getup. God forgive him—he feels like a party clown. The feeling intensifies as he examines Benson's reflection. He looks comfortable in his business casual attire, and here he is sweating his tuchis off.

"Shalom, High Priest Segal," a shopper says as she passes by.

Eleazar barely acknowledges the passing reflection, but he does notice Benson sidle up next to him. He feels Benson drape his right arm over his shoulder and watches him run his left hand up and down his body like a tailor presenting his finest suit.

"Is the respectful greeting in the marketplace really worth the hassle?" Benson asks pointedly.

"Believe it or not, I know what you're referring to," Eleazar says to Reflection Benson.

"Do you now?"

"I do," Eleazar assures. "I read that New Testament you gave me several times. It's the reason for my crisis of faith."

Benson mumbles a *Huh!* under his breath as he cordially tugs on Eleazar's shoulder, encouraging the walk to continue. Benson's not-so-subtle, *you don't say?* response is not lost on Eleazar.

"Settle down, Ben," Eleazar bids his dear friend. "Most of me thinks it's total bupkis, but a small part suspects it's not bupkis at all."

"Why?" Benson presses.

"Because I have eyes. The New Testament may grate on my beliefs, but what I see grates even more on my intellect. I can't ignore what I've read in Matthew, First Thessalonians, and especially Revelation. They predicted all that's happening right now; and if three books got it right, what else is the New Testament right about?"

Eleazar, now empowered by his confession, rolls on.

"Another contributor to my crisis is the rabbis of old insisting that Daniel was not a prophet, but here we are, living through exactly what he predicted. If they got that so fundamentally wrong, what else are they wrong about? Is Jesus really *the* Messiah?"

"Yes, Ele, He is."

Silence descends as Eleazar ruminates over Benson's confident *no ifs, ands, or buts* answer. Israel's high priest is beginning to think so too.

The quietude continues as they exit the mall and enter Jerusalem's more typical-looking boulevards. Along the way, Eleazar continues to receive greetings from Jerusalem's natives and adopted citizens alike. But like the one at the mall, he only registers them as bodiless whispers, like lonely phantoms caught in the winds of an abandoned Wild West town.

Seeing his friend's furrowed brow, Benson elbows him. "What else is going on?"

Eleazar's answer drips with sadness. "The Sanhedrin threatens to remove me from office."

"Oh yeah? Why?" Benson asks.

"Because I dared to challenge their authority."

Benson's eyes widen, requesting more input. Eleazar obliges.

"I continually remind them that Vincente's not Jewish, so how could he be the coming Messiah? You know what their retort is?"

Benson's shrugging shoulders answer for him.

"'Neither was Father Abraham.' Isn't that ridiculous?!"

"Sounds like all doctrine's out the window so long as the gravy train keeps pulling up to their station," Benson says.

"Pretty much. But here's *the straw*. I accused them of having the wool pulled over their eyes."

"And it came off a wolf's back," Benson adds.

Eleazar points at him in excitable agreement. "Exactly!"

"I'm impressed. Awfully bold of you. What was their response?"

"Rage, pronouncements of damnation, the usual."

"Anybody tear their cloaks?" Benson asks mischievously.

"No," Eleazar says with a bright smile. "They're taking a vote on Monday to decide my fate. It's gonna pass. I know it."

"I'm sorry, Ele. But maybe your expulsion will be a blessing."

"Yeah. Maybe."

Silence returns as they continue their pilgrimage to the temple, now in sight.

"I'm having...dreams," Eleazar suddenly says as if confessing to a lewd sin.

"Of what?" Benson asks, though unsurprised. Scripture says MANY Jews will have prophetic dreams in History's final seven years.

"The immediate future."

"Don't be embarrassed. I have them too. Well, I used to." Benson's last sentence is barely audible and coated in shame.

Emboldened by Benson's disclosure, Eleazar continues. "One reoccurring dream started after I read Mark 13. I don't know what the *abomination of desolation* means, but the dream feels ugly.

I have a deep dread that'll come to pass this Saturday, at Vincente's deification. He's already been canonized as a saint; now he's being canonized as God..." He trails off, swept away by the tsunami of emotions such blasphemy unleashes.

On that note, neither speak till their journey is complete. When they breach the Mughrabi Gate, Eleazar pipes up as though coming out of a commercial break.

"That's what's going on."

"So, not much then," Benson says lightheartedly.

Eleazar smiles. Benson's gift of cheeriness has always been one of his favorite attributes. They arrive at the foot of the temple steps. Eleazar pulls Benson in for an embrace and kiss on the cheek. A couple of seconds pass before he breaks the hug and holds Benson at arm's length.

"Have you talked to Josh yet?" Eleazar asks.

Still shackled by Eleazar's strong hands, Benson looks away. Tears glisten in his eyes. "Not yet. But I think I'm gonna stop with the phone and pay him a visit."

"Good idea. I don't understand much about this Christianity of yours, but I do understand what I'm seeing. Time for messing around seems to be over."

Eleazar centers Benson's head and focuses on his eyes. "You understand what I'm saying? Stop screwing around. Make peace with your son," Eleazar commands before pulling him in for a quick hug. Without another word, he releases, turns on his heel, and ascends the steps.

Benson watches before blurting out: "Shalom, High Priest Segal."

Turning his head but still ascending, Eleazar responds: "And to you, My Friend."

Benson offers a "thank you" smile as he watches Eleazar disappear inside the temple. He turns and heads back to the Mughrabi Gate. Once there, he passes through to descend the winding wooden footbridge. At the bottom, he politely cuts through the accumulating crowd of visitors bottlenecking at the covered bridge entrance and exits the congested Western Wall area. Now free of the thicket, he heads for his favorite bakery, on this side of town anyway: Benson is an unabashed pastry addict and cares not who knows it. A few hundred yards later, he reaches his fix-boutique and joyously enters, announcing well wishes to the dough proprietors.

Minutes later, he is outside, a steaming hot cup of coffee in one hand and a wax-papered Krantz in the other. Enjoying his acquired ambrosia, he hears a crash and an agitated bawl from an alley to his left. Curious by the commotion, he investigates. Arriving at the entrance, he sees a man on his hands and knees collecting random items scattered across the dirty alley ground.

Distracted by the irritating stumble over a stack of unseen bread crates, Eric doesn't notice the man staring at him. After reloading his backpack (in his haste, he didn't zip it shut so some of the donations fell out during his spill), he re-slings the backpack and stands. It is then that he notices the creeper, creeping on him from the alley opening. He doesn't know who this man is, but he does know that if he acts nonchalant, he will appear simply as a foul Anathema digging through the trash.

"Are you okay?" Benson asks.

"I am. Thank you," Eric responds as he brushes past Benson and returns to the street.

"Were you digging through the trash?" Benson yells after him.

Stopping his escape, Eric turns. He doesn't know why, but he feels compelled to answer. "Gotta eat," he says offhandedly before returning to leaving.

"Wait! Please don't go! My name is Benson Mendelsburg. Do you know my son, Josh?"

Eric, now even more uncomfortable with this encounter, searches anxiously for an answer. He knows who this man is and the power he wields. He desperately wants to skedaddle.

"Never heard of 'em. Excuse me. I need to go." After offering a silent confession prayer for lying, he breaks off into a sprint and rounds the first corner he reaches.

Just before Eric disappears, Benson yells after him. "If you do know my son, tell him I love him!" Eric never looked back.

Not sure if he heard him, but the queer encounter buoys Benson's spirits...he knows a lie when he hears it.

\*\*\*

Eric did hear and will retell the awkward encounter the next time he sees Josh. For now, he distracts himself with something far more pleasant, i.e. Emily Walsh...

*** 

Eric first met Emily (he loves the melody their combined names make—Eric and Emily, or $E^2$ if she'd only indulge his nerd tendencies) at the Mendels' house when she came on board as their newest scavenger. He'd heard there was a newly Born-Again VP joining their cause but that was the extent of it. Aside from her being an American and now a doctor at the Hadassah University Hospital, he was given no other details. Later, after their hearts were knit together, he heard her full story, and what a story it was, worthy enough to receive Movie-Of-The-Week treatment.

They've been dating for five months but kept it on the q.t. They thought this was best because they assumed Josh and Ariella wouldn't be down with it. Office relationships are always a tricky affair and since their office specializes in providing life and staving off death, it's even trickier. But apparently, they weren't fooling anyone as evidenced by Josh's abrupt admonition to *put a ring on it*. That's what he's been trying to do for the last month, nevertheless, he appreciated the unintentional blessing.

In a perfect world, Eric would've already proposed. His insistence on giving her a ring, the perfect ring, was the reason for the delay.

Well, that and he was also an Anathema; he just couldn't go out and buy one. He could, however, go out and find one, in a car, driven by Mattias Cabrera, his Scavenger buddy.

On their days off, the two scoured Israel's land looking for that perfect ring left behind in one of the many abandoned houses. Mattias didn't mind giving his time to his *brother*—what else was he gonna do? His wife went up with the rest, so he has plenty of discretionary time. Plus, his Argentineness loves the pursuit of romance in all its forms. He remembers fondly those days of wooing his dear Antonela. Living vicariously through Eric's amarè satisfied his passion for passion.

The reason for the lengthy hunt wasn't due to the number of rings; on the contrary, they'd found dozens of rings pleading to be taken home and admired once again. The problem lay in Eric's persnicketiness. Not just any ring would do; it had to be the perfect ring, the ONE ring to capture her emotions and rule her heart—a reasonably low bar...

That bar was finally reached last Friday in an Old World, Born Again's house. After searching the usual areas for an engagement ring, Eric made a pit stop in the dusky master bathroom. The only source of natural light came from the skylight, but because it was cloudy, it didn't offer much help. Once *one* was done, he approached the sink to wash his hands. Straddling the dainty mound of unmentionables lying on the floor, Eric leaned into the mirror. He saw a tired face coated in sand, dirt, and dust staring back at him. He needed a shower, but a sink bath would suffice.

As he turned the faucet handle, the clouds broke, releasing a sunray to pierce through the skylight. The natural laser cut through the dust, bounced off the bathroom mirror, and then ricocheted into the sink, which now had water pouring into it. Shocked by the cool phenomenon, he looked into the sink—what he saw stopped his heart. The sunray penetrated a beautiful diamond ring, causing it to *explode* in dazzling rainbow colors. Its flashing on the running water created even more brilliant sparkles...whoa!! The running water was about to drag the ring down the unblocked drain!

Eric quickly turned off the water while thrusting his free hand into the sink, jamming his middle finger on the bowl. The eye-watering pain was worth it—he rescued the breathtaking round-cut diamond ring.

He held it in the sunray to examine it. By no means is he a diamond expert, but as he twisted the exquisite ring, he felt confident it was over a carat and a half. If Josh's *Uncle* Halvar was still alive, he'd confirm it was just a hair under a carat and a half, but who cares: the clarity and color sat a couple of notches left of center on the diamond chart. Whoever the previous owner was, their finger carried every bit of three months' salary.

Knowing he'd found *the one*, he was determined to protect it. He scoured the vanity for something to stick Emily's ring in. He found nothing suitable. He opened the medicine cabinet. Flashing an *eureka!* smile he snatched the bottle of ibuprofen. He removed the cap to find two pills. He dumped them into his hand (his achy back sang hallelujah, and his middle finger harmonized) and replaced them with the ring. Resealing the bottle, he slid it into his cargo shorts' zipper pocket and zipped it shut. Just then, Mattias entered the bathroom. Eric smiled as he reverently patted his pocket...

***

Hand deep in his pocket, fidgeting with the future Mrs. Warren's ring, Eric continues his journey to the Hochbergs. He only has a couple more minutes till he arrives; he wishes there were only a couple more minutes till Friday evening. Now that he has his ring, the idea of waiting another four evenings is intolerable. But, alas, he must. Emily volunteered to take the hospital night shifts till Thursday (he marvels at her strength to scavenge as well), so Friday is the next time they can get together. He feels like a kid waiting for the family trip to Disneyland but knows it's still an eternity away. Mercifully, his mind will soon be distracted: he's nearing the Hochberg's backyard.

Stepping through the bushes and materializing in the backyard, he walks slowly so the elderly couple can see who he is and address the security system with minimal stress. Arriving at the back door, he raises his fist to begin the not-particularly original six-part secret jingle. The problem is, after knock one, the door swings open a smidge. With fist suspended in mid-air, his left brain takes command of the scene. Seeing there's no evidence of forced entry, he deduces that the old folks didn't latch the door securely. Contrariwise, his gut insists this is not the case. He pushes the door wide, giving a full view of the room and its corners. Even though he was a chemist, he did receive rudimentary training on clearing a building while at Quantico.

"Mr. and Mrs. Hochberg!" he yells. No response. Aside from the whirring fridge, it's a perfect *pin-drop* environment. Though his heart picks up the tempo and his adrenalin courses, he forces himself to stay in the moment and not go full-on SWAT.

Working through the first floor, stopping at each room to clear them, he periodically calls out for the elderly couple: still no answer...still deathly silent. Climbing the stairs to the second floor, he catches the faint whiff of what he's been dreading...decay.

At the top, he peeks around the left-side staircase wall to scan the hallway. He notices light coming from the bathroom at the end of the hall. To get there, he must pass three bedrooms. Instinct tells him his hunt will end at the bathroom, but he must slow his emotions and clear each room in turn.

As he walks down the hall, the fetid fragrance is only mildly perceptible, but drawing closer, the bathroom's putrid perfume increases in potency. He can no longer sweep his intensifying dread under the rug—death awaits him in this room.

Arriving at the bathroom doorframe, he takes a calming breath before peering in. When he does, his fears are realized. There, lying face down on the tile floor, hands tied behind their backs, are Mr. and Mrs. Hochberg. With the abhorrent reality finally revealed, he centers his mind as the shock wears off. His only concern is figuring out what happened.

He steps in and approaches the motionless couple. Clearly, both took a bullet to the back of the head. Their snowy white hair is matted in sickeningly brown clumps of dried blood. A pool of coagulated blood collected around the crown of their heads like a grotesque halo.

Tenderly, he unties their wrists and rolls them over. Wanting to honor them for a life well lived, he retrieves a washcloth, soaks it, and gently washes away the dried gore from their still faces. As he cleans, he reflects on their beautiful story; it's heart-wrenching and heart-warming; inspiring and harrowing. It deserves emulation and remembrance, so he does exactly that, if only for a moment...

Mr. and Mrs. spent their early childhood eking out an existence during the Holocaust. They'd met when Mrs. and her family were tossed into the same concentration camp barracks that Mr. and his family were in. They became fast friends. The two confused children leaned on each other as they endured the heinousness molesting their innocent eyes. Their bond intensified after Mrs.'s parents died before a Nazi firing squad. Mr.'s parents took her in. The two were inseparable—until that is, Great Britain separated them.

After the war ended and the concentration camps were liberated, Mr.'s family was sent to the Feldafing Displaced Person Camp. Before leaving, they attempted to take Mrs. with them, but she was sent to Great Britain with other orphans. Eventually, she was adopted by a Jewish family who was already living in Great Britain.

When 1950 rolled around, two years after the State of Israel was created, Mrs. and her adoptive family joined the jubilant Jews who'd already returned to their ancestor's land: Mr. and his family were some of those jubilant Jews.

Many years down the road the two children of the Holocaust reunited and quickly returned to inseparable status—as husband and wife. They found their *happily ever after*. Their life together began during the first Holocaust, fitting it should end during the last. Their death is monstrous, but a blessing in disguise. They'll avoid what comes next. Yes, Adolf Hitler's villainy was unspeakable, but it'll scarcely be remembered once Vincente Basile's unleashed hell hits their shores...

As the gunk gives way to Eric's gentle scrubbing, something unexpected distracts him from his mental eulogizing—there are cuts and bruises on their faces. Puzzled, he scans the bathroom for further clues. Aside from the pool of blood and the splatter on the far wall, he finds no other traces of blood. His analytical mind gets busy.

*If they were beaten, it wasn't in the bathroom. So logically, it happened elsewhere. But then why were they shot in the bathroom?*

Multiple moments pass before the macabre picture unveils itself.

*The bathroom was the end of the line; it was the furthest point in the natural flow of the house... they were dragged up here and beaten along the way.*

Wanting to test his theory, he leans over each and kisses their foreheads before exiting the bathroom. Walking down the hall, he throws a glance into each room. Sure enough, each room proves his theory: small blood stains are scattered throughout. Obviously, they were lugged into each room and beaten. Most likely their assailants were looking for something, but the Hochbergs refused to crack under the torture. Eric is confident he knows what they were searching for.

He heads to the basement. Having the same furnace room setup as the Mendels, Eric reveals the stockroom's hidden door and enters. For now, he focuses only on grabbing a few essentials. He'll send the Quarter's Scavengers to grab the rest later—this house is *burned*. Once his backpack is stuffed, he exits, closing the door behind him. After switching the breaker and reengaging the electronic lock, he turns to leave when suddenly his world is plunged into inky blackness...

# CHAPTER TWENTY-THREE

Eric's eyes flutter as they try to open. His right one eventually does; however, his left one refuses to comply. Like a jammed garage door, it only opens halfway. The last thing he remembers is a wicked right cross and then exploding pain. After that...nada.

With one and a half eyeballs now eyeballing, he scans the room, discerning just how deep this hot water is: from what he can surmise, it's not good. He's still in the basement, but now he's sitting at an antique school desk. His hands are interwoven through the cast iron frame behind him and then zip-tied. The capper to the shocking predicament—the stockroom is wide open and two sneak thieves peruse its shelves.

"Oh good, you're awake."

Eric turns to see another stranger reach the bottom of the stairs. A demure man follows.

"I was concerned we put you in a coma," the new addition to Eric's nightmare remarks.

"Sorry to disappoint you, but I can take a punch," Eric fires back, hoping his mounting trepidation didn't crack his voice.

"Please. Stop. Haven't you heard? The

Reagan-era man's man is dead. You're allowed to cry now. Nevertheless," the leader of the four-man home invasion says, looking pointedly at the demure man. "Let's pull our punches, or we'll never get what we came for."

"You came to beat up a ninety-year-old couple? Reagan would've been so proud," Eric says, still attempting to land verbal haymakers and still missing the mark.

The leader flashes a good-natured but also, *don't mess with me* smile.

"No, we came for that," he nods his head toward the stockroom. "And information."

"That's an impressive stockroom," one of the two browsers praises. Both have exited to join the meet and greet.

"Must have taken your Runners and Scavengers months to collect all that," the other concurs.

"Perfect timing, fellas," the leader attests, noticing the subtle shift in Eric's bogus tough-guy act. "We're gonna be here as long as it takes so let's get the show on the road, shall we? I'm Dino. Those two are Lazlo and Sal." Dino introduces himself and his crew. Interestingly, he doesn't introduce the demure man. "We know all about your operation so please don't waste my time. What we don't know is who's involved."

"There isn't anyone else," Eric says unconvincingly.

"That's the best you got?" Dino asks. "I'm embarrassed for you. For the sake of your piddly rebellion, I hope your fellow confederates are better liars than you."

"There *is* nobody else," Eric avows, hoping the emphasis will sell it. It's been a big lying day for him, which bothers him immensely. Lying was always his sin of choice before Jesus miraculously redeemed him. He's got some confessing to do tonight...if he survives to see the stars come out.

"You're not exactly sticking the landing. Let me explain how the subconscious mind works and how it just betrayed you. Because you put the emphasis on 'is,' you're telling me there *is*, or for the sake of proper grammar—*are*, others in your organization besides you and the old farts upstairs. Should've put the emphasis on 'nobody.' I would have been more inclined to believe you."

Eric shakes his head. "You're exhausting."

Dino bares a satisfied, *I know, right?!* smirk. "That's why I'm the best at doing what I do."

"Which is?"

"Getting what needs got from those who don't want to give it, one way or another."

"So that's what you're doing? Beating and murdering an old couple because they wouldn't tell you what you wanted to hear?"

"First of all, I didn't beat or murder anyone. My associate," he says as he coaxes the still-nameless man front and center. "Is the guilty party. It's amazing what's possible when one lowers, or in his case, abandons one's beliefs."

Dino holds up the demure man's bloody-knuckled hand, advertising his Infinity-Snake branding. He's an Anathema...or was. Dino, pleased by the sought-after reaction, flaunts a satisfied smile.

"Second, it didn't have to go that way. Trust me; all they needed to do was tell me what I wanted, and they'd be in their recliners solving murders with Angela Lansbury and gripping about their arthritic knees. Yet, instead of being helpful, they chose heroism. They have holes in their heads because they wouldn't cooperate. Pulled the trigger themselves. But, between you and me, I was moved by their refusal to cower. Bravest blue hairs I've ever seen."

Pushing *stop* on his elocution *apparatus*, Dino meanders about the basement, examining and handling the various knickknacks.

"So now it's your turn," he blurts out, jonesing to hear himself speak. "Tell me what I want, and you'll be free to go. I promise."

"You can ask all you want, you bombastic sociopath. I'm not talking."

*BING! BOOM!* Eric receives two lightning-fast fists for his disrespect. Fresh blood streams from the new cut above his right eye.

"Please, don't be rude. Yes, I can be a tad verbose, but I'm not a madman. I'm an honorable man, a trustworthy man, some might even say, a nice man. Certainly, a man of his word. I know what you're thinking. I can see it in your eyes, well your one good eye anyway. You're saying to yourself—*Can he be any more cliché?* I know I sound like an '80s' action movie bad guy spouting nonsense monologues. But the difference is, and this is a big one, the only way you're escaping is me cutting that zip-tie, not because ninjas came to your rescue."

"Do you ever shut up?!" Eric yells, sick of Dino's babbling.

*CRACK! POW!* Two more quick hooks for his troubles. Eric leans to his right and splatters the concrete floor with a mouthful of blood. Dino pulls the demure man away from Eric and swaps places with him. He lifts Eric's head to examine his surrogate handiwork. He sees Eric's left eye is now completely closed and the right threatens the same result.

"You're doing this to yourself. You talk, this ends, you go. You're forcing me to break my associate's hand on your face. Not cool, Man."

Through the bloody haze of his right eye, Eric stares defiantly at a fixed point on the wall. The reality sets in—he's dead even if he does talk.

A silent minute passes. Sighing, Lazlo elbows Sal.

"Come on. This'll take forever."

"K. Hey, Boss, care if we go get right while you deal with this?" Sal asks, nodding and pointing at the ceiling.

"Go," Dino approves. "But wait for me. I'll be up shortly."

The two spring up the stairs. Whatever *getting right* is, they're enthusiastic about doing it.

Dino turns back to Eric. "Alright, one last chance before I leave you two to get better acquainted. Thanks to Benedict Arnold, I already know this home helps the Anathemas. What I don't know is: who else is involved, and where are they doing it?"

"Why do you insist there's somebody else?" Eric asks.

Dino walks to the furnace room and points at the electronic lock.

"Because of this! Because of the high-tech security system surrounding the house. Those two old Jews don't have the brains to set all this up. I mean, C'Mon! They still have a VCR hooked up! No, somebody else is involved. But most damning..."

He pulls out an old-fashioned flip phone.

"Text from this past Sunday," he informs. "'Checking to see how last night went.' Then an hour later—'Did you see my text? Please confirm.' Yesterday—'I'm assuming you forgot to charge your phone but I still need to hear from you. FYI, Eric is in your area this week, so he'll be the one dropping off. Trust all is well.'"

Dino dramatically flips the phone shut and stares at Eric, his expression cloyingly cocky.

"I assume you're Eric?"

Eric says nothing.

"Of course you are," Dino condemns. "Whoever *blocked number* is, I've been watching their texts come in since Sunday. Let me tell ya, I struggled not to reply. But kudos to me, I resisted. I knew I'd give myself away if I did. I don't speak Fogey. Plus I ain't trying to text on a numeric pad. That's a skill I don't miss."

Eric sighs. "Please, Dino. Get to the point."

Smiling, Dino continues: "Gladly. The last

text is the smoking gun—*you* being in *their* area. *You* implies others are doing what you do. *Their area* denotes ownership of a specific geographical location. So, whoever this is, they just revealed there are indeed others. So, please, who else is involved?"

"For the last time, I'm not telling you anything no matter what you do to me."

"If you say so. I'll give you one more opportunity to make it easier on yourself. You don't need to give up the names of everybody else. Just tell me who *Blocked Number* is and where I might find them."

Eric remains steadfast. Dino shrugs his shoulders as he swaps out the Hochbergs' cell with some unseen thing from his pocket.

"Suit yourself. I'm going upstairs to make a phone call and *clear my head*," he says while making some oh-so-played air quotes. "When I come back down, perhaps you'll be more cooperative."

He turns to leave but stops perpendicularly next to the Betrayer. He whispers into the man's ear.

"Here. To keep you focused and motivated."

He dangles the retrieved thing from his pocket—a small baggie of pink powder—in front of the Betrayer's eyes. A moment of loathsome staring passes before the Betrayer snatches the baggie.

Dino smiles. "Good boy. Remember, pull your punches. I don't wanna be here all day because you knocked him out again." And with that, he heads upstairs.

"How long have you been doing meth?" Eric asks. He spies the Betrayer's quizzical eyebrow arch. "I'm a chemist. I know what meth looks like."

"Then you know what it does," he retorts as he dumps a tiny mound into the webbing of his left hand and snorts. He repeats with the other nostril.

"I do. Fries your brain and rots your teeth."

Galvanized, the Betrayer pockets his speed, approaches Eric, and *hands* him a light knuckle sandwich—no cheese and only one slice of bologna.

"Trust me, you'll lose your teeth long before I do."

Reeling from the bop on the cheek, Eric droops his head and breathes deeply, trying to hang onto his fortitude. He wants to stay faithful to Josh and Ariella and honor the Hochbergs' sacrifice by not wasting it.

"To your question, almost a month. Stuff's amazing. Don't know how I got anything done before."

"Better pace yourself. It's merciless. It'll capture you quickly."

Proving he's his own man, the Betrayer pulls two more snorts.

Eric shakes his head, deciding to attempt a reverse Stockholm Syndrome. He knows mental anguish when he sees it. This guy just needs somebody to listen to him.

"What's your name?" Eric asks.

"Jon Nelson."

"Jon, why did you do it?"

"I wanted more," Jon says, effortlessly. Eric's right: Jon does need a listening ear. "I was sick of watching the VPs coast through life while my family and I barely scraped by."

Eric seizes on the humanizing opportunity. "You have a family? How many kids?"

"Three. Two girls and a boy."

"What are their names?"

"Rachel, Esther, and Asher."

"Their ages?" *Keep him talking, Eric, my boy*, he mentally cheers himself on.

"Rachel just turned thirteen; Esther, nine; and Asher, eight."

"Wow, Asher came quickly after Esther. Having two kids in diapers at the same time must've been difficult for your wife. She sounds like a strong woman. What's her name?"

"Rebecca."

"That was my wife's name too!" Eric exclaims, silently praising God for the, "We're all connected, small world after all" feeling that's arrived on the scene.

"Was?" Jon asks. Fueled by meth's social attributes, he's engaged in the conversation.

"Yes, was. My whole family was in The States when the attack came. I was guest lecturing at the King Abdulaziz University."

"I'm sorry," Jon consoles. "Must have been hard."

"Thanks, and it was, but I'm doing a lot better now."

"How so?"

"Survivor's guilt turned me miserable and suicidal. Every day was pure torture. But now, I have a purpose, thanks to..." Josh and Ariella were the next items on the conversation assembly line. But thankfully, he mashed the emergency stop button just in time.

"Well, thanks to Jesus," Eric says. Judging by the fierce change to Jon's countenance, he might've kept his employer's heads out of the lion's mouth but may've stuck his in.

"Jesus?!" Jon yells before changing to a low-key, *whatever* tone. "Jesus," Jon snorts while shaking his head. "Please. Jesus doesn't care."

"You're wrong. He does care," Eric says with unwavering conviction. Though part of him wonders, *Then why am I getting the living daylights beat out of me?*

"Really?! Why, after choosing to suffer with His people instead of enjoying the pleasures of Vincente's world, is my life so difficult? Where's the blessing? Where's the reward?"

"You have the wrong perspective. You're assuming that just because you say 'yes' to God and 'no' to sin, life will be easy. It won't. Christ called His own to a life of hardship. But He promises that those who persevere to the end will receive way more than what they gave up."

"Fine, but why do my kids have to suffer? I'm sick of looking into their sad, confused eyes and saying, 'I know kids in the neighborhood get to have all the newest toys, but we need to be grateful we have a meal today.' What about the Sunday School song, "Jesus Loves the Little Children"? Is that for all the little children except mine?"

Eric listens to the timeworn, trite whining about God being a big meany; it's been around since Eve first bought into it. Nevertheless, instead of chastising him, Eric believes what Jon needs is to hear Truth.

"Jon, I could never understand how hard it's been for you and your family, but I promise you, Jesus does. He does love all the little children, and the big children too. If you've come to Him on His terms, not your own, then you are part of His family. I promise God will never abandon His own, even if it feels like He has. Live by faith, not by sight."

Jon rolls his eyes with top-notch theatrical flair. "Spare me the sermon. I've heard it all before. My grandfather dragged me to church every Sunday. He's why I chose to become an Anathema."

"To be with him?" Eric presses.

"No, he disappeared with the rest."

"Your grandfather was a Born Again in the Old World?"

"Evidently, if you believe in all that Rapture nonsense."

Eric stays silent, waiting to hear more. Jon catches the vibe.

"My grandmother died when I was two. In his grief, my grandfather *found* Jesus, though he says Jesus found him, but whatever. My father, having lost his mother to a drunk driver, could no longer function, so he turned to booze. My mother endured his abusive alcoholism for five years. Eventually, she found comfort in another man's arms. Because he had his own family and she didn't want me messing everything up, when my parents split, she didn't fight for custody. My dad didn't want me either, so my grandfather adopted me. From seven till I graduated, I was in church, hearing all the Bible stories and singing all the church songs. I didn't believe the absurdity, but because I loved him, I never put up a fuss when Sunday rolled around. However, when I moved out, I abandoned church. My grandfather was heartbroken but gave me my space. When I had my own kids, I let him take them to church. Felt like I owed it to him."

"You've had a hard life. I'm sorry, Jon. Thank you for telling me your story. I'm confused though. Your reasoning for becoming an Anathema doesn't add up. Why choose something you think is stupid? Your grandfather's not here to see your choice."

"Fine, I didn't do it *for* him, I did it *because* of him."

"Whaddya mean?"

"When he disappeared, I thought maybe there was something to all those sermons."

Eric smirks. "Did ya, now?"

"Don't be smug," Eric admonishes. "Shut up and listen."

Eric obeys.

"I chugged the *Kool-Aid* and got the haircut. I started praying with my kids at bedtime;

I helped them memorize the Bible verses my grandfather gave them. I even sang along with the songs I detested growing up. I completely gave myself over to the *Life*. And when the time came to choose sides, I chose sacrifice. I've never been more wrong."

The conversation comes full circle. All the chitchatting and memory lane strolling have worn Jon out—he needs a break. This break, however, won't be coming with a Kit Kat bar...

Jon ferrets the little baggie from his pocket and examines it. He's about to partake but is suddenly overwhelmed by the feeling of being watched. Obviously, Eric's doing the watching. Extreme paranoia is one of meth's many chums.

"Close your eyes," Jon commands, completely spun out.

"Why?"

"Because I don't want you watching me."

"I can barely see."

"You got two seconds before I knock you out."

Eric wisely obeys. Closing his remaining, half-working eyelid, he relies on his ears to communicate the goings on. He hears two consecutive *SNORTS* but the follow-up *CHAOS* noise is unexpected. He opens his eye to see Jon on his hands and knees surrounded by toppled boxes that once formed a stacked tower. He shakes his head, hoping to knock some sense back into him. Good idea because he just briefly blacked out.

"Jon, your brain is tweaking. You're gonna

OD if you don't stop."

Gingerly, Jon stands, trying to focus. Eric's right, his virgin brain is succumbing to the battery acid and antifreeze. In his messed up state, Jon thinks he hears Eric add, *You're gonna kill yourself, you moron.*

"What did you say?!" Jon snaps, casting an evil eye at Eric.

"I didn't say anything."

Eric's assumed bald-faced lie enrages Jon. With balance restored, Jon marches towards Eric, ready to get back to work. Suddenly, something dark scampers behind Eric, startling Jon and teetering him backward. Maniacally, Jon squints his eyes and scans the room, hunting for the prowler. Curious, Eric swivels his head, joining in the search.

Seeing there's nobody else but them, Eric's hip to what's happening. "Jon, you're hallucinating."

Angered by Eric's continued condescending Jon wallops Eric hard, harder than up to this point. If Eric was on a folding metal chair and not a heavily base-weighted cast iron desk, the blow would've tipped him over. His head droops, blackness encroaching on his consciousness. One more blow like that and it's lights out, maybe permanently.

"Stop telling me I'm crazy! I swear if I screw up this opportunity for my family because you forced me to kill you…"

Confused, Eric opens his mouth to speak, but only a torrent of blood comes out.

Eventually, he forms a gurgled sentence. "I don't understand," Eric confesses.

"If I do this job, my family and I become full VPs."

"Full? Anathemas converting to VP only get half benefits."

"That's the kicker; if I do this job, we get full benefits." Jon enters the stockroom, snags a bottled water, and returns.

"Jon, respectfully, you've been lied to. That option doesn't exist."

"It does when you know a guy who knows a guy. That's how I got the job," Jon explains as he douses his scorched throat with water.

*The job of beating up two ninety-year-olds? Must've taken all your smarts to pull it off.*

"What?!" Jon exclaims as he cuts his chug short, dribbling water down his chin. He stares hard at Eric, waiting for an explanation.

*I said, 'You're a weakling who can't take care of his family.'*

From where he's standing and the state of his twitchy brain, Jon isn't sure if Eric is speaking. But if it's not him, then who? He'd rather smash than think about it. Taking a purposeful step, Jon marches towards Eric determined to knock the sass out of him. However, he's halted by the skittering *shadow men* darting out of the corners of his eyes. Searching wildly, he sees another one pop up, run across the back of the basement, and duck behind boxes. Jon rushes past Eric and leaps behind the same boxes, ready to fight whatever's crouching there. But, unsurprisingly, he sees nobody. He scans the basement, determined to catch the gremlins pushing him to the brink.

"Jon, what was your job?" Eric blurts out.

Jon doesn't answer. He's too busy tiptoeing like a loon, hunting for the rascals responsible for pilfering his sanity.

"Convincing the Hochbergs to talk," Jon finally answers.

Distracted by the hunt, Jon unconsciously sends his tough-guy act on furlough. Eric notices the softness in his voice, especially when he says, "Hochbergs." There was a hint of fondness like he was talking about his own grandfather.

"It sounds like you knew them," Eric points out.

Still searching, not really engaged in the conversation, Jon answers as though to an inquisitive child. "Of course, I knew them...they fed me every week."

Eric's concussed brain provides the riddle's solution.

"You live in this Quarter?"

"That's why we're all here. I knew where they lived."

Continuing his fruitless hunt—Jon's fruity brain has definitely cracked—what he just said struck a discordant chord on the fretboard of his conscience.

"You know, it didn't need to go down the way it did," Jon says, disheartened by the outcome. "All they had to do was give up whoever's on the other end of those texts. I kept assuring them Vincente knows there's an underground network keeping the Anathemas alive, that their continued silence wasn't helping anybody."

No longer interested in the hunt, Jon walks back to Eric, ready to finish the job and claim his R-Chip with full benefits.

"So, one last time, you gonna follow in their footsteps, or are you gonna carve your own path?"

As Eric peers up at the tweaked-out, half-human towering over him, a thought forms in his brain. He speaks.

"Jon, eventually, the guilt of what you've done will be more than you can bear. I hope and pray that as you're being crushed under its punishing weight, you'll reach for God's outstretched hand of mercy and be forgiven... before it's too late."

Jon stares into the defiant eyes of one whose heels are dug in. A new voice speaks into his short-circuiting mind. *He's never gonna talk and you're never getting your chip unless you kill him right now. Because if you don't, he'll warn the others. If he lives, your family dies.*

As silence returns to Jon's broken brain, he reflects on how badly this simple job went sideways, backwards, and loop-de-looped. Before his family's life hung in the balance, Jon struggled to kill a spider. Now he's about to add a third teardrop tattoo to his rapidly aging face. Jon sighs as beelines for Mr. Hochberg's workbench. During his maniacal prowling, he saw something attention-grabbing—a large pipe wrench hanging on a tool pegboard.

At the workbench, he eyes the preposterously huge wrench and lifts it off the heavy-duty double hook. The unexpected weight crashes Jon's hand onto the workbench, forcing out a shocked yelp! Eric watches Jon slide out his pinned hand, shaking it wildly.

Eric knows the time has come. The wrench's weight looks substantial, and will clearly hurt (Jon's throbbing hand proves it) but the weight of finishing well is his highest concern. He bows; he prays; he struggles under Fear's raging tumult. He pleads with the One who holds his hand to help him excel in this opportunity to be named among the godly servants, those who endured stoning, swords, and being sawn in two. He is determined not to buckle. Yes, of course, Eric fears death. He is wrapped in frail humanity like all who came before. But as was their ultimate fear, so it is his—betraying the Savior.

Jon, whose hand has stopped *screaming bloody murder*, picks the wrench back up, ready to *commit bloody murder*. Now accustomed to the wrench's eighteen-pound weight, even to the point of liking it—the heft feels seductive, like that of a six-shooter's cold steel—Jon turns toward Eric, prepared to face his accusing glare. However, instead of seeing terrified, pleading eyes, he sees the crown of Eric's bowing head.

Relieved (he assumed there'd be cries for mercy, not courageous acceptance), Jon approaches Eric, ready to get this villainy over with. As he walks, he again mentally praises his new *bestest buddy*: he couldn't do what needed doing without methamphetamine's help.

However, when he's squared up in front of Eric, Jon finds it impossible to raise the wrench. Not because the weight is an issue again, but *because of what he's about to do's* weight. Fearing imminent wussing-out, Jon imagines his family suffering this same fate. Seeing a giant wrench hovering over his precious little girl's head is all he needs. Fueled by the rage at such a vile image, Jon raises the wrench and with wood-chopping ferocity, slams the wrench down. The force was so extreme, that Eric's skull succumbed to the vicious blow. But praise God. Mercifully, at the moment of Eric's prayer, he was called home. By the time the wrench made contact, Eric's tears were already wiped and the recollection of this life spread to the four corners of eternity. He never felt a thing.

Meanwhile, up on the terrace...

***

While Eric suffered in a cast-iron chair, getting beat to death, Dino and his two goons were luxuriating in deck furniture, getting high. Shortly after Eric died, the communal joint did too.

"Smoke break's over; time to check in with Andel," Dino announces as he pulls out his cell.

"You're gonna talk to the pope stoned?!" Lazlo exclaims.

"I thought it was a mortal sin to talk to a

holy man plastered," Sal comments.

Dino sneers at such nonsense. "First off, no. And second...holy man? Hardly. Andel is Vincente's puppet, a babbo, nothing more."

"Then why do you kiss up to him?" Lazlo presses.

"Because Vincente asked me to. He and I go way back. Basically grew up together joined at the hip. 'They're so much alike, they might as well be conjoined twins,' people used to say. Though, I'm the better-looking one no matter what Vincente says." A sly smile lights up Dino's exceedingly handsome face. "I endure the Pontiff's pomposity out of respect for my friend."

"You knew Vincente before he was world president?" Lazlo speaks with hushed reverence.

"I knew Vincente before his voice changed and he got his first armpit hair. I knew him when he was just Vinny."

"Vinny? I have a hard time seeing him as a Vinny," Lazlo states.

"What was he like?" Sal asks.

"A force to be reckoned with, even back then. I'll never forget watching him take on five dudes at once. Knocked all five out. I tried to help but he waved me off. Vinny loved to fight. His knuckles were always scabbed."

"Shut up! Serious?" Lazlo asks. "What else?"

"Later. Let me call this jamook so we can get out of here."

He calls while activating the speaker. Andel answers.

"Did you find a stockroom?" Andel asks,

foregoing a greeting.

"I did. I also have their runner in custody."

"Did he tell you anything?" Andel asks, his voice filling the small deck.

"Not yet, Andel. My VP-in-waiting is beating it outta him as we speak. It's only a matter of time and effort."

"Excuse me?" Andel hisses. "You will address me as Pope Vassallo. Do you understand? Just because you're the world president's childhood crony doesn't mean you can talk to me like I'm one too."

Dino rolls his eyes as he forms a finger gun and shoots the phone. His goons muffle snickers. "Begging your forgiveness, Successor of the Prince of the Apostles."

"Your mouth will be your undoing."

"It's my cross to bear, Father Vassallo. I'll work on it. Pray for me." He's laying the sarcasm on thick, and his goons love it.

"I knew Vincente turning his old Mafia thugs into private security was a bad idea," Andel bemoans under his breath.

Dino hears him and fires back. "Then why didn't you tell him?

"I did, but he has a blind spot for you nitwits. It clouds his judgment."

"I'd be careful Andel," Dino warns. "It'd be a shame if you *accidentally* drowned in the Mediterranean."

"Threaten all you want," Andel responds unflappably. "Vincente's loyalties only extend so far."

Andel's rejoinder stops Dino's *Goodfellas* routine cold. He knows the Family is binding but only if you're advancing its interests, not hindering them. Dino swallows his pride.

"You done beating your chest? Good. Let the Anathema go. If he hasn't talked yet, he never will," Andel instructs. "But follow him. He'll eventually lead us to somebody who WILL talk."

"As you wish, Supreme Vicar of Christ," Dino affirms before pressing the *END* button and successfully procuring *the last word* victory.

"Well, you heard the *buffone*," Dino says as he stands, attempting to repair his image. Lazlo and Sal get the drift and follow him back inside. Deafening silence greets them as they enter the house.

"I truly hope you didn't knock him out again," Dino calls as he descends into the basement.

At the bottom, they stop in stunned silence, gaping at what greets them. They see Eric's lifeless body still shackled to the desk, minus a head, at least not one in the traditional sense. It looks more like a smashed open watermelon resting atop drooping shoulders, and its juice, fruit, and rind scattered across the room.

Lazlo immediately throws up while Sal turns his head quickly, narrowly avoiding the same fate. Unfazed—he's seen worse—Dino notices Jon sitting on an overturned milk crate, the blood-dripping pipe wrench sitting in his lap.

"What happened?" Dino probes, his voice unnervingly calm.

"What needed to happen," Jon responds.

"How many times did you hit him?!" Lazlo grills while wiping his mouth.

"As many as it took to kill him," Jon answers emotionlessly.

Dino shakes his head in bewilderment. "I told you not to knock him out, but you thought smashing in his skull was okay?" He stops talking and paces the room.

"If we let him live, he'd warn the others," Jon remarks. "Trust me, I did you a favor by killing him."

Dino throws icy glares at Jon. "Trust me, I'm doing you a favor by not killing you," he retorts, popping Jon's undeserved ego balloon.

Sal, having regained his wits address Dino. "Whattawe do now?"

"I don't know. Let me think a sec."

After a moment of requested "thinking silence," a solution forms, but first Dino must survey the damage to see if it's feasible. He approaches Eric's motionless body, mindful to step over the parts that once formed a head and face, and leans into the grotesque mess. He leans this way and that, studying Eric like he's examining a used car. He then drops to his haunches and peers up at Eric's remaining head. Still, he can't quite get the angle he's looking for.

Pivoting while still on his haunches, he looks for his two goons. Lazlo has disappeared upstairs to get some fresh air; Sal catches Dino's gaze and shrinks back. Dino shifts his searching spotlight to Jon.

Dino whistles like whistling for a dog. Jon obeys... like a dog.

"Get behind him and pull his shoulders back."

Again, Jon obeys emotionlessly. Giving Eric's lifeless body a hard yank, Jon suddenly finds himself with a mutilated mess resting against his stomach. Stunned by the heinous head-butt, he looks down into the cavernous skull presenting itself. Jon notices blood dripping onto his shoes; quickly, he scoots them back and looks away. The reality of what he's done bum rushes his conscious, making him queasy.

Dino, irritated by the continual stymieing of the angle he's after, snaps at Jon.

"Hold what's left of his head straight so I can see under his chin!"

Jon does, drawing ever closer to a total mental breakdown. Dino gets the view he's after and smiles.

"Perfect." He stands and addresses Sal. "Grab the shotgun from the trunk."

Sal's face forms a quizzical expression. "Why?!"

"Because I told you too," Dino answers, his tone pregnant with a psychopathic quality. "You can let go now," Dino instructs Jon.

Gratefully he does, causing Eric's torso to flop forward again.

"Cut his hands loose, but don't let him fall off the chair," Dino instructs. Jon obeys.

With no further instructions, Dino heads to the laundry area, hunting for something apparently elusive. By the time Sal returns, Dino gives up the exploration.

"I don't understand what we're doing," Sal remarks as he hands over the boom stick.

"You will. Trust me. Go back upstairs and look for some bleach and rags. I couldn't find any."

Sal heads for the stairs as Lazlo appears at the bottom of them. Dino notices.

"Feeling better?"

"A little. Smoked some more to settle me down."

"Good, you can help."

Lazlo, unwilling to take another step, remains fearfully planted. Sal, now all business, continues upstairs, grabbing Lazlo's arm in a *C'mon, let's go* motion as he goes. Lazlo, grateful to be taken away from the horror, follows.

Once in the kitchen, Lazlo peppers Sal, who's searching the cupboards, with questions.

"What is going on?!" Lazlo quietly bawls.

"No idea. Apparently, the wannabe VP got a little carried away."

"A little?!" Lazlo says. "There's brain and skull everywhere!"

"I know. I was down there," Sal remarks.

Lazlo shakes his head. "Why are we still here? Let's just bounce. It's not our problem."

Sal finds his quarry and heads back to the stairs. As he passes his whiny partner in crime, he quietly mutters, "Because, we have a job to do. Plus, do you wanna ditch him?" He's referring to Dino. He disappears down the stairs, leaving

Lazlo to ponder his words.

He doesn't ponder long. Following, Lazlo mentally prepares himself for the unsavory business ahead. When they return, they see Jon donning gloves and holding a trash bag, policing the basement of the various bits and pieces.

"You two follow after him and scrub up the blood," Dino directs.

Lazlo looks at Sal with extreme angst. Sal shoots a *Don't say a word. Just get to work* look in response. They do and after roughly fifteen minutes, the basement is as close to shipshape as possible.

"Excellent," Dino praises. "Time to mess it up again." He hands the shotgun to Jon, who stands emotionless like one with incurable PTSD.

Seeing Jon's stone-cold demeanor (Dino has told him the plan), Lazlo and Sal take a step back. Dino notices their spooked reaction.

"Relax. It's not for you. It's for him," Dino assures. "We need to stage his suicide."

Sal's expression would be amusing if not for the situation. Lazlo joins him in the confusion. Dino pulls back the curtain on his plan.

"Somebody will eventually come looking for him; and when they do, I don't wanna raise suspicion. If they assume this guy killed himself, they'll be less likely to think we're onto them. It'll be sadness they're feeling not fear and paranoia. You understand now?"

"Ohhhh!" Sal exclaims, mental lightbulb blinking to life. "If they think it was a suicide and not a murder, they'll simply head back to wherever and report the news."

"Exactly."

"That's pretty smart," Sal remarks.

Whether it's bravery now signaling the battle cry, or pot's *sunshine day* brightening the melancholy sky, Dino's brilliance also blows Lazlo's mind and presses him into action.

"So, what happens next?" Lazlo is reinvigorated and happy he didn't split.

Dino nods to Jon who re-animates and sets upon his assignment. The remaining three watch Jon march over to Eric, squat in front of Eric's drooping half-head, work the shotgun muzzle into Eric's mouth and use it to push his head up. Jon speaks a warning—

"Fire in the hole…I guess."

The audience plugs their ears and waits for the gun-powder explosion. Jon whispers a petition to Eric's corpse— "I am so sorry. Please forgive me." And with that, he pulls the trigger.

The blast has the desired effect. Some of Eric's head attaches to the ceiling in the direction of the gun's angle. Also, when Eric's ricocheted body bounces off the seat back, Jon moves out of the way, allowing Eric to fall off the chair and pin the shotgun between his body and the floor. The illusion of swallowing a shotgun is complete.

Lazlo and Sal hoot and holler like they just witnessed a magician make something disappear. Dino simply smirks, satisfied with the results.

"Well, that about wraps it up. Let's go," Dino instructs, circling the wagons.

His goons head for the stairs. Jon follows but Dino blocks him.

"Going somewhere?" he asks. The two goons stop their escape to watch the drama unfold.

"Well, yeah. With you guys," Jon says nervously.

Dino tongues a *so sorry* tsk. "Yeah, see, I'm gonna need somebody to camp out here. Inside."

"With three dead bodies?!" Jon bawls. "I'm okay with keeping an eye on the house, but why can't I do it from across the street?"

"Because a search party might come and go, and you'll never see it. No, you need to be inside. Only way to guarantee you don't miss 'em."

"But what if nobody comes?" unyielding panic now setting in.

"I'll make you a deal. If nobody comes after two weeks, then you can leave."

"And then my family and I get our chips?"

"Oh, you betcha," Dino starts with a folksy Minnesota drawl before switching over to a *mess with me and you'll be sorry* inflection. "But listen closely because purported ignorance will not fly. If you leave early, your family can only hope to look as good as him. Understand?"

Jon nods in the affirmative. The three head upstairs, leaving Jon to work through his horrible circumstances. Recollection suddenly strikes.

"Wait!" he yells desperately as he bounds after them. Once upstairs, he discovers the house is empty. Seeing the open front door, he dashes through and finds the two goons already in the idling car and Dino about to step in. "Please, wait!"

Dino obliges, stopping halfway in between the world of fresh outside air and the world of noxious cigarette smoke and BO.

"Yes?" Dino asks with mock concern.

"Wait, please," Jon begins, now standing in front of Dino. "Can you leave me a little? I'm out."

Dino is confused at first but then catches on. A sly smile creases his cheeks. "You want me to leave you with a friend?"

Jon's despairing nod says, *aye, good sir.*

"What happened to the baggie I gave you earlier?"

"It's all gone." Jon gently grabs Dino's arm. He immediately lets go after seeing Dino's disapproving glare. "Sorry, sorry. Just please, don't leave me *here*, alone, with nothing."

"Ohhhh, you mean, INSIDE?" Dino enjoys his bedeviling. "Yeah, that would be uncomfortable, especially when the bugs start crawling. I went through meth withdrawals when I was younger. It was one of the worst experiences ever. But to do it with three dead bodies. The smell...the maggots...the flies. I do not envy you."

Reaching into his pocket, he heaves a satirical sigh as though this is a great burden. "Don't say I never did anything for you."

He pulls out a baggie with barely a dash of pink *poison* and hands it over. Jon's eyes, seeing only that a bag is coming, brighten with joy and relief. However, once the bag is in his grasp, and his eyes see the pitiful amount, clouds of despair quickly move in.

"I don't mean to be ungrateful, but this is barely more than I do at one time."

"Then I guess you'd better ration carefully."

Hearing the word *ration*, triggers a memory of his family. "Can you please let my wife know where I am?"

Dino says nothing, only nods his head.

"You promise?"

Again, no words, only finger-crossing over his heart, swearing an oath. Holding the silent, now awkward glare, Dino's expression turns into a *Why are you still standing there? I'm done with you* look. To reinforce his attitude, he fully enters the car and unceremoniously slams the door in Jon's face. Offering no adieus or sayonaras, Dino drives off, leaving the angst-ridden Jon to stare after them. Jon's conscience immediately activates. He hears—*Grab your family and disappear.* The rebuttal—*Don't be a fool! He'll find you and slaughter you all.*

Listening to the latter, Jon walks back inside. He made this mess, so he needs to see it through even if he loses his mind in the process. For comfort, he fingers his precious little cache as though fingering prayer beads. Somehow, he must make it last; somehow, he must keep his mind; somehow, he must survive...for three hundred and thirty-six hours.

# CHAPTER TWENTY-FOUR

When early Saturday morning rolls around, the morning of the day when history's timeline receives a major event dot, somebody does come looking for Eric. Just in time, too, because the four days of unrestrained hell Jon lived through were moments from swallowing him whole. He never would've lasted another nine.

However, the celebratory balloon drop will be delayed because when Eric's one-person hunting party does show up, Jon assumes it's just another *cricket* sailing him closer to the dark island of Stark Raving.

He had exhausted his "supply" before the end of day one. By now, he's fully ensconced in withdrawal and other contributing factors (zero sleep and zero mercy from his tell-tale heart) that he no longer has a grasp on reality. For the past ninety-plus hours, nonstop hallucinations and *shadow men* were his only house guests. But now, a new guest joins the party, one that sounds pretty and unmenacing, not like the ravenous nightmares that've been screaming, "Nevermore!" to his pleas for peace.

"Eric? Are you here?" a female voice calls

out, piercing the mortuary-like silence. "Mr. and Mrs. Hochberg? Anybody here?"

Early Wednesday morning, Jon stopped investigating the noises and shadows that ran amuck in this house. He spent the previous ten hours chasing what he could clearly see and hear while never finding any evidence that he saw or heard anything. So when this new voice raced through the house, Jon chose to ignore it and remain protected inside the sofa cushion/mattress fort he'd constructed in one of the bedrooms. This is where he spends his time, digging at the *bugs* that scurry under his skin.

She calls out again, earnestly and with a hint of dread: this new guest knows the smell of death and the house is choking on it.

"Eric! Please answer me!"

Hearing her voice again, Jon decides to peek from his fortress. The voice is different from the guttural, maleficent whispers he's been hearing for days upon days, maybe even months...he's not sure anymore. His damaged mind warns him that this is just his *guests* trying new tricks but, heaven help him, he swears this voice is human. But the tone and pitch change aren't the most convincing arguments; the voice shouting somebody else's name, not his own seals the deal.

Giving blind hope a chance, Jon tiptoes across the room. Quietly, he opens the door, giving his ears full range. He listens, not daring to breathe. Suddenly, he hears a wail of anguish; whoever it is, they're now in the basement.

Jon waits for more but hears nothing.

Feeling froggy, he enters the hallway and peers over the protective barricade of Tupperware bins he'd stacked at the top of the stairs. Obviously, this maniacal attempt to save his sanity yielded no fruit, nor did the installed hasp and padlock stop the accusations from seeping through the quarantined-off bathroom door.

More silent moments pass before he hears the cacophony of feet stomping up the basement stairs. Instinctively, he falls back to his fort but stops when he hears the back door open and slam. As if waking from a long dream, his mind reminds him of his assignment—following anyone who shows up.

With sanity's light dawning, he races across the hall and bursts into another bedroom. This room's window overlooks the backyard. If he has any hope of tailing this woman, he needs to see what she looks like.

Mercifully, he sees her just before she disappears. Without wasting another second, he dashes back into the hallway, blasts through the wall of bins, and tumbles down the stairs like a pratfall comedian. His ungraceful trip ends with him slamming his head into the wall. Leaping back up, he sprints for the back door—there's nary a second to lose.

Once he breaks through the backyard and enters the city streets, he spots her immediately. Forgetting today is the Sabbath, he assumed he'd lose her in the crowd. Instead, she's one of a handful of people on the mostly empty sidewalks. Luckily for Jon, this woman does what she can to honor her neighbors: even though she's not Jewish, she chooses not to drive just the same.

Breathing slowly, gaining composure, he decelerates his pace to a leisurely stroll and follows her. Fortyish minutes later, her journey ends when she crosses a street, approaches a fence gate, swings it open, and walks through... careful to close the gate behind her. This act was the only thing she did correctly. Not once did she check her three, six, and nine. Nor did she wait at the bus stop for five precautionary minutes before heading through that fence gate. Her mind was too dismayed by the gruesomeness to obey the established safeguards.

Standing at the bus stop, which is part of a large Park-n-Ride parking lot, Jon counts how many houses down this house is from the corner of the street. Since he's looking at only the back fences of these houses, he's not one hundred percent sure which one she entered.

After getting his count, he walks to the end of the street, rounds the corner (being mindful to memorize the street name), and walks the street in front of the houses, ticking off each as he passes. After six houses fade from his peripheral vision, he arrives at number seven—*the* house. Mental noting the house number, he reverses his trip and heads back to the bus stop. There, he beelines for the payphone.

Wanting tourists to feel safer, Jerusalem's mayor installed credit card-excepting payphones at all bus stops. Then, when all forms of money were abolished, he had the phones equipped with R-Chip readers. Even though everybody has a cellphone, he still felt their existence was necessary: cellphone batteries do die after all.

Knowing he can't make a call Jon entreats the few passerbys to hook him up with their R-Chip. It took two "no's" before getting a reluctant "yes". His appearance and odoriferousness are overwhelming.

After bashfully thanking the Good Samaritan—the more his freedom from the house of horrors extends, the more his lucidity returns: he's a disaster—Jon de-cradles the receiver and punches in Dino's digits. Three rings transpire before Dino answers.

"Hey, it's Jon."

"Jon who?" Dino asks.

"Jon. The guy watching the dead Jewish couple's house."

"Oh, right. You're still alive?" His voice is saturated with genuine surprise.

"Yes, and I'm standing across the street from what I think is another drop-off house."

"Why do you think that?" Dino quizzes.

"Because a woman showed up this morning looking for...HIM. I followed her to this house."

"No kidding? Do you have the address?"

"Yes, 13 Gaon Street."

"Excellent job. Seriously. I'm not often impressed."

"Thank you," Jon says, not remotely interested in this guy's praise. "What should I do?"

"Wait there. I'll get back to you."

***

Dino disconnects and locates Andel's number in his Contacts list. Finding it, he moves his thumb to the blue number, ready to push it but stops. An inner voice speaks up, instructing him to think this decision through. Three seconds of thought later, Dino backs out of his Contacts list and opens his Google app. There, he types in Jon's provided home address. The returned information confirms he made a wise decision in suspending his call to the pope.

Bringing his Contacts back up, he locates Vincente's private number and thumbs it. He waits, knowing that Vincente is most likely getting ready for his coronation but still hoping he has a minute. Seconds later, his wish comes true.

"Dino!" Vincente answers, delighted to hear from his old friend. "It's been too long."

"Hi, Vincente," Dino responds with like enthusiasm. "I know you've got a lot to get ready for but do you have a minute?"

"I always have a minute for you, my friend," Vincente assures. "What's on your mind?"

Glad to hear the vestiges of his old friendship coming to light, Dino continues. "Has Andel told you about the old Jewish couple and what's going on?"

"He has."

"Okay, 'cause you're not gonna believe what my VP wannabe unearthed."

"I'm listening," Vincente promises.

"I think he's found the masterminds behind the whole kit and caboodle," Dino informs.

"Dino, I'm glad your gift of gab hasn't waned, but please, out with it."

"I believe the masterminds are the Mendels."

"Joshua and Ariella Mendel? The children of two of my closest associates. Those Mendels?"

"Yes. A woman showed up at the old Jews' house this morning. My wannabe followed her, and she led him right to this house. I Googled the address. Their names came up as the owners."

"Well, this is an unexpected problem," Vincente bemoans.

"What should I do with them?"

"Nothing. For right now anyway. Tell your ambitious Anathema to keep an eye on their house for the rest of the day."

"Why not just raid the house and kill them?"

"Kill them? On what charge?" Vincente inquires.

"Charge?" Dino asks incredulously. "Vincente, you've had me killing Anathemas for weeks now. Why are these two any different?"

"Because they're the children of two of my closest associates," Vincente repeats himself. "Dino, the quickest way to destroy a business is to keep disgruntled higher-ups on staff. I still need Benson and Eleazar. Besides, Ariella saved my life and as far as Joshua...I have a special fondness for him. I like knowing he's in the world."

Dino remains silent.

"I know you don't agree with me, but I need you to trust me."

"I do Vincente. I do."

"Thank you. You've always been a good friend."

"Then may I speak frankly?"

"You know the answer," Vincente assures. "Speak."

"I don't think it's wise to show any partiality. If these two are the ones behind it all, then I feel they need to be dealt with immediately."

Silence is the only reply. Dino continues his sales pitch.

"In all the years we've known each other, have I ever steered you wrong?" Dino asks the leading question.

"Alright, my devotion to them may've created a blind spot, but why do you think they're THE ONES? Do you have any proof?"

"It's a hunch, and no, not yet. The woman could have gone anywhere, but she went to their house."

Vincente goes silent again. This is an important decision; it needs mindful reflection, not gut reaction.

"Andel says you found a secret stockroom in the old Jews' basement. Is that correct?"

"Yes. An impressive one too."

"Alright, this is what's gonna happen. Keep your man where he is. If the Mendels are the masterminds, then an emergency meeting will happen today, most likely with their co-conspirators. The whole operation could be zeroed out today."

"What if nobody shows up?" Dino presses.

"They will. This is my hunch."

"Okay. And then?"

"Knock on the door. Announce this is an illegal gathering. Perform a search. Standard stuff."

"KGB all over again."

"If it's not broke, don't fix it," Vincente says with zero emotion. "It's true...I hate the Anathemas, and I want them all dead; but because of who Joshua and Ariella are, this needs to be handled with decorum. If you do find a stockroom, you are to arrest them, NOT kill them. I repeat, bring them to me alive."

"I'll do my best."

"No, you'll do it. Period. Bring more people if you need to."

"My guys are enough," Dino responds confidently.

"You do understand who Ariella Mendel is, right?"

"My guys will be enough," Dino repeats.

"Alright, Dino. Don't fail me."

"You can count on me, Mr. World President."

# CHAPTER TWENTY-FIVE

A pair of bloodshot, weary eyes fling open. They belong to Emily Walsh, at least she thinks she's Emily Walsh; she's not entirely sure because she's wrestling through the terrifying moment of waking up in a strange place and not knowing where you are. As the moments sneak by, the disorientation dissipates. She's now alert enough to know she's in the Mendels' guest bedroom, but aside from that, all else remains stubbornly veiled. No worries though, here in this warm bed is a perfect place to solve the *head-scratchers*.

Staring at the ceiling, she arranges her choppy memories into an organized timeline. The exercise produces results, but it's not necessarily a win. The memory of finding *parts of the man she loves* head stuck to a basement ceiling pushes to the forefront. Wiping back fresh tears, she plays the scene in her mind, holding back none of the gruesome details.

Though she didn't examine the basement closely, her exceptional photographic memory steps in and fleshes out the details. As she combs through the *photos*, the obvious big picture forms; the trouble is, her intuition insists they were *Photoshopped*. Yes, at first glance, Eric killed himself, but at second glance, the evidence doesn't line up…as if the whole sordid event was concocted. The more she chews on the clues, the more confident she is in her hunch—Eric didn't kill himself. She's seen enough suicides to know this one looked off.

The most glaring evidence is there wasn't much of *Eric* on the ceiling or the walls behind him. Shotgun suicides make a tremendous mess; what was left behind seemed underwhelming. Did he shoot himself, clean up the mess, and then shoot himself again? It doesn't take Albert Einstein to prove that's a flimsy deduction; Herbie Einstein would suffice.

Another telltale clue was she knew Eric better than any other man, including her first husband. Eric wasn't remotely suicidal. His zest for life and endless optimism didn't fit the "cry for help" narrative.

But there was one more conspicuous clue —the engagement ring and piece of paper she found in his pocket.

Not wanting to leave him in that vulgar position, she rolled him off the shotgun and laid him flat on his back. As she straightened out his hips, she felt something odd in his pocket. She removed it. When she saw the ring, she gasped. She couldn't help it; it was breathtaking. But then she noticed the folded paper lying on the floor next to the same pocket. Snatching it, unfolding it, and reading it, her heart quickened more passionately than at the sight of the ring. It was a note to her, except that it looked more like crib notes for him because the subject matter was evident—he was working on his engagement speech, and based on the several "~~cross-outs~~," it was still a work in progress.

Longing to salve her broken heart, she retrieves the note from her pocket. Sitting up, she turns on the bedside lamp and leans against the headboard. Unfolding the note, she settles in, ready to pour over each word. After three consecutive read-throughs, she refolds the note and says symbolically— "Yes!" as she slides on the ring.

With anguished ecstasy, she holds out her left hand to examine the nearly flawless diamond. Wanting to better experience its exquisiteness, she pivots towards the lamp and sticks her hand under its glow. However, her ring-admiring is aborted by what must be a dirty trick: the bedside clock announcing a preposterous time.

"Seven thirty-three!!" she says not all that quietly. "How is that possible?!"

Calling her hippocampus back into service, she strives to account for the last several hours. She remembers arriving at the Mendels around nine this morning. She remembers talking a little, crying a lot, and then being guided in here to rest. *But what happened to the last ten hours?* She thinks to herself. *There's no way I could've slept that long.*

Staring dumbly at the clock, she spies a mysterious medicine bottle also on the bedside table. She snatches it. She only needed to see three words to crack the "Case of the Lost

Ten Hours": *Emily, Watson,* and *Lunesta.* Oh yes, everything makes sense now.

A few months ago, she struggled with severe insomnia. She was putting in a ridiculous number of hours at the hospital. When she'd get home, her adrenalin-spiked-brain wouldn't let her sleep. She'd lie there, staring at the ceiling or the walls or the TV for hours on end. By the time she'd sort of fall asleep, she'd suddenly wake up like she was gasping for air and see that fifteen minutes had passed. This would happen night after night, ad infinitum. Eventually, she stopped trying to sleep altogether. What was the point? She was just gonna wake up minutes later anyway.

After a solid week of this, Eric strongly suggested she get a sleeping aid. Though she hated the idea—it wasn't too long ago that she leaned a pill and booze crutch—he promised to step in should she lose her way. She took his advice. *Only to get caught up*, she promised herself. And after four straight days of uninterrupted eight hours, she did and didn't need them anymore. Even so, she thought it wise to keep them just in case it ever happened again.

With the recollection of *benzo-popping* now solving her immediate question marks, there was still the matter of who killed Eric and why? But first...

"Yowzah! Do I gotta pee!"

Tossing back the covers, she heads to the door and cracks it open to hear other voices besides Josh and Ariella's in the living room.

Wanting to attend to problema número uno before dealing with the inevitable questions, she creeps to the bathroom. Once that greatest of human needs is addressed, she opens the bathroom door to now hear silence from the living room—the flushing toilet alerted everyone to her conscious state. Knowing she can't avoid it any longer, she heads to the living room.

When she rounds the corner, she sees seven standing persons, their compassionate eyes all looking in her direction. Four of the new people were the Lassalles and Blitsteins, the husband-and-wife duos that ran the other two drop-off houses. The fifth was Mattias Cabrera, Eric's engagement ring-hunting buddy. Though the Lassalles and Blitsteins only just arrived, Mattias pulled in just after Emily fell asleep. All were here for an emergency meeting. Doing this on the Sabbath was not desirable, but it couldn't be helped: the stakes have spiked considerably.

Not wanting comfort just yet, but the longing in the new eyes to give it could not be ignored. She submitted to the hugs.

Once Emily's shoulder-dampening by sympathy tears ran their course, she was invited to sit on the loveseat.

"We had no idea you two were dating," Harrietta Lassalle says.

"We are so sorry, Dear." Bellamy nods his sympathetic agreement with his wife's condolence.

"Neither did we," Jaleesa Blitstein adds in her attempt at softening Emily's pain. "If you ever need anything, please don't hesitate to ask Hadwin and I."

Emily can only manage a faint smile of gratitude for their love.

"I knew," Mattias, standing on her left, says. "I was with him when he found that ring." He points at her hand.

Emily looks up at him. Several new tears break through the *dam* and joyously glide down her face like freed prisoners. For the first time today, Emily cries happy tears. She snatches Mattias's arm and brings him down to eye level.

"Please tell me," she urges, wanting to hear the story.

Mattias smiles. "When he found that ring, the gleam in his eyes was so bright you'd think angels had paid him a visit. I've never seen such excitement in a grown man."

Smiling brightly, she closes her eyes and presses the ring against her lips, imagining it was Eric's lips pressed against hers. After a moment, she breaks the seal and thus the spell, and shifts to more important gears. She can return to quiet moments with her fallen man at more opportune times. For now, life and death must take center stage.

"Did somebody get his body?" Emily asks.

"Yes. Josh and I did," Mattias confirms.

"Can I see him?" Emily asks.

"I'm sorry Emily, we already buried him," Mattias says.

"It was our decision," Josh speaks up, wanting to relieve Mattias of any responsibility.

"Please understand. We didn't think it was best for you to see him again," Ariella adds, explaining their executive decision.

"I understand. You made the right decision. Where did you bury him?"

"In your backyard," Mattias says. "I hope that's okay. We figured it would be the most special place for him."

She ponders their decision, realizing there would be no better place. She could plant a rose garden around his headstone and visit him often. A rose garden would be fitting for this tragedy because, after all, every rose has its thorn...

"Did you find the Hochbergs, too?" she asks, remembering there's more tragedy than just Eric.

"Yes. They were in the bathroom," Josh testifies. "We think they were executed."

"So was Eric. I'm certain," Emily says. "That was a fake suicide."

"We know," Ariella promises. "It was clearly wetwork."

"But what we don't know is why," Bellamy says.

"Or by who," Harrietta includes.

"WhoMMM," Bellamy chimes in, his twenty-seven years of English teaching barking its *know-it-all* yap.

"Now's not the time, Bellamy," Harrietta scolds.

"I know. I'm nervous. Sorry."

She gives his hand a *you are forgiven* squeeze. She's used to her grammar being corrected after all these years.

"What concerns me is, were they being watched?" Jaleesa adds.

"Most likely, yes," Josh speaks the undesirable truth.

"It was inevitable. The sheer size of what we're doing couldn't stay hidden forever," Ariella adds.

"Nevertheless, we're shutting down for now," Josh says.

Ariella silently cringes at this. While Emily slept, she and Josh had their own emergency meeting. She believes they should push on but scale back the intricacies; Josh believes they should go completely dark and let things cool off. They argued at length, but in the end, she decided to trust his more rational thinking... for once. Her not listening to his insistence that they flee Jerusalem two years ago planted a memory marker in her long-term memory bank. However, that doesn't stop her from believing his "rationality" is due to extreme cowardice.

"If they were being watched, does that mean we are too?" Jaleesa directs this question at the Mendels.

"From now on, we must be on high alert," Josh says, choosing to dodge the question.

"While still remembering God is in control no matter how intense our circumstances get," Ariella adds, pointing their attention to the One who does all things well. Each reflects quietly, knowing she's right.

Thunder crackles, snuffing out the living room's somber silence...

# CHAPTER TWENTY-SIX

J on looks up, startled by lightning's unexpected explosion. He's thankful for another distraction, the second one in a half-hour. His still sketchy brain could've done with a few more over the last ten hours. Nothing happened, aside from Lazlo dropping off a barebones flip phone.

Ever since Dino called back, relaying Vincente's instructions—which was around 9:30 a.m.—he's been camped out in the Park-n-Ride parking lot, diligently watching the Mendel's backyard while striving to be as inconspicuous as possible. His fidgetiness and chasing the tree's shadows like groupies following a rock band (the oppressive June sun is murderous) makes this no small feat. Somebody watching him for five consecutive minutes would assume a mental patient escaped the loony bin...they'd be right.

The first distraction of the last thirty minutes was a car pulling into the parking lot and four people exiting. This was noteworthy because it's the Sabbath.

*The buses aren't running yet, so where are they going?* Jon had pondered.

Watching them regroup before marching across the parking lot, Jon held his breath. He watched them pass the bus stop bench. Still, he held his breath. They approached the street. Jon's optimism spiked, but still, he kept his glass half full. They could just be out for a walk on the city's quiet streets. But they did not turn left or right down the sidewalk; they walked across the street, directly towards the Mendel's fence. And then, it finally happened—somebody entered the backyard. His job was almost over.

Forcing his nervous-energy-intoxicated hands to settle down, he opened the phone and called Dino. Seconds later, Dino answered.

"Yes?"

"It's Jon. Two older couples just arrived in the same car and walked through the Mendels' gate."

"Are you sure it was the Mendels' and not somebody else's?"

"One hundred percent sure. What now?"

"Keep watching that gate. I'll be there in twenty..."

At minute twenty-one, Dino's car pulls into the parking lot. Like an excitable child greeting Dad in the driveway at the end of the workday, Jon rushes to Dino's car. He arrives just as Dino and his goons step out. Dino smiles, not because he thinks Jon's actions are endearing, but because he knows he owns Jon—he's the quintessential bully.

"How ya doin', Sport?" Dino asks, ruffling Jon's hair. "Did you miss me?" Sal and Lazlo snicker like classic toadies.

Jon grits his teeth and submits to the humiliation. He's come too far to let his pride trip him up at the finish line.

"Their car is still there," Jon informs, pointing across the parking lot. "I'm pretty sure nobody's left."

Dino paces while melodramatically rubbing his chin like he's working through a puzzle. He's toying with Jon's emotions, and building mean-spirited suspense. His goons enjoy watching their boss do his thing.

"Fine. Guess I'll keep my word," Dino says as he unpockets his cell and thumbs out a text. "Just fast-tracked your R-Chip approval. Monday morning, you and your family will go to the RFID department at St. John's and get your chips."

Jon is unable to move. Hearing his job is finally over, he feels the weight of his exhaustion. Dino stares at the immobile Jon.

"You're done. Get out of here."

"What about them?" he asks, looking over his shoulder and thumb-pointing at the Mendel's house.

Dino enters Jon's intimate space and bores down on him. Being that Dino is a few inches taller, Jon feels the nasal exhaust warming his forehead.

"You're...done," Dino repeats.

He remains inside the *circle*, giving Jon one last chance to be on his merry little way. Jon gets the hint. He lowers his head, ducks his shoulder, and walks around Dino, careful not to shoulder him as he sidles by. He then runs into another roadblock—Lazlo and Sal. Jon gives a hard look, requesting they move; they look back, daring him to make them.

The staring contest continues until Jon sees Lazlo's gun out and dangling at his side. Jon wisely relents and veers around the goons as well. Now that he's in the clear, with only several miles of walking between him and his family, he gets on *his horse* and begins the long trek home. Mission accomplished: his family's future is secured.

The goons, after watching Jon skedaddle, rejoin Dino, who is now hyper-focused on the fence that walls off the Mendels and their neighbors.

"What now?" Sal inquires.

"We make a house call," Dino answers as he leads the trio back to their car.

"What, we gonna roll up to the front door and knock?" Lazlo mocks. This can't be Dino's strategy.

Turns out, that's precisely his game plan.

"Just like Mormon missionaries."

\*\*\*

Three minutes later, Ariella's phone dings.

The eight, with fresh coffee warming their stomachs, are entrenched in fervent prayer, waging war with the fear gripping their hearts. This prayer meeting is nothing new. Once a week for the last two years, all involved in their extraordinary mission have met at the Mendel's house for bible study and prayer. During those couple of hours, the baby Christians grew up quickly.

In the beginning, this practice felt strange because all had mocked the silly Christians of the Old World for wasting their evenings on such nonsense. But, as it is for all the Anathemas who've given their lives to Jesus in these outrageous days, they now understand why. They never would've gotten this far without the crash course in Theology, Christology, Bibliology, Eschatology, etc, et al.

The wealth of sermons, books, and podcasts of the Old World, mercifully still in existence in the New, served them well. The more they listened and read the more amazed they were at how much information existed back then. How did they miss this? What stopped them from paying attention to it all? They could've escaped all this terror. They could be up in Heaven waiting for these seven years to end, waiting to come with Jesus on the clouds to help Him set up His Kingdom. How foolish they were.

Nevertheless, they refuse to feel sorry for themselves and play the "what if" game. God has them here, right now, for such a time as this...

Ariella investigates what her phone wants. Josh, sitting next to her on the couch, leans over for a look-see. Seeing the CCTV image on the Home Screen tells them their impromptu prayer meeting is over—an idling car sits in their driveway.

"Friends, give us a minute," Ariella requests as she and Josh excuse themselves and head up to their bedroom.

After stepping in and closing the door,

she opens her security app. Together, they watch three men exiting the car and walking up their driveway. Once the doorbell rings, the app automatically switches from the driveway camera to the doorbell camera.

Seeing who stands at their front door elicits an earnest breath from the depths of Ariella's soul.

"Who's that?" he asks, sensing the added tension to the already edgy moment.

"Dino Gennari," Ariella replies. Though no longer a part of the IDF, she still knows who the major players are in Vincente's private security. Dino is one of the majorist.

"We may have a problem...Whaddya want, Dino?" Ariella says into the phone, which transmits her voice through the doorbell's speaker.

"If you know who I am," Dino says, leaning into the prominent doorbell camera, his face taking up the whole view. "Then you know I'm not to be trifled with. We're here to search your home. Either you're opening the door, or we are. I leave it to you to decide. But please know, one way or another, we're coming in."

Ariella indiscriminately scans their room, thinking.

"You're not letting him in, are you?" Josh asks.

"It'd be far worse if we didn't. Let 'em look around, they won't find anything."

"But he's probably the one who killed the Hochbergs and Eric."

She grabs his hand. "I know. It'll be okay."

Josh looks warily into her strong, confident eyes. He wishes he was stronger. His two left feet of clay constantly get in the way of their *dance*. But she's okay with this. She knows he struggles with anxiety and loves him regardless. She kisses him.

"Come on. Our silence is making things worse."

She exits their bedroom and heads for the stairs. Josh stays behind and takes a beat. Infuriated by his cowardice, he purposes right then and there to take some of the pressure of being *the Mendel Family Rock* off her shoulders.

"I'll be right down!" he announces to a descending Ariella before marching over to her nightstand.

At the bottom of the stairs, which lands in the foyer, Harrietta meets Ariella. "There's somebody at the door," she whispers, nodding at the front door.

Ariella cups the woman's arm. "I know. Please join the others. I'll take care of this."

Harrietta remains fixed to the floor, her gazing at Ariella is equally fixed. Ariella smiles and mouths *Go*. Finally obeying, Harrietta walks past the stairs throwing a look up at Josh as he descends. Josh regards her, agreeing with the obvious apprehension. He arrives next to his "all-business" commando wife. Nudging her shoulder, he flashes a newly determined look. This buoys her spirits.

"Ready?" she whispers.

Pursed lips and an *affirmative* nod are his answers. Breathing deeply, she opens the door to find a smiling Dino and two ultra-serious men bookending him.

"Evening, Dino. How can we help you?" Ariella asks.

Dino enters without being invited in. Ariella closes the door behind them.

"Lovely home ya have here, Mrs. M," Dino remarks.

Ariella ignores the fake pleasantries and repeats her early question. "What can we do for you?"

"Well, Ariella, I'll respect you by speaking succinctly. We have reason to believe the two of you are running a network that aids Anathemas. If this proves true, it'd be considered high treason and could warrant the death penalty. Since both of your fathers are a considerable part of the world president's administration, surely you know this."

Dino and his goons push deeper into the house. After a few steps, they've come to a "T": kitchen on the left and living room on the right.

"Pardon me," Dino says to the six people sitting in the living room staring at him. "I apologize for intruding on your..." he addresses the Mendels. "What *is* going on here?"

"Nothing illegal," Ariella says. "You boys want some coffee?" Ariella asks as she heads to the Keurig, ready to play hostess.

"None for me, thank you." Dino turns towards the kitchen, leaving his back exposed to the living room. "I'll be up all night."

Lazlo and Sal enter the kitchen, grab coffee mugs staged on the island, and await those mugs' future filling.

Dino smiles. "Excellent. Now we're getting on. See, this doesn't need to be unpleasant. Just let us do our odious task, and we'll leave you good people to carry on with your night."

"What gives you the right to harass us?" Hadwin pipes up from the living room.

Dino turns at the unanticipated voice to find an old man standing defiantly in the center of the living room. Lazlo and Sal, who moments ago were waiting with outstretched coffee mugs like beggars pleading for alms, have joined Dino. Their abandoned mugs now replaced by drawn handguns.

Seeing their extreme overreaction, Dino scolds them. "Boys, where are your manners? We are guests in this home. Put your guns away."

They unenthusiastically obey. Dino turns his attention back to the belligerent firecracker. "What's your name?"

"Hadwin Blitstein," he says with no trace of fear. This isn't his first rodeo. He knows well the trappings of being Jewish.

"Ah, a Jew, that explains it. You are a mouthy, contemptuous bunch. But, I suppose you'd have to be. Things haven't exactly worked out for your people, have they? Can't seem to catch a break."

Dino stops toying with his feeble prey and turns his attention back to the matter at hand.

"So, as I was saying, we have reason to believe there is, in fact, something illegal happening in this house. You will allow us to search your home. You have no choice in the matter. The easier you make this, the smoother it will go, and the quicker we'll be on our way."

"On whose authority?" Ariella asks.

Dino plays his hand by upping the ante. "I've been given full authority to deal with the situation as I see fit. My merciful side hopes, for your sake, I find nothing. But my sadistic side hopes, for my sake, I find something. I've recently discovered that a part of me I thought long dormant has been awoken. Like a dog biting a human, I can't help myself; I want to bite again."

"Then you need to be put down!" Hadwin, running his mouth again.

"Hadwin. Sit!" Josh yells at the fiery senior while at the same time grateful for the opportunity to open his own pressure valve. The *steam* was becoming critically impacted.

Dino, enjoying the confrontation immensely, approaches the still-standing Hadwin and regards him with bemusement and respect.

"Hadwin, I have no doubt you were a scrapper in your day, but that day is over. Best to obey your master."

Hadwin, refusing to back down even one iota, ignores this disrespectful hooligan and focuses on the kitchen where he sees Ariella shaking her head with unmistakable *sit down and shut up* ferocity. He finally relents and returns to the couch where he joins a relieved Jaleesa. In his youth, Hadwin was indeed a brawler. Many a scrape has she spread Neosporin on in their decades-long marriage, so she knows his propensity for *putting up his dukes* when backed up against the wall. She's not ready to dig him a hole just yet.

"Good boy," Dino praises. He turns his attention back to Ariella. "Okay, Madame, lead the way."

"Where do you want to start?" Ariella asks.

"Let's start with the basement and work our way up, shall we?"

"As you wish."

"Excellent!" Dino exclaims with impish enthusiasm. He turns to his goons. "You two stay here and keep these nice folks company, especially my new friend." He's pointing at Hadwin.

With no further words, Josh and Ariella open the basement door, flip on the lights, and lead the way down. They stop at the bottom and stand off to the side. Dino arrives and parks himself dead center in the finished basement's main room. He looks to his left, then to his right. He then turns around and examines the wall behind him. It's a spacious room with three secondary doors leading deeper into their basement.

"Unless you're gonna save time and come clean, this basement ain't gonna search itself," Dino says, his menace thinly veiled.

"Which way?" Josh asks, trying to sound

nonchalant. This situation is volatile enough; it wouldn't do to throw his spiking emotions into the fray as well.

Dino points at the closest door. Josh opens it, allowing Dino to step through. This is a small empty room. After a quick eyeballing of all four walls, Dino steps back into the main room and waits for Josh to open the next door. This is the laundry room, somewhat bigger. But still nothing in it other than the washer and dryer. Not even a hamper of dirty clothes joins the scant furnishings. Dino does his thing again before exiting and waiting to be ushered through the final door. Josh obliges. During the searching process, Dino remains silent, but gabbers be gabbin', eventually.

"It was smart to have different basement setups. The Hochbergs didn't look like yours," he comments as he follows. His announcing they were at the Hochbergs wasn't a slip of the tongue, it was very much intentional. Mind games are his jam.

With Dino in the rear, Josh can rearrange his angry expression without being noticed. He must keep his emotions in check.

Not getting the reaction he was looking for Dino twists the knife. "But I'll tell ya. Whoever moves in has a serious mess to deal with. My overzealous familiar got a tad carried away with your runner."

Josh, now standing at the final door, clutches the doorknob and transfers all his rage into the inanimate object by squeezing the stuffing out of it. It was either it or Dino's throat.

While Josh strives to stay silent, Ariella works through the possible scenarios should Dino find the stockroom. The one common denominator...Dino meets his maker, period. The only question mark is how. All her weapons are upstairs so she's gonna have to improvise. Dino continues chiding.

"My instructions were to keep him alive, but it's hard to find good help and all that..." Dino pauses. "The whole sordid affair plopped into MUBAR territory before I could stop it. Eh, whaddya gonna do, am I right? It is what it is."

Josh looks over his shoulder and glares at Dino. Ariella spots the percolating rage in her husband's eyes. She needs to let the air out of his tension balloon post-haste before the *POP!* gets them all killed.

"MUBAR?" Ariella asks.

"Messed Up Beyond All Recognition. Didn't wanna cuss in front of the lady," he says chummily while throwing a friendly wink at Josh.

That did it. Josh can no longer abide this fool's flippant twaddle. Letting go of the doorknob, he steps towards Dino while keeping himself in front of the third door.

"Do you know how many people are starving, who are waiting for a reprieve from this living hell?!"

"Joooosh..." Ariella's eyes widen as she slowly but oh so ultra-seriously shakes her head. Dino catches her attempt at de-escalating the situation.

"Don't worry, Ariella, I won't hurt your man. Just so long as he stops stalling and opens this door. I'm sensing I'm not supposed to see what's inside."

Josh refuses to open the door. Dino takes an intimidating step toward him. Ariella, knowing she could take them both out with scarcely an extra breath, walks behind Josh and opens the third door. The two junkyard dogs hold their ground a blink longer before Dino snorts mockery and peers through the opened third door. He sees that this room is much bigger than the other two and contains a sub-door on the far end.

"Ooh, exciting! Now we're getting somewhere." He steps in and heads to the sub-door, confident treasure is hidden on the other side.

Josh and Ariella join him in the new room but stay back by the third door, breathlessly watching Dino approach the furnace room door. He rests his expectant hand on the doorknob, psyches himself up for the *SURPRISE!* and then...

The drumroll beat rollicking in his head crescendoed to the climactic heights of unbridled suspense only to abruptly lose its rhythm and awkwardly tumble into the cymbals.

The aggressive whipping open of the door delivered the most anticlimactic gut punch imaginable. The glorious percussion once producing such grand euphoria was heartlessly replaced by a comical *sad trombone*. All he finds is a small room; all he sees is the hot water tank, the furnace, and cobwebs swaying in the *whoosh* of the flung open door.

He takes a moment to regain his composure. He can't afford to lose his emotional leverage by broadcasting his disappointment. Besides, it doesn't mean there *isn't* a secret stockroom, it just means he needs to look harder. Suddenly, the lightning and faint distant thunder percolating for the last fifteen minutes, make its presence heard and felt.

"Whoa! Somebody got a strike!" Dino exclaims, reacting to the bone-jarring thunderclap.

The Mendels ignore his folksy schtick as they step back into the main room, grateful for the stockroom's continual clandestineness. The problem is, Dino remains, pacing and musing as though ambling through an art museum, albeit one with no paintings on the walls. In fact, there isn't anything on the walls, or furniture, or stuff in general, anywhere. Nothing to make one think the finished basement served a purpose at all. They return to the third room and peer in.

"You have an exceptional basement," Dino remarks. "Clearly, you put a lot of work into it. Though, it's lacking that *lived-in feeling*."

"We haven't gotten around to giving it," Josh answers.

"It would seem. Don't get me wrong, you guys did a bang-up job. First class all the way. Problem is, I don't get the sense a she shed, or man cave was your ultimate goal. I do, however, have an overpowering hunch  this is meant to be a smoke screen to hide a much larger objective…"

He continues pacing. "My gut's never let me down before, but there's a first time for everything. Così è la vita," he says, shrugging his shoulders like a teenager saying *whatevs?* "Let's head upstairs, I guess."

Josh and Ariella sigh in relief as they lead the way, putting the source of life for hundreds in their rearview mirror. But just before reaching the clear, thunder strikes again. And this time, as the boom dies out, the electricity dies with it. The swallowing up in total darkness lasts but a blink before Dino has his phone out and pointing its LED flashlight at the couple like a fast-draw artist in an old Western.

With the spotlight glued to the Mendels, the phraseological *pin-dropping* comes into play as the trio remains in their silent stand-off. The deafening silence doesn't drag on for long. The faint but undeniable sound of an electrical lock disengaging blasts from the furnace room and barrels towards them at 767 MPH. The breaker's small, backup generator adds its defectiveness to the unfolding drama…

Distressed grimaces contort the couple's faces as they stare into the opposite expression forming on Dino's face. Lost in rapture, Dino disregards sound judgment by turning his back to his enemies and returning to the furnace room. His cell's flashlight leads the way like a leashed-hound dog on the scent.

Drawing closer, the flashlight's cone

expands across the wall. Eventually, some light spills into the furnace room, highlighting its features and flaws. Dino's snake-like intensity focuses on one specific flaw: a split in the wall by the hot water tank.

Arriving at the furnace room door, he does not throttle back but accelerates up to the fake wall. Standing there, savoring the saccharine palatableness of success, he reaches out and pushes the newly revealed door inward. With the secret room now open, his flashlight starts from one end and tracks across to the other end. He lets out a stunned whistle.

Regrettably, his ecstasy is cut short by his sixth sense sounding the alarm. Casually, he retrieves the 9mm from its concealed carry holster and whips around, ready to confront *Death's* reaching hand. A blast of light and sound erupts in the room. However, it originates not from Dino but from a shocking source. Dino's phone drops, lands at his feet, and casts the flashlight upwards, bathing himself and Josh in light. The glow encapsulates and accentuates the smoke seductively emanating from the gun in Josh's hand.

Utterly stunned by the reversal Dino, gun still in hand but no longer pointing, looks at the red blotch expanding across the lower half of his shirt like ripples in a pond. The bullet ripped through his stomach and pierced his bowels. He might as well have been shot in the heart because the same result is assured: he's a dead man.

Looking into Josh's equally stunned eyes,

a thought blinks to life. It is a thought often accompanying a drowning man—*If I'm going down, I'm taking him with me.*

Galvanized by thoughts of revenge, Dino quickly points his gun at Josh. But Josh, adrenalin still filling his veins, fires two more shots into Dino's chest—the final two nails sealing the coffin shut.

When Dino made his way back to the furnace room, Josh and Ariella remained back, hoping what they heard *wasn't* the stockroom's lock unlocking. Watching Dino push open the secret door removed all doubt. Whether Josh was thinking clearly or not, he jumped headfirst into the fray. Ariella, who was a few steps behind Josh as he charged after Dino, screeched to a halt, stunned by Josh's first shot. Because of the suffocating darkness, she never saw him pull out the gun.

She may've missed the first shot but was on him immediately after the final two. She snatches the gun away and gives it a once over. She really didn't need once; she knew where it came from.

"You took this from my bedside drawer?" she asks as she also removes the inside waistband concealed carry holster from his pants, slides the pistol in it, and attaches the duo to her waistband.

Josh, ensnared by shock, doesn't answer her. He's focused on the long-dead Dino. His mind labors through the implications of what's happened, on the finality administered by his hand.

"Boss! What's happening?!"Sal's voice fills the darkness.

Josh doesn't react. Ariella does, removing the firearm once again. She's in the zone now, ready to escalate the situation so it can be de-escalated quickly. She sprints to the door leading back into the main basement room and takes cover behind the door frame. Peering out, she watches the dancing cellphone flashlight spilling out of the stairway tunnel grow large. She steadies her breathing, ready for the close-quarters combat that's about to play out. She waits but not for long. The second she sees the goon's drawn gun leading the way, she fires two shots into the thin stairway wall. A dead Sal tumbles forward, flopping onto the ground.

She breaks cover and scampers to the stairway where she snaps back into cover against the stairway wall. She peers up the stairs, waiting for the second goon to show his soon-to-be-dead head. Again, she doesn't wait long.

"What's going on down there?!" Lazlo hollers as he appears at the top of the stairs, gun also drawn. Ariella fires. This time her shot misses wide, causing him to duck, lose his balance, and fall on his back end.

"Whoa!" he yells as he crab-walks backwards. Rather than firing back, he scurries to his feet, dashes to the kitchen sliding glass door, and bounds into the twilight.

Ariella steps over the dearly departed Sal and flies up the stairs, two at a time. Arriving at the top, she dashes to the glass door. There, she covers against the wall, gun at the ready. Ducking, making herself small, she sneaks a quick peek before snapping her head back in. No shots. She peers out again for a longer look. Seeing that the backyard is empty and the fence door wide open, she stands, breaks cover, and relaxes her weapon hand—Lazlo has safely escaped.

Slowing her breathing, deciding whether to give chase, the power comes back on. Peering at the newly illuminated can lights, her attention is drawn to the six terrified faces staring at her. Oh yeah, they have guests...

Understanding the situation is abated, she allows her emotions to return to DEFCON 5. After holstering her firearm, she holds up her hand to say—*all is well*. Silently, she returns to the basement: she needs to check on her husband.

She finds Josh sitting, both knees up to his chest and his arms wrapped around them. He's not hugging them or rocking like he's in an upright fetal position, but more like he's sitting at a campfire. However, he's not staring at dancing flames, but rather a bleeding corpse. She pads over and joins him on the floor.

"I hate guns," he eventually mumbles. "I only grabbed it for self-defense."

"I know, Love. When did you take it? When we were in our bedroom?"

He nods. "I took it after you went downstairs. But the madder he made me, the more I hoped, BEGGED, he'd make me shoot him."

"You made the right decision. It was either him or us."

"Was it though?" he asks, guilt hovering like a tidal wave. "My rage fueled this. I didn't have to murder him. We could've subdued him."

"Josh, that's a normal human reaction, but not one based on reality. He was a dead man the second he found that room. I was gonna snap his neck, but you got to him first."

Silence descends as Ariella leans against Josh and rests her head on his shoulder. She's affording him time to process. Working through the taking of life is a delicate moment. Many emotions vie for center stage. She remembers her first time; she felt a lot like this.

"Umm, Guys?" Emily adds her voice to the fragile moment.

Ariella sits up to see Emily stepping over Sal still at the stairs.

"In here, Emily."

Emily enters the third room, her gaze landing on Dino's motionless body. As a doctor, she's seen her fair share of dead bodies, but knowing it could've been, SHOULD'VE BEEN her own body...well, this is a new sensation. She's a tad shaken up.

"We're not sure what to do," Emily informs, referring to herself and the other five souls.

Ariella, who spent these quiet moments forming a plan, answers. "You and the others will haul up food and supplies to be packed into our car, Mattias's and the Lassalle's. We're taking as much as we can because when we leave, none of us are ever coming back."

"Where are we going?" Emily inquires.

"The mountains," Ariella answers. "Quickly. We need to be in the wind before Vincente's coronation begins. Everybody will be focused on getting to the Temple Mount. We should have no trouble leaving the city."

"What do we do with these two?" Emily is referring to Dino and Sal's final resting place.

"Let 'em rot. If somebody comes looking for them, we'll be long gone."

Emily says nothing, only walks into the stockroom and grabs an armful before heading upstairs: her mind's in the game. Ariella gifts Emily with a grateful smile as she walks by; her hyper-focused unflappability is much appreciated.

Ariella stands to her feet, encouragingly hoisting her husband up with her: he can finish brooding later. Once both stand, Ariella looks deep into his troubled eyes before bringing him in close.

"Love, can you please get the Lassalle's car?"

He says nothing, only looks into her squared-away eyes. The two share a silent, affirming moment; a kiss; and her handing out a loving yet motivating slap on Josh's *wallet*. She needs his full focus. He offers a faint smile: message received.

But before Josh saunters off, Ariella says: "We need to pray."

Josh agrees, but his mind is not in the best place for prayer. Ariella, as all couples should do when their spouse is not operating at their best, picks up the slack.

She begins, offering an impassioned plea to the God of Heaven, empowered by one of the first bible passages Benson taught her during her early days as a new Christian. She prays this back to God.

"Father, You tell us in James one, five through eight that if we lack wisdom we are to ask You for it because You will give it to us generously without rebuke. However, You also offer a warning. We are to ask You with full faith, no doubting. You tell us that if we act like that, we're indecisive and unstable. Father, we don't want to be unstable. Help us resist our doubts and fears. Lord, we don't know what's coming. We don't know if our part in Your Grand Design is over. But we know You know. Lord, please. Show us the way. Send us somebody to point us to the next thing. We ask this in Your Son's Holy Name, amen."

*\*\**

Once Josh returns with the Lassalle's car, it's quickly filled so that the two older couples can be on their way. Ariella wanted them back at their respective homes quickly so they can leave a note for the Anathemas coming for Distribution Night in a couple of hours. The note will say: "It's not safe. Do not go back to your homes. Leave immediately."

Emily and Mattias sit patiently in the Mendel's packed car, in the driveway, backed in closest to the garage door. Mattias's own packed-full car sits first in the driveway, ready to zoom away. The two are giving their leaders, who are sitting on the hood of Mattias's car, a moment... hopefully, not their last. The power couple will be splitting up for a few hours.

Mattias's car has had a busy day. It's been Eric's hearse, soon it will be food transport, but for right now, as Ariella explained to Josh, it will be his Uber.

While Josh was grabbing the Lassalles car from the Park-N-Ride parking lot, Ariella called his dad to keep him in the know. Hearing all the gritty details, Benson pleaded with Ariella to convince Josh to meet him at his office building before they fled. Ariella has just done that and to her surprise, he did not put up a fuss. He simply said, "Okay."

With the assumed difficult conversation over, she and Josh sit quietly, watching the overly active night sky. Jerusalem's heavens appear to be in an epic battle. At the Temple Mount, several roving spotlights paint the darkening clouds. They are beacons, encouraging the world to —"Come one, come all, and witness the greatest event in human history!"

But there is more going on in the sky. The looming storm that's been toying with Jerusalem's residents for the last hour has stopped its advancement, appearing to be biding its time like a Siberian tiger waiting to pounce on an unsuspecting village. Josh and Ariella watch the electrical storm warily.

The sky resembles a Chinese ceremony playing out in the dark clouds. The constant firecracker-like electrical explosions, which appear to be tearing the heavens to shreds, are unnerving, exhilarating, and definitely spooky. It seems Somebody else has something to say. However tonight plays out, tomorrow will be the dawn of the end.

"You get back to me ASAP, understand?" Ariella, overwhelmed by the sky, the circumstances, and her human frailty, suddenly breaks the somber silence.

Josh may not have put up a fuss, but she is; mentally, anyway. She hates the idea of them splitting up. Her only reason for contacting Benson was to keep him in the loop, not to let him pull Josh OUT of the loop.

As per the emergency plan they created back at the beginning of their rescue mission, a secret rendezvous spot was established should the whole kit and caboodle go belly up. Their escape plan is solid, leaving very little room for unexpected hiccups. However, Josh heading deeper INTO the city instead of OUT is a major hiccup. Her normally cool-customer aura has been obliterated by the boulder-sized dread crashing onto the situation.

Josh slides off Mattias's hood while offering a hand to Ariella to do likewise. Taking a second, allowing her frustrated tears to flow freely, she wipes them away and slaps the same tear-soaked hand into Josh's.

Drawing her close, now his turn to take up

the slack, engulfs her in his arms. Leaving for the Lassalle's car did wonders in pulling him back from Despair's edge. One of Susan's strategies for dealing with his mental health was, "Do the next thing." Sometimes the disrupted mind just needs something, even trivial, to break the destructive spiraling it's stuck in.

After allowing her time to cry it out, he pulls back, looks into her eyes, and says nothing, only kisses her. Heart and emotions steeled, Josh climbs into Mattias's car and leaves. Ariella remains, watching the car disappear around the corner at the end of the street.

Seeing and sensing her commandant's disquietude, Emily exits the Mendel's car and joins Ariella in her private war. Her arm lands across Ariella's shoulders.

"Who's in control?" Emily asks the leading question.

"I know. But what if He takes Josh."

"Then that's what He wants and that's what's best for all of us. Don't lose sight of Truth. We need you. You're our leader. Now lead."

Pep talk is over. Emily releases Ariella, walks over to the driver's side door, and opens it, waiting for Ariella to climb in behind the wheel.

"Let's go," Emily commands.

Ariella resets her focus and obeys. Seconds later, her car is at the entrance to their development, stopped at the same stop sign Josh turned left at. Ariella peers in that direction, hoping to see his glowing backlights. Wishful thinking...he's long gone. She mentally sends him a quick *I love you* across the ESP airwaves before turning her wheel to the right.

***

Eleven and a half minutes later, Josh sent his dad an, "I'm here" text. Now, he's pacing outside his dad's office building. He's nervous, not because of the impending danger, but because he'll be seeing his dad for the first time in two years. There's a lot to say but not nearly enough time to say it.

As it turns out, the time spent dreading the moment didn't even last a full minute. Benson, not bothering to waste a second in the revolving entrance door, bursts through a secondary door. He's huffing; must've skipped the elevator and opted for the steps: two at a time it seems.

When he sees his dad, chest heaving like he's having a widow-maker, all apprehension melts away. In its place—calm assurance. The world may be settling comfortably into its *handbasket*, but in this place, all was right with it. Wasting not one more of their precious few seconds, Josh sprints to his dad and collapses into his fatherly arms. The hug lingers; the tears flow.

"Josh, I am so sorry." The words fall out of Benson's mouth with great relief. He's been wanting, NEEDING, to say them for a long time.

"Dad, I forgive you, but I have a lot to say, and this might be the last time I can say it."

Elder Mendel says nothing, only leads them to a nearby bench. Sitting, Josh stares at the ground and collects his thoughts: he wants to be concise while still saying everything that needs to be said.

"You've been my whole world my whole life," he says. "You've been on a pedestal for so long, I can't remember a time I wasn't looking up to you. Wanna hear what my shrink figured out?"

Benson says nothing. Only waits.

"That most of my issues stem from trying to be you instead of me. That every time I failed to be like you, through doing something ridiculous or not doing something up to your quality, the shame sent me spiraling into my ever-present pit of self-loathing."

"Josh, my son, I never wanted you to be like me."

"I know, Dad. Putting you in such a precarious place wasn't fair to you, and definitely not healthy for me. It was just a matter of time before you came crashing down. I'm not sure what hurt most: your betrayal or seeing you broken and crumpled next to that pedestal."

"This may not matter now, but if I could take everything back, I would. I don't know what happened to me in Vincente's office. One minute I'm resisting his charms and the next, I'm completely beguiled. I never should've taken that meeting. I let my pride and ego overrule what I knew was a dangerous situation. I was so seduced by the notion that the most powerful man on the planet needed me, that I blindly marched in. Trust me, I've been suffering the consequences ever since. I blame only myself. You don't know this, but it got so bad, I was suicidal. But then something happened to take the focus off myself and put it back on God."

"What?" Josh asks, stunned by his dad's confession.

"My assistant died."

"I don't understand."

"I know, and you don't need to," Benson assures his confused son. "Just know I've been hard at work mitigating the damage I've done."

Those last three words— "damage I've done"—sent a wave of guilt crashing into Josh's wind-battered little *boat*. Lost in this moment, he forgot about the blood on his hands. His dad catches the dispirited vibe.

"I know what happened," Benson informs. "Ariella told me."

"I caused a lot of damage too."

"You didn't have a choice."

"There's always a choice, Dad."

"Not according to Ariella. Son, he had to die."

The stunned look on Dino's face involuntarily splashes across Josh's consciousness. Violently mushing his eyes shut, he squeezes both temples with his right-hand thumb, and fingers as though trying to squash the image out of existence.

After Ariella's call, Benson debated if he should tell Josh about the other matter dominating his mind of late. But seeing the anguish on his son's face assured him now was the perfect time.

"Once my relationship with God was

restored so were my nightly dreams," Benson begins. "They were foggy, but I have no doubt they were mostly about you."

Josh opens his eyes and bores them into his dad, excitingly waiting for more details. Is he about to get an answer to Ariella's prayer already? Boy, that was fast.

"From what I can discern, God has something profound for you to do next. I think your job of feeding the Anathemas is over. Now, your job is feeding the VPs."

"I don't understand," Josh says, dishearteningly. He was hoping for a crystal answer, not a cryptic one. "They have more food than they know what to do with."

"I don't think it's physical food."

"What then?"

"My guess is spiritual food," Bensons says with a shrug. "I know you want more answers, and I wish I could give them. But take heart, my son, I get the impression they're on their way."

Josh's pocket breaks into a jingle—it's Ariella's theme song. He answers. "Hi, Hon."

Benson also unpockets his phone but for time-checking purposes. He doesn't like what he sees.

"Are you out of the city yet?" her words enter his ear.

"Not yet. I'm still with my dad."

"Not for much longer," Benson informs, his voice ripe with forewarning. Ariella hears it.

"Please say hi for me as you're saying goodbye. It's almost nine-thirty. Vincente's ceremony will begin soon. You need to leave. Now."

"Okay. I'll see you soon. Love you."

"Me too. Hurry," she commands. They both hang up.

Benson takes the lead by standing. Josh doesn't budge. He's paralyzed by the cruel sting of their brief time together. He wants to remain a little longer, but he can't, and he knows it. Reluctantly, Josh stands. Benson grabs his shoulders, arresting his attention.

"Son, thank you for forgiving your prodigal dad. You've given me the courage to do what still needs doing." Benson falls silent, searching for the right parting words. "Listen to me; obey God, no matter what. We only have a few years left, and then it's all over. Let's both finish well."

They hug each other, but no tears accompany the embrace this time. After sufficient time for one last hurrah-hug passes, Benson releases his son.

"I love you, Dad."

"I love you, Josh."

Sighing deeply, Josh crosses the street to the small, executives-only parking lot where his car resides. He opens the door, but before he hops in and flees the rushing *tsunami*, he steals a final glance at his father. They stare at each other with the intensity of those who know they'll never speak again, because they won't, at least not in this lifetime. Lord-willing, the next no longer tarries...

# CHAPTER TWENTY-SEVEN

E nergy and anticipation surge through the throng like dolphins galloping through the ocean depths. The chattering of the multitudinous blend together, infecting everybody with exhilaration. It's peaceful mob mentality at its finest. This is happening among the gathered people outside the Temple Mount—those not lucky enough to secure a place inside. They are jammed together in the Western Wall Plaza where two Jumbotrons stand side by side, providing the visual proof of prophecy being fulfilled.

Because it was impossible to fit everybody inside the Temple Mount the Sanhedrin agreed to this one-time-only desecration by allowing the Plaza to be turned into a sports arena.

And for the other roughly 4 billion people not in Jerusalem, the event is being broadcast live so that all may witness. It is a moment in time that will be remembered for all time and is moments away from commencing.

\*\*\*

Growing restless, Aaron D'Angelo stands at an open window in one of the temple's upstairs private chambers. His being in this room is also a one-time-only allowance made by the Sanhedrin. The thought of letting Gentiles into the recesses of their sacred temple is a tough pill to swallow, especially a *pill* as unclean as a pill-poppin' junkie.

He was sent up here to get ready, but he's been ready for some time. Now there's nothing to do but wait for his summoning to join Vincente on stage. This is of great consternation to Vincente's inner circle. Against their counsel, he insists Aaron be close by for the big event.

*He's a walking disaster and completely unpredictable. He could ruin everything. It makes no sense!* was the basic gist of their griping.

Vincente's only reply was, "It doesn't need to make sense. Just obey." Case closed.

Still at the window, a breeze blows in, sending a chill through Aaron's broken body. He's always cold even when it's "sweaty weather," which tonight most certainly is. Based on the huddled masses waiting for Vincente to be crowned Messiah, the humidity isn't dampening the rock concert-like vibe. Though dusk is nearing total darkness, the outdoor lamps are enough for Aaron to see the enormity of the crowd inside The Mount—the house is packed.

Another breeze blows in, causing him to step back. Clutching his long-sleeved arms around himself he looks down and notices his uncovered wrist. Un-hugging himself, he slides up his sleeve, revealing a grotesque mess. Disgusted, he slides up his other sleeve and stares at his bare arms as though he'd forgotten what they look like. He studies the bruised and collapsed veins dotting his arms; they look like a tourist map highlighting points of interest.

Sadly, this putridness doesn't stop at his arms; the horrors extend across his gaunt, sickly body. His entire body resembles a ravished World War I battlefield. There's hardly a vein he hasn't jammed a spike into. Most have been hit multiple times like persistent mortar shelling from the Germans. Whenever he's sober —which isn't often and doesn't last long—the pain is immeasurable. The levels of despair and hopelessness have reached such dizzying heights that Aaron will do anything, short of suicide (it is a mortal sin after all...pesky Catholic upbringing), to escape his captor's cruel clutches. But all past attempts to flee failed.

Normally, being around Vincente makes him nauseous. But tonight, he's craving the opportunity. He believes he's finally found the exit door.

\*\*\*

"Are you ready?" Andel asks. He's just entered.

"I'm dressed, aren't I?" Aaron chides.

"No. I mean, are you *ready*? Have you jammed a DISGUSTING needle into your DISGUSTING body and pumped DISGUSTING poison into it yet?"

"I was just about to. Wanna watch?"

"Not in the slightest, but I have no choice."

"Wait, you serious?" Aaron's caustic

sarcasm backfires.

"Yes, I'm serious. I'm required to witness your filthy habit. Vincente wants you on your best behavior. Why he doesn't just burn down your revolting drug den with you in it is beyond me."

"That doesn't sound very loving, especially for a... 'Man of the Cloth.'" Retrieving some of his old spunk, Aaron chooses a lofty voice and air quotes to mock Pope Vassallo. Clearly, his Catholic superstitions only extend so far.

Andel doesn't appreciate the obvious disrespect. "Aaron, hear me. Vincente will eventually tire of you, and when he does, I will personally snuff you out."

"My, my, my, that's not very Christianly of you!" Apparently, all his quips are only of the *clutching his pearls* variety.

"Lucky for me, Christianity is dead." An equally pitiful comeback. The laughable power struggle tête-à-tête mercifully reaches a stalemate. Scorecard: both are losers.

Aaron rolls his eyes as he heads for the chair and end table where his syringe-carrying case awaits. Arriving and plopping, Aaron settles in. Unzipping his case, he removes the required tools for his awful habit. When he removes the drug baggie, he holds it out and flicks the bottom of it. He steals a glance at Andel to see if he's still watching—he is.

Aaron silently thanks the drug gods that he prepared this special concoction beforehand. Aaron's confident Andel knows diddly-squat about cooking, but he's pretty sure crushing some Adderalls and tossing them into the mix would raise suspicion.

As he begins the vile process, he mutters to himself for having to inject this loathsome medley of evil. Being forced to daily continue this debased lifestyle lost its thrill long ago, but mixing stimulants with his H was a whole nother beast. He wishes there was another way, but if he wants to succeed tonight, this is how it must be. The scag is necessary to keep his out-of-control heroin addiction at bay; the Adderall, however, is to keep his mind focused and his senses centered.

*Just a little bit longer, my boy, and you'll be free...*

Another couple of minutes and the abhorrent process is complete. Aaron sinks into the chair, looking on the verge of melding with it.

"You ready?" Andel sneers.

"What's your problem?" Even with closed eyes, Aaron perceives the peevishness. "The burden of playing second fiddle weighing you down?"

Andel ignores the chiding attempts which annoys Aaron: he wants to quarrel.

Aaron opens his eyes to slits. "You know what your problem is? You're a fussy, jealous, pathetic little man."

Andel looks at his watch—it's almost time. He says nothing, only opens the door and walks out. He does, however, speak to the large security guard furnished with an MP5 slung across his chest, standing outside the room.

"Get him downstairs even if you have to carry him."

The guard nods understanding and steps into the room. Aaron sees his aggressive attitude won't fly with this mountain of a man. He stands immediately, maybe a little too quickly—he must lean against the wall to shoo away the dizzy birds. Yeesh, this is a potent batch.

After a moment, settled repose appears on Aaron's face. "Lead the way, my good man."

The guard says nothing. Only shakes his head and nods towards the door, demanding Aaron walk in front of him. Aaron shrugs and does as he's told. The big moment has arrived. This is it. Don't get scared now.

\*\*\*

As he traverses the stairs, depending substantially on the handrail (hopefully the discombobulation wears off soon; his plan is heading towards epic-fail territory), the tumult of the expectant faithful grows louder.

The stairway eventually leads into the Holy Place, a yawning open space adorned with such elegance that being here should make any visitor feel unworthy. Well, those visitors who aren't Aaron anyway: he has a perverse satisfaction in knowing his presence is probably causing major garment rending. A perverse smile joins the ongoing perversity.

Aaron's intrusion IS causing quite a disturbance. The Sanhedrin are beside themselves knowing that Aaron is traipsing through their temple; he could have exited the side entrance and walked around to the front, but Vincente insisted Aaron walk this path. Vincente is not doing this for Aaron's sake. Oh no, he's doing this to remind the persnickety, sanctimonious Jews who the Alpha Dog is and always will be...or so he thinks.

Nothing lasts forever, and the Jews are quietly orchestrating an uprising to prove just that. They have their temple and their nation: these things are their true Messiah. Crowning Vincente is simply part of the show. Total control and autonomy are what drives them, even to the point of joining forces with their centuries-old enemy to eradicate each other's, common enemy. But this is down the road; more planning is needed. For now, they keep up pretenses; mustn't raise any alarms.

Aaron halts in the center of the Holy Place, scoping out its etherealness—it truly is jaw-dropping. His one-man entourage exits the stairway, approaches Aaron, and *shoots* a drive-by warning at him:

"Don't make me come back in here."

Aarons says nothing to his passing escort, only stares at him as he approaches the large archway granting access to the temple's porch. Aaron assumes Vincente is on the porch, waiting. He can only assume because the walking *tree trunk* blocks much of his view. Stepping through the archway, the guard joins the other no-necks in Vincente's private security scattered around the porch.

With a clear view through the archway, Aaron now sees Vincente and he is on the porch. His back is to him as he waves to the excited crowd. Aaron's stoned eyes catch the flickering light from the nearby torches highlighting his enemy. The trippy effect reminds him of his video game days, as though the game's final boss is now revealed.

Inspired by the nostalgia of his first and comparatively harmless addiction while being reminded of his humanness, Aaron steps forward, swearing he hears Hero-Music. As he goes, he reaches into his pocket, making sure a key item is still there. Verifying it is, he strokes it like massaging a lucky rabbit's foot.

His march is determined, his eyes glued to the prize—the back of Vincente's head. Aaron steadily shrinks the gap separating the looming planetary collision. With each purposeful step, another yard is erased. Inch by inch, it's a cinch.

Suddenly, his subconscious pulls up the emergency brake, nearly giving him emotional whiplash. Danger appears up ahead.

With no warning, Vincente turns his head as though hearing his name called. He bores his eyes into Aaron's. This unanticipated reaction jars Aaron, sending him into a panic. He freezes mid-step, daring not to breathe. Terror's vice grip around his unstable mind drains the blood from his face and ratchets up the BPMs. Every *Busted!!* moment in his life combined couldn't compare to the shame, embarrassment, and fear he now feels.

What caused this queer turn of events? How did Vincente know he was behind him? Did he feel him? Did he hear his thoughts? Is this some instance of clairsentience? Vincente has powers no man has—this is well documented—but his reaction smacks of expectation like he was warned beforehand.

The strangeness continues. From out of left field, another occurrence zooms in and tags Aaron's sprinting sanity. The flickering torchlight's hypnotic glow dancing across Vincente's calm, smiling face supernaturally unleashes a torrent of childhood memories and sweeps Aaron out to the exhaustlessness of Innocence Lost...

Every summer, Aaron and his six-member family (he was the youngest of four) spent a week camping at their favorite national park. Hiking, canoeing, swimming, and goofing around were the general order of business. As a young boy, it was the highlight of his summer. But his favorite memory was everybody gathering around the campfire on the final night to listen to Dad's fantastic ghost stories. The fire's glow on Dad's gentle face is a core memory from his childhood.

Young Aaron loved this night because every summer he swore things would be different. That, this was the summer he would not let his overactive imagination get the best of him; it would be this summer that he didn't have an accident; this summer, without a doubt, he'd finally show his bladder who's boss.

Dad knew about his youngest's weak

bladder; it was a personal challenge for him. He knew that if he crafted the perfect scary story, invariably, Young Aaron would wet himself. Most writers base their success on how many NYT Best Sellers they have; Dad based it on successful pee-pee pants summers.

Every summer, both combatants entered the campfire circle. Pee-pee pants, or no pee-pee pants: who would win this year? Both loved the challenge and both loved the outcome no matter what. The other three kids adored this summer ritual as well; they got to be spectators to the glorious struggle. The only real loser in this contest was Mom—she had to clean the laundry when they got home.

As Dad got rolling, everybody kept a gleeful eye on young Aaron, waiting for the moment. Like gladiators, each fought hard to outdo the other. But, eventually (at least during his single-digit years), Aaron always gave up and succumbed to the tinkles. When Dad finally saw the telltale look on his youngest's face, he pantomimed an *air signing pen* and said, "Check, please!" At that, everyone fell into a fit of giggles because Dad did it again.

Mom may have feigned annoyance, but deep down she enjoyed the summer tradition just as much. Even if she did get irritated with Dad, it didn't last long. She was charmed by his creativity and zest for life. He seemed to never run out of either until brain cancer took one and eventually the other.

Some patriarchs are so massive, so larger

than life, that when death rips them away, the family never recovers. The D'Angelos were never the same again, especially Mom. She fell into a crippling depression and never recovered. Aaron's paternal grandfather did the best he could to mitigate the loss. Aaron loved him dearly for that, and he saw a lot of his dad in his grandfather, but it wasn't the same. He just wasn't...Dad...

As his third eye wraps up the unexpected flashback, allowing tears to flow from his physical eyes, a thought flowers—*what would Dad think if he saw me now?*

Guilt engulfs Aaron in shame, causing his anger to burgeon. Being forced to associate his precious father with this foul devil adds motivational fuel to his fire. The opportunity to redeem himself in his father's eyes empowers him with fresh determination. However, as quickly as his rage blazed up, the energy going out of his legs doused it just as fast. A voice spoke to him.

Truthfully, what Aaron heard couldn't technically be considered a voice, that would denote humanness. No, what he heard was more akin to euphonious warbles piping into his dizzy brain. He's unsure where it came from or who made the sounds. Unsettled, Aaron labors to understand but doesn't need to for long. The answer is obvious—the *voice* didn't come from this realm. He's in danger of reliving his childhood disability...

Really, this oddity isn't that unusual. He's

had many parleys with residents of the *Other Side*, especially when messing with Uppers. Speed and all its filthy variants tend to make his brain more active than usual. Like the irritating neighbor who insists on introducing everyone to everyone else at a neighborhood block party, Speed likes to drag thoughts and voices out of the isolated *lawn furniture* up to the center of the revelry.

But despite the experiential expertise of the drug, Aaron doesn't believe this *voice* is coming from the amped-up land of Amphetamine. The reason—he's never heard a dialect like it before. He isn't left in confusion for long. An English-speaking voice joins the soiree, giving Aaron the interpretation.

"Not yet but hold tightly to your vehemence," the English voice says. "Go, join him on the porch. Soon, your time will come. Soon, you will express your fury to its fullest measure. Until then, watch and wait."

As though being cc'd on the conversation, once the interpretation concludes, Vincente nods to the side of the porch, beckoning Aaron to park himself over yonder.

Aaron disobeys, refusing to move. All this craziness is more than his tweaked-out brain can handle. The *voice* shows up again, but this time, instead of using just sound, he includes sight.

Aaron and Vincente are suddenly transported to a peaceful meadow. There is no sound other than the breeze rustling through the tall blades of grass. The two hold their gaze, but only for a tick. A warm smile creases Vincente's face as he motions for Aaron to join him. Still, Aaron remains steadfast while Vincente continues beckoning. Words fill Aaron's brain.

*Come, all will be well. The voice can be trusted.* These words were undeniably Vincente's.

And with that, Aaron is imbued with supernatural strength and clarity like he's never known before. He understands now; he is at peace. As he takes his first forward step, he is transported back to the temple as though leaving one room and entering another.

Propelled by this new inclination, Aaron steps onto the porch. Vincente nods approval as Aaron walks by and takes his mark out of the audience's view.

The porch is wide and positioned high above the courtyard, giving the apotheosizing worshippers a perfect view of their savior, their almost Messiah. This vantage point is perfect for Vincente as well. From it, he can look out across the sea of adulating adorers clamoring for his gaze to fall on them, to give them the blessing of basking in his glory.

Now outside, Aaron marvels at the restrained pandemonium. The atmosphere is exhilarating and diverting, amusement to its fullest definition. It takes but a moment of exposure to the controlled anarchy before Aaron is swallowed in its emotionally driven undertow and swept out to the sea of bliss. He's never experienced anything like it.

While Aaron is bewitched by the

reverential blustering, danger lurks in the grass of his inattentiveness. He is unaware of the conviction slithering towards him like a serpent stalking a preoccupied mouse.

With guard down, the conviction clamps onto Aaron's psyche and injects its pestilence into his stream of consciousness. His mind is altered; reason escapes him. Now, he is overcome with an inconceivable emotion—unbridled, unmitigated, unimaginable love for Vincente Basile.

Fully embracing the deception, a new sensation overtakes him; it is akin to an out-of-body experience. He's endured many OBEs while toying with *chemistry*, but this differs from the other previous adventures. This altered reality is not due to the dirty heroin/amphetamine concoction. It is its own unique experience. He's not flying like in times past but is instead earthbound. A mystical far-off quality is present —he's here, and he's not. If his creative mind was still functional he'd explain the experience as thus...

Both the activity he's seeing and the words he's hearing play out as though happening on a pool deck while he sits on the pool floor, submerged underwater, watching. The action has a shimmering, squiggly quality, and the words are muffled and flat. Everything feels surreal.

He watches Vincente wave energetically like he's part of a parade. But then he sees Eleazar Segal, dressed in high priestly apparel, exit the temple and glide across the porch.

Next, he sees a demure temple servant holding something soft and squishy nestling something hard and shiny exit the temple. Eleazar stops next to Vincente, his body perpendicular to Vincente's right side; the servant also stops, waiting in the wings. Vincente halts his waving and stands at attention. The audience (both present and watching virtually) falls silent and waits for the ceremony to begin.

Vincente breathes slowly, centering his mind. Focused, he faces Eleazar. The two are now parallel to each other. Vincente drops to one knee and bows his head, waiting to be crowned king of kings and lord of lords.

Eleazar motions for his servant. He approaches, allowing Eleazar to lift the hard, shiny thing off its soft, squishy nest. He then raises it to the heavens. At that moment, Aaron's reasoning mind fills in the blanks—the servant was holding a pillow that held a crown.

With the dark, menacing sky serving as the backdrop for the gorgeous crown, Eleazar recites a Prayer of Dedication. Aaron strains to hear but, alas, no such luck. This has nothing to do with his current psychological residence, but rather, Eleazar is speaking Hebrew. Even so, Aaron's spellbinding remains.

Eleazar finishes his prayer, nearly concluding his role in the ceremony. All that remains is crowning Vincente's head. He does this with considerable regality. Eleazar then steps aside, allowing Pope Andel Vassallo to perform his part. Vincente remains on one knee, his newly crowned head still bowed.

Andel rests his left hand on the top of Vincente's exposed head and raises his right hand to the *Throne Room*. Words spill out of Andel's mouth, and, like before, Aaron has no chance—they are in Latin.

The men's roles were similar, but their tasks accomplished a specific purpose. Eleazar's was to entreat YHWH to bless the crown; Andel's was to beseech Adonai to bless the man who bore the crown.

Once Andel wraps up his prayer, he shifts his hand from resting on Vincente's head to cupping his arm and coaxing him to his feet. As he does, Andel takes a step back and holds out his hand to Vincente. He speaks:

"Watching World, those in attendance and around the globe, it is my distinct and profound privilege to present to you...your Messiah."

At that, Vincente faces the courtyard and the cameras, takes a symbolic, headship-establishing step forward, and waits. He doesn't wait long. Andel and Eleazar drop to one knee and bow their heads in reverence. The rest of the VP world, including those watching virtually, follow suit by taking a knee and bowing.

Vincente speaks, but, as it's been for this crazy mind trip, the words are muffled in Aaron's ears. At least they're in English, so he picks up a few words. He points his right ear at Vincente, desperately straining like one hard of hearing.

But, without warning, a new abnormality materializes, vying to be king of this oddity hill. The late contestant distracts Aaron from his auditory frustrations. The watery-like haze distorting Aaron's view dissipates from the middle of Vincente like a camera shutter opening on a picture-worthy subject.

Again, if Aaron's creative pencils weren't dulled by drugs' fading, he'd describe the moment as being born and Vincente being the first thing his new eyes see.

Overwhelmed by emotion, his mind reveals to him an unexpected truth. With unwavering conviction, he now knows Vincente is his Messiah. Feeling irreverent (he was the only one standing; thankfully, everybody else was bowing and unaware of his flippancy), he quickly takes a knee and bows his head.

While staring at the intricate porch floor stones, he strives to decipher what his Messiah says—his vision may be restored but his hearing is still choppy. After considerable concentration, he catches a few phrases— "Glorious new dawn," "Faith in me," and, "Never abandon you or forsake you." The last thing he hears before a roar erupts is, "Rise and behold your Christ!"

Aaron looks up to see Vincente standing with his hands raised like he's signaling a touchdown. A fitting simile since the crowd's jubilation is equivalent to witnessing the Super Bowl's winning touchdown.

Swept up in the euphoria smothering the Temple Mount, Aaron also leaps to his feet and joins the celebration. Clapping, whooping, and hollering, he walks to the top of the steps and peers out at the throng. Though it's dark, and the only sources of light are the outdoor lamps and raised cellphone screens' glow, what he sees inflames his passions. The courtyard appears not to be full of individuals worshipping in their own way, but rather a collective, pulsating blob of impassioned humans vibrating in a hypnotic blur.

Aaron has attended many stadium-filling concerts and witnessed similar scenes. He's experienced the phenomenon of groupthink taking over a crowd and turning them into one mutual mass, all sharing and feeling the same emotions. He's felt those moments when all lay aside their ideologies and prejudices, and accept and love each other as the universe intended.

Yes, he's experienced moments like this before (he has the T-shirts to prove it), but what he's feeling and looking at right now is extraordinary, otherworldly. It is intoxicating and enticing. He longs to be with the ardent, to join them in their bacchanalia. All that separates him and they are forty-three steps. He takes the first one...

"Stop!" the *voice* speaks abruptly.

Caught in between the first step and the porch platform, Aaron obeys. The cloud of ecstasy previously engulfing him was snatched away by his troubling psychosis. The sudden disorientation is tormenting. He feels cold, as though stripped naked and left in a barren field to die.

"I wanna join them," Aaron says as he

points at the crowd.

"You have a job to do," the *voice* reminds him.

"But you stopped me."

"No, I detained you."

"What's the difference?" Aaron fires back, acting like a snotty teenager.

"The difference is, it wasn't time yet," the *voice* responds.

"And now it is?"

The *voice* doesn't answer. It's obviously, "Yes."

Determined to get his way, Aaron switches to another classic teenager strategy—whining.

"But things have changed. My eyes are opened now."

"They've never been more closed. You've been duped."

"How do I know you're not duping me? Maybe you're just a dissociative mind trip."

Aaron suddenly stumbles forward as though shoved from behind. He stops his momentum at three steps, narrowly avoiding tumbling to the bottom. He whips around and scans the porch platform. He's amped up, ready to rumble with the rascal responsible for this monkeyshines. Only a second is needed to see there is nobody within twenty feet of him.

"Get...back...up...there," the *voice* commands.

Aaron remains defiantly fixed to the step.

"Don't make me repeat myself," the *voice* warns.

"Or what?" He asks with childish impudence.

"Aaron, I don't count to one, let alone three. Obey. Now."

Aaron still doesn't budge, until something does the budging for him. He's shoved from behind again, this time with greater force. Aaron lands hard on the three steps, ramming his knees and forearms into the jagged edges. Aaron crawls up to the platform, taking a seat.

"Now, get back to your spot," the *voice* orders.

Aaron inspects his knees and arms. His shirt sleeves and pants are torn, revealing nasty scrapes and seeping blood. Aaron raises an eyebrow and smiles as he rubs his palms together like he's rubbing off dirt. He stands back up. Feet planted on the first step; calves pressed firmly against the platform's edge.

"You're gonna have to do better than that. I'm so doped up I can't feel anything. I'm going down there. Period. So, unless you kill me..."

Aaron trails off, not bothering to finish his sentence. The implication is obvious. But what isn't obvious is why he's being so audacious?! HE'S COMPLETELY FREAKED OUT!! Love truly does make you do stupid things. But, as the Brits say, *in for a penny, in for a pound...*

He lifts his foot up, ready to descend. Continuing with the spoiled teen routine, he keeps his foot in mid-air, daring the *voice* to stop him. The *voice* takes up the gauntlet.

Out of the darkness comes a screeching,

535

disembodied, hellish face flying directly at Aaron's smug face. The sight of the hideous face, combined with the force of it smashing into Aaron and continuing through him unabated, sends Aaron reeling backward and tripping over the platform edge.

He lands on his backside, but physics maintains its strict laws by bouncing the back of his head off the stone ground. Immediate and fantastic stars explode in his brain, making him woozy. He props himself up on his hands and scans his environment. Unfortunately, the horrible face was not a one-time occurrence. The comprehensive attack of multitudinous horror-faces rushing fast and hard sends him scurrying backward in a kind of half-crab-walk. The barrage of abject heinousness pelts him as though shot from an attack helicopter's rapid-fire missile launcher. He scampers quickly, determined to find safety.

The panicked scuttling comes to a painful halt when his back slams into the temple wall. He's now back where he's supposed to be. The moment his back hit the wall was the same moment the devil-faced *hellfire missiles* stopped… thankfully. He pulls his knees into his chest and leans against the wall. The upright fetal position gives him a tenuous sense of security, freeing him up to get squared away. He is disoriented and dazed, most assuredly concussed. He closes his eyes and covers them with his hand, hoping to scatter the stars.

The nastiness ramps up its cruelty. A

cacophony of blood-curdling screams erupts in both ears; its intensity is like an audiophile's dream surround sound system. This fresh hell is taking its job of driving Aaron completely bats seriously. He removes his hand from his eyes and assigns it to sound-muffling duties just as its twin is already doing. Together, his hands strive to block out the shrieking, but to no avail.

Terror-stricken, Aaron presses his palms against his ears even harder as though trying to squish his head...whatever stops the agony. He swivels his head manically, searching for the source of these beastly screams. But he can't find them! He cannot locate the assailants whose screaming mouths seem like they're right up against his ears, close enough to nibble on them.

Full-blown panic sets in. He's experienced a few bad acid trips over the last couple of years, but they were an afternoon at a cat café compared to this terror. He needs to release the pressure, or his mind will snap. Out of ideas, he scrunches his eyes shut and adds his own backup screaming to the Norwegian death metal-like "song" playing in his head.

Finally, mercifully, the screaming stops. He cautiously opens his eyes and takes in his surroundings; he finds nothing out of the ordinary. Though, that's not entirely true. He does notice one glaring curiosity—nobody is looking at him. This boggles his mind.

*Did nobody see my meltdown?* he wonders. *Did I even have one, or was it all in my mind? Was everybody too busy worshipping to notice the crackhead having a freak-out?*

Knowing the answers will never come, he decides to test the waters by unblocking his ears. He hears only the celebration still going strong. His rapid breathing abates and his heart returns to normal junkie-levels of beats: the drugs combined with the terror...his heart still working is a miracle.

The *voice* speaks again, but this time there is gentleness included with its imperiousness.

"Are you listening now? Do I have your attention?"

Aaron, feeling like he's just gone twelve rounds and lost, only nods his head feebly.

"Good. Look at Vincente."

Aaron turns his gaze on Vincente and sees he's already gazing back. Vincente wasn't looking before; Aaron is certain of that. The look on his face is not concern, but bemusement accompanied by an approving smirk. His attitude smacks of the school bully watching his underlings harassing a nerd at his locker.

"Do you see how he regards you? You are only his slave. Don't you want to break free from him?"

"I did, but not anymore."

"Shall I remind you of all he's done?" The *voice* doesn't wait for an answer.

Similar in intensity to the screaming, a gang of memories crashes through the restaurant-like kitchen door separating his subconscious from his conscious. They invade his mind with Dark Ages-like cruelty. Aaron grimaces, stabs his temples with both index and middle fingers, and closes his eyes as the memories he thought were long destroyed by drugs play out in agonizing detail. They are abominations that not even a PTSD diagnosis can adequately account for.

Graciously, this doesn't last long. The memories stop and are relegated back to the windowless, concrete cells of his unconscious mind. The fingers that were previously stabbing his temples now massage them as he takes deep, meditative breaths. His eyes remain closed.

"Aaron, stand up," the *voice* commands. "Go and see."

Opening his eyes, Aaron instinctively understands he's to walk to the steps and look out. Leaning into the wall, he stands carefully, attempting to get his sea legs back. Feeling good to go, he presses onward, unsure of what awaits him. Arriving at the steps he sees not peaceful ecstasy as before but rather unmitigated anarchy and brutality.

The scene reminds him of the many mosh pits he's witnessed and been a part of while at heavy-metal concerts. The stomach-churning gore is extreme. It's like watching clans of hyenas spread out across the savannah each mutilating their own wildebeest.

Through sickened eyes, he watches ill-fated individuals being torn limb from limb by ravenous, suddenly crazed worshippers. He endures the putridness briefly before returning to the temple wall. How did things change so drastically for him? Moments ago, he was awash in euphoria; now, all he wants to do is put a gun to his head. His seesaw emotions are making him seasick, exactly as the *voice* intended. Like experiencing sensory deprivation, Aaron's humanity was stolen from him.

"What you saw is not a hallucination," the *voice* says. "But it is a vision."

Aaron listens intently. "You mean, that wasn't real? That's not really happening right now?"

"No, not yet, but it will be...soon. And it will be at Vincente's behest. Unless you stop him."

"You mean kill him."

"That's why you're here."

"No, I'm here because Vincente told me to be here."

"Just like he'll tell the whole world to kill those who don't bow the knee."

Aaron falls silent. The *voice* starts closing the deal.

"You can either have the blood of one on your hands or the blood of millions. It's up to you."

A last-ditch excuse germinates in Aaron's mind. "But if I kill him, his entourage will kill me."

"Wasn't that the plan?" the *voice* reminds Aaron.

Like the mind tricks one plays to remember why they came into the kitchen, Aaron walks back through the last few hours. A lot can happen to distract you on your journey from the living room to the kitchen: the ambrosial smell coming from the neighbor's barbecue; the new Sports Illustrated on the dining room table waiting to be read; seeing a sinister vision of multiple thousands dismembering a few dozen with their bare hands...you know, normal everyday stuff. Eventually, Aaron recalls why he came into the kitchen—he came to die.

With fresh resolve, Aaron turns his attention back to Vincente. However, unlike the other creepy times when Vincente was already staring at him, Vincente is instead staring into the distance. His empty expression looks like one psyching themselves up for a colossal moment.

"This is your opportunity," the *voice* says. "Don't waste it."

Jarred back into action, Aaron moves to fulfill his destiny and enjoy a martyr's death. Taking a final empowering breath and exhaling through gritted teeth, Aaron advances. In that same moment, Vincente turns to square up with the approaching Aaron and waits.

With hidden gun, now freed from his pocket and pointing, Aaron marches smartly toward Vincente. All excuses are settled; all fears are a distant memory; emotionlessly, he puts the pistol's semi-automatic capability through its paces, not stopping until he hears *click, click, click.*

It was fast and unanticipated. None of Vincente's security noticed what was happening till it was too late. They were expecting danger from without, not from within.

Because it was a surprise attack, two

security guards positioned behind Vincente took a stray bullet to the temple and died instantly. One guard took a bullet in the arm, but it was only a flesh wound. Three bullets went wild and landed harmlessly elsewhere. Of the ten rounds fired four hit their intended target. One hit Vincente in the forehead, killing him instantly. He crumpled like clothes dumped from a hamper.

Trigger finger throbbing from exertion, Aaron drops the gun. The metallic *clunk!* of the gun bouncing off the stone steps is loud in the stunned silence of those present and those watching at home. It was the *clunk!* heard 'round the world.

With his adrenalin still doing its thing, Aaron fans out his arms like he's been crucified and tilts his head back, staring into the dark, crackling sky. His response may be a touch melodramatic but he's about to eat a whole lotta lead...can't deny a dying man his final wish.

At that moment, after a couple of hours of labor, the pregnant clouds give birth. Aaron closes his eyes against the heavy raindrops pelting him in the face. In quasi-Shakespearean-esque fashion, the rain  symbolically washes away his sins; the guards' forthcoming return fire will atone for them. Aaron waits for the latter.

Meanwhile...

*\*\*\**

At the same time Aaron was approaching the steps to witness the carnage happening in the crowd, a weary trawler carrying its equally weary trawlers struggles to get off the choppy Mediterranean waters. They just need to push through 140 nautical miles more of intensifying sea and they'll land at Port Said.

"Is a hurricane brewing?" Alex Wright, the newest greenhorn nervously asks.

His question is directed at Newlyn Kendrick, the vessel's veteran boatswain. He's leaning on the gunwale and staring into the darkness, acting like he didn't hear the question. A handmade cigarette hangs lazily on his lower lip. The greenhorn remains a couple feet back, giving the old sea dog his space lest he be *bit*: his bite AND bark are equally upsetting. If not for the cig's cherry occasionally lighting up and then smoke billowing from his nose, Alex would assume the man was asleep.

"C'mere," Newlyn unexpectedly commands.

Alex stays put. He's already battling a case of the heebie-jeebies; dealing with the gruff sailor's usual guff is not high on his agenda.

Newlyn regards him over his shoulder. "Relax. Come here," an eerie softness coats his normally aggressive, drill-sergeant-type veneer.

Alex joins him on the railing. Newlyn turns back to the troubled sea. He removes a box of premade cigarettes from his breast pocket.

"Cig?" Newlyn asks.

Alex accepts the offer. The box is then swapped out for a lighter. Newlyn flicks his Bic and waits for Alex to light up. Overwhelmed by this absurdity, Alex nonchalantly sniffs the handmade cigarette to see if it's a different *kind* of cig. Analysis completed—nope, not dope. He leans in for a light, cupping the flame (the spark wheel was thumbed several times) from the wind and rain.

"The Mediterranean Sea don't have hurricanes, they have Medicanes," Newlyn informs. "And it's not the season yet."

Silence descends once again, allowing Alex to meditate on whether the aliens who obviously abducted the real Newlyn were friendly or hostile. In the nearly four weeks Alex's been aboard this vessel, not once has the crusty old curmudgeon offered him an olive branch much less a cigarette. What he did offer was around-the-clock tongue-lashing as though it were his personal mission to berate him into oblivion.

But, in all that time, the incessant verbal abuse rarely caused a blip on Alex's emotional radar. Truthfully, he found it kinda amusing, even nostalgic: a momentary change for the early twenty-something from constant sea sickness to welcoming homesickness.

Growing up in the Marines-like tyranny of playing adolescent East Texas football, he's witnessed and experienced all manner of ear-bleeding, foul language. His coaches relished the opportunity of making one of their players cry.

*It's our job to turn these whiny snowflakes into men!* was their rehearsed rationalization for the equally whiny helicopter parents when they "stopped by for a chat."

So his boatswain's hurled abuses—much

of it unbelievably shocking: he obviously takes great pride in living up to the "swearing like a sailor" idiom—ain't nothin' but a thang. They mostly bounce off his iron-strong skin like a marshmallow shooter pelting a rhinoceros.

The real motivation behind Alex's earlier promise to the heavens of hanging up his waterproof bib should he make it home is his experience with East Texas weather.

He was eleven when Harvey hit the Gulf and only one when Katrina unleashed her damnable villainy. Though they didn't do any significant damage to his hometown of Corpus Christi, he's seen enough to know he ain't down with hurricanes, or Medicanes, or whatever this is. His boatswain's unexpected civility does more to agitate his *jar* of already a-fluttered butterflies than anything else. According to Newlyn's unyielding braggadocio, he's seen and experienced everything one can on the open water, real and mythical. If he's spooked, which he clearly is, then something's amiss.

Isaac Green, the first mate, joins the two-member powwow.

"Everything battened down? Captain's confident we'll be docked before it gets worse, but just in case."

"It is," Newlyn assures, still leaning on the railing, not bothering to look at his first mate. "Does the radar show anything?"

"Nothing noteworthy. A pop-up storm maybe."

"I don't think so. This is something else,"

Newlyn corrects as he continues watching the west like a hawk.

"What then?" Isaac presses.

"I don't know. Something about the air. It feels…heavy."

Isaac and Alex allow Newlyn to think in silence.

"No, my gut tells me our problems aren't from above," Newlyn says as he peers at the sky. "But rather…from below."

Uneasy silence fills the implied "heavy air." Still focusing on the open seas, a surprising reality presents itself to Newlyn—the horizon is shifting to the right. He stands erect and flicks his butt into the sea.

"We may have a problem," he informs.

"What?" Isaac asks. The answer reveals itself, so he speaks it. "The vessel's turning west."

"Why is it doing that?" Alex asks, sensing the ramped-up tension.

"Because we're being pulled," Newlyn answers simply.

"By what?!" Alex squawks.

"By that," Newlyn says, pointing out into the growing darkness.

Isaac and Alex approach the railing, squinting to see what Newlyn sees.

"What is that?!" Alex asks.

Isaac has a suspicion but says nothing; the idea of such a thing is too fantastic. He grabs a nearby spotlight and shines it at the figment turning into reality.

"Is that what I—"

"A maelstrom?" Newlyn says, cutting off the consternated greenhorn.

"Wait, so it's not a whirlpool?" Alex asks hopefully.

"No, it is. Just a much bigger one."

"Impossible," Isaac says, pooh-poohing such foolishness. "We're too far out in the open."

Newlyn points his hand at the evidence; a "whaddya call that?" expression highlights his face.

"Alright, fine," Isaac concedes. A new reality pops in his head. "But that would mean something happened on the…"

"Exactly," Newlyn says, knowing no further conversation is needed between the two experts. For the amateur at best however…

"I don't understand. What happened?" Alex asks, annoyed he has to reach for the answer instead of it being handed to him.

"What happens when you pull the bathtub plug?" Professor Newlyn asks his only student.

"It makes a little tornado."

"Right, but in the water, it's called a vortex," Newlyn says nothing more because, in his mind, the *school bell* rang, and class was dismissed. But by Alex's watch, there are still three minutes left. Alex looks to Isaac for more information, but he's no help, so he looks back to Newlyn—still nothing.

"Ahhh, shouldn't we do something?!" Alex blurts out.

"Like what?" Isaac responds.

"Like move in the opposite direction!"

"Unnecessary. We'll be fine," Isaac replies.

"Won't it suck us down?"

"Sure, if we were in a Jules Verne novel," Isaac says, delighted by his witty response. "Relax, kid, that's just fantasy. No big deal. Ship's too big. Worse it'll do is spin us around for a while, possibly make you puke, and get us home later than we'd like."

Newlyn leans into Isaac and whispers: "Like the fantasy of a maelstrom in the first place? Do you really want to stick around and see what uncorked the sea?" At that, the heavens dump their rain.

Eyes blinking against the sudden deluge, Isaac nods in agreement. He steps out from the three-person palaver and stands in the center of the deck. He sucks in wet air to help project his voice over the deck's hustle and bustle and the pelting rain. But before he can shout orders, somebody with more clout interrupts him

"World President Basile was just assassinated!" The captain yells as he exits the bridge, open laptop balancing in his hands.

Everybody within shouting distance freezes and gawks at their captain. However, the stupefied sailors have only a second of sallow stupefaction to slosh in before the next startling occurrence arises. *Something* rises out from the maelstrom and flies directly over the now silent-as-a-tomb fishing vessel.

The gawking faces all look up as they attempt to track whatever it was that just exited the deep and entered their world. Based on the silhouette against the flashing sky and the amount of rain being blocked, this "flying thing" is horrifyingly huge.

Isaac remembers the powerful spotlight resting limply in his now white-knuckled hand. He quickly mashes the "On" button and chases after the flying behemoth with the luminous cone.

In the driving rain and the speed at which this monstrosity flew, nobody got a clear view before it was out of range. After the craziness passed, the unplanned game of freeze tag ended, and the chitchat of "WHAT just happened?!" died down, there were only two details of this destined to be *the greatest fish story ever told* that everybody agreed on. It had a huge tail, and it was headed east…directly towards Jerusalem.

Meanwhile, meanwhile…

\*\*\*

At the same time Aaron approached the porch steps, bracing for what his stomach assured him would not be a Kodak moment, and Alex's valiant struggles to quell his tumbled tummy, a lone nondescript man sat serenely on a bench overlooking the sacred Jordan River: stomach status—A-Okay.

The Jordan River Man (JRM) mentally gathers himself from his quiet repose. Standing to his feet, he turns and sets his eyes to scaling Mount Nebo which overlooks the Jordan River. He blinks.

Atop Mount Nebo, another nondescript

man stands close to the edge and gazes at what daylight's waning seconds offer. With the sun's full power, Mount Nebo normally offers a spectacular view of much of the Holy Land. It's a favored destination for pilgrim and tourist alike.

JRM, now also on the Mount, sees Mount Nebo Man (MNM) and approaches him, not bothering to pay a single farthing of attention to the "points of interests" scattered across this semi-holy site. If you've seen a small chapel and information plaques before, you've seen them all.

"Quite a lot of... stuff up here," JRM remarks to MNM.

"More than the last time I was up here," MNM responds. "That certainly wasn't here."

JRM looks in the direction of MNM's blind pointing. No "Where's Waldo" levels of focus are needed to spot MNM's highlighted feature—it's the focal point up here. He's pointing at a large brazen serpentine cross that stands tall, casting its pious aura over the gawking wayfarers who come to pay homage to a man long in the grave.

"Huh," JRM mutters with similar indifference given to one enthusing over seeing Spring's first robin. "Nice."

"Isn't it? How's the Jordan looking these days?"

"Anticlimactic compared to this eyesore," JRM comments.

"Yeah, kinda ridiculous."

"But, as one man said, 'There's nothing new under the sun.'"

"I think even he'd be impressed by these,"

MNM says holding out one foot and showing off his snazzy sneakers. "Would've made all that walking around a lot more comfortable."

JRM snorts an appreciative laugh for MNM's wry wit.

"Has it shown up yet?" JRM asks with a *time to get down to business* lilt to his voice.

"Not yet. Any minute now."

They stand silently and gaze out across the desert, focused on one location—the Mediterranean Sea. They wait but not long. The enormous beast suddenly blasts out from its watery tomb and races toward Jerusalem with the same single-mindedness of a medevac hastening to the scene of a major accident.

*\*\*\**

The sky rushes past in an instant; the deafening din of whooshing wind is comprehensive; the wall of pelting rain offers no resistance. What is happening at this very moment? Are these sensations being experienced by an adrenalin junkie soaring through the air in a wingsuit? Or perhaps these are the sights and sounds someone strapped into a VR headset experiences as they dive like a Peregrine falcon at break-neck speeds.

It is neither of these things but rather the beast from the sea's first-person perspective as it hastily closes the gap between itself and its objective. Minimal minutes pass before it breaches Israel's shores. There, the giant beast starts losing its girth like a balloon steadily losing its air.

The snarling, savage thoughts and voices that ping off the walls of the beast's mind, a kind of intensity no mere mortal can handle while remaining sane, urge it on. They plead—*faster! Not a moment to lose! Go! Go! Goooooo!!!!*

The beast doesn't need the voices' spurring. It knows not to dillydally. It knows because it's laid dormant for this moment for untold millennia, waiting to be called in to save the day.

In seconds, it's within Jerusalem's airspace where it shrinks even more. With the Temple Mount now underneath, the beast descends at astonishing speeds. Each passing second creates a smaller and smaller beast. And with each second ticked off, the more obvious it is that Vincente Basile is ground zero.

With Vincente's lifeless face rushing towards him—his gaping mouth clearly the bullseye—the beast completes its final round of shrinking. It's now the size of a gnat, small enough it zip inside Vincente's mouth unnoticed.

The last thing the gnat-sized beast sees before sacrificing its life is the pitch blackness of Vincente's throat engulfing him. Once the gnat-beast is submerged in Vincente's deceased depths, it erupts in a blinding explosion of electrical sparks.

The electricity shocks life back into all of Vincente's vital organs, creating an immediate response. The moment electricity surges in Vincente's brain is the same moment the rain stops. Suddenly, a moment from earlier in the day replays in Vincente's new mind. He is sitting in a dark room—the place where he now exclusively talks to his messenger, the place where his messenger first revealed his physical form—listening to his messenger's sobering predictions:

*Tonight, your house boy will kill you, for I will put it in his mind to do so. But fear not—this is not the end; it is the beginning. There is much to do, but first, you must die. Since your humanness alone is insufficient, I will send you my most powerful servant. He will willingly die so that his power may indwell you. He will swap out your deficiencies for his superfluities. Tonight, you must both sacrifice your lives for the other, but in the end, you will both rise again...as one.*

Vincente's eyes fling open. The first thing he sees is the people on their hunches surrounding him standing erect and stumbling backward.

"He's alive...he's alive..." one of the nearby temple servants remarks quizzically. Eventually, he can no longer deny his senses. He races to the top of the steps. "HE'S ALIVE!!" he heralds to the world with uplifted hands.

The temple servant stares at the silent audience. Stunned and annoyed by their disbelief, the servant looks over his shoulder in time to see Vincente rising to his feet. A smile as bright as the sun beams across the servant's face. He turns back to the crowd and yells, "See! And believe!" He steps aside and presents their risen savior.

Vincente joins the servant and rests his

hand on his shoulder. The servant bows and steps out of sight. Once they see the truth standing before them, a loud gasp ripples through the audience. None dare breathe lest this be a cruel sleight of hand or trick of the mind. Eventually, all must breathe. In an instant, and with one united cry, the world erupts in praise.

As the world basks in his sovereignty, Vincente turns around to see two hulking guards dragging Aaron back inside the temple.

"STOP!" Vincente shouts. "Wait."

Confused—surely, he wants a bullet in this traitor's skull—but still, they obey. Vincente approaches them.

"Thank you, but I'll take care of this personally."

They release Aaron but remain close by. Vincente drapes his arm around Aaron's shoulders and leads him into the Holy Place. He whispers, "If you thought things were bad before…Aaron, my dear friend, your mind cannot comprehend how bad life is about to get. Alright, you two," Vincente calls to his guards who then enter the temple. "Get him packed. He's coming with."

"We goin' somewhere, Boss?"

"Yes. Back home," Vincente informs.

They take Aaron back into custody and lead him out the side door. Andel, who remained on the porch while Vincente dealt with Aaron, now comes inside.

"Did your messenger tell you this would happen?" Andel asks.

"Yes."

"You're supposed to tell me everything he tells you. We're supposed to be in this together," Andel reminds him, annoyed by his relegation to the dark.

"We are, and I'm sorry, but it had to be this way. He didn't want you knowing because he knew your hatred for Aaron would drive you to stop what needed to be done."

"No more secrets," Andel requests.

"No promises," Vincente returns.

Vincente recognizes the internal struggle in Andel's eyes...and understands it all too well.

"Go, my friend," Vincente says, doing what he can to placate his *almost* equal. "It's time to put the bow on this charade."

Andel understands what the *bow* is and is ready to get on with it. The two go in opposite directions: Vincente, back onto the porch; Andel, into the Holy of Holies.

On the porch, Vincente beckons Eleazar, who's currently huddled with the Sanhedrin, to join him. Eleazar breathes deeply and leaves the four remaining Sanhedrin to continue discussing what just happened.

"I don't understand what's going on," Eleazar confesses to Vincente. "How's this possible?"

"Praise the Lord. Clearly, He wasn't done with me yet," Vincente responds.

"I guess not," Eleazar agrees, his head spinning from all that's happened.

Vincente becomes quiet, reserved even,

seemingly infected by a sudden case of uncharacteristic sheepishness.

"I humbly ask for your permission and for your blessing," he spits out.

"For what?" Eleazar asks, detecting the flagrant irregularity that's creeped onto the scene.

"I would like to honor Yahweh by offering the sacrifice. To thank Him for what He's done."

"Ummm…" Eleazar stammers. He looks at the Sanhedrin who are all staring at him. Before leaving them, they reminded him to walk the tightrope of status quo and to go along to get along—*We need him a little bit longer, Eleazar. Don't lose sight of the prize.*

"But I would like to use my own personally picked out sacrifice. Please." For a wee bit longer, Vincente also must stay inside the precarious boundaries of status quo. *Keep coming, filthy Jews. Just a little more…*

"Okay, Vincente," High Priest Segal accedes. "But this is a one-time thing. Are we clear? Do you understand?"

"Of course, Eleazar," Vincente steadies his boiling rage. How dare this arrogant Jew treat him like a spoiled child! "Thank you."

The two peel off from each other and go in separate directions: Vincente to the altar where he busies himself with final preparations; Eleazar to the gaggle of Sanhedrin, anxiously waiting for a report.

"What did he say? What does he want?" asks one of the fastidiously dressed leaders.

"Yes, Eleazar, tell us what he said," another of the sanctimonious squad reiterates.

"He asked for my permission," Eleazar says nothing more, foolishly hoping to avoid elaboration.

"To do what?!" the third member asks peevishly. "Why are you being cagey?"

Eleazar mentally moans at the *NO DICE!* cruelty.

Seeing the discomfort in Eleazar's eyes, the fourth member of the band, most likely the *lead singer*, takes a different approach—placid diplomacy.

"Eleazar," Lead Singer starts as he genially squeezes the high priest's tense shoulder. "It's okay. We just want to know what's going on."

Lead Singer's shoulder squeeze has its desired effect. Eleazar takes a courage-producing breath before delivering the tunic-tearing news. "He asked permission to perform the sacrifice."

"He what?!" one of the holy Hebrews roared. The other two's faces turn to a raging-red hue.

Lead Singer holds out a steadying, "calm down" hand at the blustering, righteous-indignant three. "And you said?"

"I said..."

He doesn't need to answer, because the sudden *SQUEAL!* erupting in the night air answers for him. All five search for the source of the noise. Call them crazy, but they swear it's coming from inside the hallowed halls of the Holy Place.

Andel steps through the temple entrance

with a leashed pig as though exiting a different dimension. Horrified, they watch Andel lead the unholy pig toward their Holy Altar.

He MUST'VE come from a different dimension; it's the only explanation for this outrageous behavior. Surely, he's not so foolhardy to think they're gonna allow this desecration?

The "Protectors of the Temple's Sanctity" pursue Andel but immediately run into a roadblock. Four of Vincente's elite guards, their MP5s at the ready and safeties off, step in front of the advancing, dithers-spiked "Fearsome Five." The pleading looks on the guards' steely faces exclaim, *Just give us a reason.*

The finicky fussbudgets wisely halt their advancement but not their tongues. A torrent of rapid-fire, emotion-laced Hebrew pours out of their mouths like a dam breaking loose. For these unfortunate guards, they've been instructed to ONLY take drastic measures should the Sanhedrin become violent. Otherwise, they were to remain mellow like Buckingham's finest. That's a lot to ask of these former Goodfellas; smack around first, consider the consequences second was always their way.

The riled-up Jewish leaders tire themselves out and fall silent. They helplessly watch Vincente slip on a butcher's apron while calling over two more of his burly guards. Arriving, he directs them to take the leash from Andel's extended hand, lift the heavy hog onto the altar, and strap it down. Andel turns his attention to preparing the altar. He motions to a meek temple servant to perform his part of the ceremony—handing Andel a nondescript pitcher. Taking it, Andel pours out a dark liquid into a small trench that wraps around the altar's edges and channels into a small reservoir under the pig.

Once everything is ready, Vincente places one hand on the pig's head to calm it while also holding it still; his other hand brandishes a butcher knife and puts it on the pig's neck. He holds it there. His forearm muscles tighten, ready to violently jerk his arm sideways and unleash the pig's blood all over the altar.

The pig's unexpected arrival silences the crowd's furor. Apart from the random "WHOOP!" circulating through the masses, Vincente's congregation is subdued—they are supremely curious to see what comes next.

Not wanting to stomp all over this sacred moment, Vincente searches for the perfect words for the sacrificial prayer. As it turns out this is wasted energy: his new tenant took charge and spoke the perfect prayer.

Like a foul stench escaping from an opened casket, the voice and words that blasted the balmy night air twisted Eleazar's stomach. These were not the words of any language he was familiar with. He's not sure the voice is even human. It may have originated from Vincente's mouth, but it was not his voice.

Surprisingly, something unexpected happens. The longer Eleazar listens, the more his stomach settles. And with the nausea disappearing, his mind blankets him in serenity.

Yes, the voice isn't Vincente's, and the words are indecipherable, but their appeal is undeniable. They are both soothing and frightening, awesome and awful all at the same time.

The prayer stretches on, as does Eleazar's awestruck state. For him, time blurs and loses its rigidity. He's at total peace, unaware that the strange voice and words have whisked him away to a psychedelic plane. Hopefully, this won't be a twelve-hour journey, but just a quick trip down the rabbit hole. For now, mesmerization ensnares him in the sights and sounds. It's the most incredible thing he's ever experienced. Vincente's new tenant is powerful indeed.

As the ecstasy continues, submerging Eleazar deeper into his own mind, his sixth sense suddenly chimes in, drawing his attention away from Vincente.

Looking up, he sees clouds from every direction inconspicuously slink across the sky and gather into one central location, as though being drawn by a magnet. As each cloud arrives, it's absorbed by the already amassed clouds, becoming an even bigger cloud. Eleazar gapes, eyes growing wide as the phenomenon continues. But as unexpectedly as it started, the gathering together stops. At the conclusion, a gargantuan cloud hovers above. Eleazar keeps his attention on the craziness, waiting for the next act to begin. He doesn't wait long—the heavenly show continues.

From the giant cloud, a blue light pulsates like a strobe light. It is slow, similar to a resting heartbeat. Eleazar takes his eyes off the heavens and sets them to scanning life on the ground. Amazingly, nobody else is looking up; their entire focus is on Vincente, who's still uttering his ethereal prayer.

*Is another storm rolling in?* Eleazar takes counsel with himself. *I've never seen the sky act like this.* He mulls over what he sees, eventually arriving at a conclusion.

*No, this isn't a storm. This is something else. Like Vincente's voice, it's not of this realm. I'm confident of that. Realm...*

Eleazar chews on that word.

*If an alien voice is coming from Vincente, are aliens about to come from the sky?*

Scowling, rolling his eyes, Eleazar castigates himself for wasting energy on such hooey. *Come on, Old Man! You don't believe in aliens. Think! What is happening?!*

Eleazar's unconscious mind wanders off to the dusty annals of his neocortex. There, it thumbs through Eleazar's extensive *memory file cabinets* looking for the answer. After a moment of purposeful hunting, his unconscious finds the desired memory folder, removes it, and reads. The information is grim. Without delay, his plucky unconscious races the folder upfront, to Eleazar's consciousness. Receiving the folder, Eleazar opens it and sees the answer...he wishes he kept it closed.

"I do, however, believe in..." Eleazar speaks out loud but stops short, not revealing the answer.

Instead, he turns his attention to the altar, onto the pig who's stopped thrashing and gone still. Startled, Eleazar sees the pig staring directly at him. Marveling over the pig's unwavering focus, Eleazar gives in to the bizarreness and locks eyes with the pig. His mind's eye, still spellbound by Vincente's otherworldly charm, rewards him with an extraordinary illusion—the pig's heartbeat.

As though gifted with x-ray vision, Eleazar sees the pig's pulse throbbing inside its jugular. The transcendent phantasm doesn't stop there. His mind's eye then superimposes an image of the giant cloud over the pig's head, overlapping the sky's pulsating blue light with the pig's jugular like stacked transparencies on an overhead projector. Startling illumination awakens in the high priest's overstimulated mind —the fate of this pig and the fate of mankind are linked.

Once Vincente stops speaking, the supernatural blue light and the pig's pulse quicken. Both know what comes next. Just before the beats reach heart attack level, Vincente slices.

The thin layer of skin protecting the pig's jugular splits, allowing the dammed-off river of blood to spew outward, violating the altar. At that exact moment, the gargantuan cloud splits open like an invisible hand unzipping the sky. Though similar to the explosiveness of a sliced throat, the sky doesn't gush blood, but rather a slurry of quick-moving things.

Even though Eleazar foresaw this outcome,

the shock of seeing his premonition prove true drowns him in dread. Through tempestuous chattering teeth, he finally declares what he believes in...

"Demons."

Terror-stricken, Eleazar helplessly watches the *machine gun* blast of dark man-sized creatures shoot out from the tear in the sky. Untold millions flee the scene—where they're headed is anybody's guess—while a smaller number form an enormous black canopy a mile or two above the Temple Mount. And there they stay, suspended in midair.

Eleazar's eyes remain transfixed by the steadfast air brigade. They seem to be bidding their time, waiting patiently for orders.

*Am I the only one seeing this?* the terrified Jew asks himself. He takes a quick scan of his fellow porch dwellers. *Nope, all are clueless. Maybe the crowd sees it.*

He unsticks his feet and commands them to carry his trembling body to the top of the steps. Peering out, he does see distaste on some of the faces. However, it appears their discomfort is due to the gore on the porch, not the blanket of evil hovering overhead.

Accepting it's his responsibility to save these people, he draws in a breath, preparing to unfurl his stage voice. But just before he proclaims his life-saving message, the hovering mob receives their orders. With astonishing precision, the armada rolls out and falls into dive-bombing formation.

Terrified, Eleazar watches the fierce denizens of hell swooping down on the clueless crowd. This attack draws to mind the behaviors of swarming locusts. Their descent upon lush crops is driven by one goal—total destruction. When the mission is complete, the never satiated swarm moves onto the next field, leaving behind a swath of carnage as though a nuclear bomb went off. This act of instinctual savagery by a remorseless insect is an unsettling sight to behold, and what's transpiring has all the earmarks of grim similarity.

Eleazar desperately wants to sound the alarm, but he knows it's too late. These people are seconds away from being devoured and there's nothing he can do. A handful of yards remain before touch down; Eleazar squeezes his eyes shut, unwilling to witness the massacre.

Seconds pass, surely enough time for the symphony of bloodcurdling screams to begin, yet nothing happened. In fact, there was no sound coming from the courtyard at all. Were they all destroyed, and only Eleazar remained, or was it the other way around?

Unable to take the suspense a second longer, Eleazar opens his eyes. At the first evidence of sight through slitted eyes, he sees a full house. Stunned, he opens them fully. Yes, they are all still there.

Although not everything is copacetic. A disquietingly blank, thousand-yard stare has settled on every face. Also, nobody is moving: not a nose itch nor arm twitch as far as the eye can see. It's as if the pause button on a giant cosmic remote was thumbed.

*What...just happened?* the unnerved high priest questions as he scans the crowd. *Why is nobody mov...wait, did he just move?*

Eleazar halts his scanning and homes in on one specific person a few rows from the front. He waits breathlessly for the person to move again...he does, and not just him. Interspersed throughout the crowd, Eleazar now sees a few dozen heads swiveling slowly, examining those nearby. These bewildered few are also unsettled by the radical change overtaking the crowd.

After a few moments of concentrated observation, the creepy vibe is more than they can handle. Thinking it best to vamoose while the vamoosing was still good, the Noncatatonic began filing out. Worming their way through, the fleshy statues dotting the Temple Mount offer no resistance apart from the minor effort needed to nudge The Frozen aside.

The Fleeing eventually submits to the hysteria of the situation. Creeping across a stranger's view, occasionally stopping to peer into their dead eyes and finding no response as though staring at a zoned-out junkie, can rattle even the stoutest of heart. (*Hello? Is there anybody in there? Just nod if you can hear me. Is there anybody home?*)

And for those few deeper in the middle, claustrophobia ensnares them, igniting a panic like those trapped in a burning building. No, this was all too much. It was time to get out...now.

Abandoning all politeness, the few dozen ram through the crowd like a running back pushing to the end zone. The guilt entangling their hearts makes the situation even more unbearable. These Fleeing Few have no business being here. They are all Born Again Anathemas.

Eleazar turns his attention away from the crowd to the porch. *Is the same thing happening up here?* He thinks to himself. The answer is apparent: there are only five operating persons —himself and his four holy compadres, who are also panicked.

Eleazar shifts his attention to Vincente and Andel. Both are standing at the altar and staring straight ahead. Vincente is in the front, bloody butcher knife still dangling at his side; Andel is a step behind and to the right. Neither move, but Eleazar suspects it's because they choose not to. As scrutinizing moments pass, his bewitchment broken long ago, Eleazar catches Vincente's slow head-tracking of The Skedaddling.

Eleazar turns back to the crowd. Vincente's eerie staring births in him a fresh fear—he's no longer worried about the *Air Force*; he's now worried about the *Marines*.

"SSSTTTOOOP!"

Vincente's unexpected, authoritative command—reminiscent of the heart-jarring voice of a professor announcing, "Time's Up!" during a final exam—stuns the Still Moving, freezing them like the rest. Eleazar returns his focus back to Vincente, who's now pointing his killing knife at the crowd.

With all eyes on him, including the previously Frozen, whose heads all moved in unsettling unison to gaze at him, Vincente begins his final speech of the night.

"The time of mercy for and nonviolence against the Anathemas is coming to an end. The time for depurating is about to begin."

Without taking his eyes off the crowd, Vincente stretches out his knife-holding right hand, making it perpendicular to the right side of his body. Seeing his cue, Andel springs into action by removing the closest torch from its stand and swapping out the knife for the stick of fire.

With torch in hand, still outstretched from his body, Vincente freezes in place and milks the moment for all its worth. He knows all eyes are on him and the fire; he knows all are waiting to see what he does next. He doesn't make the world wait long. He thrusts the torch upward and holds it; the sudden movement swishes the flame, making it crackle. He looks like he's holding a beacon, signaling the dawn of a new era.

This overwrought display of pomp and circumstance is him basking in what he's worked tirelessly for, a way of celebrating over his conquered foes like Roman triumphs of antiquity.

Throughout history, once a throne's been usurped it's paramount for the new king to wipe out all memory of the previous administration. One of the most effective ways of doing this is eradicating the previous king's followers. It's never wise to allow a remnant of faithful to continue existing, unhindered from orchestrating an uprising. This will not happen in Vincente's kingdom. He is focused like a cobra ready to strike.

Vincente waited long enough for the Anathemas to confess their sin and beg for his forgiveness. It's time to slam shut the door of his mercy. For those still transitioning to a VP, well, too little, too late.

"We are on the precipice of a new world," Vincente says, continuing the flagrant farce of a ceremony. "But first, the cancer that has long been free to fester and spread needs to be addressed; the malignant tumors ripped out and tossed into the trash can of history. If we are to ever move forward, intensive chemotherapy is needed. The pain will be difficult, and the nausea at times, unbearable. But in the end, hate and its practitioners will've been purged, damned to the hell they so readily condemn us with. The unquenchable fire they promise will engulf their own souls, snuffing them out for all eternity. My loyal followers, my brothers, and sisters, the healing begins...now."

At that, he joins his left hand with his right, transfers the torch, and brings it down to the altar. The moment the torch's dancing flame licks the canal of flammable liquid the entire altar ignites, drowning the bled-out pig in blazing fire.

The burning pig reanimates the crowd as though the fire melted their frozenness. Thousands of eyes suddenly flutter and blink back to consciousness, making them aware of the shifty, vile Anathemas. Like yellow jackets responding to a threat against the hive and their queen, they strike zealously. The stinging is unfathomable.

As the fire consumes the pig, Eleazar watches a large group of crazed VPs fall violently on the closest Anathema with blazing quickness. The brutality is supercharged by superhuman strength, as though all the VPs were injected with a rage-inducing drug. The carnage was boundless and unbearable.

He need only see one person's limbs ripped off and then their head effortlessly plucked from its neck like playing the age-old dandelion game before he was ready to call it a night. He squeezes his eyes shut, stops his ears, and turns his back to the courtyard.

That's all well and good for him, but the savagery didn't stop just because he stopped looking at it. The violence didn't end just because he stuck his head in the sand. The trampling, the beating, the mangling, the mutilating will continue until there isn't a single Anathema left intact, whether he acknowledges it or not.

He doesn't get to hide from the repugnance for long, however. The distinctive, rhythmic blasts of automatic gunfire open his eyes. Panic sets in as he sees one of Vincente's private security marching towards him. The butt of his MP5 is pressed squarely into his shoulder pocket, and the barrel pointed at Eleazar's face. As the guard comes in close for an accurate kill shot, Eleazar sees the emptiness in the guard's soulless eyes. Whatever pity or remorse that may've existed has vanished; cruelty and indifference are all that remain.

This lack of humanness is not limited to Eleazar's assassin only. Behind the advancing devil, Eleazar sees the other guards standing over the now motionless Sanhedrin. With their guns pointing down and the blood seeping from the multiple gunshot wounds across the Sanhedrin's bodies, no mystery exists as to what befell Jerusalem's anointed.

Seeing his finale is also seconds away, Eleazar closes his eyes and prepares to meet Yahweh.

"Stop! Not him. Vincente still needs him."

Eleazar opens his eyes to see Andel's back. He is standing between himself and the guard.

"Join your team and escort Vincente back to his vehicle," Andel instructs the emotion-whiplashed hitman.

The guard lowers his weapon. Eleazar sees the disappointment in his steely eyes. Remaining fixed between the ravenous lion and its prey, Andel waits for the guard to about-face, and obey. The guard relents and joins his team ushering Vincente through the temple archway. Andel turns to address Eleazar.

"You're welcome."

"Why me?" Eleazar probes. "Why do I get to live?"

"Misguided loyalty. C'mon. Vincente wants you safe in his home," Andel says as he pulls Eleazar toward the temple entrance.

"Which one?" Eleazar asks. Vincente has three homes and they're each in different countries.

"Iraq."

"Iraq? Why not here?"

"Because his time here is done."

"Then let me call my daughter, please. She'll be worried."

Andel halts his towing. He wants Eleazar's complete attention.

"It's you that should be worried about her. She's no longer off limits. She and her husband are now at the top of Vincente's hit list. They'll find them and all the other Anathemas. They won't stop till they do."

Andel points at the courtyard, wanting the terrors to imprint on Eleazar's brain. Eleazar notices that the crazed lunatics have finished mutilating the available Anathemas and are now filing out into Jerusalem's empty streets. Their movement speaks of a single-minded, undaunted purpose. They leave...they prowl.

# CHAPTER TWENTY-EIGHT

J on Nelson ducks inside a dead-end alley and hides in a large dumpster's shadow. Freezing in place, slowing his huffing and puffing as quietly as possible, he waits for the demon-possessed death squad to pass.

Oh, how he wishes he listened to his inner, sensible voice. But he couldn't; its reasoning sounded so boring. It was hard to heed it when his other, more adventurous voice's counterargument sounded so exciting. He just HAD to see what was happening at the Temple Mount, to see what all the fuss was about...

After Dino released him, Jon's original intention WAS to head home and hide out for the next thirty-six hours as he and his family waited for their R-Chips. But instead, he found himself on the outskirts of the Western Wall Plaza. Since the walk was a few miles, he arrived after the ceremony already began. He had to stay on the shores of the sea of people staring worshipfully at the Jumbotrons. This is why he's alive to regret his choice. At first, after the violence erupted in the outside crowd, he didn't know who the slaughterers and the slaughteries were. It was when a flung from the scrum severed arm landed near him that he figured it out: the snake-infinity-sign-tattooed hand gave it away.

After unconsciously looking at his hand and then at some deranged crazies who had spotted him, he understood the situation—he was gonna die if he stuck around. He quickly gotta steppin'...

Hearing only silence, Jon creeps out from the shadows and slinks towards the alley exit. Pressing his back into the final three feet of building wall, he cautiously peers around the corner. Seeing the coast is indeed clear, he breathes deeply before plunging into the unknown. Having walked several yards in the open streets, he suddenly feels like a shy streaker. He quickly returns to the alley to calm his panicky heart.

"Come on, Jon! This is ridiculous!" he whispers out loud. "You didn't go through five days of torture just to die in an alley. Your family needs you. Go home! Now!"

Having psyched himself into putting on his big boy pants, he steps back into the streets and double-times it. To help keep his courage levels maxed, he visualizes his family no longer living in squalor but in a gorgeous house where the food pantry bursts at the seams and the garage houses two nice cars. This image has the desired effect. Liking the idea, he expounds further on the life that awaits him and starts adding toys, both kid and adult versions, to his new castle. Oh yes, things look a whole lot sunnier. He knows he made the right decision, especially after seeing what just happened to the foolish Anathemas.

*Why are they so stupid?* he thinks as he hoofs it home. *Holding on to some foolish belief. Where did it get them? Dead, that's where! Their faces smashed in, that's how!*

A new image of his family pops in his head —tonight's atrocities happening to them. His running downshifts to a slow gait as he closes his eyes and confronts the abominable images.

*My family can't wait till Monday. They may not live through the night!*

Stopping in the middle of the street, he digs into his pocket, searching: "Please be in here," he begs the heavens. Sighing in relief, he finds Dino's flip phone and yanks it out.

"Now, please answer." Four fruitless rings chime. "Of course," he says, snorting frustration at the robot lady insisting he leave a message.

"Dino, it's Jon. Please, I need help. I don't think I'll last through the night. Something crazy is happening. People are being slaughtered and I think they're Anathemas. Please, I'm begging you, for my family's sake, call me back. We need a safe place to hide till Monday morning. I'll do anything you want. Just help us, please."

Hearing commotion coming from a cross street up ahead, he jams the phone back into his pocket. Blind panic returns as he searches for the closest escape route. He desperately wants to take the thru street to his right but the dead-end alley on his left is closer, so he ducks in. Luckily, he doesn't put much stock into signs, or the constant dead-end alleys he's forced to hide in would harsh his adrenalin buzz.

This alley has no dumpster to hide behind, so he invites the building shadows to swallow him, and not a moment too soon either. Barely three seconds in the shadows expire before the frenzied rabble passes the alley entrance. They looked like a pack of hyperactive Jack Russells hunting for rats.

Silence again. This time he wastes no time. He launches himself back into the open and heads for the thru street he previously wanted. Feeling Death's cold hand reaching out, its bony fingers centimeters from his neck, seconds away from grabbing it and snapping it, pushes him ever faster. In and out he weaves through the city streets, all the while keeping his ears pricked up for shouting mobs.

Driven by his fear, feeling its smothering debilitation, triggers an unexpected wave of empathy. For some reason, his mind abruptly reminds him of Eric. Perhaps it's because he watched several people being beaten to death, just like he did to Eric.

*He must've been terrified, yet he didn't resist or fight back,* Jon ponders the absurdity. *Where did his courage come from? I'll scratch and claw till my dying breath! So, why didn't he?*

Shame and guilt pummel him, slowing him to a leisurely walk—his legs are rubber by now anyway.

"How did this get so out of control?!" he blusters out loud. "I've never touched a drug in my entire life; never even seen one in person.

And now I'm a junkie?! Never so much as ran over a squirrel, and now I've killed somebody? Three somebodies!" he corrects himself after the accusing images of the Hochbergs explode in his brain.

"I was just trying to take care of my family!" he says louder than he should. He's no longer worried about being caught. He's furious and he wants God, should there be one, to know it. "To provide them with a better life. To give them a future..."

He returns to silence. Complaining out loud benefits him not one iota because nobody's listening. All he has is himself, and he's all he needs. Sadly, his rant lasted a hair too long: a gang of crazies rounds the corner and spots him.

"There's one!" the voice echoes down the empty street. Jon looks in their direction. He guesstimates there are close to thirty killers who have him in their sights...and they're only a block away!

Intoxicated by the most powerful fight-or-flight imaginable, Jon scans his surroundings. He wasn't entirely sure where he was until he saw the cross-street sign in the opposite direction of the mob. Eternal hope immediately sprang.

He knows that hanging a Louie at the recognized cross street between several buildings will bring him to the giant wall that surrounds the entire city. From there, it's only a football field away from one of the city's nine gates.

His mind berates him. He could've used one of those gates a long time ago and been home-free by now. But when the slaughter at the Western Wall broke out, he let his fear paralyze him into hiding instead of empowering him into escaping. By the time he came to his senses, it was too late, the hunt was already on. The plague of psycho killers had spread throughout the city, forcing him to take unnecessary twists and turns. But all that is water under the bridge; his salvation is around the corner. He sprints in that direction.

Having entered the cross street, now seeing the wall, he needs only to hang another left, run a few dozen yards, and he'll be gone. With spirits freshly buoyed, he finds another *gear* and blasts forward, putting much-needed distance between him and his demented exterminators. At the end of the cross street, he rounds the final corner as planned, and immediately targets the desired gate (so far so good). But then, the wheels fall off. Jon slams on the brakes and hastily returns to the cross street where he's hidden by the closest building.

"Oh, come on!" Jon mutters through gritted teeth. He leans into his knees, trying to catch his breath. Standing erect, he angrily shakes his head as he paces, swearing silently all the while. Eventually, he leans his back into the building and stares up at the sky. A temptation to pray grips his troubled heart. Feeling helpless and hopeless, he caves and closes his eyes, but that's as far as he gets. The second he closes his eyes his panicked mind reminds him of the encroaching mob. Opening them, he looks back the way he came—they haven't arrived yet. Allowing that somewhat good news to embolden him, he ignores the previous impulse, scoots down the wall, and stops at the edge of the building. He peers out.

His disheartened eyes stare at the new, bigger mob in front of the sought-after exit gate. They didn't notice him, but he noticed something obvious about them—they were standing, not roving. The thought, *probably there to snatch anyone trying to escape*, pops into his mind.

*Now what?* he wonders.

His mind works through his options, none are ideal. He can go back; he can try to climb the wall; or he can go right and dash for the next closest gate. He looks to the right; the coast is clear. Obviously, the only viable solution is hanging a Ralph; the problem is, he has nothing left in the tank to run one more foot let alone two thousand. Nevertheless, this is the answer. He pulls himself back in for one last rest period. It better be brief—the Previous Mob is seconds from rounding the corner.

"Dig deep," he says, pumping himself up for another 700-yard dash. "You can't quit now. Go!"

Energized, he peers the way he came for one last look: still clear. He leans back out and looks left: Gate Mob still standing there. It's now or never! The second his striding foot lands on the ground, it instinctually pushes against its ball and sends Jon reeling backward—a car motors past, shorting out Jon's plan.

"What the?!" he exclaims.

Dumbfounded, his head tracks the car as it

heads for the gate. He doesn't get to stand slack-jawed for long—Previous Mob rounds the corner, putting him square in their sights. Hearing the commotion from behind propels him back into the street, heading right, the way the car came. He's banking on the car drawing Gate Mob's attention, and if he's lucky, Previous Mob as well. However, he doesn't get to test that theory before he's stopped dead in his tracks yet again. He's staring at a brand-new mob, most likely chasing after the car, heading right toward him! Can't this poor guy catch a break?

Frozen in the middle of the street, wild-eyed and nearing a mental breakdown, Jon looks down the street he just left and sees Previous Mob is about to spill out. With New Mob and Previous Mob closing in on him, he does the only thing his maddening mind can think of—chase after the car and hope it'll be a diversion for him to sneak through the gate.

Only seconds after Jon vacates the middle of the street do Previous and New Mobs converge and morph into one Super Mob. Without breaking stride, Super Mob pushes after Jon like a horse striving for the finish line. Jon has one chance at this. If he trips, he's done; there are no do-overs.

Running as though a chariot on fire, Jon sprints after the car, doing his best to catch it. But suddenly, the car's brake lights glow, and the car stops. The driver-side door flings open followed by Josh half stepping out, hand reaching, bidding him to come.

"Hurry up! Get in!" Josh yells after Jon.

Stunned, Jon lets off the gas...that was his undoing. By the time he blasts forward again, deciding to take this stranger's offered help, it was too late—Super Mob was on him. Like a surfer being swallowed up by a massive wave, Super Mob pounces on Jon, slamming him onto his stomach. There, on top of him, they begin pummeling him to death.

As his mind and body succumb to the brutality of fists and feet buffeting him, what flashes before his eyes is not his life but rather the last thing Eric said to him...

*Jon, eventually, the guilt of what you've done here will be more than you can bear. I hope and pray that as you're being crushed under its punishing weight, you'll reach for God's outstretched hand of mercy and be forgiven...before it's too late.*

The moment the jackals fell on Jon was the moment Josh knew there was nothing he could do. Since leaving his dad, he's come across more scenes like this than his mind will ever forget. Climbing back into his car and closing the door, his side mirror gives him a view of Jon. Taking an ill-advised second to stare into the mirror, Josh watches as the dying man's hand reaches out fervently, his watery eyes pleading. Not sure why, but Josh gets an overwhelming sense this man isn't reaching for him but for something unseen.

Knowing the end was mercifully nigh for the poor man, Josh focuses out his windshield. However, his top peripheral vision gives him an out-of-focus view in his rearview mirror of a boot crashing down atop the mauled man's head and smashing it to smithereens like Halloween pranksters stomping jack-o-lanterns. Jon's death was poetically apropos and utterly deserving, but then again, so was the thief's on the cross. Man needs not a lifetime to be right with God, just a moment...

Seeing that Super Mob is finished with their kill, Josh assumes they'll turn their attention to him next. After all, half that mob has chased him for blocks; he's certain they want satisfaction. Like Jon, Josh has been forced to look for the road less traveled. Every gate he's come across looks like this one. Sure, he could've plowed through the fleshy blockade, but he couldn't bring himself to kill another VP, despite the situation. He just kept on motoring, looking for a way out without having to kill anybody.

Seeing this latest Gate Mob convinces him to stow away his nonsensical scruples. He's tired and time has run out. Scraping a few VPs off the hood of his car is a small price to pay if he's to get back to Ariella. Being alive with more blood on his hands was far better than dead with an olive-branch-holding dove perched on his forearm. The problem is, he shouldn't have stopped; now his life hangs in the balance—Gate Mob surrounds the front of his car, attacking it.

As Josh steps on the brake while grabbing the shifter ready to put it in DRIVE, a flurry of fists blasts through the windows. He throws up his arms to cover his face. His shielding arms successfully block some of the glass shards but not all. Some contact his face and slice through his skin like a hot knife to butter. Ignoring the free-flowing blood, Josh returns his hand to the shifter and puts it in REVERSE. But before putting the pedal to the metal, Super Mob arrives from the rear and joins the carnage.

Several crazies climb on and begin stomping the car into submission. Both the windshield and back window are kicked in. With the side windows already smashed, there is no barrier between Josh and the mob. Hands reach in from every direction, grabbing Josh's flailing arms and turning him into an old Stretch Armstrong toy. One way or another, whether whole or in parts, he is coming out of that car. Knowing there will be no escaping this time, Josh closes his eyes and prepares himself to meet the Creator...

Suddenly, there is silence. No hands are pulling him asunder. In fact, nothing touches him. Is he in heaven? He opens his eyes and sees three things in rapid-fire succession—he's still in his car; what looks like black snowflakes softly settle everywhere; and two nondescript men stand casually in front of his car looking at him. Mightily mystified, Josh creeks open his door, steps out, and walks to the front. The dark, fluffy flakes collect on his head and shoulders. He holds out his hands, allowing the flakes to land in his palms. He scans the innocuous stillness of the previously tumultuous war zone. His mind flashbacks him to peaceful snowfalls at night.

"What happened?" he asks the two

strangers standing a few yards away. "Where did everybody go? Am I dead?"

"No, Josh. You are very much alive. THEY are not," one of the men informs as they amble up to Josh.

Josh's intuitive light blinks on—this fluffy stuff is human ash. But then, as an afterthought, he realizes one of them called him by his name.

"You called me Josh."

"We did," the second man says plainly.

"How do you know me?"

"We know you because He who sent us told us about you," the first man says matter-of-factly.

"Who sent you?" The answer should be obvious. After all, they are clearly the ones responsible for the instantaneous nuclear cremation of more than a hundred people.

Neither responds. They simply smile as they patiently wait for Josh to catch up.

"Ahhh. I see," Josh says nervously.

He backs up mindlessly and sits atop the dented hood of his abused car. He scrunches his eyelids as he attempts to take it all in. They join him, one on each side, sandwiching him in. The three men sit quietly, their feet propped casually on the front bumper, creating a picturesque image. Josh feels comfortable and at home nestled in between these two unique men, but somebody needs to talk.

"So, who are you?" Josh asks.

"We are His witnesses," the man on Josh's right says.

"Witnesses to what?" Josh asks, silently

hoping this isn't all a big ruse and they are Jehovah's Witnesses.

"Of great and terrible things to come. And no, we're not Jehovah's Witnesses," the second one assures.

Josh is so relieved that he doesn't ask how he read his thoughts. Instead, he continues. "Are you angels then?"

"No, we are men, like you," the left-hand man informs.

"Well, I can't obliterate people, and I can't read minds, so you're not exactly like me."

"You're right. Thousands of years ago we were like you."

A new thought rises in Josh's mind. His mental gears are whirring along nicely now. "I think I understand. You've come from a different realm, right?"

"The Third One, yes."

"Josh," the man on the right starts. "I'm Moses. He's Elijah." This is said with zero pretense and so effortless; it was like they were introducing themselves at a party.

Amazingly, this does not take Josh by surprise. Before the Rapture initiated a seismic shift in mankind's history, he and Elizabeth attended an End Times seminar at their church. He remembers absolutely nothing about it except for the possibility of Moses and Elijah returning in the Tribulation. He was skeptical. How could two famous prophets from the Tanakh have anything to do with the New Testament? Nevertheless, he listened, if for nothing more than curiosity's sake.

The teacher cited two reasons to support this theory. One—no one truly knows where Moses was buried, and Elijah never died. And two —both prophets appeared to Jesus, Peter, James, and John on the Mount of Transfiguration as recorded in Matthew, Mark, and Luke. These two reasons were fantastic enough to intrigue him into remembering.

"But you're dressed in modern-day clothes," Josh states the obvious.

"Should we be dressed in tunics and sandals?" Moses asks offhandedly.

"Moses is quite fond of his Nikes," Elijah explains. Moses stretches out his legs appreciatively, admiring his 21st-century footwear.

A muffled guffaw escapes Josh's mouth. The sheer silliness of the situation amuses him.

*Ariella will never believe this,* he thinks to himself. *Ariella!* Her piercing eyes blaze in his mind. *Is she okay? I need to get back to her, pronto. But am I supposed to? Would it be rude to abandon MOSES and ELIJAH?! Am I supposed to show them around?*

"No, Josh. It wouldn't be," Moses responds. "And yes, she's okay."

"You don't need to show us around either," Elijah assures.

Feeling foolish for thinking such an absurd question (obviously they know the way), Josh scoots off the car and faces Moses and Elijah who remain on the hood. "What are you gonna do now?"

"Get the Anathemas to safety," Moses informs. He has a bit of experience in this area.

"And address the dead. Like him," Elijah snaps his head back slightly, drawing Josh's attention over his shoulder.

Josh leans to his right to peer around them and the car. He spots Jon's mangled body in the middle of the street. "Who is he?"

"One who lost heart," Moses responds. His tone is more disappointed than sad.

"And his way," Elijah finishes the verdict. "He won't be the only one. There will be some who do all they can to end their suffering, even desertion."

Josh's dejection at such terrible news is self-evident.

"But take heart, Josh," Moses adds. "There will be untold thousands of VPs who will abandon Vincente's dark world and come to the Light, especially from our own people."

"The Jews?" Josh clarifies. It suddenly dawns on him that he shares the same DNA with these two men!

"Yes. And it will be your privilege, along with thousands more, to present that Light," Elijah announces.

This doesn't elicit joy but rather trepidation. Sure, Josh prayed for direction, and it does line up with his father's dream, but he doesn't deserve such esteem, especially not after what he did tonight.

"What is it?" Elijah asks, seeing the

disconsolation in Josh's eyes. He knows what "it" is; dealing with this issue is next on their agenda. Josh needs to talk it out, or he'll be stuck and thus unusable.

"I killed a man earlier tonight," Josh informs.

"We know," Elijah assures him.

"But wouldn't that discredit me? How can I still be useful?"

"Joshua," Moses begins, like a mother drawing the attention of her preoccupied child. "Is your understanding of the Gospel really that lacking?"

Josh regards him with bemusement. "But it's the sixth commandment." He pauses for effect. "You wrote it!"

"You're right. I did. But I killed somebody too, remember?"

"Oh yeah," he remarks sheepishly, remembering Moses' shameful murder.

"In fact, I did A LOT of things that SHOULD'VE discredited me. But thankfully, there is grace and forgiveness with God, otherwise, none of us could do anything."

"God chooses to use imperfect, undeserving people to accomplish His purposes; He delights in it," Elijah adds. "You know these truths. Let them settle deep into your heart. Now is not the time for an incorrect view of God because life is about to get very scary, very quickly."

"How so?" Josh asks, fear rising to dangerous levels.

"Heaven's silence is drawing to a close. The

Eternal One is about to speak...loudly."

"Don't let your heart be troubled," Moses says. "The same command God gave to your namesake after I died, I now fittingly say to you: 'Be strong and courageous. Do not be afraid; do not be discouraged, for the Lord your God will be with you wherever you go.'"

"He specifically instructed us to remind you of that," Elijah says encouragingly.

Josh's breath catches in his throat. "You mean...*He*?"

"Yes. *Him*," Moses confirms.

His anxious heart is now still, at peace. He's ready to get to business. "What now?"

"Now, you get back to Ariella and take her and those with her to the Judean Hills."

"And wait there," Elijah adds to his partner's instructions. "We'll be along shortly."

"You will? When?" He's excited by this news. He knows he needs to get back to Ariella, but he's in no hurry to leave either. He's aching to spend more time with them.

"Soon," Elijah returns, removing all ambiguity of Josh getting a more definitive answer.

Josh accepts this is the end of the information road and that it's time to get on the concrete one. The problem is, they remain fixed to the hood of his road transporter. If he's driving there—and, judging by the car's condition, he's not sure it'll even start—then they need to let him.

"Don't worry, Josh. You're not driving

there," Moses says.

"I'm not?" Josh asks.

"No. We're sending you there," Elijah says.

"You're doing what now?"

"We're transmitting you to Ariella," Moses kinda explains.

They notice the consternation blink to life in Josh's peepers.

"It won't hurt," Elijah promises, putting Josh's heart at ease.

"It is disorienting," Moses warns. "You'll probably get sick."

"You'll get used to it eventually. Call it a preview of what's to come."

"Right," Moses says cheerily. "You'll be doing a lot of it after all this is said and done."

Josh doesn't know what that means, and he's certain they won't explain. So he offers his hand to Moses. Moses shakes it warmly. He then presents his hand to Elijah. Elijah smiles as he holds onto Josh's hand.

"See you soon," Elijah says. And with that, Josh is gone.

Elijah and Moses scoot down from the car and brush off. Moses heads to the rear of the car. "I'll take care of him," he announces.

Once at the back bumper, with Jon in sight, Moses looks at him pointedly for barely a second before Jon's body bursts into a poof of weightless fluff. Moses returns to Elijah. And like Josh, they are gone as though they were never there.

What remains of Jon's physical body begins to settle: ashes to ashes, and dust to dust. As far as where his soul settles...only God knows.

*** 

The storm clouds have moved on, leaving behind a melancholy, sparkly sea of blackness. Ariella Mendel stands alone, staring up into the infinite, wallowing in sadness. She's not prone to depression, but tonight, with all that's gone on, she battles with her emotions as much as she battles with the chilly night air.

She is standing on the Mount of Olives. From this vantage point, she can see the Old City but not what's happening within her walls. Good thing: it wouldn't improve her heavyheartedness.

Behind her, pops and crackles from a campfire add their voices to the desert night chorus. She could be there, sharing the warmth with the other six, but she needed to be alone to battle the thoughts in her head.

A small blanket helps with one of the battles, but the other requires help from an outside source. She takes her eyes off Jerusalem and turns them loose in the heavens once again. With her eyes swimming unfettered amongst the stars, they chase after each one as though completing a majestic "connect the dots" astral puzzle. It doesn't take long for her mind to see the hidden picture; obviously, it's God. She prays.

"I know You're in control," she says out loud. "I know Your way is best. I know You won't give me more than I can handle. But right now, I'm struggling to believe any of it. Please, help my unbelief."

Typically, God doesn't answer prayers immediately, but sometimes He does. She suddenly hears what sounds like a giant rubber popper toy flipping over, followed by the kind of violent retching accompanying a night of bad sushi.

In a flash, the blanket is off her shoulders and her sidearm is out, pointing. She sees the shaded outline of somebody doubled over, *abusing* a poor helpless bush.

"Let me see your hands!" she commands. She advances on the intruder, adrenaline and blood pressure spiked, ready for action.

"I said, show me your hands!"

"No, you said, 'let me see your hands,'" Josh corrects. Ariella recognizes the voice.

"Josh? Is that you?" she asks, lowering her weapon as she squints into the darkness.

"More or less," comes his wearied reply. He has wrapped things up and is now stumbling towards her.

She returns her .45 to its hidden holster and rushes to him. Unconcerned with his unattractive state, she throws her arms around him, smothering him in a huge bear hug. Even if she hadn't pinned his arms to his side, he was too weak to return the hug.

Mattias appears on the scene. "Ariella? Are you okay? We heard you shouting."

"We're okay, Mattias," Josh assures, not bothering to take his head off his wife's shoulder.

"Josh? When did you get here?"

"Just now," Ariella reports. "Go tell

everybody all is well and we'll join you in a minute. Okay?"

"Can do," Mattias vouches for his ability to follow orders.

When their privacy returns, Ariella pushes Josh backward and holds him out for observation. "Where DID you come from? I didn't hear you pull up. And you're bleeding! Are you okay?"

"Ariella, my love, please, I need to sit."

"Of course!" she remarks. "Sorry." She helps him sit on a nearby boulder and then retrieves her small blanket. After she's wrapped him up, she forks over a bottle of water. He gratefully accepts and begins gargling and rinsing. She hands him a much-needed stick of gum as well, to which he responds with a *good-thinking* grunt and nod.

Once he feels a little less worse for wear, Josh holds out his right arm and the blanket like Dracula holding out one side of his cape. He is inviting her to share the warmth. She needs no further prompting. Once she's burrowed in next to him, he seals her in, creating a two-person cocoon. Her head drops to his shoulder.

"What happened? Where's your car?" her emotions functioning at even keel now.

"I didn't drive here."

"You walked?"

"Right now, I wish I had."

"I don't understand. Either you walked, or you drove, or you appeared out of thin air."

"The latter, I guess."

"Now's not the time," she rebukes. "What happened?"

He says nothing more. She pulls out of his arm and turns perpendicular to him, giving her a view of his right-side profile. His gaze remains fixed in the distance. A few silent seconds pass.

"Are you being serious? How?"

He gazes at her and responds with a bewildered, wild-eyed, shoulder shrug. "I have no idea. One second I'm down there in the city, and the next I'm up here."

"You're gonna have to do better than that."

"I know, and I will," he assures. He falls quiet as he reflects on the last hour, especially his run-in with Moses and Elijah and their prophetic words. The recollection inspires and motivates him.

"But not right now," he says, finishing his thought. He rises from the boulder and stretches out his tired back. With energizing blood igniting his body, gumption propels him forward to the cliff edge. He stares at the Judean Hills.

To look at him, you'd never guess he was the same man hurling on shrubbery a few minutes ago. And Ariella is doing just that...looking at him, confused by what she sees. In the three years they've been married, Josh never struck her as a man's man, but she didn't see him as a cream puff either. He's just extraordinarily unextraordinary. Despite his truant pluck, it never affected her love or respect for him. In fact, she appreciated his milquetoast demeanor: it made being herself that much easier.

But now, seeing him glowing in the moonlight, standing tall and formidable, maddeningly alluring and bewitching, she feels like she's looking at a completely different man. He has an aura emanating from him, a chutzpa that demands inattentive wastrels to sit up and take notice because somebody of great importance stands in their midst.

*Did that back stretch swap out his impotent backbone with a titanium one?* she jokes to herself. *Is it even Josh, or is he a demon look-alike? The way tonight's going, it wouldn't surprise me. It'd explain appearing out of thin air.*

"Josh, where were you when you found out I became a Born-Again, and how did you feel?"

He regards her with a raised eyebrow. "What?"

"Just answer the question. Please."

"At the airport Starbucks. Fear and guilt."

"Why?" she continues the inquiry.

"Because I never expected to fall in love with you. Because I felt like I was betraying Elizabeth. Why are you asking?"

"Just checking." Accepting it's him, she puts the skepticism to bed and marvels at his transformation from Faintheart to Braveheart.

They stare at each other, enraptured in a kind of love few ever experience. He holds out his right hand, beckoning her to join him. She does, taking his hand in hers.

Emily walks into the area from behind, hoping to motivate the two to come and give them direction (she and the rest are growing weary of waiting). However, once she sees the silhouetted "M" of her co-leaders standing side-by-side, holding hands, she stops and returns their privacy to them. The group can wait a little longer.

"We need to go there," Josh says, pointing with his left hand.

"Where?" she asks, trying to discern where he's pointing.

"The Judean Hills. Tonight."

"Why tonight? Everybody's worn out."

"Because that's what I was told to do."

"By who? Your dad?"

"No, definitely not my dad," he corrects, a mirthful smile cresting on his dirty face.

"Josh, please stop being cryptic. What's going on?"

"I'll tell you as I tell everybody else. A lot has happened but not a lot of time to tell it."

She's not down with being left in the dark but accepts now's not the time for husband-and-wife privileges.

"Can you at least tell me if your dad's okay? Even from here, things don't look good."

"He is."

"Then what? Please. Give me something."

Sensing her frustration, he turns to square up with her. She does the same. He then takes her other hand. The scene resembles them standing at the altar, ready to marry all over again. But instead of saying, "I will" he says...

"What did we ask God for tonight?"

"For direction. To send us someone to lead

us onto the next thing," she answers.

He smiles, steps into her circle, cradles her head with both hands, and kisses her. After a period of G-rated passion passes, he pulls his head back so his eyes can focus on hers.

"Ariella...He has."

INTERMISSION

First look at, "The Conquering King"...

Ariella's cut off by machine gun fire coming from the direction she's pointing towards.

"Get down!" Ariella yells as she instinctively grabs for the sidearm no longer housed on her hip. Frustrated by its absence, and the feeling of being naked without it, she calls *Improvise*, *Adapt*, and *Overcome* into action.

Thirty seconds of rapid-fire powder-explosion *cracks!* echoe off the rubble and the few still-standing cavernous buildings before the air turns deathly silent again.

Josh wrestles with the flashbacks of piercing Dino Gennari's soft body with three bullets. Ariella, long desensitized by multiple killings and the unknowable minutes spent in combat, breathes easy, working through their options.

On her hunches at the front of the van, Ariella scoots around Josh towards the van's left side. With sight lines restored, she sees the other four sitting with their backs pressed into the van. Each scrunches their eyes and stops their ears against the previously deafening violence. Ariella quietly snaps her fingers. Emily, closest to Ariella, opens her eyes and looks to her right. She observes Ariella holding her index finger to her lips and then flattening her hand and pushing down, requesting silence and staying put.

After seeing Emily nod understanding, Ariella grabs

Josh's arm, directing him to follow her lead. Josh looks into his special forces wife's eyes and finds them calm, cool, and collected. Empowered by her razor-sharp mien, he too nods understanding and obedience.

Remaining crouched, Ariella stops at the edge of the van's front bumper and peers out, taking stock of the street's happenings. Hearing and seeing nothing, she stands up, bravely leaves cover, and enters the deadly wide-open. No artillery greets her brazenness. Taking a few steps further away from cover and still no retribution for her arrogance, she accepts they were not the assailants' target. Probably don't know they exist. Good. They have the element of surprise.

Ariella looks back at Josh and motions for him to follow her, but to stay low. Breathing deeply, centering his mind, Josh joins his wife, who leads them quickly through the dangerous openness and back into the safe shadows of nearby buildings.

Confident the gunfire originated down the same street where Inner Divine Harmony resides, Ariella presses her back into the building and scoots to the end of the block, coming to a four-way stop. Looking back, finding Josh on her heel, she signals for continued silence and a pause to their advancement. Cautiously, she peaks her head out and looks to the right side of the four-way stop, assuming the shooting took place in this direction.

She doesn't see anything at first, but continued scrutiny reveals the backs of three heads, each positioned behind separate cars. Their snake-like focus is on a specific storefront, the third business in the line, housed in a building kitty corner from the building she and Josh hide behind. Ariella looks at the store's name—Inner Divine Harmony.

*No harmony here*, she scoffs to herself.

Grateful her assumptions prove true, that she and the group are not the targets, she sets her mind to concocting an escape plan for Emma, if she's indeed in there.

Obviously, she and Josh are not using the front door. Maybe there's a back door. Peering further up the street they're on, she sees two staggered cars parked in the middle of the cross street, perfect for her and Josh to hide behind as they work their way unnoticed to the desired building.

She also looks to the left side of the four-way stop. She notices this direction is full of abandoned cars and concrete waste-high barriers dotting the street. If she created an obstacle training course, it would look like this. Plenty of safe places to hide behind in a gunfight, for both good guys and bad. She stores away this information should their escape go sideways. For now, she needs to get her and Josh safely to the first car.

She puts her mouth to Josh's ear and whispers: "I'm pretty sure Emma's in trouble," she begins, Josh grimaces. "If we move quickly and quietly to that building, stopping briefly at each of those cars—"

She points at the planned cover spots and the destination. Josh nods understanding.

"—we can go in through the back door. If we're lucky, we can sneak her out."

"How do you know she's in there?" Josh whispers the fair question.

"Hunch. Three gunmen are focused on Inner Divine Harmony. Can't be coincidental."

Josh nods slowly, agreeing this can't be a fluke.

"Are you ready?" she asks.

"Yes," Josh says evenly, amazed at how exciting his life has become. Encountering the occasional raccoon squatting in vacant homes was kinda exciting. Enough to get the ol' ticker pumping a little extra blood. But now he's teleporting across the world and engaging in urban warfare with his exhilarating wife. Moses and Elijah were right—this will be a fun 3 1/2 years.
Seeing the sublime sparkle in his eyes, (his brain has just doped him up with yummy adrenaline) Ariella kisses his cheek and squeezes his arm.

"Follow me," she commands as she crouches low and moves silently to the first cover spot, careful not to kick any potential noisemakers. Josh follows suit, safely joining Ariella at the first car.

Gaining control of her breath, Ariella makes sure the coast is still clear before setting off for the next car. This tactic continues for nearly two minutes before the Mendel Commandos arrive safely in the destination building's shadows. Taking a well-earned rest, the duo catches their breath and slows their heart. Breathing normally, Ariella regards her husband and holds up the universal "okay?" hand signal. Josh answers with a wink and a Fonzie "thumb's up!" This earns him a smile and a love-backhand-slap to his bicep.

Ariella jerks her head forward, instructing Josh to keep following. Not waiting for a response, Ariella presses her back into the new building's wall and scoots toward the back. Arriving at the end of the line, again she stops for a check down the back alley. Quickly, she locates the third back door, confident it belongs to Inner Divine Harmony. To get there, they must pass two dumpsters and other random obstacles.

Seeing that only the two dumpsters are large enough to conceal potential danger, she watches both like a hawk, looking for movement. Her effort is rewarded, but it's not a win for Team Mendel.

At the second dumpster, the one closest to Inner Divine Harmony's delivery door, she sees the barrel and muzzle of an assault rifle peak out—an assailant is waiting in the back should Emma try to escape.

Ariella ducks back behind cover and scoots Josh toward the middle of the building's side wall. Josh senses her frustration.

"What's up?" he whispers.

She doesn't answer, choosing instead to hunt her surroundings. Glistening from a few yards away catches her eye. A smile flashes, transforming her frustration into satisfaction. She quietly retrieves the discovered thing and brings it back to Josh. In her hand is a large shard of broken glass. Concern lights his eyes.

"What's that for?" he asks.

"For the person hiding behind the dumpster's jugular," she states emotionlessly.

"No!" Josh commands. "Our mission is to offer eternal life, not deliver eternal death."

"Right now, our mission is to safely rescue Emma. This is the only way to do that."

"Can't you just knock the person out?" Josh asks.

"Love, this isn't the movies. The element of surprise lasts less than two seconds. After that, the situation gets dangerous. It's why stalking predators go for the throat, to incapacitate quickly. Otherwise, the deer has time to kick."

"I hear you, but we must trust God. There has to be another way."

The look of determination in his eyes captures her, overpowers her. Never has she allowed anybody, especially one with a Y chromosome, to overrule her instincts. Then again, she's never met a Y chromosome worthy of her respect, apart from her dad.

"Ariella," Josh begins, gently placing his hand on hers, the one holding the glass, eager to slice flesh. "I love you and I know this goes against your fundamentals. But please, the killing has to stop."

In this powerful moment, Ariella's highly trained, cultivated instincts rage and thrash. Years of experience and close calls scream within, insisting she listens to them not this untrained civilian.

*Who does he think he is?!* the elite warrior deep inside demands. *He's never been in combat, never tussled with the dogs of war!*

Her mind goes silent, ready to submit to her instincts, not to the one who has dreams...
The random recollection of Josh's prophetic dreams silences her warrior's battle cry. She is unsettled by the unusual silence. Her drill sergeant persona is never silent, always does it bark orders. A new voice whispers. It is soft and gentle. Its insistence that she listen to Josh is evident.

*It is he that El Shaddai speaks to. It is he that speaks for the God who sees.*

Silence returns apart from the phrase, "The God who sees" ping-ponging off the walls of her mind. It refuses to fade away. It denies her peace. Her inner voice responds.

*If the God who sees is speaking directly to Josh, I should probably listen to him.*

A different, insidious voice trumpets.

*This is a dangerous precedent. Allowing him to lead in spiritual matters is one thing. Allowing him to lead in life and death matters is entirely different. He will get you and everybody else killed. God can't use you if you're dead. God wants you to make safety your highest concern. He does not want you taking unnecessary risks when you're smart enough to know a better way.*

Ariella suddenly understands what is happening, and who it is that holds the mic. The cold feeling accompanying the moment is powerful and intense. It is a moment that all of God's children throughout all of history have experienced. It is a feeling deep inside that insists they listen to the revealed truth and reject the counter lies.

Many saints have ignored the clear truth ringing in their hearts. Abraham lied to Pharaoh, telling him that his wife was his sister. David pretended to be a madman so the Philistines would leave him alone. Intimidated by a little girl, Peter swore and lied, insisting he didn't know Jesus.

All three knew that God promised never to leave them or forsake them. All three previously experienced God's faithfulness in their lives. Yet, in a moment of fear, they listened to the enemy of their souls instead of listening to the God who sees. They chose safety over trusting God's sovereignty. All reaped the whirlwind of shame and suffered the fallout.

One of Ariella's favorite scripture passages explodes in her mind. It was something she and Josh memorized early in their marriage. She recites it back to the vexatious serpent.

*"But he gives more grace. Therefore it says, 'God opposes the proud but gives grace to the humble.' Submit yourselves therefore to God. Resist the devil, and he will flee from you. Draw near to God, and he will draw near to you." James four, six through eight.*

As God's double-edged sword swooshes through the dark and dangerous caverns of her mind, a promised outcome occurs—Satan slithers away; no rebuking required. Curious...

Free from the internal battle, Ariella breathes easily. She releases the hand holding the broken glass from Josh's grip and quietly sets it on the ground. She returns her empty hand to Josh's grasp and looks deep into his eyes.

"I'm choosing to trust what you say because I know

you speak for God," she pledges. Josh raises a quizzical eyebrow at her cryptic, random statement. "I will trust God to help me subdue whoever is hiding behind that dumpster without getting anybody killed."

"Including that person?" Josh confirms.

"Yes, but you need to stay back until I get control of the situation. Understand?"

He doesn't like the stipulation but he nods approval. She squeezes his hands and mouths, thank you.

Releasing his hands and returning her mind to the psychological domain needed for dangerous situations, she scoots back to the end of the building. Looking in the alley, confirming everything remains the same, she psyches herself up and enters.

Sidling down the alley, moving like a ninja, her footsteps are light and measured, careful not to disturb any dormant alarms. Each tip-toed stride brings her closer to the second dumpster, the potential gate to her eternity. As she slinks, she notices feet shuffling in the gap between the ground and the dumpster. She stops a yard away from the ensuing encounter, preparing herself for possible fisticuffs. Several seconds pass with no drama.

Ariella is no stranger to raids. She has successfully led many breaches through an insurgent's nest, leaving no one unnecessarily alive. Aside from her first time, she's never been abused by the fears of the unknown.

Training creates muscle memory, the ability to act aggressively and swiftly unhindered by the mind and its humanness. It's why she was a perfectionist, it's why she insisted her team ran the training gauntlet twice a week. She's never lost anybody on her watch. All her members were elite. All were perfectly honed administrators of death. All were ghosts.

But now, at least three years removed from her last incursion, fear dominates her mind. She's unsure of herself, her memory muscles—gangly and atrophied. Special forces members are encouraged to restrict all ties. It keeps them razor-sharp and acute. But she has willingly disobeyed that wisdom. Josh is her world. She will never forgive herself if she gets him killed.

Looking back, she sees Josh's head peaking around the building. She waves him back, demanding he return to safety. She cannot focus on what she must do if she's afraid of a stray bullet piercing his brain. Josh's face stubbornly remains in harm's way. Ariella puts her hand over her heart and slowly mouths—*PLEASE...*

Persuaded by her pleading eyes, Josh relents and ducks back into cover. Relieved, Ariella breathes deeply and prepares herself for the upcoming two-second adrenaline rush. Creeping to the edge of the dumpster, she closes her eyes, centers her mind, psyches herself up, and plunges into the unknown...

The encounter lasted a hair over a second though it felt like she was in slo-mo. As her limbs performed their deft dance all sound disappeared like inserting ear plugs. Her prey morphed into a hazy blur as techniques gained from her mastery of Krav Maga disarmed and incapacitated.

In the end, the man's rifle is burrowed into her shoulder pocket; her eye boring down the sites; and the sites zeroed in on the man's face, hidden behind his cowering, crossed arms. With no resistance, she'd taken his rifle, offering only a swift kick to the face as payment. It happened so fast, that she never saw his appearance. Judging by the physique of the man backed into the wall, whimpering from the pain of a bloody nose, he is petite, posing little threat.

Just then, Josh shows up. Disobediently, he'd watched the electrifying moment, awed and a little intimidated by his lethal wife. She shifts her focus from the rifle's sites to her husband, irritated he didn't wait for the all's clear signal but thankful he's okay.

"You alright?" Josh asks. "I'm pretty sure that's Emma's bicycle from my dream. She must be here," he says, pointing at a nearby bike resting on its kickstand.

"I think I tweaked my shoulder but I'll live," she answers while acknowledging the bike's presence. "But as for you," she says coldly turning her gaze to the man still covering his face.

"You won't if you don't do what we tell you. Lower your arms."

The man obeys. As he does, Ariella lowers the rifle, a tick off from being synchronized. Shock engulfs her. What stands before her is not a diminutive man but rather a pitiful boy.

Thanks for reading! Choosing to spend your time and money on my book is not lost on me. Your support means a great deal. Lord willing, the sequel will be out soon!

www.ingramcontent.com/pod-product-compliance
Lightning Source LLC
Chambersburg PA
CBHW050838030726
47503CB00007BA/2216